LIES UNSPOKEN

the flawed love series
book 1

Lisa DeJong

Danielle —
If you follow your heart,
you'll have no regrets!

Lisa DeJong

Edited by Madison Seidler

Cover by Mae I Design

Formatting by Klassi's Kandids Formatting

LIES
UNSPOKEN

This book is dedicated to my friend Jessica who believed in me from the start.

PROLOGUE

As a little girl I'd always dreamed of the day I would get to put on that white dress—the one with the ballroom skirt and strapless fitted bodice. I dreamed of my daddy walking me down the aisle in a nice black tuxedo, proudly giving me away to the perfect guy—the one I'd waited for my whole life.

And during high school, I met Derek. He was my dream come true. We were together our junior and senior year, and when he was offered a baseball scholarship to UCLA, he'd asked me to follow him.

This might sound crazy, but I knew pretty early on that he was the one. I couldn't even think about spending a day apart from him, so when he proposed the weekend we graduated college, I said yes. It was the best night of my life.

But as the wedding approached, I felt a slight distance between us. I thought it was the stress of planning a wedding for three hundred people, or the pressure he was under trying to get a spot on a minor league team. We didn't see each other much, and when we did, things weren't as natural as it used to be.

I thought we'd be okay. I loved him, and he loved me. I couldn't imagine being with anyone else. He was my life.

And then one day I realized I might be wrong . . . about everything.

It just happened to be the same day I had my last fitting for my wedding dress. He'd offered to pick me up at my house after, and I thought he was going to take me to dinner.

What I saw as I climbed in the passenger seat would forever be burned so deep into my memory that the scars may never fade. It was the way he looked at me. Right at me. His eyes told me everything yet nothing at all.

"What's wrong?" I asked, pulling the door closed behind me. He hadn't said anything, but I could tell. I knew practically everything when it came to him.

His long fingers danced along his square jaw. His dark brown eyes were so vacant . . . of everything. A pit lodged itself in my stomach. "I can't do this," he finally said.

"Can't do what?"

"Us," he replied quietly.

The pit became a boulder, crashing into the cage that was supposed to keep my heart safe. "You mean the wedding? Are you saying you want to postpone it?"

All oxygen must have been sucked out of his car because I couldn't breathe. Hours could have gone by, watching him stare out his stupid windshield, and the whole time, I couldn't breathe.

"Derek," I pled, holding back tears.

He finally faced me, eyes glistening with his own unshed tears. "Lila, I love you, but it's not the type of love that's going to keep us together forever."

I braced myself against the leather seat. As if the whole world flipped upside down, time slowly suffocated me.

He continued, even though I didn't want to hear more, "I didn't want things to end this way, but I can't let them go on any longer either."

"Is it the stress of the wedding? We can fix it. I mean . . . I mean, we could do something small. Maybe a beach wedding with our close family." The words poured out before I had much time to process what he really meant . . . what it meant for me.

"Lila," he whispered, leaning across the seat to cradle my face in his hands. "I never wanted to hurt you. I never wanted to think about a second of my life without you in it, but the fact that I've been able to says something. We were so young, and I think we've grown up and grown apart. I'm sorry."

I shook my head, not able to find the right words.

My soul was torn. My heart was broken. How the hell could this be happening? I'd tried to convince myself it was just a bad dream, that I was seeing something that wasn't real. But no matter how many times I blinked my eyes, he was still there staring at me.

"Why? I mean . . . everything was fine this morning."

I looked into his eyes. It was like watching a drop form on the spout of a faucet. Slowly growing bigger. And then it fell, leaving a wet trail down his cheek.

"I'm sorry," he repeated. "I never wanted something so bad, but I can't. No matter how hard I try, I can't make myself want this anymore. Not like I should."

I thought about asking if there was any way I could change his mind. I wanted him to love me the way he used to. I wanted to go back and patch all the holes that were punctured in our relationship—the ones that drained it to this point. In the end, I knew in my heart that there was no changing this.

"So this is it?" I asked.

He pulled back, letting his hands drop away from me. "It has to be."

Tears fell quickly down my cheeks. By far, the worst moment of my life. But that was what unexpected heartbreak would do to you.

"I guess I have to learn how to not love you," I said before quickly opening the door and running back toward my house.

Something so beautiful turned ugly in a matter of minutes. I was wrong about so many things. Were there signs I missed, things that were right in front of me?

The tears fell down my cheeks, leaving a path of black mascara as I tore up the sidewalk.

I was almost there when I heard him yell my name. I didn't turn around; I just kept going. I thought about everything I'd lost and everything I'd never have. I'd trusted my heart to him, and he left it in a million pieces.

I said goodbye to my happily ever after.

THEY SAY RUNNING WON'T SOLVE your problems, but it certainly helps mask them.

Ignorance is bliss.

What I don't see won't bother me.

The things I can't hear won't eat me up inside.

Call me a coward, or maybe I've just been temporarily weakened by circumstance. Either way, the only way to escape it is to get away from here.

As I slowly board the plane, a whirling mixture of excitement and sadness fills me. I've lived in the same place all my life, and now I'm going to leave behind all the comfort that's had me wrapped up tight for over twenty-four years.

I'm also leaving the bad memories. Those constant reminders everywhere I look: places Derek and I went on dates, people we hung out with together. All our firsts and lasts happened in the same small town, and this is the only way I'm ever going to make the memories fade.

I follow the line of people, taking my seat ten rows back, right next to the window. With any luck, the person who sits next to me will be the quiet business-type who checks emails the entire flight or, better yet, a sleeper. Sleepers and suits are my favorite, but I brought my headphones just in case it doesn't end up that way.

After tucking my oversized handbag under the seat, I sit back, resting my forehead against the cool window while waiting for the rest of the plane to board. November in the Midwest is unpredictable as far as snow goes, but the cold is always guaranteed.

Surrounding the Omaha Airport are miles and miles of fields, a serene view I'm leaving behind for my chance in the big city. Skyscrapers. City lights. Trains and taxicabs. I'm looking forward to all of it.

A fresh start.

A new beginning.

A life I'm creating for myself.

Four months ago, I thought I knew everything about love and happiness, but I realize I didn't know a damn thing. I'd always assumed that time bound two people together. I was naïve. I've learned that people can fall out of love just as quickly as they fall into it.

I can't imagine hurting anyone the way Derek hurt me, and I've asked myself every day if I could have done something different to change the way our story was written. Some days I wonder if there was something I could've said to make him stay . . . to make him fall back in love with me.

But love doesn't work that way.

We met up a few days after our breakup to return things to each other. I'd had time to think about everything, and looking at him made me sick. I pretty much dropped a cardboard box at his feet with a *Fuck You* note lying on top. He hurt me in ways I will never be able to explain—not to him anyway.

Now, he's living out our dreams all on his own.

He sleeps in the bed we'd purchased to put in the house we never bought.

He finally got the baseball contract he'd been waiting for but couldn't get his fingers on when I was his girl.

I hate him for all of it. He's able to move forward, and I'm left trying to figure out where it all went wrong. It's a question I could spend a lifetime asking myself.

"Saying goodbye can be rough," A smooth male voice floats from my right, pulling me out of the ocean of misery I'd been swimming in. It's deep and smoky . . . in a different state of mind I might even classify it as sexy.

"Not as hard as it might seem," I chide back, chancing a look. He's a vision in a gray pinstripe suit, tailored to fit his strong, muscular body perfectly. His dark hair is just the right length to wave a little at the ends. A shadow of facial hair peppers his jawline.

"Is Chicago home for you?" he asks, a slight smirk pulling at his full lips. They're a shade of dark pink—distractingly beautiful, really.

When I don't respond right away, he clears his throat, pulling me back to reality. Only then does it dawn on me that he asked a question, and I haven't bothered to look up into his eyes. When I finally do, I realize his lips were nothing but an appetizer to something better. Those eyes—dark green on the outside and fading to a dull gray inside.

"Long day, then?" he asks, reminding me it's my turn to speak.

"Sorry," I mumble, shaking my head. "I'm moving to Chicago, and yes, it's been a very long day of packing."

"Are you from here?"

I shift in my seat, checking again to make sure my seatbelt is secure. The flight attendant stands at the front, going through all the safety instructions I've heard so many times before. "I'm from a small town about thirty miles north of here. You?"

"I live in Chicago. I'm here on business."

"What do you do?"

He smiles. Perfect teeth, go figure. "I'm an architect. I design hotels all over the country."

I nod, suddenly at a loss for words. I'm two years out of college, and, until three days ago, I'd been working in a furniture store. If I had to guess, I'd say this guy is in his early-thirties, at the most, and he's designing freaking hotels. The universe is proving to me loud and clear how much of an underachiever I am.

"What do you plan on doing in Chicago?" he asks, eyeing me carefully.

I suddenly feel underdressed next to him, and I wish I'd covered myself in something nicer than ripped blue jeans, a T-shirt, and an oversized cardigan. "I have a degree in design, but I'll probably end up waitressing for a while . . . until I can find something more permanent."

He nods, bringing a water bottle to his lips. "What type of design?"

"Interior," I say, watching him take another slow sip.

"Well, do you have a copy of your resume?"

I shake my head. "No."

I watch as he pulls his black leather briefcase from under the seat and unlatches it. It's full of perfectly organized files, not that I expected anything else. "Here's my card. Send me your resume, and we can talk."

Grabbing it from between his fingers, I glance down at the name. *Pierce Stanley, President, Stanley Development.* "I don't have a lot of experience yet," I admit.

He laughs. "I'm not putting you in charge of the design team. We have over fifty design positions, interns to assistants to designers."

"Okay," I say, tracing my fingers along the card's edges. It would be the beginning of my dream, but everything that's happened has shaken my confidence. I don't know if I'm in a place, emotionally, to succeed. Not yet.

"Why don't you write down your information so I can contact you, just in case."

It could turn out to be a really good opportunity for me, but this man is going to forget about me five minutes after getting off this plane. He'll take phone calls and attend important meetings. I'll entertain it anyway.

"Do you have a piece of paper and a pen?"

He hands me a small notebook and a pen that probably costs more than the sweater I'm wearing. "Name, email, and phone number should do."

I scribble everything he asked for, taking enough care to make sure it's readable. I hand the pad of paper back to him, watching his lips curl again. "Lila? That's a pretty name for a beautiful woman."

"If I'd done more than roll out of bed this morning, I might believe you."

He smiles. "Believe it or not, Lila, I don't have to lie to please a woman. You're beautiful . . . don't let anyone tell you differently."

There's no way to hide my blush, even with only the night sky out my window. "Thank you."

"Sorry, that probably comes across as pretty forward."

"Something tells me you know exactly what to say and when to say it. You didn't get to where you are in your career without that kind of skill."

"You're right, but I didn't get to where I am by lying either."

"Touché."

Crossing my arms over my chest, I stare back out the window. I rest my head against the glass, my mind drifting to a million different things until I see Chicago in the distance— tall, lit up buildings coming closer and closer.

In just a few minutes, I'll officially be a city girl. I'm not dreading it by any means because I'll be surrounded by coffee shops, clothing boutiques, and art. I'm ready to be swallowed into a sea of people where nobody knows who I am.

Glancing to my right, I take in the amused stranger. "How am I going to survive in this city? I'm used to being able to cross town in less than two minutes."

He rests his head back against the seat. "I moved here from a small town almost twelve years ago. It takes a little getting used to, but you'll do just fine."

"You? A small town boy?" I ask, lifting a brow.

"We all have to start somewhere." He smiles. If nothing else, Mr. Stanley is easy to warm up to.

We're both quiet as the plane begins to descend on Chicago's O'Hare Airport. The sky has turned from gray to black and the city lights illuminate the night for as far as I can see. I never thought anything would beat the serenity of the country, but this might just be it. It's peaceful . . . in a different way.

I wonder where my new apartment is in the vast city. I know it's a ways from downtown, but from my view, Chicago looks like nothing but a complex maze of lights. My moving here worked out perfectly because my college friend, Mallory, has a place she was looking to rent. She's studying in Europe for a few months, finishing her Master's Degree. And to sweeten the deal, she offered it to me practically rent-free. It'll buy me some time to find a steady job, and then I can find a place of my own.

"Do you need a ride somewhere?" Pierce asks, tearing my eyes from the cityscape. It's a question with an easy answer, but yet I still somehow ponder it.

"No, I've got one figured out," I reply, bending to pick up my handbag from the floor.

"It wouldn't happen to be a yellow cab, would it?"

I bite back a smile. This guy is annoyingly perceptive. "Probably."

"I'd be happy to give you a lift."

"I'll be fine, but thank you. I need to get used to Chicago cabbies anyway."

He nods, standing to pull his carry on from the overhead. "You have my number. Don't hesitate to call me if you need anything, Lila." My name rolls off his tongue slowly with a hint of deliberate sexiness.

"It was nice talking to you, Pierce." With one last smirk he saunters down the narrow walkway. My eyes are trained on his retreating form, but I don't take a step to follow him.

"Excuse me, miss?" I shake my head, realizing I'm holding up the plane.

My fresh beginning is already looking up.

CATCHING A CAB WAS EASIER than I thought it would be, but sitting in a dark car alone with the driver is proving to be the opposite. His English is broken, and when I ask him if he can turn up the heat, he mumbles some nonsense about putting on my coat. The interior smells like a mixture of sweat and fast food. And to make matters worse, when I slid across the leather seat, my fingers pressed into something sticky.

I make a mental note to find a job close to my apartment so I don't have to worry about transportation. This is a part of the city I may never get used to.

As I attempt to relax in my seat, I reflect on the day . . . on the road that led me here.

Chicago is about me. I'm going to be the person I always intended to be, do what I want to do. To be happy, content, and live a purposeful life. I deserve better than Derek . . . better than the way we ended things. I deserve a second chance.

When the cab finally pulls alongside the curb in front of an old brick building, I breathe a sigh of relief. It's three stories, maybe four, depending if you count the half windows that stick out above the ground floor. It's hard to make out much else in the darkness.

"This is me?" He could drop me off miles from where I need to be, and I wouldn't have a clue.

The driver doesn't turn, but I see him looking at me in the rearview mirror. An amount flashes on his meter: thirty-seven dollars.

I dig through the side pocket of my purse and hand him forty-five. I came here without a job lined up and only a few thousand dollars to my name; every penny spent is going to give me anxiety until I have work lined up. "Keep the change."

He nods, and his expression lightens. "You need help, miss?"

"Sure," I answer, curling my fingers around the door handle. As I open it, he opens his, meeting me at the trunk to pull my suitcases out.

"You have good night," he says as he sets the second piece of luggage on the curb. He wastes no time climbing in his little yellow car and disappearing down the street until all I see are his bright red taillights.

This is it, I think to myself as I look down the barren street.

I inhale a deep breath and spin around, getting a closer look at my new home. The street is lined with buildings that are just like it: brick, with simple glass doors and dim light shining through. It's a far cry from the historical, wooden two stories that make up my hometown.

After picking up my overstuffed suitcases, I start the short walk to my front door. It's not long before I have to set them back down to pull the key card from my pocket. Mallory sent it in a care package, along with a key to her apartment shortly before she left. It was the day I decided there was no turning back; I'm going to do this no matter how much it scares me.

I take one flight of stairs then another, my fingers aching from the weight of the suitcases. By the time I reach the third floor, I'm praying that Mallory has a bathtub and a bottle of red wine. There's no other way to end a long, exhausting day.

To my relief, the key turns easily, giving me a full view of the tiny apartment. A small kitchen sits right inside the door, opening to a tiny dining and living area—one just big enough for a futon, beanbag, and a small wooden coffee table. There are two doors off the living room—one on each side. The first one opens to a bedroom, which looks like someone took a dresser full of clothes and scattered them across the floor. In the corner is an easel with paint supplies strewn all over, making it look much like a preschool classroom. It's definitely not Mallory's.

I step back, carefully closing the door behind me. The other door has to open to a more organized setup, or I'm definitely in the wrong apartment. Mallory was borderline obsessive compulsive in school. She was the one straightening the bathroom after each of us was done, and her wardrobe and desk were meticulously orderly . . . annoying really.

I wrap one hand around the knob while the other searches for the light switch. I close my eyes like the special guest at a surprise party waiting for the big reveal. When I open them, not a doubt lingers that this apartment belongs to Mallory. A simple mahogany four-poster bed sits in the center, covered with a white down comforter and bright blue pillows. The dark wood floors are partially covered with a white shag rug, and three colorful abstract paintings cover her walls. Maybe she picked up art as a hobby since the last time I saw her; that would explain the other bedroom.

I run back into the entryway to grab my luggage and double check the deadbolt. Living in the city is going to be a huge adjustment for me. Sirens. Trains. Tiny little apartments. It's not what I'm used to.

Once I'm back in the bedroom, I throw the first of my suitcases on the bed and quickly start unpacking.

I lift the second suitcase onto the bed, and as I'm unzipping it, I hear the door to the apartment creak.

My heart races. My mind flashes through all the episodes of *48 Hours* I've watched over the years, hoping in the end I only think I heard it. Maybe it was my tired mind playing tricks on me like a psychological Houdini.

That hope is crushed when I hear footsteps. My eyes lock on the bedroom door, and every muscle in my body tenses. There's nowhere to go unless I can magically escape out the window, and there's no way to make that happen without drawing attention to myself.

If this is it . . . if this is how I'm going to die . . .

"Who the fuck are you?" a shadowy figure asks, sounding more irritated than anything else.

I step back again, my legs hitting the bed. My brain cells abandon me, and my ability to speak goes right along with them. Scanning the room, I search for anything that could be used to render him unconscious long enough to make my escape, but my flighty mind can't concentrate.

"You have two fucking seconds to answer me, or I'm going to pick your ass up and throw you out!"

I inhale then exhale, trying to calm my jittery nerves. *Please let this be part of one of those God-awful reality shows, like* What Would You Do? *or something.* "Lila. My name's Lila," I answer quietly.

He steps forward, until the light of the bedroom gives me the first glimpse of his face. I didn't know scary could be so easy on the eyes. "And what the hell are you doing in my apartment, Lila?"

Shaking my head, I try to get a grip. If I had anywhere to run, I would. I'd like to get as far away from here as possible.

"I thought . . . I thought this was my friend Mallory's apartment. The key worked and—"

"Wait, Mallory knows you're here?"

Unable to stand on my shaky knees any longer, I fall back on the bed. I think my dreams of a hot bubble bath and glass of wine just went out the window. "Yeah, she's letting me stay here until I find a place of my own. Who are you?"

"Her brother," he bites back. A few more steps and he's fully in my view. Gorgeous, not in the magazine cover way, but the kind that makes you drool because there's no way you can take him home to Mom on Christmas. He's the type of guy a girl wants to be with for one night just to see how good it could be, to fuck away every bad sexual experience she's ever had in her life. Dark blond hair, partially covered by a gray beanie. A light sprinkling of facial hair along his jaw. Black leather jacket. Faded blue jeans. Black motorcycle boots. And from what I've heard so far, a dirty mouth to match.

"What are you doing here?" I ask, crossing my arms over my chest.

His eyes scan my breasts before meeting mine again. The muscle in his jaw ticks as he scrubs his hand over his face. "I live here."

My eyes widen. "What do you mean *live here?*"

He raises an eyebrow, giving me a glassy stare. Those sapphire eyes could end me, but I'm not going to let them. "As in this is where my mail comes."

"Shit," I mumble under my breath. *This is never going to work.* A couple minutes in the same room, and I already know that much.

"Let me guess, perfect Mallory didn't mention that when she handed you a key to this place." His voice drips with heavy sarcasm.

I swallow, trying to dislodge the huge lump in my throat. "No."

He laughs, covering his hips with his paint-stained hands. "That's typical. How long are you planning to stay? A few days?"

"A few months probably. Mallory's not coming back until spring, and she said to stay as long as I need."

"That's just fucking great," he groans, and, without another word, walks out of my room. A door slams, and the whole apartment goes quiet as I lie back on my new bed. I have an asshole as a roommate. A sexy asshole, and the only thing that's keeping me from pounding on his door is the exhaustion that's taken over my body. All I want to do is fall asleep—to forget most of this day even happened.

I reach for my purse, rummaging through it until I find my phone. I don't care what time it is in Spain; Mallory owes me an explanation.

After three rings, I'm fuming. Four rings means voicemail, and I'm not in the mood to wait.

"Hello," she answers, sleepily.

"Mallory," I groan, skipping pleasantries.

The sound of blankets shifting comes through the phone. "Oh God. You met him, didn't you?"

"Mallory, I swear—"

"Look, I didn't think he'd be home tonight. He's going through one of his phases where he usually disappears for a few days to paint and sort his shit out."

I sigh, rubbing my fingers over my forehead. "So when exactly were you going to tell me?"

"Tomorrow, or maybe the next day . . . after you got all settled."

"I can't live with him," I say, honestly.

"Look, just give it a few days, okay? He's not home often so you won't even know he's there," she pleads.

"I hate men."

"I know," she mumbles, sounding tired again.

"I'm going to kill you the next time I see you."

"I know." She's drifting off. Her voice is fading.

"What's his name?"

She yawns. "Blake. Can I go back to sleep now? It's four in the freaking morning, Lila."

"Fine, but I hope the bed bugs bite."

"Love you, too," she whispers.

"You're lucky there's an ocean between us," I add. I don't feel like all the pissed off energy has evaporated yet.

"Night."

"Night," I answer back, throwing my phone across the bed.

Pans crash together in the kitchen, waking me from a deep slumber. I open one eye just enough to read the time on the alarm clock. *7:00.* There has to be a roommate ordinance against this.

Folding one side of the pillow over my head, I try to fall back to sleep. It works, for a few short minutes, until I hear metal clanking in the kitchen again. *This is not going to work,* I think to myself. After getting only a few hours of sleep the night before, I was looking forward to sleeping in before I have to begin my job hunt . . . and apartment hunt.

When the rustling continues, I throw my covers off and roll out of bed. My bare feet pad against the cool hardwood floors as I make my way into the living room. Wiping the sleep from my eyes, I focus in on a shirtless Blake standing in front of the stove with his strong back to me. His body is sculpted. Wide shoulders. Waist tapering in at just the right angle . . . there's probably not a pinch of fat on the guy.

I quietly walk up behind him, tapping my finger on his shoulder. "We need to talk."

He spins around, his arm brushing against mine. His hair is mussed—a look he wears well . . . too well, as much as I hate to admit it.

"I only made enough eggs for me." He smirks, and two stupid dimples form. He's cute—stupidly so.

"I'm a cereal kind of girl," I say, crossing my arms.

His smile widens. "Fruit Loops or Captain Crunch? I'm guessing you like the ones with the cute little cartoon characters on the front of the box."

"Wheaties. I prefer to stare at a sexy athlete while eating my breakfast." I stop, moving my hands to my hips. "Look, can we make a rule? No loud noises until at least nine. Some of us need our beauty sleep."

His brow lifts. "Now that you mention it, your eyes are a little dark and puffy. It's nothing a little make-up won't fix."

"You're an asshole!"

He laughs, nibbling on a piece of egg at the end of his spatula. "That's nothing I haven't heard before."

"Are you done? Because I'd really like to crawl back into my nice warm bed."

He looks back to the stove. "Yep, breakfast is served."

"Good. I'm going back to bed."

I start to walk away, but his voice stops me. "Hey, Lila?" He says my name with extra emphasis on the second syllable—in a way I haven't heard it before. I turn around, taking in his dark, hooded eyes. "If you're going to walk around looking like that every morning, I might be okay with this roommate thing."

Looking down, I'm suddenly reminded that all I have on is a sleep shirt that reads: *"I don't hate morning people. Mornings have nothing to do with it."* It barely covers my ass, and the wide neck falls off my shoulder. It's certainly not something I'd want to be caught in by him.

"Definitely an asshole," I groan as I hurry to my room and slam the door shut behind me.

I hear him laughing through the wall, which just irritates me more. This is so not going to work. Either he's going to push me to the point of wanting to return to Nebraska, or I'm going to kill him.

After a couple additional hours of restful sleep, I wake to a mostly quiet apartment. *This is how it should be every morning*, I think to myself. A band of light shines through the space between the mini blind and windowsill. My first full day in Chicago, and the sun is shining, which has to be a good sign.

The first thing I need to do, before I go job hunting or anything else, is call Mom. The short text from yesterday won't hold her off for long. I grab my phone from where I left it on the other side of the bed and press HOME in my contact list. No matter where I go or what I do, it will always be home.

After just one ring, she answers, "Hey, how's my city girl?"

"I'm good. How are things back home?"

She sighs. "Is it bad to admit that I miss you already? I didn't have anyone to drink my coffee with this morning."

I smile sadly. Mom and I have had breakfast together every morning since my relationship with Derek ended. A lot of internal crap was sorted out during those mornings; it's how I ended up here.

"I miss you too."

"What are your plans today?"

"I need to finish unpacking, and then I'm going to see if I can find a job," I reply, resting my head against the mahogany headboard.

"Any idea where you're going to look?"

I stare up at the plain white ceiling like it might hold an answer . . . it doesn't. "I think I'm just going to walk around the area and see what there is."

"You'll find something. They'd be stupid not to hire you."

"Spoken like a true mom," I say, rolling my eyes.

She chuckles. I love when she does that, because it's so contagious even when I try my hardest not to catch it. "Yes, but it's true. You're smart like your momma. So how's the apartment and everything?"

"The apartment is small but really nice. The bedroom is very Mallory, but I love it." I pause, trying to decide what else to tell her about my current living situation. Blake is something I hadn't figured into the equation. "And I have a roommate."

"What? Who?"

"Mallory's brother. I didn't realize anyone else lived here until he came through the door last night. Seriously, I thought I was going to die at the hands of a crazed lunatic my first night in Chicago." Just thinking about it makes me shiver.

"At least you'll have somebody to watch out for you. Is he anything like Mallory?" she asks. Mom met Mallory a few times during my college days. She's so close to perfect, she makes me look like the devil's spawn.

"Not exactly."

"Is he nice?"

"Umm," I answer, smacking my lips. 'Blake' and 'nice' have a slim chance of ever being used in the same sentence from what I've seen so far.

"Oh boy, well, maybe you'll find a job today, and you can move into your own place soon, then you won't have to worry about it," she says in her matter-of-fact mom voice. I love her and that voice. She's been my best friend for as long as I can remember. Anything I need, she's there for me.

"I should probably go if I'm going to make a dent in my job hunt today."

"Okay, call me tonight and let me know how it went."

"I will." And if I don't, she'll call. It's a guarantee.

"Be safe. I love you."

"Love you, too, Mom."

I hang up the phone feeling calmer, but also missing home. Somehow, I need to find that here. I need to meet people and make Chicago *home*.

As I step outside in the light of day, I realize this neighborhood looks much like I pictured it last night. Blocks of tall brick buildings as far as the eye can see, but they're dressed up by the colorful leaves on the trees that line the narrow street. Fall in Chicago isn't that different from my hometown.

I start walking down the sidewalk, hoping there's a business district tucked in here somewhere with a few restaurants or coffee shops. I'm not going to be picky, especially if it allows me to avoid the public transportation system, or even better yet, get far away from Blake.

The air is cool and crisp against my skin, forcing me to pull my black pea coat closed tighter. The street is pretty quiet, but then again, it's Friday afternoon and people are probably working.

I head north, seeing more businesses come into view. There's nothing big and flashy about it. It kind of reminds me of the downtown in my hometown: quaint shops, wrought iron benches lining the sidewalks, and shoppers gazing inside store windows.

I decide to start on one side and work my way to the other. When I don't see any HELP WANTED signs, I leave my nervousness and reservations behind and start going inside to ask, hoping for a little luck.

The first three places quickly turn me away. The next, a coffee shop, hands me an application, but says they'll keep it on file because they don't have any open positions at the moment. Next, I go into a flower shop and craft boutique without any success.

There's one place I skipped: a bar with a rough-looking exterior—faded sign, beer lights only half lit. Feeling deflated, I take a deep breath and pull open the door. The first thing that hits me is the smell of stale beer.

I walk up to the wooden bar, feeling completely out of place. This isn't a yuppie hang out. There are no suits or classy dresses; it's T-shirts and tattoos.

"Can I get you something to drink?" I look up to see the bartender eyeing me up and down, the corner of his lips turning up. He's a little older—maybe forty—and his black T-shirt is pulled tight against his muscled chest.

"Actually, I was wondering if you're hiring," I say, squeezing in between two bar stools.

He laughs. "You want to work here?"

I swallow, glancing around to see most sets of eyes on me. "Yes."

He licks his lower lip, seeming to contemplate something. Just being here makes me nervous, but I'm not in the position to be picky. I watch as he walks to the other end of the bar and opens a drawer, shuffling through a stack of papers. When he comes back, he slides a single piece of paper in my direction. "Fill this out."

In front of me is the shortest job application I've ever laid my eyes on. It asks for my name, address, what position I'm applying for, and if I've ever been convicted of a felony.

Hesitantly, I fill in all the information and slide it back to him.

"When can you start?"

My eyes widen. "What about the interview?"

He grins. "Sweetheart, around here, this is your interview."

Shit. Do I really want to do this? Then I remember my depleting bank account. Sometimes, life doesn't give us a choice.

"I can start right away."

Please don't make me regret this.

Actually, no, I'm already regretting this.

"I had a waitress quit a couple nights ago. Couldn't handle the pressure apparently. Come in tonight, around seven. And," he starts, reaching under the bar, "this is your uniform."

I lift the tiny black tank top, which reads: *Charlie's Bar and Billiards* across the front in white print. It's cut low; I'll be lucky if it covers my chest, and that shouldn't be hard to do.

"Is there a problem? You're a size small, right?" he asks.

"Umm . . . do I just wear jeans with this or black pants?"

He leans forward on the bar. Usually, I like it when people smile, but his scares the crap out of me. "Jean shorts or skirt. The shorter the better."

"But it's cold outside," I reply.

"Wear pants and change when you get here. Besides, with you serving drinks at night, it's going to get awfully warm in here."

I think I threw up a little in my mouth. This probably won't last more than one day, but I need to try. This is all I got.

"Okay." I nod, rolling up the shirt and tucking it into my oversized bag. "I guess I'll see you later."

"Can't wait," he remarks, tucking a toothpick between his teeth.

As I'm walking out, two guys walk in, their glassy eyes raking over my body as if they've never seen a woman before. If it's this bad when I'm fully clothed, I'm in for a shit storm tonight.

When I finally get back to the apartment, Blake is sitting on the couch with his hand wrapped around a beer bottle.

"I was hoping you'd moved out," he says, bringing the brown bottle to his lips.

Rolling my eyes, I say, "You're not going to get that lucky. Not that I imagine you ever do."

"Don't worry about me." His eyes follow me the whole way to my bedroom, and the only way to rid myself of him is to slam the door. If I have to deal with rowdy bar patrons tonight, I need sleep. Lots of it.

When I wake up, it's quarter to six. Just enough time to get dressed and grab a quick bite to eat before work. I skip taking a shower, deciding I'll probably need one when I get home. There's no way I'm going to fall asleep smelling like stale liquor.

Thumbing through my drawer, I find a black bra that provides full coverage and throw it on under my new tank top. I didn't plan on wearing any shorts or skirts this time of year so those won't be here until the rest of my stuff arrives next week. I search Mallory's drawer, pulling out a pair of short, black linen shorts.

When I'm dressed, I assess myself in the full-length mirror. It's worse than I thought; the tank showcases the top of my cleavage no matter how much I try to hide it. I wear more than this on the beach most of the time.

I take a few extra minutes to braid my long red hair, letting it fall over one shoulder, and then apply a thin layer of makeup. Not too much but enough so I look like I care.

Blake steps out of his room just as I'm walking out of mine.

"What the hell are you doing?" he asks through gritted teeth.

I cross my arms over my chest, looking down at my bare legs. "Getting ready for work."

He comes closer, standing in the center of the living area. He's changed from earlier, wearing a red and blue plaid shirt and a pair of faded blue jeans that hug his muscular thighs. And as much as I hate to admit it, he looks good.

"Your top," he says, pointing his finger toward my chest.

I shift on my feet. "That's where I'm working. Don't worry . . . I don't usually walk around town like this."

"You've got to be kidding me." His voice is louder as he rubs the back of his neck.

"Nope," I say, continuing on to the kitchen.

As I open cupboard doors, I feel him behind me. "You moved all the way to Chicago to work at Charlie's?"

"No." I pull out a box of crispy rice cereal.

He groans. "Have you been in there?"

"Yes."

"And *you* want to work there?"

I turn, practically running into his chest. He smells fresh, with a blend of spice and wood . . . I love that smell. "No, I don't *want* to work there, but it's all I can find right now."

He shakes his head. "You won't last more than one night. I'm tempted to bet on it right here, right now."

"You don't know me," I say, passing by him to open the fridge. No milk. *Great.* I push it closed and reach my hand in the box, shoving a mouthful of dry cereal in my mouth.

"Sure I do," he says, lifting himself up to sit on the counter. "You're a friend of my sister's, which means you'd probably qualify for nun-hood. You probably grew up in a perfect little house with flowerbeds under each of the fucking windows, and you probably see this city as an adventure. Tonight is going to be anything but an adventure. I'll guarantee that."

I stand in front of him, careful not to touch his knees. "You don't know shit."

He grins. I'd like to slap it off his face. "Mallory would never say that."

"Exactly."

"Do you know what you're getting yourself into?" he asks, his expression more serious this time.

"I'm a big girl. I can take care of myself."

"How do you plan on getting home tonight?"

I shrug. "It's only a couple blocks away. I'll walk."

He groans, running his fingers through his blond hair. "Those creeps would be more than happy to help you home, I'm sure. What time are you off?"

"No idea."

"That's fucking great," he says, sliding off the counter and disappearing inside his room. I don't understand why he even cares, but I'm not going to let him get to me.

BEFORE LEAVING FOR WORK, I pull on a pair of oversized black sweatpants and wrap my black coat tightly around me. I head out the door, making sure to lock it behind me. I heard Blake leave a few minutes ago while I was shut inside my bedroom. It's probably better that way since all he's good at is getting under my skin.

It's only six-thirty when I step outside but it's already pitch black. Feeling uneasy with very little light along the street, I walk quickly, anxious to get to work. I never thought I'd say that about Charlie's.

When I reach the front of the bar, I take a few deep, cleansing breaths. I really don't want to be here, but I need to be. Life's circumstances don't always allow us to make our own choices.

"You going in?" a husky male voice says from behind me. I look back to see a bald guy with neck tattoos standing a foot or so behind me. I hadn't realized it, but I'm standing right in front of the door, blocking the path of anyone who wants to go in or come out.

"Sorry," I say, pulling the door open.

I hold it, letting him pass before following him inside. My stomach rolls when I get a look inside. It's much more crowded than before. Pulling my coat even tighter, I make my way to the bar, noticing the guy who hired me pouring drinks.

His brows pull in when he sees me. "You come in to tell me you quit?"

"No," I answer, flattening my hands on the bar. "But can you tell me where I can change?"

He nods toward the back where a wooden restroom sign hangs. "When you're done, I'll tell you what I need you to do tonight."

"Thanks. By the way, what's your name?"

"It's written across your chest, sweetheart." He smiles, and all I can do is walk away before I change my mind and leave out the same door I walked through less than a minute ago.

As I make my way to the back, I notice that three-quarters of the people in here are men. Some are younger, around my age, and the crowd is a better mix than it was before. Maybe you don't need a tattoo and a rap sheet to hang out in this place after all.

I change quickly, not wanting to be in the rundown bathroom any longer than necessary. It looks like it hasn't been decently cleaned in months—the walls are covered in words I could never say around my mother.

I tug the bottom of my shorts as I make my way back out to the lion's den. This time, the stares I get are hungrier. Eyes don't stop on my face—they travel down, taking in my bare legs. I hate being the center of attention, especially this kind. Sex sells, but I've never wanted to be in the business.

Charlie nods his approval when he sees me. "Looking good. Next time, I'd prefer heels, though."

"I'll remember that," I reply, staring down at my chucks. "What do you need me to do?"

His eyes scan the bar until he finds who he's looking for, waving them over. "Dana has been with me a long time. She'll show you the ropes."

A perky, big-breasted blonde comes up beside me. "Yeah, Charlie?"

He points to me. "This is Lila. I want you to show her how it's done out there, and then let her take a few tables on her own."

Her eyes scan over me before she sticks her hand out. "It's nice to meet you."

"It's nice to meet you, too," I say, wrapping my hand around hers.

She lets go of me, gesturing to the sea of tables. "Follow me."

I stay close, tugging the hem of my shorts down one more time along the way. The thought of talking to any of the people in here makes my palms sweaty. This isn't my scene; in fact, I rarely drink.

"Our job is to take orders and read them off to Charlie. He makes them, and we serve. If you do a good job, on a night like tonight, you can go home with a couple hundred dollars. The key is to smile, and it doesn't hurt to flirt a little, too."

I quicken my pace to catch up with her. Even in four-inch heels, the girl could beat me in a foot race. "I'm not very good at flirting."

She stops, glancing over her shoulder at me. "It won't take much. You're freaking gorgeous."

I shyly tuck a piece of loose hair behind my ear. "If you're trying to boost my confidence, nothing you can say is going to make this any easier."

"Fine, just watch," she says, visibly rolling her eyes.

I watch her work, staying far enough back to let her do her thing but close enough that I can hear every word. She's good at this, letting all the little comments and innuendos go in one ear and out the other. And when one guy tries to pull her down on his lap, she brushes his hand away and saunters off like it's nothing.

When we make it back up to the bar, she rubs her temples, blowing air from her full red lips. "Ugh, I don't want to go back to that table. I don't mind flirting, but I hate when they fucking touch me. Who does that?"

"What are you going to do?"

She gives me a sideways look. "I'm going to take his drink back to the table, but I'll be careful not to stand next to him. The rest of the group isn't that bad."

I nod, deciding it's exactly what I would do in her situation.

Charlie comes up, leaning in to hear the order Dana just took. He begins pouring liquor into glasses and quickly places them on her tray.

"Time to get this over with," she says as she picks up the tray and makes her way through the crowd. She does exactly what she said she was going to do, setting the jerk's drink down from the other end of the table.

"Anything else I can get you?" she asks, a fake smile stretching across her face.

"Aren't you going to come sit?" the jerk asks. He sticks out his lower lip, and instead of making him more alluring, it disgusts me. Overweight, stomach pulling at his faded Budweiser T-shirt, he's definitely not a prize.

"No, I have more orders to take, but I'll be back after a while to check on you." She winks and motions for me to follow her.

"Maybe you should take his next drink and pour it over his head. The guy's an idiot," I whisper as we walk away.

"Charlie would lose his shit. If things get too bad, he'll kick them out."

I follow behind her for a couple hours. She does a great job of putting on her game face when she's in front of the customers, but I can tell some of them are getting to her.

"Ready to take a couple tables?" she asks after reading Charlie the latest round of drinks.

I'm not, but I probably never will be. "Sure," I answer, swallowing down my inhibitions.

"Okay." She smiles, scanning the room. "There are two tables in the corner by the door. One of the guys who just walked in can't keep his eyes off you, by the way."

While taking a calming breath, I slowly count to three. *1 . . . you can do this. 2 . . . quit thinking so much. 3 . . . just be yourself.* I grab a small pad of paper from the counter and spin around. I'm a few steps out before I spot the nightmare that sits in my section. Blake is with another guy and two women. With exception to him, the group is laughing and having a good time. His eyes are glued to me.

Not ready to face him, I walk up to my other table first. It seems safe—a group of middle-aged guys each sporting a wedding band. *How bad can it be?*

"Hey, how are you guys tonight?" I ask, forcing a smile.

"I think it just got a whole lot better." One winks, his eyes roaming down to my chest.

"Happy to hear that." The furniture store was a breeze compared to this. "So what can I get you?"

"Bud Light."

"Captain Coke, please."

"Make that two Buds."

The only guy yet to order is the one who can't seem to keep his eyes focused on my face. "And you?"

He doesn't answer right away, probably enjoying how uncomfortable he's making me. "Why don't you come over here to take my order?"

I panic, remembering what Dana taught me about staying away from the creepers. He hasn't touched me, though, so I move to the other end of the table, careful to stay a couple feet from him.

He scoots his chair over, coming a bit too close. "I'd like an Old Fashioned, and if you're available later," he starts, running the back of his finger up my thigh, "I'll show you what else I like."

I step out of his reach, feeling tears prick my eyes. I should say something, but I can't. This isn't me.

"Don't fucking touch her." I know that voice. I've heard that tone. Blake angles his body in front of mine. "Did I make myself clear?"

The guy sitting in front of Blake is larger, but Blake's got more muscle.

"Loud and clear," the guy says, turning back around in his chair.

"Good, now apologize."

The guy spins back around. "Fuck off, asshole. Any girl who walks around like that is asking for it."

My chest heaves up and down as I take a step back. Blake grips the front of the guy's blue T-shirt, pulling him up until their faces are only inches apart. "Apologize or you'll find out just how much of an asshole I can be."

"Blake," I interrupt, sliding up behind him. "It's fine. I can take care of myself."

He doesn't look back. Nothing. His voice softens as he addresses me. "It's okay, Nebraska, I got this one."

I step back, knowing this is a losing battle. It's obvious Blake doesn't listen to anyone.

"Now, apologize you little fucker," Blake spits, tightening his fingers around the blue cotton.

The guy raises his arms in surrender. "Dude, chill. I'll behave, okay?" He looks around Blake to where I stand. "I'm sorry."

Blake lets go of his T-shirt, sending the asshole back into his chair with a thump.

I nervously rub my fingers together, waiting for Blake. He turns slowly, a look of concern etched on his face. It's different than the arrogant way he usually looks at me. "You okay?" he asks.

I nod, closing my eyes to try and calm my nerves. "I can take care of myself."

He scoffs. "This isn't the place for you. I know you need a job, but I think you should look for a new one."

"Don't tell me what to do." I start walking off toward the bar, but he grips my arm, pulling me back.

"Trust me on this one," he says, his mouth so close to my ear I can feel his warm breath. What that and his woodsy scent do to me . . .

Get a grip, Lila.

I shake my arm free, facing him. "I know you think I have this perfect little life. That I'm some goody two shoes who moved to Chicago for an adventure. But you're wrong, Blake. I've been through my share of shit, and this bar is nothing compared to it. Now if you don't mind, I need to get back to work."

Without another word, I walk off to give Charlie my order. He puts it together quickly while I drum my fingers against the bar.

"How's it going?" Dana asks.

"Well, I went to my first table and met my first jerk. I guess some people think it's okay to grope a girl just because she has short shorts on."

She puffs air, sending her bangs flying up. "Are you sure you're up for this?"

"I have to be," I reply, honestly. "I need the money."

She nods. "I know the feeling. It's the only reason I stay."

"What's your story?"

"I moved here for a guy right out of high school. Things went well for a while, then he traded me in for someone else.

32

I'm not ready to move back home and admit failure so I stay, and without a college degree, this is all I can manage."

"That sucks." I rest my elbows on the bar and look up to the clock. It's just past midnight. Hopefully my shift doesn't last too much longer.

"I almost have enough saved up to pay for my first year of school. I'm not staying forever."

"What do you want to go to school for?"

She shrugs. "I want to be a nurse."

"That sounds better than this." I wink, watching Charlie deliver my drinks to the bar. "Hey, how do you get home after work?" I ask.

She stares at me curiously. "I drive."

"Would you mind giving me a ride? I only live a few blocks from here, but after everything tonight, I don't feel safe walking."

The thought of the guy in the blue T-shirt following me makes my stomach churn. It would be a while before anyone noticed I was even missing. I hate that I even think that way, but I watch way too much true crime TV.

"No problem," she says, picking up my tray to show me how to balance it. "Just watch out for anyone stepping in front of you."

I take it from her hands and carefully make my way through the packed bar. I go around to the opposite side of the table where I stood before, and set the drinks down one by one. To my surprise, the jerk in the blue shirt doesn't even look up at me. "Anything else I can get you guys?"

"We're good," two say in unison.

I turn my attention to Blake's table, noticing the way his eyes burn into me. The guy he's with has longer dark hair and piercings along his lip and eyebrow. He's wearing a dark gray hard rock band T-shirt that showcases the tattoos up and down his arm.

And the women they're with are pretty . . . beautiful actually. Both model thin, one with a short, trendy blonde bob and the other sporting dark, naturally wavy hair—the kind you see in shampoo commercials.

"Sorry it took me so long to get over here. What can I get you guys to drink?"

"I'll take a Cosmo," the woman with longer hair replies.

"Vodka and cranberry, please," the other adds.

I focus my attention on Blake, but he doesn't say anything, not at first. "What time do you get off?" he asks, zero amusement in his voice.

"I don't know," I reply, tapping my pen against my notepad.

"Ask." The way he says it makes it sound more like a command than a request. He's irritating, but this isn't like home where I can tell him to screw off and slam my door.

"What can I get you to drink?" I ask, changing the subject. Everyone at the table is looking between us like we're two tennis players in the middle of a long volley.

The other guy clears his throat. "I'll take a shot of whiskey."

My eyes lock in on Blake again. He's annoyed, that much is obvious, and I'm starting to feel the same way. "Would you like something to drink, Blake?"

"Water," he says simply, eyes narrowing in on me.

I walk away without replying, quickly making my way back to the bar. When I'm close enough to grip the top of the bar, I pull myself up against it. It's my shore after a long swim. The finish line after a marathon. It's just too bad I have to go and do it all over again.

Just when I'm starting to settle down, two strong arms cage me in. Every muscle in my body goes rigid. "What time do you get off work, Lila?" *Blake.* Why does he care so much? Up until yesterday, he was just another guy.

I lean forward until my chest meets the bar. He's too close . . . way too close. "I'm getting a ride home. You're off the hook, okay?"

He steps closer, his chest pressing to my back. "Who?"

He makes it hard to breathe. Hard to think. "Dana, the other waitress."

"Sure?"

"Positive."

"In that case, I'll take a shot of whiskey." His warm breath tickles my ear, sending a trail of shivers down my back. I want to scream for him to leave me alone, but my body is thinking something entirely different.

I nod, tightening my grip on the bar.

"Good. And, Lila, don't think I didn't notice how your body reacted to me just now." The tip of his nose brushes my ear before he walks away, leaving me flustered. I want to hate him, but my body is drawn to him like a magnet.

"Who the hell is that?" Dana asks, startling me.

"My new roommate."

"I give it one month," she says. I glance over, taking in her oversized smile.

"One month for what?" I ask, signaling for Charlie.

"Before you sleep with him."

She couldn't be more wrong. Or at least, that's what I keep telling myself. I'd be lying if I said I haven't imagined what his skin would feel like against mine a time or two. "Whatever."

She laughs, leaving me standing alone.

THE MORNING SUN SEEPS through my curtains a little earlier than I'd like. It was almost three in the morning when Dana finally dropped me off at home. By the time I showered the bar off my skin and relaxed enough to fall asleep, it was well past four.

Rolling over to my side, I notice I only slept four hours. If I'm going to be working at Charlie's, I might need to replace Mallory's pastel curtains with something darker, or invest in one of those little masks to cover my eyes.

Before I left last night, I asked Charlie about my schedule, and he said he needed me every Thursday, Friday, and Saturday night. It didn't sound like much, but Dana divulged that the place is pretty much dead every other night. The tips are good—enough to get me by while I have cheap rent, but maybe I can find another job during the week to get me out of this apartment sooner.

I nestle myself between the pillows and pull the warm down comforter up past my eyes. I don't have to be to work until seven, and if I don't get more sleep, I'm going to regret it. Especially if the crowd is anything like last night.

After a few minutes with no success, I throw my arms up. My mind wanders to Blake. Even last night, when I was trying to fall asleep, my mind drifted to him. He's the epitome of what I don't need or want in my life right now. He's too intense and a little rough around the edges.

I won't allow him to control me. I'm certainly not going to let him pop up at my place of employment and act like he has a say in what I can and can't do.

Just as my eyelids start to grow heavy, music blares from the other side of the apartment. Head-banging, wood-splitting music ricocheting off the walls. *Asshole.*

After a couple minutes of trying to ignore it, I gather my wits and throw my comforter off. I yank my door open with such force it hits against the wall with a thud. Without hesitation, I stalk across the living room and push Blake's bedroom door open, ready to tear him in two.

I'm stopped dead in my tracks before I get the chance. The woman with short blonde hair straddles Blake's naked body. His eyes are closed tightly, his hands gripping her firm ass, moving her carefully against him. I clench my teeth to keep myself from screaming out as a burning sensation fills my chest then seeps down into my stomach. Seeing him with her shouldn't bother me, but it does. Feeling defeated and annoyed, I disappear into my bedroom and sink into my warm bed without being noticed.

When I wake up hours later, the house is quiet again. For a while, I lay still, listening to the sound of the wind against my windowpane. A light dusting of flurries falls from the gray sky. It's one of those days I just want to stay in bed in a pair of sweats and devour a good book, but my stomach growls, putting an end to that idea.

I pull my thick terrycloth robe from the back of the chair and tie it tightly around me to chase away the chill.

After taking a deep breath, I slowly open my door. If Blake's home, there isn't any sign of him. His door is closed, and the apartment is silent.

I can't keep doing this. There's no way I'm going to be able to live here with him; I feel like a prisoner sequestered to her cell. I don't want to think about what he's doing, or what I might walk in on.

I pour myself a bowl of cereal and sit down at the small dining table. *This is how it should be*, I think, pulling my knees to my chest. Quiet. Peaceful. Comfortable. Alone. My eyes fixate on the snow falling outside as my mind wanders off.

There's still so much I want to do with my life. Coming here was obviously the first step, but the last thing I want is to get stuck working at Charlie's for the next few years just to escape my old life. I want to live in a place I love, spending my days doing what I love. No matter what it takes, I'm going to get there.

After finishing my cereal, I grab a pad of paper and pen from the table and scribble House Rules across the top. Blake and I are both adults; we should be able to make this work until I find a better solution. Besides, if I have to find my own place, it's going to take a while longer before I have enough savings to make it happen.

When I'm done, I have exactly five rules. They sound fair enough, not asking him to do anything I wouldn't do for him. I set it on the end of the counter and take one more look out the large window in the living room. The light coating of snow on everything makes it look peaceful, and I wish I could take the rest of the day to just explore. I want to find the art scene, to make new friends.

Maybe tomorrow when I have a day off.

My phone rings from the bedroom, pulling my attention away. I run across the cool floors, anxious to hear a familiar voice.

I slide my thumb across the screen to answer and lift it to my ear. "Hello."

"Hey, just thought I'd call and see how your first day in Chicago went." It's Mallory.

"Well, besides living with your brother, everything's fine."

She sighs. "Is he giving you a hard time? 'Cause I'll kick his ass."

"I think you already know the answer. Can't he stay somewhere else?"

"That bad, huh?"

"He's the most stubborn, inconsiderate—"

"I know," she interrupts. "I've had to deal with him for twenty-four years."

"Why didn't you just tell me he was living here? I would've made other arrangements." Like maybe stay home for a few more months to save money for a deposit on an apartment and make damn sure I had a good job. It sucked staying in that town, but it wouldn't have killed me.

"He didn't move in until just a couple weeks ago . . . after we talked about you using it while I'm out of town. He's been going through a lot, and I couldn't tell him no."

I sit on the edge of my bed, pulling at the belt of my robe with my free hand. "I made some house rules. Hopefully that will help."

She laughs hysterically at the other end of the phone.

"Shit," I mutter, falling back onto the mattress.

"Yep." I hear her tongue click. "Anyway, it's getting late here. I have class early in the morning, so I'm going to go to bed. I just wanted to check in."

"Yeah, I need to get ready for work."

"You got a job! Why didn't you tell me you found something?" she asks, excitedly.

"It's not anything to brag about."

"Well, where is it?"

I hesitate, nibbling on my lower lip. "Charlie's. It's just a couple blocks from here."

There's a short pause before she says anything else. "I don't think I've ever been there, but be careful walking through that neighborhood alone at night. Maybe you should have Blake pick you up when your shift is over."

"There's a girl I work with who doesn't mind giving me a ride. And as far as never being there before, you're not missing much." The cruddy, outdated interior flashes through my mind. The smell. The people. I could live without ever having to go back there.

"Ugh, well hopefully you'll find another job soon. Go downtown and check with some of the design or architecture firms," she suggests.

"I will early next week."

She yawns. "I better let you go before I fall asleep. I'll call you again in a couple days, okay?"

"All right. Sleep well."

"Have fun at work," she says, right before she hangs up.

Noticing the time, I clear my head and get ready for my second night at Charlie's. *God, help me.*

There's only a little more than an hour before closing time. The place was packed for three hours straight, but things are finally slowing down. I've made enough tips to pay a month's worth of student loans, though, so I can't complain about that.

"My feet are killing me," Dana says, sliding up next to me at the bar.

I look down at her four-inch heels and roll my eyes. "You should get a pair of chucks."

"Charlie is going to be pissed if he sees those on your feet."

"He'll get over it."

She smiles. "You're probably right. He's not going to fire a hot little piece like you."

"Great, just what I always wanted. A job that I keep simply based on my looks. Besides, I'm tired and I could care less what I look like."

Her brows furrow. "Did someone party after work last night?"

"I wish. My nightmare of a roommate brought that blonde home from the bar, and I guess he's not all that quiet when he screws." The whole messed up vision crosses through my mind again. *If only magic eraser worked for everything.*

"Wait, are you jealous?" she asks, her lips pulling into a smile.

Defensiveness rises in my veins. "Hell no. I'm annoyed, Dana. There's a big difference." *And, maybe I'm a little bit jealous.*

She laughs.

I growl. She's so wrong, or I'm in denial.

Charlie appears at the other end of the bar, staring at us. Besides reading countless drink orders off to him, I've barely talked to him all night. "Do you girls need help finding something to do?"

"No, Charlie," Dana says, "We're just trying to . . . regroup."

"Whatever. I don't pay you to regroup. Get out there and check drinks."

With a collective groan, we disperse to our respective tables. Tonight hasn't been as bad as last night. No comments that crossed any lines. No touching. If every night were more like this, I might be able to handle it for a few months.

41

"Hey, baby!" a balding, middle-aged man calls as I maneuver my way between tables. "Can I get another Bud Light? I've been empty for over ten minutes."

"Sorry," I answer, backing away. "I'll grab you another."

I swivel on my back heel to get to the bar, but I run smack dab into a muscular chest instead. "You should really watch where you're going," Blake says, grinning down at me.

Crossing my arms over my chest, I say, "If you sat down at a table, we wouldn't have that problem."

"Oh, trust me, we'd still have a problem. It might not be this one, but we'd definitely have one."

"Look, I don't have time for this shit tonight." I try to push past him, but he grips my upper arm, halting my progress.

"What section are you working?" His body is so close to mine, the heat from it scorches my skin. I can only imagine what his naked body would feel like against mine. *Stop it, Lila!*

"There's two of us; that gives you a fifty percent chance of guessing right. Sit down and find out." I yank my arm away, but I can still feel the impression of his hand on my skin. "Good luck!" I shout, heading toward the bar.

My night was going so well, but now I'm irritated with a side of extra pissed off. *Why can't he just leave me alone?*

"Your hot roommate checking up on you again? Or is he trolling for another woman to take home tonight?" Dana asks when I come up beside her.

"He's not that hot," I reply, staring straight ahead. *He's not hot . . . he's freaking gorgeous.*

"Whatever."

"Can you do me a favor?" I look at her, watching her eyes narrow on me. "Wait on him. I can't do it."

She picks up two ice-cold beer bottles and starts walking away. "No can do. Besides, he's here to see you."

I clench my teeth, trying to bite back my anger. He can't keep doing this. He can't keep coming in here and acting like we're anything but roommates who barely know each other. He's not my friend. He's not my enemy. He's just a guy . . . an attractive one at that.

Charlie puts the tray full of shots I ordered in front of me, pointing toward the back corner. "There's a guy sitting all alone in the back, waving his hand. Make sure you get his order after taking these. You girls are going to cost me a lot of business."

I don't have to look over my shoulder to know who it is. *I'm going to kill Blake. A slow, excruciating death.*

"I'll take care of him," I say, flashing a smile made purely of fake sugar.

While I deliver the shots to a table full of intoxicated college guys, I don't let my eyes wander to Blake. He's watching me . . . I feel it. I decide to play a little game, an attempt to get a one-up on him.

One of the college guys can't seem to keep his hands to himself. The backs of his fingers graze my bare thigh, and instead of knocking it away, I place my hand on his shoulder and smile.

"Are you guys out celebrating tonight?" I ask. His fingers move upward, brushing against the bottom of my shorts. Inside I cringe, but I don't let my smile falter.

"Just blowing off some steam," one of them answers.

Without warning, the guy who'd been touching me pulls his hand away and yanks me onto his lap. I feel his excitement pressed against my ass, and scoot forward to avoid the intrusion. This is just flirting, I tell myself.

"And you picked this place?" I ask.

"This place has the best view in the city. What are you doing after work tonight?" the guy whispers against my hair.

"I'll probably just go home. It's going to be pretty late."

He grins at me, licking his lower lip. My stomach rolls.

Before either one of us can say anything else, a warm hand wraps around my arm, pulling me up. "This one's going home with me tonight!" Blake growls, trying to shove me behind him.

I do my best to step out of his reach. He's the Hercules to my Popeye without spinach. "No, I'm not."

"Yes, you are," he seethes, glaring back at me.

"Fuck off, Blake. Or better yet, find someone to fuck and leave me alone." I use anger to loosen my arm from his grip and walk back to the bar. If Charlie saw all that, he's going to kill me. Luckily, he looks preoccupied with a couple of guys at the other end of the bar.

I feel Blake watching me but don't look back. It might give him some satisfaction, and I don't want to give him anything of the sort. I grab another round of drinks, taking my time to set each glass on the table with ease, knowing Blake's tracking my every move. He can suffer; I doubt he really came here for a drink anyway.

On my way to his table, I stop to wipe off a few that are now empty and push in chairs. Charlie's probably watching me, wondering what the hell I'm doing, but I highly doubt he'd fire me over this. I've mastered this job in a matter of days.

I saunter up to the small table Blake occupies all by himself. It's a sad sight really—an attractive guy sitting alone in a shit hole like this. "What would you like to drink tonight, sir?" I ask.

"Sit," he says simply.

"I'm working."

His brows knit together as his eyes scan the room. "There are three fucking tables. Now sit."

I cross my arms over my chest like the defiant only child I am. "You're going to get me fired."

"That old prick won't fire you. Trust me . . . you could walk out of here right now and you'd still have a job tomorrow."

Looking over my shoulder, I spot Dana leaning against the bar, watching us intently. She nods, mouthing, "I got this."

As I turn back around, I see the smirk on Blake's face. He saw the whole exchange and knows I'm all his. I'm really starting to hate this guy.

"Fine," I say, sliding in across from him. "Did you need me to sit to take your order?"

"It didn't look like you were having any problems sitting a few minutes ago. You better watch yourself, Lila."

"Maybe I like him," I tease, pulling my bottom lip between my teeth.

"You're not that stupid." He stares at me, eyes smoldering.

"Or, maybe I am, and you just haven't figured it out yet. What's your deal anyway? Nothing better to do than follow me around?" I ask, leaning in.

He shrugs. "My sister would kill me if anything happened to you, and believe it or not, she's the only person I give one fuck about besides my parents."

"By the way," he adds, pulling the list I left on the counter from his pocket, "this is bullshit."

"You came here to talk about the house rules?" I ask, feeling even more annoyed.

"These aren't house rules. It's pure fucking bullshit."

Regular Blake is good-looking, but there's something a little extra special about pissed off Blake. Naughty Lila wants to pull him into a closet and shut him up with her body, but Nice Lila would never allow it.

I rest my elbows on the table, leaning forward even more. "I don't think so. No loud music before noon seems pretty reasonable."

He laughs, leaning in. "Is it the music that bothers you or the sex?"

My face flushes. *Good thing the lighting sucks in here.* "Music," I answer, swallowing hard. The sex bothered me. It bothered me a lot because it made me feel stupid jealousy that I probably shouldn't.

"And what's this shit about being quiet in the kitchen? I can't fry an egg without a pan, Lemon Drop."

"Did you just call me Lemon Drop?"

His eyes twinkle, even under the dull bar lights. "I'm pretty sure that's what I just said. Answer the question."

"I'm a light sleeper." Our faces are inches apart, but I'm not backing away. It would be an admission of defeat.

"Then get some earplugs."

"It would be a lot cheaper for you to be quiet."

For a matter of seconds, we just stare at each other—a simple battle of wills. It's a variation on one of those stupid staring contests I used to have as a kid. Eventually, one of us will blink, and it's not going to be me.

He finally leans back, dropping an arm over the back of his chair. "See the garbage can next to the door?" I don't have to look. I know where every stupid garbage can is in this place. "That's where this list is going on my way out."

"How mature of you," I say, trying not to show my frustration. He doesn't deserve to know how much he gets under my skin. I stand up and push in my chair, anxious to get as far away from Blake as I can.

"I meant what I said about being your ride!" he yells behind me.

I keep walking, tired of him—the way he looks at me, the crap he says. It's a good thing I already asked Dana for a ride. He can wait around here all he wants, but as soon as my shift ends, I'm sneaking out back with her.

AFTER ONLY TWO DAYS OF WORK, it already feels like my days off are well deserved. I spend the day at the Museum of Contemporary Art, and then head off to the store for some much needed groceries. Dinner, wine, and a good book sound like the best medicine after a difficult week. Besides, a snowstorm is blowing in, and I'll be lucky if I get out for the next few days.

It's a little after seven when I finally get back to my apartment with a full bag of groceries in hand. Seeing that it's quiet and completely dark, I breathe a sigh of relief. Almost twenty-four hours, no work, no Blake—it's almost as if I've landed in the life I was supposed to live.

My stomach growls as I unpack everything, leaving the ingredients for homemade pizza on the counter. It's something my mom makes all the time on cold winter nights, and I could use a slice of home right now.

I plug my iPod into the docking station and blare Boyce Avenue throughout the apartment while I chop peppers, mushrooms, and onions. While waiting for the sauce to simmer, I pour myself a glass of red wine, bring it to my nose, then let the first sip coat my tongue. *This day was exactly what*

I needed, I think, as I relax against the counter. It's these little things in life we should never take for granted.

As I swallow down the last sip from my wine glass, the lock clicks and the door to the apartment swings open. Blake appears in the same clothes he had on last night. No jacket, just his signature gray stocking hat. His dark eyes find me right away.

"Found another ride home last night, did you?" he asks as he sets a brown paper bag on the counter and stands over the stove, inhaling the tomato and garlic aroma.

Last night, after I snuck out back with Dana, I was sure he'd come barging through our apartment door and cause a scene. He didn't.

"Dana gave me a ride," I answer, pressing the fresh pizza dough into a round stone.

"I was going to give you a ride." He uses the wooden spoon to swirl the sauce around. His shoulders are tense, and he sounds tired. Exhausted actually.

"Dana offered. I accepted."

He sighs, running his long, thick fingers through his hair. "Why are you so stubborn?"

I still can't figure out why he feels this need to wiggle his way into my life, to protect me. Maybe Mallory had something to do with this. Whatever it is, I don't need it.

"Can you just drop it?" I ask. "If you were so worried about how I was getting home, you should have followed up sooner."

"I made sure you made it home okay," he replies in a low voice.

"How did you do that?"

He shrugs. "I followed you."

"That's not creepy."

"Some day you'll thank me," he answers.

Maybe he's right.

"Can I have that please?" I ask, holding my hand out for the spoon.

He just stares at me, eyes locking for longer than I'd like— longer than I can bear. His Adam's apple dips as he places the spoon in my hands. "What are you making?"

"Veggie pizza. It's my mom's recipe." I train my eyes on the pan, watching the sauce simmer. Anything to keep from looking at him.

"Smells amazing. I don't remember the last time I had a home-cooked meal . . . besides eggs, of course."

I stir, trying to make myself look busy.

He stares, increasing my discomfort.

I don't know him well enough to make easy conversation. I keep my hands and eyes occupied, until I remember he didn't walk in empty handed.

"What's in the brown bag?" I ask, pointing to where he'd set it on the counter. When my eyes find him again, I notice he hasn't moved. He's been standing right behind me, just far enough back that we're not touching. He'd been staring . . . I can tell by how long it's taking him to react to my question.

"Tequila."

"Do we have limes?"

A sexy grin spreads across his face. "Bottom drawer of the fridge."

Glancing out the window, I see huge snowflakes falling across the light from the street lamp. Blake wouldn't be my first choice to spend a snowy night with, but it doesn't look like either of us will be going anywhere.

"If you share your tequila, I'll share my pizza."

Without hesitation, he says, "Sounds like we have a deal. Do you need any help? My end of the bargain is already met."

I wave him off. "I got it."

"I'm going to jump in the shower," he says. He holds my waist, gently moving me aside to place the tequila in the fridge.

His hands apply the perfect amount of pressure. I shiver, imagining what else they could do. Then, without another word, he disappears behind his bedroom door.

I pour myself another glass of red, taking small sips as I place the sauce, veggies, and fresh mozzarella over the homemade dough. I slide the stone in the oven, my mouth watering at the mere thought of having the reminder of home against my taste buds.

Blake walks out of his room in a pair of navy lounge pants that hang low on his hips and a tight white T-shirt right as I'm about to pull the pizza from the oven. The mere sight of him causes me to hesitate. I can't remember the last time someone affected me like this.

"Is it ready?" he asks, sliding up behind me. His body doesn't touch mine, but I still feel the heat as I breathe in his scent.

I shake all thoughts of him and his allure from my mind. "I was just about to take the pizza out of the oven."

"Do you need help?"

"Umm, you could take out some plates and silverware."

He steps away from me, allowing me to relax. I turn the oven off and carefully take the pizza stone out. It looks amazing, crust perfectly browned, cheese bubbling . . . exactly how Mom makes it.

"Do you want me to cut it?"

I shake my head, handing him a cup of fresh grated cheese and crushed red pepper flakes. "Set these on the table, I'll be right over."

"The only place I'm going to let you have any control around here is in the kitchen." He winks, then walks away from me. I'm not exactly sure what he meant by that; there's not one aspect of my life I'm going to let him control.

I cut the pizza, placing two perfect slices on each plate, and carry them over to the table. His eyes widen like it's nothing he's ever seen before. "Is this all you can make?" he asks, sprinkling some Parmesan over his.

I take my first bite, the hot sauce burning the roof of my mouth. "I have lots of tricks up my sleeve," I reply, wiping the corners of my mouth.

The sexy smirk returns as he fixes his gaze on me. "I'll bet you do."

"So do you have any plans after dinner?" I ask, almost hoping for a night to myself.

"I don't think so. They're calling for at least a foot of snow overnight. I'm thinking about watching a movie or something."

I groan. "I hate TV."

"How about a game? I know one in particular that could be interesting."

"And if I say no?"

"We could talk about your rules. I didn't quite get through all of them last night." He takes a big bite of pizza, but his eyes never leave me.

"I'm serious about the rules."

His head tilts to one side. "And I'm serious about not following them."

I feel my face heating up. I didn't ask him for too much, or at least I didn't think I did. "We better just let the rules be then."

"Finish your pizza, and then I'll explain the game. Since we're going to be roommates for the foreseeable future, Lemon Drop, we should probably get to know each other better."

For the next ten minutes, we quietly devour our pizza. Even without words, it's nice to have someone to sit with. There's no arguing at least.

When we're done, he picks up our plates and rinses them off while I disappear inside my bedroom to change into a pair of black jogging pants and a matching hoodie. I tie my long red hair up into a bun and step back out into the living room, noticing the supper mess has been completely cleaned up.

Blake's in the kitchen, slicing limes and bobbing his head to the rhythm of some heavy rock song. When he spots me, his eyes scan my body, head to toe. "I like that look much better than your Charlie's uniform."

"No you don't," I say, rolling my eyes at him.

His eyebrows knit in.

Sighing, I plop myself down on one end of the couch, pulling my knees up in front of me. "Let's get this game started, or I'm going to go read a book."

He comes around the counter with two shot glasses, a bowl of sliced limes, and a full bottle of tequila in hand. "Did they not have shitty bars, books, and cheap rent in Nebraska?"

I'm back to wanting to kill him. "They sure did, but there were also a bunch of things I wanted to leave in Nebraska."

"I get it. You're running from your past."

"The game, Blake. Let's get to the game."

He arranges everything on the wooden coffee table, settling in on the other end of the couch. Then, he glares at me until I can't even look at him anymore. Maybe I'm afraid that I might see too much in him . . . or maybe it's that he might see too much in me. Before he says anything, he grabs my knees and pulls me closer. Not on top of him or right next to him but still too close.

"Have you ever played truth or dare?" he asks.

"When I was like thirteen."

He smiles. "This one is a little different . . . there won't be any dares."

"What's the point?" I ask, scrunching my nose. "Besides, aren't we a little old for this?"

"Maybe, but I just want to get to know you better. Is that so hard to believe?" He watches me carefully, and when I don't respond, he fills both shot glasses and slides one to my side of the table. "Here are the rules. We take turns asking questions. If you don't want to answer, you have to take a shot."

"I'll play, but I get to go first."

"I figured that," he says, resting his feet on the coffee table. "Let's hear it."

"How old are you?"

"I see you're starting with the good stuff." He smirks, tilting his head to get a better look at me. "Twenty-seven. My turn."

"Great," I mumble.

"Oh, come on, Lemon Drop, this is going to be good." He licks his lower lip. "Where's the riskiest place you've ever had sex?"

This one I actually have to contemplate. I've only been with Derek, and I wouldn't necessarily say our sex life was exciting. I mean, he's all I've ever known, but we didn't join the mile high club or sneak off into a closet or bathroom stall. No elevator or balcony sex. It was all extremely vanilla with an occasional drip of chocolate syrup—as in Derek literally licking it from my breasts. Maybe I should just throw the shot back, but it's a stupid question to waste a drink on.

"Umm, I'd probably have to say in a tent." Undoubtedly, my cheeks have a cherry red tint to them. One look at him, and I can tell he wants to laugh. He's good at holding it in. "My turn."

I give it a little thought—trying to decide what it is I want to know most—in case he decides this game isn't so fun after another question or two.

"Where do you disappear to . . . when you don't come home all night?"

The expression on his face hardens. I know when he does leave, he's never in the best of moods, but he comes back acting like everything's okay. I'm curious. "I'll take a shot."

He pulls a half slice of lime between his teeth, bites, and then throws the tequila back. He winces—the aftershock of his first drink.

"My turn," he says, eyes narrowing in on me. "What are you running from?"

I swallow hard, unable to free the lump in my throat. "Who said I was running?

"There's a reason you're here. Answer the question or drink."

"Well, I actually like tequila so I'll drink."

I squeeze the lime between my teeth and throw the liquid back, feeling the burn in my throat. With the wine I already had, I'll be a goner after a couple of these.

Blake reaches up, swiping the lime juice from my mouth. I focus back on him, watching as he sucks the pad of his thumb to get a taste of his own. I swallow, trying to get a grip on myself. I want to know more, but I don't want to tell him more. "Looks like we're back to you. What do you do for a living?"

He shrugs. "I'm taking a break right now, but before that, I painted murals, mostly in large commercial buildings, hotels . . . that sort of thing."

"What do you live off of?" The question just rolls from my tongue. It's none of my business, but that doesn't mean I'm not curious.

"That's more than one question. I'll answer it, but you have to take a shot if you're going to break the rules," he remarks, pointing to the bottle of tequila.

When he first proposed this game, I didn't consider it a game at all, but now I see the whole point is deciding which question is worth a shot. It's teetering between opening myself up and getting flat ass drunk. In the end, I want to know more so I throw the shot back.

He continues, "It's something called a savings account. I have enough of it to last me a while."

I nod, deciding that probably wasn't worth a drink.

"My turn." His eyes brighten, and he licks his lower lip. It's hard to keep my eyes up, away from his perfect mouth.

"I'm waiting," I say, feeling breathless.

The corner of his mouth quirks. "How old were you when you lost your virginity?"

Very few people know the answer to that; sex isn't something I talk about with just anyone. "That's a lame question, don't you think?" I ask, curling my legs up under my body.

He shrugs. "You either need to answer or drink."

It's none of his business whatsoever, but my head is already starting to swim from the alcohol . . . this isn't a big deal. "Eighteen," I mutter, focusing my attention on the wood grain of the coffee table. Talking about it makes me think of Derek. He was the first and only person who has ever been inside of me like that. Sometimes, I wish I could go back and undo it all. I could have saved myself so much heartache.

Needing to forget, I fill my shot glass again and pour it down my throat, skipping the lime all together.

"Bad experience?" Blake asks.

"Just makes me think of someone I'd rather not think about."

Blake's gaze falls to the floor, his thumb brushing over his lower lip. He either wants to say something or avoid the subject. I can't always tell with him.

I clear my throat, wrapping my arms around my folded knees. "Since I already know you have a sex life, let's talk about love. Have you ever been in love?"

He inhales a deep breath, looking up to the ceiling. I recognize the emotional pain—deep-seeded, damaging pain. Without saying a word, he pours himself another shot and brings the glass to his lips, tipping it back until it's empty. He barely looks at me.

"Have you ever been in love?" he asks, probably wanting to catch me the way he'd been caught.

I nod, feeling the effect of the alcohol in my blood. If I stood right now, I wouldn't get far without someone holding me up. "My turn," I say. "Before I started working at Charlie's, did you hang out there?"

He laughs. "Not near as much as I have been lately." He stops, giving me a second to roll my eyes. "Did you move here to try to put together a broken heart?"

He's not going to let this go, and I'm not going to talk. I fill my glass yet again and down the liquid. My head spins to the point where it's hard to even form questions.

Nothing comes besides the one thing I've wondered since I met him a few days ago. "How can you and Mallory be so different?"

"I'm male. She's female."

"That's not what I meant."

He shrugs. "We grew up in the same house with the same rules, but once we turned eighteen, our lives took different paths."

"Can you be a little more specific?" I ask. My eyes feel heavy, the mix of wine, pizza and tequila weighing me down.

"I answered your question," he says tiredly, laying his head back against the sofa.

The room is quiet again as I wait for him to ask me another question. It doesn't come. At least I don't remember it.

MY HEAD THROBS.

My stomach turns.

I'm not in my bed. There's no pillow for my head, no soft mattress under my body. I rub the sleep from my eyes, focusing my attention on the light coming from the window—the living room window. The sun isn't shining, which is a good thing because it would do nothing for my pounding head.

Warm skin brushes against my stomach, a muscular arm wraps itself around my waist. Turning my head, I see Blake sleeping behind me—our bodies perfectly aligned on the couch.

I don't remember how we got this way, but if the ache in my head is any indication, there's a good reason for that. I haven't been like this with anyone in a long time. Even when I was with Derek.

I shift, trying to get out from under his hold before he wakes up. I slowly work myself free, and just when I think I am, his arm tightens around me, tucking me back against his warm body. There's no way to tell if he's actually awake without looking.

I'm not going to look.

In many ways, I'm starting to feel like Blake and I are similar. Not so much in personality, but how deep we bury ourselves in our secrets.

And the feeling of being wrapped up in him is different than I ever could have imagined. It's something I want, but I don't. Having someone hold me again fills a hole I didn't even realize I had. I understand the idea of a rebound guy, and I'm not going to let myself go there, but this is just as good.

"Aly," he mumbles behind me, ripping me from my thoughts.

"Who?" I ask, louder than I intended.

"What the fuck," I hear him mutter, his mouth against my hair. He stirs, and his whole body tenses right before he lets go of me. He's coming to his own realization, but it seems like he's not going to take it as well as I did.

I sit up, the throbbing in my head unbearable.

"What are you doing here?" he asks, his voice angry and confused.

"Trying to wake up." Scanning my body for the first time, I'm relieved that I'm in the same clothes as last night.

"No, I mean, what the fuck are you doing here . . . with me?" Out of the corner of my eye, I see him come up beside me. He rubs his own temples but keeps his eyes off me.

I think about standing and simply walking away, but I can't. "I think we passed out. Don't you remember how many shots we had last night?"

"We didn't." He signals between us with question in his eyes.

"We still have our clothes on. Asshole," I groan, rubbing my temples.

"I don't want you to think this meant something, because it was nothing."

"I didn't want it to be anything," I whisper. *Or maybe I do, and I won't admit it.*

A giant ball of tangled emotion forms in my throat, and I do my best to swallow it down. I didn't expect anything from him, but hearing him voice it without invitation is a cruel rejection. Even if I admit that I want him, he wouldn't want me.

"At least we're on the same page," he mumbles, standing and hurrying off to his room. His door slams, causing me to startle.

He was cold.

Then he was warm.

And now, he's back to cold again. It's probably better if I don't let him in . . . to avoid the chill that's sure to follow. Wanting to be hidden away should he decide to come out of his room, I stumble to my own. I should jump in the shower to wake myself up, but I fall into my bed instead. The headache, the rejection . . . I just want to fall back asleep.

Pounding music—the kind with enough bass to shake the floor beneath you—wakes me. He's back to his old self, and I want to kill him. And more importantly, I hope he didn't bring someone else back here just to prove to me that I'm nothing. I heard it loud and clear.

I hear his bedroom door fly open, but only one set of feet sound on the hardwoods. A weird wave of relief sweeps through me. Curling myself into a ball, I try to drift back to sleep, the covers pulled up high against my neck.

All is right in the world again until I hear pans clanking in the kitchen. Two rules. He's broken two rules already. If I walked out of this room, he'd probably be standing in his boxers. That would make three.

Pam sprays. Eggs crack. The smell of breakfast fills our small apartment. The TV clicks on and SportsCenter drowns out the music that still plays. If I wasn't pissed before, I'm pissed now. I march out of my room, hitting the power button on the TV before stomping off to Blake's bedroom to turn down the music.

I'm almost back to my room when a hand wraps around my elbow, pulling me back. "If something's not yours, don't touch it."

I crank my head, looking down at his fingers wrapped around my arm. "Then get your hands off me."

His eyes sparkle. "You're right," he says, letting go of me. "And, if I'm following that rule, you can too."

Turning around, I cross my arms over my chest. "I'm starting to think you can't follow rules."

He comes closer, but I stand my ground. I've spent months convincing myself that I'm not weak. I'm not going to let someone like him bring my weakness back to the surface.

"I do what I want," he spits, "So stop trying to change me."

"Don't worry, Blake. I'm well aware that I can't wash the jerk off you," I say, spinning on my heel.

One point for Lila.

When I finally get out of bed, everything is quiet. I stretch my arms up, noticing a new voicemail lighting up my phone. It's probably Mom or Mallory, I think to myself as I roll over to retrieve it.

I press play, putting it against my ear. "Hey, Lila, it's Pierce Stanley, we sat together on the plane to Chicago." He laughs lightly before continuing, "I wanted to see how things were going in the Windy City and if you had any luck on the job front. My company just had a design apprenticeship open up that you might be interested in. Anyway, give me a call if you're interested. I'd really like to tell you more about it."

It's not that I have short-term memory problems, but I'd almost forgotten about Pierce Stanley until just now.

The thought of getting a real job—one I might actually like—makes me want to call him back right away, but I can't.

I want it so badly, my dream job, but I'm scared of failure. Not because I don't have the education or the eye for it, but because I've failed before. I'm not going back down that road again.

FOR THE FIRST TIME SINCE I moved to Chicago, true loneliness consumes me. It's been almost two days since I last saw Blake. Two days since I've talked to anyone outside of this apartment besides the nice guy who delivered my Chinese food last night.

The snow trapped me inside.

Then it was my own anti-social mood that kept me in. This isn't who I am, or who I promised myself I'd be after Derek wrecked me. I'm stronger than this, or I should be.

Last night, I started to wonder if Blake was right, if moving to Chicago was a stupid idea. I'm wasting the opportunity, doing the same thing I would if I were still at home.

Picking up my phone, I dial one of the only sane people I've met since moving here.

"Hey," Dana answers.

"Hey, what are you up to?" I ask, nibbling on my lower lip.

"Actually," she groans, "I was just getting ready for a date, and I feel like I have nothing to wear. What are you up to?"

My smile falters just a little. *It looks like I'll be spending another night home alone.* "Who's the guy?"

"Just a guy."

"Someone from Charlie's?" I ask. Chances are I don't know him, but it doesn't lessen my curiosity.

"No, you've never met this one. He's not really the type who frequents Charlie's."

"That's probably a good thing." It's true. There's not a single guy at Charlie's who I would agree to see outside of work. I'd probably end up murdered in a ditch. And without a stable roommate to report me missing, it would go unnoticed for days.

"So what's up?" she asks, changing the subject.

"I was calling to see if you wanted to do something tonight, but we can make plans for another time."

"That sucks," she says, and then backtracks. "I mean . . . it doesn't suck that you called but just that I have other plans. How about next week on one of our nights off?"

We work the next three nights, but at least that means I won't be stuck in this apartment. Alone.

"If you can squeeze me in," I tease, feeling a little unsure.

"It's a date. Tuesday . . . put me on your calendar for eight o'clock. I know this cute little bar that has cheap tacos and margaritas." *A girl after my heart . . . if I can bring myself to drink tequila again.*

The door clicks open, and I look up to see Blake coming in. "It's a date. By the way, have fun tonight."

"You too. I hope you find something to do."

I hear Blake's heavy boots on the floor but force myself to keep my eyes off him. "It's about to get interesting."

I throw my phone down on the couch and pick up my Kindle, trying to get lost in my book again. It's usually the best sort of distraction, but I smell his soap and hear him moving around me.

My eyes scan a whole page, but I can't repeat a single word I read. My heart races and all that flows through my mind is what he'll say, or if he'll even say anything at all.

"When is your date?" he finally asks, standing at the end of the couch. I try not to look, but I can't help it. He looks good in

63

fitted black jeans and a muscle-hugging gray henley; my eyes linger a little longer than they should.

"Next week." I force my eyes back to my book.

"Did you meet him at work?" He places emphasis on the last word. I'd never date anyone I met at Charlie's, but he doesn't know that.

If I didn't know better, I'd say someone is a little too curious—jealous even. "Hmm, kind of. Except he is a she, and it's the type of date where there's zero chance we'll end up in bed together at the end of the night."

"Sucks to be you." His voice is lighter, teasing. Silence follows, but I know he's still there. No footsteps. No doors opening or shutting. He's appraising me . . . I feel it. He doesn't have to report his findings because I guarantee the value isn't all that high right now.

"Is this what you do every night?" he finally asks.

"Nothing better to do." All I've done is read on my days off. It's too cold to go out and explore more of the city, and my one attempt to get out of here and be social was a bust.

"I'm going with a couple guys to watch a band downtown. I think you should come."

I shake my head without looking up. "No thanks."

He yanks the quilt off my bare legs. My tiny cotton shorts seemed like a good idea until just a few seconds ago. "Maybe it's not optional."

"You can't tell me what to do, Blake." I try to pull the blanket from him, but he steps back until it's out of my reach.

"If all you want to do is read, go ahead, but you're bored. I can tell."

I purse my lips, not at all sensitive to the fact that I have no make-up on. "How's that?" I ask.

"For one thing," he says, coming up next to me, "your reading machine is upside down. Kind of hard to read that way, don't you think, Lemon Drop?"

Asshole. I flip my Kindle around. "I was just finishing a phone call. And why the hell do you keep calling me Lemon Drop?"

His thumb brushes against the corner of his mouth. "They remind me of you."

"That's one of the most asinine things I've ever heard."

"Have you even left the apartment since Monday?"

I shake my head, trying to focus on my book. Maybe he'll get the point and walk his sexy ass out of here. Not likely, but I can hope.

"Get dressed. We're leaving in thirty minutes."

Lifting my eyes back to his, I say, "I never agreed to go with you."

He starts walking away. "And I never asked. Thirty minutes, Lila. Go!"

Blake yells at least six times to let me know the cab is waiting downstairs. I've been ready for a few minutes, but I want to keep him waiting, to either piss him off or make him leave without me. Maybe both.

I open the door to the outside, pulling my black coat tighter around my waist. I never asked what type of band we were going to see, or where they were playing. There's a chance I'm overdressed or underdressed, but either way, I know I look good. A form fitting heather dress hits at my knees, black knee-high boots taking care of the rest of my exposed skin. The high neckline and long-sleeves may not be most people's idea of sexy, but this dress hugs . . . everywhere.

I'm going to prove a point tonight. I'm not his toy to play around with; I never will be. It doesn't mean I can't dangle myself in front of him. Tonight is going to be about fun and games, and this time, I'm the master of ceremonies.

Irritation pours off him as I climb in the back seat. It's enough to make my lips quirk with happiness.

"Next time, I'm going to lie about the time," he remarks. I feel him staring at me, but I don't meet it.

"Who said anything about a next time?"

He laughs. "You may not realize it now, but there will be. Getting people to do what I want is one of the many magical powers I possess."

Rolling my eyes, I ask, "Are you saying you're a wizard?"

"No, I'm saying I'm a clever person who's unraveled the complex workings of the female mind. Believe me when I say it's not that fucking easy."

"You're crazy."

"Not crazy enough to keep you away from me." *Jerk.*

The rest of the ride is quiet. It's dark outside, but the lights of downtown illuminate the cab. Blake has been tense since our exchange, but I ignore him for the scenery. This is the first time I've been down here this time of day, but I can already tell I'm going to love it. There are so many people. So much radiant life and energy. With the Christmas lights decorating trees and buildings, I could easily get lost here.

The cab pulls down a side street, coming to a stop along the curb. "We're here," Blake announces, bumping his shoulder against mine.

Without much hesitation, I slide out, stepping onto the busy sidewalk while he pays. The air is cold, and when I inhale, a mixture of food tickles my senses. It reminds me that I forgot to eat dinner, which means any alcohol I drink will go straight to my head. *Great.*

"Ready?" Blake asks, bumping my shoulder again.

"Yep," I reply, letting his touch guide me.

We end up in front of a blues club that advertises barbeque on the canopy; my stomach growls just thinking about it. "They serve food here?" I ask, sounding more desperate than I intended.

His mouth comes inches from my ear, his breath tickling my skin in his attempt to speak over the crowd. "Great food."

I shiver. I don't know if it's him. Or the thought of smoked brisket. Or maybe the cold air.

He opens the door, his eyes scanning the packed room. I'd almost forgotten that we were coming here to meet some friends of his. Maybe I should have spent my time in the cab praying that they're nothing like him.

The longhaired guy he was with at Charlie's a few nights ago and another waves us over to a table in the corner. I'm pretty sure they're smiling at *us*. I grimace, not liking the feeling of an *us*.

"Dude!" the guy I hadn't met until now exclaims, "What the fuck took you so long?"

"Guys, this is Lila. Lila, this is Ronny," he says, pointing to the guy with the loud mouth. "And this is Mark." He points to the other guy, the one who was with him the other night. "Lila's my new roommate, and she takes a long fucking time to get ready before going out."

I slide my jacket off my shoulders, feeling three pairs of eyes staring at me. Blake's fall to my chest before slowly coming back up. His mouth gapes open . . . exactly the reaction I was going for when I chose this dress.

"Sorry," I say confidently. "I wasn't planning on going out tonight so I had to throw myself together."

"Doll face, you look anything but thrown together. Why don't you slide in next to me," Ronny remarks. By the way he looks at me, I can tell he's a pig—the kind that works really hard to pick up a girl in a bar only to have her sneak out a side door to avoid him.

Because this is all harmless fun, I sit next to him in the booth. Blake slips in across from me. Our eyes connect. He sneers. I smile.

"So what band is playing?" I ask, tapping my fingers against the tabletop.

"The same one that plays every night," Mark replies, breaking his silence.

"Oh." Before I can ask anything else, a blonde waitress appears next to our table in a short black miniskirt and white top, buttoned down just enough to show the edge of her red lace bra.

"Can I get y'all something to drink?"

"Rum and Coke," Mark says.

Ronny moves a little closer to me, wrapping his arm around my shoulders. "I'll take a Sam Adams and whatever Doll Face here wants."

I shrug, hoping to shake him off, but I fail miserably. "I'll take a shot of whiskey."

"Make that two." I catch Blake's eyes across the table. He swallows hard then breaks contact.

Not to my surprise, Ronny does most of the talking while we wait for the waitress to return. I guess he used to work with Blake, but now he paints houses. Honestly, the more I listen to him talk, the more I think there's something to taking in too many fumes. He's kind of funny, but that's where it ends.

The waitress reappears with our drinks. "Do y'all want to pay for these or start a tab?"

"I'll pick up the first round," Blake says, sliding a plastic card across the table. She quickly walks away with it.

"I wanted to buy the lady a drink," Ronny rebuts. His fingers slip down my arm, tracing circles around my elbow.

Blake leans halfway across the table. "Give up, asshole. She's not going home with you." He's talking to Ronny but looking at me. I don't understand him.

"Is he like this at home?" Ronny whispers, his breath hitting the side of my neck.

I keep my attention on Blake. His jaw is locked so tight; it's got to hurt. "Pretty much," I whisper back. "I'd say he needs to get laid, but I know that's not the case."

Mark whistles low, bumping Blake with his elbow. "Did you hear that? I think someone may have finally met his match."

I lean in toward Ronny's ear, resting my hand on his shoulder. This is pissing Blake off, and I kind of like it. For his part, Ronny squeezes my thigh.

"Fuck this," Blake mutters, leaving the three of us alone as he stalks off toward the bar.

Victory. Immediately, I slide away from Ronny, smiling apologetically. Maybe he thought he was getting somewhere, but this is nothing but a game. Men play them all the time, so why can't I?

I figured Blake would come back after a few minutes, but he doesn't. I finish my whiskey and instantly regret it. With an empty stomach, I'm feeling the drunken tingle after just one drink. Mark and Ronny talk, but I don't listen. My head spins as if it's stuck in the eye of a hurricane.

The place is packed, but I feel like the only person in here. I scan the bar again, anxious to find Blake and get the hell out of here. Maybe pick up a pizza along the way. I'm lost in my own world when cold lips press against my neck. I jerk my head in response, hitting Ronny in the face.

He cups his nose, wincing. I quickly move away. "I'll be back." I pick up my coat from the back of the booth and pull it over my shoulders.

"Hey, I just wanted to have some fun!" Ronny yells after me.

A path clears for me as I make my way toward the bar, ignoring him. Another drink—or five—might be all I need to fix this messed up night. I hate when my plans don't work out the way I want. What was I hoping to achieve tonight? Did I expect Blake to fall to my feet and beg for something I don't even want? Or maybe I do want it, and that's what bothers me so much.

The bartender appears in front of me as soon as I slide up against the bar. He smirks, his eyes exploring my body before coming back up to mine. He reminds me of Blake—full of himself. There's probably a girl waiting outside the door to go home with him and his dimples after every shift. Another fucking wizard.

"What can I get you?" he asks.

"Whiskey, tall."

That only widens his smile. He splays his hands on the bar top, allowing him to lean forward even more. "Straight?"

I toss my hair behind my shoulder and rest my elbows against the old wooden bar. Tonight was supposed to be about fun, and life is what you make it. "Twisted whiskey isn't really my thing."

"Mine either," he says, darting his tongue out over his lower lip. He moves in to say something else, but I step back. *Too much, Lila. Too much.*

"I could really use that drink."

He nods, turning to pull a glass from the back shelf. Music starts, and I spin around to get a glimpse of the band—three guys about my dad's age. The singer's voice is a soulful cry to the slow, beautiful melody. I rest my elbows on the bar, letting the music sway my hips like the wind does the leaves on the trees.

My eyes close. I want to forget where I am and just pretend for a second that I'm on a private beach with soft sand under my feet. The song changes, and when I open my eyes to find my drink, Ronny is standing in front of me. He's watching me with thick perversion.

Before I can say anything, his hands encase my waist, pulling me against his body. "Dance with me." I hate the smell of beer on his breath.

"No." I shake my head and push down on his arms. His hands clench into fists, but he doesn't step back. This whole fucking night has been ridiculous. I unclasp my clutch and throw money on the bar to pay for the whiskey I didn't get to drink. I could use a whole damn bottle right now. "Tell Blake I said bye."

I expect him to follow me, to yell like he did before, but he doesn't. Without looking back, I head out the door, letting the city air wash over me. Coming here with Blake wasn't a good idea. I should have known the second he asked me.

Blake and I aren't meant to mix. We're a mistake—an experiment that results in toxic fumes.

Before heading back to the apartment, I stop at a small pizzeria and buy a slice of hot cheese pizza. My hollow stomach can't wait the few minutes it will take to get home so I devour it as I walk down the city streets. It's pitch dark, and I don't know a soul out here, but it doesn't matter to me. If the world wants to swallow what's left of me, let it. Maybe that's where life's path is leading me . . . down a dark, narrow hole.

As much as I hate them, I hail a cab and crawl into the backseat. The driver and I exchange nothing but my address as the downtown streets turn into residential ones. When he pulls in front of my house, he asks for fifteen and I hand him a twenty.

Once I'm safely tucked in my apartment, I change into my sweats and curl up on the couch with my e-reader. This is what I should have done in the first place. Besides the pizza, the entire night was a waste.

I disappear into the land of alpha males and the weak heroines who love them. It's the kind of book I love to hate. I tell myself I'll never be one of those girls, but since Derek, I've felt like maybe I was one with him at times.

It's a struggle—constant and fierce—but in the end, I know I'll be okay. What doesn't kill us is supposed to make us stronger, right?

I hear the door unlock, and quickly beeline for my bedroom. I didn't expect Blake to come home tonight, and I'm not in the mood for a meet and greet with his nightly pick-up.

"Lila!" I hear him yell as soon as my door shuts. "Damnit, Lila, come out here now."

My hand stays on the doorknob. I'm scared that if I move, he'll hear my bare feet against the old hardwood floors. He'll know I'm still awake.

"Lila. Come. Out. Here. Now!" Blake wears a permanent asshole patch on his shirt, and I'm tired of it.

When I still ignore him, his fist hits hard against my door. "I know you're awake."

I know without a doubt if I don't open the door, he's going to keep yelling and eventually he'll wake up all the neighbors. Hesitantly, I turn the knob and get an eyeful of his pissed off expression. Every muscle in his body goes rigid.

"What?" I ask, crossing my arms over my chest.

He takes a step toward me, his chest brushing against mine. "What the hell were you thinking leaving without telling me? I spent a whole fucking hour searching the club for you, thinking some asshole had gotten a hold of you!"

"I told the guys."

"Well, you didn't tell me!"

I swallow hard, taking the smallest of steps backward, hoping he won't notice. "Honestly, I didn't think you cared. I agreed to go with you, but I never said I'd leave with you."

His eyes burn into mine as he makes up the space I'd gained. "When you come with me, you stay with me, and if you think you need to leave, we'll fucking leave, but you should not be walking around this city by yourself at night. Especially wearing that piece of fabric you call a dress."

"You know, Blake, I'm a big girl, and I can take care of myself," I say, poking my finger into his chest. "Besides, you're the one who left me alone at the bar so I didn't think you'd care."

"Do you want to know how much I fucking care, Lila?" he asks.

My eyes widen, and my heart races as he steps closer, pushing my hand right back into me. He's not just being an asshole . . . he's genuinely, seriously pissed.

His arm wraps around my lower back. I push against his chest, but his grip on me is too tight. "There's not a whole lot in this world I care about, but every time I look in those green eyes of yours, I don't have any control." His lips are mere inches from mine. His hand practically burns into my cotton-covered skin. "I hate not having control."

Confusion is all I feel as I stare at his dark shadow with no idea of what to say. He tore in like the first wave of a windstorm sweeping away all my thoughts.

"Say something." His voice is lower but not without edge.

"I made it home safely, didn't I?" *Daring in my current predicament if I do say so myself.*

"This time."

"And the hundreds of other times I've walked home at night."

His grip on me tightens. "Why are you so stubborn?"

I shrug. "Why do you have to be such an asshole?"

Without warning, his lips crash into mine. At first I fight it, pushing hard against his chest, but he tastes like whiskey. Woodsy and smoky like a campfire, matching the intensity of his kiss. He melts away my anger with his mouth, leaving days' worth of unrealized sexual tension in its wake.

He tastes.

I lean into him.

He sucks.

My knees go weak.

He isn't something I wanted. Not three weeks ago. Not even three minutes ago. But as his hands slide up my back, coming up to circle my neck, I'm drowning in want. He tilts my head back to allow himself better access. My tongue tangles with his. Never in a million years did I envision this . . . how much pleasure I would feel from a simple touch. I guess sometimes we have to have our desires at our fingertips to realize their true depth.

When his lips leave mine, his hands stay. We went from one extreme to another so quickly . . . I'm not sure what will happen when he pushes the brakes. His face is close, like he wants to kiss me again, but his hands fall away from me instead.

"Don't—"

One step back.

"Ever—"

Another step.

"Let me—"

Another step. His back hits my bedroom wall.

"Do that again."

As he exits the room, I'm left wondering what the heck just happened. That kiss took all the cells in my brain and tangled them. I never imagined this, and I hate to admit it but I liked it.

But the way he left me leaves a nagging burn deep in my chest.

It's just another reason I need to find my own place. Getting any deeper into this with Blake is going to get messy . . . that's a guarantee.

"WHAT'S EATING YOU TONIGHT?" Dana asks.

I've been standing in front of the bar staring at a tray of dirty glasses for God knows how long. I hadn't even realized I was doing it until just now.

"I'm just tired," I answer, shaking myself out of Lila-land. The truth is, Blake was gone when I woke up this morning, and he hadn't come home before I left for work. I don't want to think about him, but there must be part of me that cares or I wouldn't feel this way. It's like someone burned a tiny hole in my chest and the pain keeps spreading the longer I go without hearing from him. I hate feeling like this.

"Liar."

Tapping my fingernails on the old wooden bar, I contemplate how much I should tell her or if I should tell her anything at all. It bothers me that he disappears all the time without any explanation, not that he really owes me one. He's said that he doesn't work so what does he do for days at a time? Where does he go?

I try to chase any twisted yet viable explanations from my mind, but that's easier said than done. Does he have women across town who he spends the night with? Is that who Aly is? I've been thinking about her since he said her name the other morning, hoping she's nothing more than a character in his dreams.

"It's Blake."

That sparks her interest right away. "What did he do now?"

More nail tapping. "He kissed me."

Her eyes double in size. "I knew it. You lasted longer than I would have, though."

"It's not like that."

Sure, he kissed me. It was nice, but then he just left after—the epitome of romantic.

"Well! Spill it," she demands, glancing around to make sure no one is within earshot. She knows me well enough to know I'm not the kiss-and-tell kind of girl.

"It was the best and worst kiss I've ever had. How is that even freaking possible?" I'm more expressive about it than I thought I would be, throwing my arms up in the air.

"You're going to have to elaborate."

"He came in all mad because I left the bar without telling him. He yelled at me, then he kissed me, then he told me to never let it happen again."

She steps back, shaking her head. "I'd say he likes you, but he doesn't want to. And, I'm sensing a bad case of commitment-itis."

"So what do I do? I have to live with him."

"First off, don't you dare fall for him. He doesn't deserve you." She pauses, a huge smile spreading across her face. "I'd fuck him, though. Just once because I bet you all my tips that he knows exactly what he's doing."

She's crazy. Nuts actually. I turn back to the bar, signaling to Charlie that I need another round.

"Lila, listen to me for once."

I keep my back to her.

"How many guys have you been with?" she asks when I don't react.

I turn to glare at her.

She continues, "From your nice non-answer, I'm going to guess that you're a virgin, or you've had, at maximum, one or two partners. Nothing to be embarrassed about, but Lila, Blake could rock your world. At the very least, he'll show you how good things can be under the sheets."

"When you say it like that, it sounds pathetic."

For the first time since I've worked here, I'm actually happy to see Charlie standing in front of me. He saves me from Dana and her insane ideas. "What do you need?" he asks.

"Two Bud Lights, and a shot of Jager," I blurt, hoping he puts the order together just as fast. I already told Dana more than I should have, handing her enough ammo to make the situation worse.

"Look, I know you don't want to talk about this anymore, but be careful. Seriously," she says, squeezing my shoulder.

As she walks away, I realize there's only one option. I have to move, get my own apartment so I don't have to deal or think about Blake. It's the only way.

My whole life is in a tailspin. Blake hasn't come home, and I have no way of getting ahold of him, not that I'd try. Charlie's is keeping me busy, but it's not challenging me in the ways I want. It's not why I sat in crowded classrooms for four years.

Since I left work last night, I've been thinking about Pierce's offer, and how stupid I've been for not calling him back right away. It's an opportunity that most of the people I graduated with would kill for.

I pace my room to keep my nerves at bay. He called three days ago, and there's been nothing but radio silence on my end.

I'm quieting the voices that keep telling me I'm not good enough or qualified enough because I need this—a reason to stay in Chicago.

"Stanley." Pierce's deep voice floats through the phone.

"Hello, Mr. Stanley." My voice shakes. I quicken my steps to chase the nerves away. "It's Lila."

"Lila?" The way my name rolls off his tongue stops my maniacal pacing. It reminds me how easy he is to talk to.

I run my fingers through my hair, inhaling deeply. "Yeah, airplane Lila. I'm sorry it took so long to call you back. I didn't know if I should respond, but I've had time to think about it, and I'd like to apply for the apprenticeship. If it's still available, that is. I—"

"We're still hiring," he cuts me off. "Would you be able to come down for an interview this afternoon?"

"Today?" *Shit. I don't have anything to wear to a real interview.*

He laughs. "This afternoon would be today."

How bad do you want it, Lila? Do you want to crawl back to Nebraska with your tail between your legs? "Yeah, I can make it. What time is good for you?"

"Two o'clock."

"Don't you need to check with your secretary or something first?"

"No, Ms. Fields, if there's something scheduled then, I'll cancel it. Just make sure you're here."

"I'll be there," I say, opening the closet door.

We both mutter a short goodbye before I toss my phone onto the bed and start thumbing through Mallory's closet. I need to look professional with enough edge to showcase my eye for color and design. Mallory is a basic-with-a-hint-of-elegance type girl; this will take every bit of my creativity. Not that I'm a fashionista by any means.

I pull a sleek black pencil skirt off the hanger, and then shop her closet for the perfect shirt. Nothing catches my eyes.

Frustrated, I throw the skirt over the end of the bed and shower. If this interview doesn't pan out, I might not get another chance anytime soon. Everything has to be perfect. I can't go into it thinking I can't do it. I can't go in thinking about Derek or Blake or all the other reasons my life hasn't been going the way I want.

After drying and straightening my hair, I pull it back in a perfect bun at the nape of my neck, letting a few wavy strands stay loose around my face. It makes me look older—professional.

I wonder what Blake would think if he saw me like this, in my element, reaching for my dreams. Would he find it attractive? Would the skirt I picked out bring on a replay of the other night? I shake my head, trying to chase it away. *Stop thinking about him, Lila. He's not worth it.*

I select a blush-colored lace bra and panty set to give myself some needed confidence. Feeling sexy always allows me to keep my head up, no matter what I'm doing, and I definitely need that today.

There's a silk blouse I brought with me—white with black polka dots that will look great paired with my pencil skirt. I pull it from my small corner in Mallory's closet and put it on, leaving the top three buttons unfastened.

After a layer of make-up, a toothbrush, and a pair of black pumps, I'm ready to go an hour before I need to leave.

To kill time, I sit down with today's paper. If I get this job, and continue working at Charlie's, I'll be able to afford my own apartment. Looking at the ads, it seems that apartments in this area are some of the most affordable. I circle a few that I think will fit in my budget and set it aside, hoping I get to call on some later.

Thinking about Charlie's reminds me that I'm supposed to work a shift tonight. With no idea how long the interview will take, I text Dana and ask if there's anyone who could possibly cover my shift. In case there's not, I grab the little pieces of fabric Charlie calls a uniform and tuck them into my purse.

Bored and anxious, I throw on my black coat and head to the train stop. It takes me less than thirty minutes to get downtown, and the map on my phone leads me straight to Stanley Development. It's a high rise with wall-to-wall windows—the kind of building I always dreamed about working in one day. Like the big shot executives in the movies.

The lobby has white and black granite floors, gray walls, and a huge antique chandelier hanging high up above. It's a timeless design—one that only requires a change in accessories every now and then.

"Can I help you?" the doorman asks. He's an older gentleman who smiles as if he has the best job in the entire world.

"I'm looking for Pierce Stanley's office."

His smile widens. "Twelfth floor. Elevators are down the hall to your left."

"Thank you." I wave and start walking, trying to stop myself from gawking. I hit the up button and wait with two men dressed in ill-fitting suits. When the door opens, we squeeze in with several other people. *Here goes nothing,* I think to myself. The higher we climb, the harder it is to breathe. My life isn't dependent on this, but it sure as hell feels like it.

I follow the two suited guys out when we reach Pierce's floor, noticing they're around my age—fresh out of college.

"May I help you?" a professionally dressed woman with a perfect blonde bob asks, a welcoming smile on her face.

"Yes," one of the guys answers, "I'm here to interview for an apprenticeship with Mr. Stanley."

"I'm here for the same," the other guy pipes in.

I stay back, waiting for her to see me, but in the back of my mind I know if this is my only competition, I'm a shoe in. Both of these guys came dressed like they don't give a damn. There's no flair—nothing that says they want to be remembered after they're gone.

"Take a seat," the woman says to them. "Someone will be with you in just a few moments."

They walk away, and the receptionist's eyes focus in on me. "How can I help you?"

"Hi. I'm Lila Fields, and I have an interview for the apprenticeship at two."

Her eyes travel my body, but quickly come back up. "Oh, yes, Ms. Fields. Mr. Stanley will be seeing you soon. Please have a seat, and I'll let him know you're here."

"Thank you."

I pull off my coat before taking a seat. Each second feels like an eternity as I wait nervously, memorizing every detail of the swanky office. This really is where I aspire to be . . . my dream.

Out of the corner of my eye, I see two sets of eyes on my crossed legs and adjust myself so I can't see them at all. At least I know the skirt is a homerun.

"Lila." It's the way he says my name, more than his actual voice, that's distinctive. Looking to my right, I see Pierce standing there in a light gray suit with a baby blue button-up underneath. His dark hair is slicked back away from his face. He's a breath-taking vision—the kind I've only seen in designer suit ads.

"Mr. Stanley."

I stand on shaky knees, ready to shake his hand, but he grabs the coat from me instead, walking it over to the receptionist. "Can you put this in the closet please and make sure Ms. Fields gets it before she leaves." It's a command, not a question.

He motions for me to follow him, and I do. His hands are tucked into his pockets, lifting his suit coat just enough for me to get a peek at his perfect backside. It should be illegal to look that good in wool. At least the scenery keeps my anxiety at bay.

At the end of the hall, he opens the door to an office that is bigger than my whole apartment. The floors are the same as the entry, but a plush white rug sits in the center. An oversized mahogany desk sits on one side, and a couch and bookcase on the other. A large table sits in the middle displaying models of high rises. I'm tempted to go get a closer look, but my legs are too wobbly to venture too far.

"Do you like it?"

For the second time today, I catch myself gawking. "It's huge."

He laughs, running his thumb along his lower lip. "The bigger, the better, right?"

My face turns a bright shade of red. "That's what they say."

"Take a seat," he instructs, pointing to one of two black leather chairs in front of his desk.

I do as he asks, forcing one foot in front of the other. Once I'm comfortably seated, I feel a little more in control. "Do you conduct all of the apprenticeship interviews?"

He grins. "I don't. But I thought you'd be more comfortable interviewing with me personally."

"Why do you want me?" I shake my head, realizing the weight of my words. "For this position, I mean."

"I saw something in you, and I want to explore it." His voice is deep and masculine; I could listen to it all day. "Tell me, where did you go to school?"

I open my purse and pull out a copy of my resume, handing it to him. "UCLA."

"And you're from Nebraska?"

"Yes, long story," I answer, crossing one leg over the other. One simple question, and my heart is already racing.

"What is your goal? What do you want to be when you grow up, Ms. Fields?"

"I want to design commercial spaces. I don't want to arrange furniture or put together centerpieces. I know I have to start at the bottom, but I'm willing to do whatever it takes to make a name for myself."

"What inspires you?"

I sit back, a little more relaxed. "It's usually something small. A piece of art or fabric. I take in the colors and the lines and imagine it on a larger scale."

"Name the last space that made you think, *I wish I'd come up with that.*" His eyes never leave me. So intense. So powerful.

"I'm not sucking up when I say this, but whoever designed your entrance is a genius."

"Really?" he asks. He's going to tell me he hates it, or it's outdated. I feel it. "Because I designed that myself."

I stare openly.

He laughs. "It's okay, Lila. Very few people know I did that."

I nod, darting my tongue out to moisten my dry lips. "So what does this apprenticeship involve?"

"We're working on two hotel projects in the next couple months. The Design Apprentice will assist our design team in transforming them, and if all goes well, take on a permanent role in the company."

I wonder if he notices my eyes lighting up. "When will you be making a decision?"

His lips curl. "I think I already have. Can you be here Monday morning at eight?"

"Seriously?" I ask, wanting to jump from my chair.

"It's yours. The pay isn't much, but if you succeed, it'll be worth it in the long run." He probably closes quite a few business deals, layering the good with the bad.

"What is the pay? Can I ask?"

"It would be stupid not to. Fifteen dollars an hour during the apprenticeship." Right now, that's a lot for me, but he doesn't have to know that.

"I'll take it." I want to jump up and hug him, but I don't.

He gets up from his chair, coming around his desk. "You made my day, Ms. Fields," he says, offering me his hand.

"Likewise," I say, placing my hand in his. "Thank you. For everything."

The second he lets go of me, I head to the door, anxious to call everyone I know. "Did I dismiss you, Ms. Fields?"

Every part of my body stops moving, heart included. Once I regain my composure, I look back. "Sorry. I thought you were done with me."

He takes long strides toward me, only stopping when we're a couple feet apart. "I don't think that's possible."

"Excuse me?"

His eyes drink me in. The way he does it leaves me feeling exposed and naked. "Is there a man in your life right now?"

What does this have to do with the job? Why would he be asking me this? He's a powerful man behind a very successful business. What does he want from me? On top of that, the question is totally illegal. I learned that much in Business 101.

"Technically the interview is over," he says, putting an end to the swirling thoughts in my head.

Blake's face flashes through my mind, but I dismiss it. We're nothing but an inconvenience to each other—definitely not dating.

"No," I mumble, shaking my head to confirm the same. Since Derek, there's been no one. I don't think someone special even exists.

"Good." He smiles then walks back to his desk. "You're free to go now."

I'm in a complete daze as I walk down the hall. Another strange Chicago job interview, but like the first, this one goes my way. It doesn't mean I don't question Pierce's motives. We shared forty-five minutes of non-life altering conversation on a plane, and it landed me here. I would have run ten miles in heels if it meant the job would mine. I just want it to be for the right reasons.

The receptionist hands me my coat before I even ask for it, and I quickly shut myself in the elevator, afraid Pierce will change his mind. As I ride down, I pull out my cell phone and see a text from Dana, letting me know she found someone to cover my shift. I could have made it since the interview didn't take as long as I thought it would, but it gives me time to celebrate.

I text Mom and Mallory, letting them know I'm on my way to living the dream and step back out into the cold winter air.

A SMILE CURVES MY LIPS as I make my way down the narrow hallway that leads to the apartment. Today was unexpectedly amazing . . . I haven't had many days like that lately.

My phone was full of unread texts I'd ignored during the train ride home.

Mallory: I knew you'd find something. Details . . .

Mom: So happy for you. If it doesn't work out, you always have a place at home.

Mom had mixed feelings about me moving here. She was happy I'd finally started to move on from Derek, but she was hoping I'd do it a little closer to home. The only thing that will give her reassurance is time.

I tuck my phone away and pull my key out. It turns easily, and my mouth falls open when I see Blake leaning against the kitchen counter waiting for me. I wasn't expecting him today . . . or tomorrow . . . or even the next day. Not after what happened the other night.

"Hey," I whisper, tucking a piece of hair behind my ear.

He pushes off the counter, eyes locked with mine as he stalks toward me. My heart pounds against my chest, enough that I hear it between my ears.

He stands so close that moving forward even an inch would have us touching. Reaching behind me, he slams the door shut. I shutter. From head to toe, a jolt rips through me. He's not even touching me, but I feel him. The heat radiating from his body. His warm breath. I read the intense desire in his eyes, and then it all becomes too much.

Shaking my head, I try to push past him, but he wraps his arm around my waist, pulling my back to his chest. "Please don't go."

"What?" A part of me wants to snuggle against him—to feel the warmth of his body—while the other part is begging for space.

He walks us forward, pointing at the marked up newspaper I left on the table this afternoon. "Don't go," he says again.

"I have to. I'm done with this. One of us has to go."

"I'm not going anywhere," he says, tilting my chin with his finger so my eyes are level with his.

"Then I am. I can't do this hot and cold bullshit. I moved here to make life less complicated, and you've turned it into a freaking Rubik's cube." I want to be angry. I need the strength to put distance between us, but I can't. Not when his skin is against mine. He paralyzes my ability to be the strong woman I strive to be.

"I don't want you to go." His nose is pressed against my hair. He inhales, curling his fingers around my silk shirt.

"Blake." As his name leaves my lips, the fabric moves up my stomach. When I feel his fingertips brush across my skin, the hair on the back of my neck stands up. It's been too long since I've felt this way—needing to have someone else's skin against mine. Blake might be the last person I should be doing this with, but he makes me aware of my own heartbeat, strong and thunderous.

Laying my head back against his shoulder, I allow him to explore my neck with his mouth. His calloused hand runs the length of my stomach, increasing my desire. I've never wanted in the way I want him. His touch is wiping all doubt from my mind.

I shouldn't do this.

I can't do this.

A guy like Blake will only distract me. He'll grip me tight, and then when I think I'm safe—when I think my heart's safe—he'll let me go. I can't afford to take that risk. I can't afford to have my heart shattered again by a guy like him.

"I can't," I whisper, trying to loosen his grip on me. He doesn't let up.

"You can," he says, crossing his arms over my stomach. "Because I'm done fighting you. I'm done fighting this." He turns me in his arms, holding my face in his hands. "I don't want a relationship, but I want you. Be with me . . . just like this."

I close my eyes. *I don't want a relationship, but I want you . . . what does that mean exactly?* Is he making an exception? What if I don't want to be his exception? The sensations he sent through my body just a couple minutes ago linger, making it hard to think.

"I don't understand," I finally say, my voice shaky.

His hands still cupping my face, he walks me back until I'm against the wall. His gaze is powerful, paralyzing me. No one's ever looked at me like that. Not Derek, not anyone. "I want to fuck you so good that you'll be begging me to fuck you again. Then tomorrow, I'll do it all over so you don't forget how good my cock feels buried inside of you."

He slides his fingers down around the base of my neck, then down my arms, letting his thumbs brush against my breasts. "The way your body curves into mine, the way you shudder under my touch; I feel it, Lila. You want this. I know I want this."

If I could orgasm from words alone, I'd be clenching around every single syllable that just fell from his lips. He grips my hips pulling me into him. *So big.* I'm like an alcoholic that's been given a sip; there's no going back.

Standing up on my tippy toes, I brush my lips against his, pulling his lower lip between my teeth. I savor him, not sure where this is going or what I'm doing exactly. When he pulls away from me, my heart shrinks.

"Before we do this, you have to agree to one thing."

I nod nervously, anxious to just have his mouth on mine again.

"No feelings. No attachment. Just you and me, like this. Can you do that?"

Can I? I don't want a relationship, but am I ready for this? He'd be a distraction—a welcome one . . . or maybe not. It's a decision I'll probably end up regretting either way.

My gaze travels between his eyes and lips. He has me so hot and full of want, or want to be full of him. I answer the only way I can, fisting his T-shirt while licking my lower lip. A sexy, half-smile highlights his mouth, then it's on me, everywhere my skin has been exposed. He encircles me in his arms, tugging my skirt up from behind. Then he lifts me, forcing me to wrap my legs around his waist. If it weren't for his jeans and my thong and panty hose, he'd be inside me. God, I want him inside me.

"Do you know how sexy you are? Dressed all professionally and shit," he mutters against my neck. "I've always wanted my own little secretary."

I moan, arching my body into him. "What are you going to do to me then, boss?"

"Fuck," he groans. His thumbs flick over my nipples, and I realize I've never needed someone so badly.

Snaking my arms over his shoulders, I bury my face in the crook of his neck, breathing in his usual scent. I nibble and suck while he walks toward his room, his arms holding me tightly against his strong body.

I have seconds to change my mind. The sane part of me is screaming to put an end to this madness, but the mind is a small part of the body as a whole.

He rests one knee on the bed, allowing me to fall back. He kisses me. Deeply. Desperately. My world is spinning so fast; it's going to fall right off its axis. He expertly undoes all my buttons, exposing my lace bra. A low growl escapes his lips, as he sucks my nipples through the thin material. I pull his hair between my fingers, feeling the need to drive him as insane as he's driving me.

His tongue trails a path down my stomach, tracing a circle around my belly button, and then going down to the top of my skirt. He rests his chin on my abdomen, looking up at me, eyes hooded. "You have way too many damn clothes on."

I'm thinking the same about him. Finding the zipper along the side of my skirt, he slides it down and makes easy work of discarding it. My hose and panties follow.

I watch as he stands and pulls his shirt over his head, his eyes never leaving my naked form on the bed. This is the first time I've let myself be exposed in front of someone I didn't love—someone I'm not even sure if I like most of the time. I thought it would be strange, but the way he looks at me makes me feel wanted. I don't think I've ever felt this sexy.

I wiggle on the bed, squeezing my legs together to keep my body occupied. There's a growing hunger; the longer I watch him, the more I feel it.

I stare as he pulls his zipper down and pushes his jeans and boxers down over his throbbing cock. It's impressive, I have to give him that.

"Open your legs for me," he demands, walking over to his nightstand. I don't comply. I can't because I'm too busy watching him. He pulls out a condom and glances over at me, shaking his head.

Lisa DeJong

"Legs, Lila," he says again, a little louder this time. I comply as he makes his way back to the end of the bed, carefully rolling on the condom along the way. His body could be a sculpture; it's well proportioned—lean and muscular. He sets one knee between my legs and runs his fingers against my opening. Arching my back, all I can do is look at him.

A grin spreads across his face as he wipes his soaked fingers against the inside of my thigh. "Who are you wet for, Lila?"

Unable to form real words, I attempt to reach for him, to pull him down to me, but he presses against my chest to keep me away. This is not normal—the amount of desire I have for him.

His fingers brush against the top of my thighs, so close to where I actually want him, but far enough away to deny me what I need. "Who, Lila . . . who did this to you?"

"You," I whimper, reaching my hands toward him.

He lifts his other leg up and holds his body above mine. "Tell me what you want."

I lift my hips, but it's no use. It doesn't give me what I want. "You. I need you inside of me. Now."

He lowers himself on top of me, his lips parting as he enters me. There's nothing slow and sweet about it—he pushes in as far as my body will allow him. "Fuck," he mutters, pulling back out. "You feel so fucking good wrapped around me."

I moan, feeling the pressure build as he thrusts himself into me over and over. With Derek, it was all about him. He didn't touch me like this. He didn't wind my body like this. He wasn't Blake.

Blake holds my hands above my head, kissing my lips and neck. I wither under him. Every time I think I'm going to scream, he captures my lips, swallowing my cries. The tingle between my legs intensifies. I'm going to lose it, and by the quickening of his movements, he's going to come right along with me.

"Who are you going to dream about tonight in your sleep? Who's going to be touching you?"

91

I pant, arching up to take in more of him. "You, Blake. I'm going to think about you."

His lips curl up at one side. "Good girl."

Without notice, he lets go of my hands and uses my leg as leverage to flip me over onto my stomach. I lift my ass, making it easier for him as he pounds into me. When he presses his hand against my lower back, my body falls over the edge clenching tightly around him.

"Jesus Christ," he mutters, wrapping his arm around my stomach. He's throbbing inside of me as my body grips him. When I come off the high, we both fall onto the bed. I'm sated, tired, and more relaxed than I've been in months. I'd do it all over again right now if he asked.

Blake rolls off me and lays at the edge of the bed. I hear him breathing heavily, but I don't know what I'm supposed to do. What do two people who aren't dating do after sex?

"Are you okay?" he finally asks, breaking my thoughts.

I turn to face him. He's staring up at the ceiling, rubbing his hand along his jaw. "More than okay."

"Good." He glances toward me, and then rolls off the bed and heads to the bathroom without another word. When he shuts the door behind him, I take that as my cue. There's not going to be any post sex cuddles. No bed sharing. This is what he meant by leaving our hearts out of it.

I slip off his bed and hurry to pick my clothes off the floor before making my way back to my bedroom. I thought I was okay with this, maybe I still am, but it's not what I'm used to. It doesn't mean I wouldn't do it again.

FAMILIAR SOUNDS COME FROM the kitchen. I groan, concluding that Blake's never going to follow that rule. I pull my pillow over my ears, but when the blender starts pulsing, I give up and throw my robe on. This is getting ridiculous.

When I open my bedroom door, I spot Blake in only a pair of gray sweatpants, pouring a pink liquid from the blender. I smell strawberries and bananas—one of my favorite flavor combinations.

He spins around when he hears my bare feet on the hardwood. "Good morning." He smiles. It's hard to stay mad at him when he does that.

"Breaking the rules again?" I ask, leaning against the counter.

He shrugs. "I didn't think they were still effective, after last night and all."

"I don't see how that changes anything."

He drops the spoon on the stovetop and steps to me, caging me in with his arms. "It does."

I swallow, doing everything I can to back away. It's no use. "But you said . . ."

"I promised to fuck you today, remember? You need to eat first," he interrupts, his perusing eyes seducing me.

Oh, God. I didn't forget it, but after how things ended last night, I didn't take it too seriously. I certainly didn't think he wanted an early morning screw.

"Cat got your tongue?" he teases, smiling down at me. I want to kiss his perfect, full lips, but I'm not sure that's allowed. This is all foreign to me.

"Why do I have to be up this early? We have all day."

He cups my chin in his hand, tilting my head to give his mouth access to my neck. "I'm leaving town this afternoon, and I won't be back until Monday," he announces, nibbling on more of my delicate skin. "I need one more taste before I go."

Resting my hands on his bare shoulders, I'm torn between rubbing them and using my leverage to push him away. In a way, this cheapens me. If I'm going to be at his beck and call, letting him fuck me when he needs his fix, what am I going to get from that? There's no doubt he feels amazing, but what am I really doing?

"What if I don't want to?" I ask, lightly pushing against him.

He stops, leaning back to get a better look at me. "Jesus, Lila, I'd never make you do anything you don't want to do. Don't make it sound that way."

"Sorry," I say, shaking my head. "I'm not a morning person so this is what you get when you wake me up."

"Really?" He brushes his thumb against my cheek. "What if I feed you? I made smoothies."

I love smoothies. "Can I have some of your eggs too?"

His head tilts. "Now, you're pushing it."

"I'm hungry. Someone made me work up quite an appetite last night."

"I'll think about it."

I smirk, a new deck of cards falling in my hands. "What if I told you that I have nothing on under this robe?"

He growls, eyes darting to my exposed cleavage. *Men can be so easy.* "Nothing?"

"Nope."

He reaches back, grabbing a glass of the smoothie concoction he made and handing it to me. I put the glass to my lips, swallowing down the delicious strawberry-banana drink. He watches me, zeroing in on my mouth. I decide to play with him, licking the cold liquid that lingers on my lips. "That's good," I murmur.

Blake presses his body against mine, pulling the glass from my hand. He kisses my chin, then finds my eyes again. "You're right. That's delicious."

He lifts me up on the counter, standing between my spread legs. His hands brush against the inside of my thighs until his thumb makes contact with my clit. Breakfast is burning, but the need to be wrapped in each other is stronger than the need to save a few eggs.

It's not long until my robe is open, and I'm completely exposed, crumbling in his arms again.

I toss and turn, unable to sleep with my first day of work looming over my head. It's a test, one I will either pass or fail. It wouldn't be so bad, but failure means being stuck at a place like Charlie's for the rest of my life. That I can't live with.

It's been two days since Blake and I had sex in the kitchen. When he left soon after, there was no goodbye kiss.

And for the last two days, I've missed him, or maybe I've missed his hands on me. He said we had to leave our hearts out of this, but I'm starting to wonder if I'm really cut out for that. When I fall, I fall quickly. Love doesn't come with a parachute; I learned that the hard way.

I quickly shower and blow-dry my hair. Since the rest of my things finally came, I have a whole wardrobe to choose from.

I dress, curl my hair, and carefully apply enough make-up to brighten my appearance but not look too overdone, and head out the door a good ninety minutes before my shift begins to catch the train. If I'm lucky, I'll have time to grab a latte along the way. I'd kill for one to chase away that Monday feeling.

My body shakes from nerves while I wait for the train and then again while I ride. Feeling as if everything is going to reach a boiling point, I pull my cell phone out and call Mom.

"Hello," she answers. Just hearing her voice makes everything ten times better.

"Hi, Mom, how are things on the farm?" I ask, noticing other passengers watching me. It's crowded and being so close to all these strangers is making me claustrophobic.

"Things are good. Just putting up with your father being home during the day, but it will be spring before we know it. This is the best way to wake up, by the way."

"I'm on my way to my new job, and my nerves are shot," I confess, tapping my foot against the metal floor. The older woman sitting next to me narrows her eyes so I stop.

"You're going to do great. Don't forget how talented you are." She always knows the right thing to say to calm me down.

"I needed to hear that."

"I'll remind you all day."

I laugh, earning myself a few more stares. "I'll be okay."

"I saw Derek in town the other day." She pauses, and then adds, "He looked really thin. I don't think he's taking good care of himself."

I want to pretend that it doesn't matter. Derek is the past, but you don't spend six years with someone and drop every feeling you ever had for him in four months. "It's probably the workouts." That's not what I want to think. I imagine him pining now that I'm gone. I want to be his one that got away.

"He asked about you, but I didn't say much. I was in a hurry."

"It's none of his business anymore," I answer. "Look, can we just talk about something else?"

I hear the buzzer on her oven go off. She bakes fresh bread every morning so it's as familiar as my alarm clock. "Give me just a second. I need to grab that."

"Oh no," I stop her. "I need to get going anyway. I'll talk to you later, Mom. Thank you for the pep talk."

"Knock 'em dead or whatever it is they say." Her smile travels through the phone line.

"I will."

For the rest of the ride, I watch Chicago go by through the window. As strange as it sounds, it's starting to feel more like a place I can call home. I'm surprised I'm even thinking that, but the snow-covered streets and chance to live my dream make it feel that way.

The train stops a couple blocks from my new office building. I walk out and look at my watch, realizing I have just enough time to grab a quick cup of coffee from the coffee shop at the corner. I wait in a long but fast-moving line, grabbing my latte and a blueberry muffin before making my way to Stanley Development. I take a long, deep breath and open the glass door to the expansive entry.

One more inhale, and I'm at the elevator. It dings, and I cram myself inside with about ten other people. It stops a few times before reaching the twelfth floor.

I head straight to the granite desk, smiling at the same blonde receptionist who was working the other day. "Good morning, Lila. Are you ready to begin?"

I'm taken back. She remembers my name. Who does that? "Yes." I pause, looking at her nameplate. "Ms. Dwyer, I am."

She motions to the waiting area with a bright smile. "Call me Jane. Take a seat. Someone will be out in just a minute to get you."

I do as she says, setting my breakfast on the table so I can pull off my jacket. I want to look ready to work when they come out to get me.

"Here, let me take that." I turn around, seeing Jane behind me with her hands extended.

"Oh, thank you."

She walks to a hidden closet, wrapping my coat around a hanger. "When you're ready to go, it'll be in here."

I nod, taking a seat in one of the leather waiting chairs. I cross my legs and nervously clasp my hands in my lap. A few people whiz by without giving me a second glance. It's torture—being shut inside a box with a bunch of strangers.

"Lila." My eyes shoot up, taking in the view of Pierce Stanley in a charcoal suit and black tie. His suits obviously don't come off the rack; they're made to fit every part of his strong body.

"Hi," I reply, standing on unstable knees to offer him my hand.

He obliges, enveloping my small hand in his. "Follow me to my office. I have a few things I want to go over, and then I'll hand you over to human resources."

As I follow, I can't help but wonder if he meets with all of his new employees on their first day. It doesn't seem a guy like him would have the time.

He ushers me into the same oversized office he'd interviewed me in. "Have a seat," he says, rounding to the other side of his mahogany desk. "How was your weekend?"

My vision fills with a naked Blake, and my cheeks burn red. "It was good. How was yours?"

He chuckles, deep and throaty. "Not too exciting, but I'm hoping this one will be better."

"Big plans?"

"Actually, Lila, I was hoping you'd accompany me to a benefit. There will be lots of people from our industry you can mingle with. Networking is an important part of the big picture."

I was expecting a '*Welcome to the company*' or something along those lines. "Isn't fraternization against company policy?"

His lips curl as he leans across his desk. "Not necessarily. Besides, it's a business meeting, not a date."

My cheeks flush, the product of being caught jumping to conclusions. I've spent time with Pierce. I know we can carry a conversation, but this is a lot to take in on your first day of work. Besides, there's this whole thing with Blake. It's not exclusive, and he doesn't have any hold on me . . . it just feels weird. "Okay," I finally answer.

"Good, my car will pick you up at seven-thirty. Leave your address with Jane, please."

"Is there anything else, Mr. Stanley?"

He smiles. "Yeah, call me Pierce."

I smile back; his is contagious. "Anything else, Pierce?"

"No, I'm leaving for New York, but have a nice week, and I'll see you Saturday."

I nod, standing from my chair. "Thank you. You too."

When my hand curves around the doorknob, I look back one more time and see Pierce staring—actually, more like drinking me in. I do what I'm good at when things get uncomfortable . . . run. Too much intensity. Too much risk.

The rest of my day isn't quite as interesting as the first few minutes. It's filled with paperwork and boring videos, thinking about Pierce and replaying his words every chance I get. By the time five o'clock hits, I'm more than happy to walk out the door, but I take my thoughts of Pierce with me.

AS I SLIDE MY TIRED, achy body into the warm bath water, all I can think about is how I'm going to hold two jobs. One day at Stanley and I'm wiped. Just thinking about going from there to Charlie's two nights a week exhausts me.

The lavender bubbles cover my breasts as I lay back against the porcelain claw foot tub. I've wanted to sink into it since I moved here, and now with Blake gone, I need a distraction.

He said he'd be home this afternoon, and even though I have no claim to him, I've been worried. I wanted to text him, but that's not possible since I don't have his cell phone number. What kind of person does that make me? I fucked a guy—twice—and I don't know his number, his middle name, or much of anything about him besides what he likes for breakfast and that he can be a pain in the ass.

Closing my eyes, I seek my happy place—wherever that is. It's been buried underground for the past few months, but I'll find it again. I have to.

Human resources promised I'd get to do some actual work tomorrow. That should help—get me back in my element and meet the people I'll be working with. I just hope my apprenticeship means more than professional coffee fetcher and copy runner.

I sink down a little further, covering my bare shoulders with the fragrant bubbles. This is definitely the beginning of my rainbow.

Just when I'm finally settled in, I hear the faint sound of the door clicking and pry my eyes open. Footsteps follow, then silence again. "Lila!" Blake yells.

I breathe a sigh of relief. "Bathroom."

More footsteps, then the bathroom door swings open. He walks in looking exhausted—dark circles, blood shot eyes— and leans back against the vanity. His jeans are covered in colorful paint stains, and his red flannel is unbuttoned, showcasing an old Nirvana T-shirt. Even with all that, desire pools between my legs. I adjust my position in an attempt to chase it away, but that only makes it worse. It's been two days, almost three, since he's been inside me. I thought it was okay, that I had absolutely no attachment to him, but my body remembers exactly what he's capable of.

"You're home," I finally say, unable to find any other words.

He rubs his palm against his forehead, staring down at my covered body. "It's been a long day. I think I'm just going to go to bed."

I narrow in on him. He's not acting like himself—no snide comments or teasing. I don't like it. "Are you okay?"

"I will be," he answers, connecting his eyes with mine. They're a window to something much darker. I don't know him all that well, but I don't need to in order to recognize it.

This is new territory for me because if Blake were mine— really mine—I'd pull him in my arms and hold him tight until all the darkness disappeared. There has to be another way to make this better.

"Do you want to join me?" My voice shakes. Sharing a bath seems so intimate, but I can't watch him stand there like that for much longer.

His Adam's apple bobs as he assesses the bubbles again. I close my eyes because I can't watch. One more second of this and I'll be climbing out of this tub and wrapping myself around him.

"I can't," he murmurs right before the door opens and closes again.

Without any way to argue, I sag even deeper into the water. My chest tightens as I realize that I want to know more about him. I want to know what made him the way he is, why his moods shift like the blade of a windmill.

When my skin prunes, I grab a towel from the hook and climb out. It appears the only way I'm going to make this day better is to climb into my nice warm bed and drift off to dreamland.

I pull on a light blue camisole and matching pajama pants and run through my nightly bedtime routine before falling onto the pillow top bed.

Sleep doesn't come as easily as I'd hoped. I'm tired, I feel it in every single muscle in my body, but my brain won't shut off. It shifts from work to Blake then starts the cycle over again.

After trying with no luck for over an hour, I throw the covers off and stalk to the kitchen for a glass of milk. Before I get too far, the light shining under Blake's door stops me. I swear he hasn't slept in days, and God knows he needs it.

I carefully walk across the living room and put my ear to the door, hearing the faint sound of his paintbrush on canvas. I teeter between going in and just letting him be. It becomes an easy decision when I hear something crash to the floor.

When I open the door, my breath leaves me. He's not okay. Not at all. He's crouched on the floor, pulling his hair between his paint-stained fingers. His back is to me so I can't see his face.

I chance a couple more steps, and he still doesn't glance back. I'm suspended on a tight rope, and one wrong move will send me crashing to the ground. It's the risk I'm taking— ending whatever Blake and I have before it even really starts.

"Blake," I whisper, scared of disturbing something.

His shoulders sag further. I want to touch him, soothe his demons. He's motionless, like a sculpture at the museum. I hesitantly kneel behind him, placing my palm in the center of his back. He flinches, yet I keep it there. Something deep inside tells me I should.

After seconds of nothing, I crawl to his side, trying to get a glimpse of his face. His jaw's clenched, the muscles in his neck twitching. Somewhere under that anger is misery and heartache. I see it.

This man is drowning, and I'm trying to save him.

If only he'd let me pull him to the surface.

"Blake," I whisper again, barely brushing the side of his cheek with the back of my fingers.

Instead of pulling away, he leans into my touch. For a moment, it's as if I found him under the water, and I have some sort of grip on him. I want that to be true.

"You should go back to bed," he finally says, his voice strained.

"You should go to sleep."

"Lila, I'm not your fucking problem. You don't have to be here."

"I want to, and I'm not leaving until you sleep."

He sighs, gripping my wrist to pull my hand from his face. Battles with Blake are always complicated, but this one might take the cake. He stands, careful not to look at me in the process, and hurries to his bathroom. If he wants, he can stay inside for hours, but I'm still going to be here, sitting against his bed, waiting.

Seconds later, the shower starts. I lay my head back against the mattress and do my best to evaluate everything that's happened since I moved here . . . how lost I feel with Blake. The two things he's made me feel are pissed off and turned on; the disparity between them frustrates me. This whole thing was a bad idea. Blake and I were never meant to be "us." I was naïve to think I could do this without letting my feelings get in the way.

The water shuts off, and two minutes later Blake emerges wearing only a pair of sweatpants. When he sees I'm still in his room, he pauses, letting out a frustrated sigh. "Go back to bed."

"I'm staying until you fall asleep," I announce.

"I'm not sharing my bed," he bites back, his large hands resting on his hips.

Frustrated, I stand in front of him. "I don't want to sleep in your bed, Blake. I just want you to sleep. Period. When was the last time you slept?"

He grips my arms, bringing his eyes level with mine. "I'm not doing this with you tonight. Go. To. Bed."

I've never had someone look at me like this. There's a fuse on the verge of being flipped yet it doesn't stop me.

"I don't think you really want me to."

His face twists. "The fuck I don't."

I wriggle my arms free, and cradle his face before he has time to react. He attempts to pull away, but I'm strengthened by determination. My lips search for his, and when we touch, I wait for him to give in. He needs this as much as I do.

His hands land on my shoulders. He pushes, but then my lips melt him. His rough fingers brush against my collarbone then slide up my neck. He's conceding, and there's no going back now.

As he deepens the kiss, I trail my hand down his stomach and slip it into his pants. He groans when my fingers wrap around his hard cock, and when I start stroking him, his breathing quickens. I relish in this—in giving a man like him pleasure. It does just as much for my self worth as it does his psychological wellbeing.

He's going to be my vice and virtue all in one—my wrongdoing and good deed. Every game has a winner and loser, but when he's buried inside me, the end game is the last thing I want to think about.

With a quick motion, I'm lifted into his arms and my back's against the wall. He's pressed between my legs, but I need more. Leaving one arm wrapped around me, he uses his free hand to pull the collar of my shirt down below my breasts, sucking my nipples with his perfect mouth. I move against him to satisfy my own need.

Blake lifts his head, his lips a mere whisper from mine. "What do you want, Lila? Do you want me to fuck you?"

I swallow, unable to find the right words. All understanding of what the hell I'm doing left me a long time ago.

He wraps my ponytail around his hand, using it as leverage to pull my head back. "Stand up," he demands, never letting go of my hair. As soon as my feet find the floor, he pulls my pants down, covering my sensitive flesh with his fingertips. A few strokes and I'd be done for. He tugs my hair harder—it's pleasure, not pain. My knees buckle. His fingers stall, but his hand is still on me. I want to beg him to do it all over again . . . I'd do anything.

"Do you want more?"

I nod. Another stroke.

"Fingers or cock, Lemon Drop?"

I hesitate for only a second, and he removes his fingers. *Jesus, this is unfair.*

"Cock. I want your cock," I choke out. I've never craved something so much.

He lets go of me and leaves me standing alone against the cold wall as he retrieves a condom. He stands a few feet in front of me, putting on a show of discarding his pants and rolling it on. He's throbbing . . . ready for me.

"Strip," he instructs, watching me. I pull the camisole over my head and step out of my pants while his eyes follow my every move. This isn't playing out like I imagined it would, but I've never been more turned on.

He saunters over and lifts me up again. Wasting no time, he buries himself deep inside me. There's nothing gentle about it. Rough and heady; just what we both need.

I think of all the reasons I should run while he's giving me multiple reasons to stay.

He pins my arms above my head as he pounds into me over and over again. There's an overwhelming urge to touch him, and the fact that I can't is turning me on even more.

"Do you like when I bury myself in your tight little body? No one else fucks you like this, do they?"

I can't speak, but he's right. I love when he fucks me, and he's the only one who's truly ever fucked me.

"Look at me." I open my eyes, not wanting to test the already rough waters. "Come for me, baby."

I gasp, and my walls squeeze his cock over and over again. "Blake," I moan, feeling an intensity I've never felt before. He follows right behind me, letting go of my eyes to bury his face in my neck. I scream out when his teeth sink into my skin.

When our breathing returns to normal, he kisses my lips softly—nothing like what we'd just done. He looks sated. The pain that was etched on him earlier has been replaced with the afterglow of sex.

"Do you think you can sleep now?" I ask, throwing my arms over his shoulders and pecking him on the mouth.

"I might be close. Maybe after another round or two."

My eyes widen.

He lowers me to the ground, withdrawing himself along the way. "Hey, I'm kidding. You better get some sleep," he says, brushing the pad of his thumb over my cheekbone.

I nod, fully aware that I have to be up for work in a few hours. "You too, or I'm crawling into your bed until you do."

He smirks. "I dare you."

My hands rest on his muscular chest. "Blake, you need to get some sleep."

He expression falls. "I'll see what I can do."

"Let's make a deal," I say. "If you go to sleep, I'll make you breakfast before I leave for work."

The smile I love so much is back. "Now that's a deal."

Rolling my eyes, I pick my pajamas up off the floor and head toward the door. Blake doesn't move or say a word. It would be so easy to turn back around and let him sink into me again.

It won't be good for either of us. He's someone I miss when he's not around, and I can't afford an attachment like him. He's hiding behind me—in me—when what he really needs is to face whatever it is that's eating him up inside. Just thinking about it makes me feel like a hypocrite because I ran to Chicago to get away from my shit. I guess we're both lost in our own way.

MY ALARM SOUNDS JUST AFTER five, really early for a girl who stayed up past her bedtime trying to counsel a damaged man with the feel of her body.

After rolling out of bed, I quickly shower and dress. Not wanting to mess with my hair, I tie it up again, and attempt to hide my tired eyes with a thick layer of make-up. One last look in the full-length mirror, and I'm satisfied.

I didn't hear a peep from Blake after I went back to my room. I'd heard him turn the lamp off, and the sound of his bed shifting shortly after crawling into my own. I tossed and turned, thinking about him. I want to know what set him off last night . . . what thoughts were running through his mind as he buried himself inside me over and over.

As I make my way to the kitchen, I notice the ache that still lingers between my legs. It's going to remain there all day, reminding me of who I may or may not get to come home to tonight. That's the thing about *us*—nothing is certain.

Searching the fridge, I find Blake's beloved eggs. I've never been much of a cook so this should be interesting. Usually, when I'm in the kitchen with him, we're bickering about something so I don't know how he likes them exactly.

I crack two eggs and let them sizzle in the pan while I place some bread in the toaster. Blake emerges from his room just as they pop up.

"What's going on in here?" he asks, wiping the sleep from his eyes.

"I owe you breakfast." Looking down at the eggs, I add, "How do you like your eggs?"

He smiles. "Over-easy."

He comes to stand beside me, which just makes me nervous. I flip. He narrows his eyes on the pan. "Does this meet your standards so far?" I ask, hating the silence.

"It'll do," he muses.

"Good, because this is what you're getting."

I pull the toast out and set it on the plate, trying to remember what he puts on it. Opening the fridge, I spot two kinds of jelly and a big container of butter. *Shit.*

"Strawberry jelly," he says, reaching over me to grab the milk.

"Thanks."

He laughs. "All you have to do is ask."

While I occupy myself, putting his plate together, he sits down at the table with a newspaper. This feels too much like a relationship and not so much like me making good on a bet.

When everything is done, I put the plate in front of him. He looks up at me, eyes widening. "Breakfast is served," I say, sauntering away from him.

"You're going to make someone a nice wife some day," he teases. *I almost was someone's wife,* I think to myself as I walk back to the kitchen. I hate being reminded of my failures. "Did you dress up to play the part?" he adds.

"I started my new job yesterday."

"Ditching Charlie's already?"

"No," I answer, wiping down the counters. "I'm working both to save up money for my own place."

His fork clangs against the ceramic plate. "We already talked about this."

I walk across the living room to my purse, ignoring him for a minute. As of right now, I'm staying until Mallory comes back but making him sweat isn't necessarily a bad thing. It's not like he hasn't done it to me a time or two. "Settle down. I'm staying until Mallory gets back unless you give me a reason not to."

"Is that what you're wearing to work?" he asks, picking his fork back up.

"Yep," I answer, putting a little extra sway in my step. The skirt pulls against my ass, and I'm pretty sure he's looking. The apartment goes deathly quiet as I pull my purse over my shoulder. When I turn back around, he's staring at me, his mouth hanging open. "Are you staring?"

His lips curl. "You're walking a little funny today. Is everything okay?"

I narrow my eyes at him as I head toward the door. "I've been better."

The chair screeches across the floor. I count . . . one . . . two . . . his arm wraps around my waist, pulling me back into his body. "Take that back," his breath whispers against my ear.

"Take what back?" I ask, folding against his body even though I don't want to. My body is a stupid traitor.

"No one's ever made you feel better than I do."

"You don't know that."

His grip tightens. "Yes, I do. Admit it."

"Fine, Blake . . . if you don't let me go, we're going to be up against that wall or in your bed or on the counter. You pick."

"Mmm, we haven't tried the counter yet," he groans, pressing his lips to my neck.

"Seriously, I need to go."

"Five minutes."

Pushing down on his arm, I try to free myself. It's a pathetic attempt. "Blake, please, I need this job."

"Have it your way . . . just this once. But tonight, Lemon Drop, you and I have a date on the counter." He's doing that thing again, bringing me to the brink of a sexual high with words alone. At some point, I know this has to stop, but that time is not now. I haven't had my fill of him yet.

After he lets go of me, I adjust my clothes, assuring everything is still perfectly in place. I hold in my breath, trying to calm my racing heart then look at him one last time. "Bye, Blake."

He winks.

Work reminded me of my first day of school this morning. *Here's your desk. There are the supplies. I'll be your supervisor. Ugh.*

My phone dings with a new text message.

Dana: We still on tonight??

Me: God, yes! Margaritas?

Dana: You know it. Meet me at Marco's at 7.

Just what I need after a day like this. I tap my nails against the desk and stare at the clock. My cubicle ended up being on the fifth floor, which is nothing like the twelfth. Inspiration and good-looking men are minimal. I'm so bored out of my mind, I'd file, staple, enter data; I'm not too picky.

My mind wanders to Blake, and the date he promised me on the counter. Maybe I should let him know I won't be home until late. Or maybe I shouldn't because we're not really dating—this isn't a relationship where I have to report my every move.

Still, I don't want him to worry so I pull out my cell phone again. After all the angst of not knowing where he was this weekend, I still didn't ask for his number.

Looking at the time, I'm pretty sure Mallory is out of class for the day so I try her first.

Me: What's Blake's number?

A couple minutes tick by. More clock watching.

She texts me with it, and I quickly program it into my phone.

Mallory: Why did u need his #?

Me: Need to tell him something.

Mallory: Did he leave the toilet seat up?

I ignore her, typing out a text to Blake.

Me: Won't be home until late tonight.—Lila

A reply comes right away.

Blake: I thought we had a date.

I smile . . . it's hard not to. Every time I've walked around today, I've thought of him. When I look at the desk or the counter, I think of him. Even the walls make me think of him.

Me: Climb up on the counter and take care of that little problem yourself.

Blake: There's nothing little about that problem. It's a big problem, and your sexy-librarian-ass is going to take care of it tonight.

Me: I'll be too tired, and maybe drunk. Sorry.

A couple minutes pass, and when I'm starting to think he's pissed that I canceled, the phone dings again.

Blake: Still feel me between your legs?

Me: . . .

Blake: Good. Where are you going tonight?

I debate telling him, but finally concede to our little game.

Me: Marco's

Then there's nothing. Air silence.

As soon as the clock hits noon, I jump in the elevator, following the masses. The mixture of cologne and perfume fills the overheated space as the doors open at every floor. It's a waste of time; there should be a *It's fucking full, and I want to get the hell out of here* button.

When it finally stops on the ground floor, we parade out like a herd of caged animals. I'd gotten a tour of the cafeteria yesterday so I'm not surprised how big it is, but now that it's full of people, it's ten times scarier.

Not wanting to deal with lines, I head straight to the salad bar and load my plate with chicken, veggies, and fruit. I grab a bottle of water and pay before looking for an open place to sit. Surprisingly, there's a single open table in the corner, and since I don't know anyone here, I gravitate toward it.

I barely have my first bite in when a brunette—about my age—stops next to me. I'm admiring her mass of curls when she clears her throat. "Excuse me."

"Hi," I reply, not quite sure what else to say.

"Are these seats taken?" she asks, motioning to the three chairs that surround me.

"No."

She exhales audibly, setting her tray down beside mine. "Oh, good. You're the only person in this room who looked cool to sit with."

"It's kind of like high school, isn't it?"

"Exactly. Everyone has their own little cliques, and I'm sort of the new kid, trying her best to work her way to the top. I thought adulthood would put an end to this," she says, peeling the lid off her yogurt. "I'm Reece, by the way."

"I'm Lila, and I'm new here too. Yesterday was my first day."

Her eyes widen. "Me too, Architecture Apprenticeship. Ugh, the whole reason I picked Stanley was to work under Pierce Stanley, and my mentor told me he's never here."

I bite my lower lip, thinking about my meetings with Pierce. He's the type of guy most girls would sell their soul to touch. "I have a Design Apprenticeship, and I've been staring at the clock since my mentor went into a meeting this morning. They don't even trust me with a stapler yet."

"That sucks. I'd staple all day if I could get one glimpse of Pierce."

"What's his story anyway?" I ask. There's no way I'm going to tell her that I've met Pierce on numerous occasions—even had my interview with him. From what she's said so far, she'd probably tackle me and beat every little fact about him out of me.

"You don't know?"

I shake my head . . . Pierce is a big unknown. The little bit of time we've spent together hasn't even scratched the surface.

"He's talented, well-respected, and successful at a very young age. On top of that, the guy's gorgeous. I've never seen him in person, but if he's even half the man he is in pictures, I'll die." She sounds and looks like a teenage girl talking about a hot new boy band.

I've never seen a picture of Pierce, but the man's beyond gorgeous—at least half Italian, perfect body, and impeccable style. "Is he single?"

She snorts. "You need to Google him. Seriously. He dates but nothing serious. They always post pictures from events and red carpets online, but he's never had the same woman with him twice." Something tells me she'd be satisfied with just one shot. One date. One kiss.

"Interesting."

I wonder if I'm just a game piece to Pierce. Why does he want to take me to the benefit when he could have his pick of gorgeous women?

Chasing all those thoughts and doubts away, I spend the rest of my break talking to Reece about where she grew up and how it compares to here. We both groan while sharing our orientation stories. She reminds me a little of Mallory—super book smart—but she's also funny and quirky.

"How long have you lived in Chicago?" I ask, pushing my half-eaten salad away.

"Since Saturday. It sucks because I don't know anyone."

"I'm going out with a friend tonight if you'd like to join us. Nothing too exciting, just tacos and margaritas, but it will get you out of the house." Maybe I should have asked Dana first, but I don't think she'll mind. Reece is more straight-laced, but they're both guy crazy.

"Are you sure?"

"I wouldn't ask if I wasn't."

"Oh my God, yes." I swear she's going to jump out of her chair and hug me. Tonight will be fun, or at least it will be a good break from the mundane life I've been living—besides when I'm with Blake.

MARCO'S ISN'T QUITE WHAT I expected. It's a bar like Dana said, but one end resembles a dance club. I wanted low key, relaxing, but this is more of a go out, have fun, get drunk, and hope to God you don't have to work the next day type of place.

"I don't think I would have come here if you hadn't invited me . . . ever," Reece chides next to me. Dance music blares, making it almost impossible to hear her.

"Hey, it wasn't exactly my idea. Besides, we're only staying for a couple hours then we're leaving."

She bumps my shoulder when two women in short—barely covers their ass—skirts walk by. It's something I wouldn't have worn even if I'd known the place. "Do we have a safe word?"

"A what?" I ask, wrinkling my nose at her. I can't tell if she's serious or joking.

"Don't you read?" Her eyes bug out like I've grown two heads right before her eyes or something.

"Yes, I read." *Probably more than I should actually.*

"What genre?" she asks, tapping her heel against the hard floor.

I shrug. "Women's Fiction or Romance mostly. Sometimes James Patterson or John Grisham."

"No BDSM?" Even in the dimly lit room, the blush on her cheeks is evident.

"No, that's not really my thing," I answer, scanning the crowded room for Dana.

She continues, "Safe words are used to get out of uncomfortable situations. For example, I hate dancing so if anyone asks, I'm using our word."

With a roll of my eyes, I say, "Seriously, Reece? I really don't think that's what they're for."

"I don't care. So what's it going to be?" *Dana needs to hurry up.* The sooner she gets here, the sooner we can all leave. I want to go home, maybe find Blake, and let him fuck me on the counter like he promised.

"Your pick," I answer, simply to satisfy her.

She taps her index finger on her chin. It's entertaining just to watch her spend so much time picking out a word we'll probably never use. This is nothing but an outdated bar slash dance club . . . not the bedroom. "Pierce." She says it with so much excitement, you'd think he was an old friend she hadn't seen in forever standing across the room.

I shake my head, forgoing any response. I wonder what Reece would say if she knew I was going to a benefit with the hot shot CEO this weekend. Trepidation builds inside me every time I think about it. What will people think when I show up with him? What will Blake think?

Cold, bony hands cover my eyes, breaking me away from all thoughts of the upcoming weekend. "Boo!" Dana shouts, giving me my eyesight back.

"I was starting to think you'd punk'd us," I remark, crossing my arms over my chest.

"Sorry I'm late. I got hung up at home. Wait, who's *us?*"

I motion toward Reece. "Dana, meet Reece. Reece, this is Dana, a friend of mine."

Dana smiles warmly, lifting her hand in a short wave. "The more the merrier."

Tonight will be fun. Over the years I've learned that it's not so much about where you are as it is who you're with.

"Let's grab a booth before there's none left," Dana says, motioning for us to follow her.

After we're seated, the waitress brings us some chips and salsa and takes our order for three margaritas. The first chip tastes like pure salt-covered heaven on my tongue, and before I know it, I've downed a handful before Dana and Reece even get a taste.

"What are you guys going to get?" Reece asks.

"Should we order a taco platter? We can share," Dana suggests. I swear the more time I spend with Dana, the more I like her.

Reece and I both throw down our menus in agreement. The waitress returns to bring our drinks and takes our order. She's not even a foot away from the table before our lips are plastered against the salted rims. The icy tequila is some of the best I've had. Chicago has a one up on Nebraska in the drink department.

"God that's good," Reece moans, pressing her thin lips to the rim. She sounds like a woman in the throes of wild sex.

"Well, hurry up and finish those, and then we can have another," Dana says. She has half her drink gone while Reece and I still savor our first sip.

"You do realize that Reece and I have to work in the morning, don't you?"

She waves her hand like it's nothing. "Oh, come on, we're young enough. We'll bounce back quick."

I roll my eyes and take another drink, realizing just how easy it goes down this time. Tomorrow morning is going to come with one hell of a headache.

Our food arrives, and we put it away like a table of post-game football players. It's been almost eight hours since I ate a few bites of salad . . . anything would taste good to me right now.

"So, Reece, what's your story?" Dana asks between bites. I'm curious myself since I just met her today.

"All twenty-five years of it, or would you prefer me to narrow it down to one chapter?"

Dana rests her elbows on the table like she's going to soak up each and every word. "Let's start with the juicy stuff. Boyfriend? Virgin?"

Reece's narrows her eyes at her. "Why does everyone assume that I'm a virgin?"

"I'm not assuming anything. Spill." Dana grabs a handful of chips and sits back like she's waiting for the main feature at the movie theater.

"I've had boyfriends. Lots of them. Like more than I can count on one hand. One was even a football player in high school." She talks so fast that it's hard to discern. It's like she doesn't necessarily want us to retain it all.

"Do you have one now?" Dana asks, popping yet another chip in her mouth.

Reece snorts. "No, I'm keeping my options open since I just moved here. I don't want to be tied down right now, you know?"

I pipe in, saving her from more of the Dana inquisition. "I'm the same. The last thing I want to be is tied down. Besides, I just got out of a relationship a few months ago, and it didn't leave me feeling warm and fuzzy about men."

The waitress brings yet another round of drinks. The steady stream of tequila is loosening me up . . . a welcome feeling after the past couple weeks.

"Don't let her fool you," Dana says to Reece. "Lila's got a man."

"Shut it, Dana. I'm not tied to anyone right now."

She laughs. "Oh, he hasn't broken the handcuffs out yet and hitched you to his bedpost? Poor girl . . . I totally took him as the type."

I narrow my eyes at her. "What about you? Do you have a boyfriend?"

She scoffs. "Hell no! I work them like monkey bars, jumping from one to the next."

Reece and I share shocked expressions. Through high school and college, I knew plenty of jumpers but never one that would admit to it.

"Chill out. I don't end up in bed with all of them."

As if that makes it any better. Dana and I are different, but sometimes dissimilarity is needed for two parts to fit together. She's the blank to my tab.

We spend the next hour talking about the duds we've dated while on our journey to find Mr. Right. And that just leads to us discussing how Mr. Right probably doesn't even exist.

After three, or maybe four, margaritas Dana finally convinces Reece and I to join her on the dance floor. I'm uncoordinated, I always have been, but the alcohol gives me enough courage to fake it.

My body flows freely to the beat of the music. The three of us form a circle, laughing and having a good time. Strands of hair fall from my once perfect bun, sticking to my face. The best part of it all is I don't care . . . alcohol is a wonderful thing.

One song ends and another begins. Unable to make out the words, I close my eyes and let the rhythm carry me. This is freedom at its finest.

"Pierce!" Reece yells. My eyes shoot open, immediately scanning the dance floor. I find her a few feet away, her ass shoved against a guy's crotch.

My instinct is to laugh, and then I put myself in her shoes. I cringe when strange men touch me. There's a layer of unpredictability—not knowing the guy's intentions or where the hell his hands have been. I literally pry Reece from his arms, not stopping until we're back in our booth.

"Thank you. I tried to get away, and he thought I was grinding against him. It was so gross."

"You said you wanted to make friends," I tease.

"Who wants to make friends?" I'd know that voice anywhere. Deep and sexy. My mind shifts to all the seductive words that have slipped from those lips over the last couple weeks. I never imagined that thoughts of the past would leave my panties wet.

"And what are you doing here?" Dana asks, coming up behind Blake. She slides in next to Reece, glaring up at him along the way. For her part, Reece can only stare, smitten with the stereotypical bad boy—ripped faded blue jeans, fitted navy henley, hair tousled in the most perfect way possible. His parents should have just named him The Panty Dampener.

He grins, and maybe it's the alcohol or the dancing, or the memory of how his hands feel on me, but I'm finding it hard to catch my breath. "My plans for tonight got canceled."

"Oh, shucks," Dana chides, "Guess you'll have to find something else to do."

"I already have," he responds, sliding in next to me. His arm brushes against mine. Sparks fly too easily. I should move away from him, to extinguish them, but I don't. It's been a long time—maybe even never—since I was turned on by the mere presence of a man.

He runs his finger over my blushed cheeks and damp hair. "You look so damn sexy right now," he says as he leans in close. "But I prefer when I make you wet."

"Can you keep your voice down?" A deeper shade of red paints my cheeks. I glance across the table, noticing Dana and

Reece locked in a whispered conversation. Maybe they didn't hear a thing, or maybe they heard it all and they're having a nice little chat about my screwed up arrangement.

"Am I embarrassing you in front of your friends?" Blake asks, a little louder this time. His words are embarrassing me, as is the obvious way my body reacts to him. Whenever he's within a couple feet, I become a withering, flimsy petal rolled between his stupid, magic fingers.

"Will you two stop already?" Dana groans from across the table.

"I'm confused. Is this the guy?" Reece pipes in, eyes gleaming with a newfound excitement.

"They're fucking," Dana remarks matter-of-factly. *Oh God.* I want to be anywhere but here. Blake is going to know I have a big mouth, and Reece is probably wondering how she picked the company slut as a new friend.

"What's the difference?" Reece pipes in.

I grimace, draining the rest of my margarita in an attempt to hide my face. For his part, Blake is quiet. He's either grinning at how uncomfortable this is all making me or pissed that the whole world suddenly knows our business.

"There's a huge difference. I'll explain it to you when we're sober," Dana adds.

There is an immense difference between a relationship and fucking . . . I'm just learning that myself. He doesn't take me to dinner or pull me close like a second skin after sex. We just have this thing—an intense, sanity-stealing chemistry—that makes it impossible to keep our hands to ourselves. In some ways, it's more powerful than the connection I had with Derek. No feelings—just a fierce, undeniable attraction.

I didn't move here with any intention of starting something like this so soon, but sometimes we don't get to choose where we land. Life has taught me that over and over again in both good and bad ways. With Blake, I must have had a choice, but I don't remember choosing him.

Shaking my thoughts, I bring my focus back to the group around me. Reece stares at me incredulously, and it dawns on me that I haven't officially introduced her to my . . . whatever he is. When I finally take a chance and look up at him, he's staring at me with this amused expression on his face. Watching me squirm is entertaining to him, I guess. "Blake, you've already met Dana, but this is Reece. She's a friend from my other job."

"Like a peanut butter cup?" Blake jokes, shifting his eyes to Reece. I instantly want his attention back. He's not mine, but he is.

"Blake, stop!" I groan, just loud enough that my group around the table hears me.

"These two seem like they could use some alone time. Let's go dance," Dana suggests. Her wide eyes shift from me to Reece, silently begging her to agree so they can get out from under the awkwardness at our table.

"Only if you promise to keep me far away from Crotch-to-Ass guy," Reece responds.

"Don't worry. We'll find someone sexy for you to grind with."

Reece looks like the music just cued up on that popular shark attack movie, and she's about to be clamped in the jaw of the giant fish. "Or we could just leave."

Dana laughs. "Nope. Come on."

My shy new friend wrings her hands together as she stares at me from across the table. A good person would rescue her from the water, but being around Blake doesn't necessarily put me under the best light. "Go, I'll join you guys in a couple minutes."

After one last narrowing of her eyes, she begrudgingly follows Dana. As they disappear into the crowd, I look over and meet Blake's gaze. There's a sparkle in his eye I rarely see. A gorgeous smile curves his lips. He makes it incredibly hard to remember why I was angry with him just seconds ago.

His hand moves between my barely covered legs, his fingers slowly working their way upward. My breath hitches. He wouldn't go there . . . not here with all these people surrounding us. A little higher, and I know I'm wrong. This man has no inhibitions. "Come home with me."

"I need another drink first." I alternate between swallowing down my rebuttal and squeezing my thighs together. Swallow. Squeeze. Swallow. Squeeze. If our waitress doesn't come back soon, I'll have no choice but to throw back whatever I can find on the table to help drown these nerves.

"I can do so much more for you than a drink ever can. You should know that by now." His voice purrs, his breath hitting my cheek. He's not exaggerating, but I'm not leaving just yet.

The waitress reappears before I get a chance to turn him down . . . or that's what I think I was going to do. "I need another margarita, please. The largest one you've got."

She glances between Blake and me, shaking her head. "You got it."

As soon as she turns her back, Blake surprises me by pressing his lips to my neck—that magical spot right below my ear. I moan softly, feeling the familiar tingle travel down my spine.

"That good, huh?" he whispers against my skin.

Maybe it's just the tequila, but I need his hands on me—all over me. My next words surprise even me. "Dance with me."

His grin could melt thousands of panties and break a million hearts. *Damn him.* "I don't dance."

"Not a big deal," I say, pushing against his shoulder to hint that I want out. "I'll find someone else to rub their hands all over my body."

He groans, angling himself to cage me in. "I dare you."

"Well, Blake," I say, patting his strong chest. "A dare is something I never walk away from."

His attention darts to my lips and just when I think he might kiss me, he slides out of the booth. "This should be fun," he announces, crossing his arms over his chest.

Without a second thought, I scoot out and bring myself up so we're chest to chest. There's a playful glimmer in his eyes—one I usually only witness seconds before he devours me. It's taking every bit of my self-control not to beg him to take me home and do what he promised earlier.

I lift myself to my tiptoes, using his shoulders as leverage. I close the gap between us, and when he smiles like I might kiss him, I change paths until my lips are against his ear. "I'll be back in a little while . . . maybe."

I spin around, swaying my hips to show him what he's missing. I'm probably not very good at it, but the alcohol helps.

"Hey, Lemon Drop!" he yells when I'm a few steps away.

I look over my shoulder. "Yeah?"

"You'll be back."

IT TAKES ME A COUPLE MINUTES to find the perfect target on the dance floor. If I'm going to toy with Blake, I need to make him believe that whoever I find is just as good, if not better than him. He needs to feel challenged.

That's not going to be an easy find around here—the good-looking part. This isn't exactly one of those hip downtown clubs.

Then I see him—a guy leaning against the wall, the neck of a beer bottle wrapped in his fingers. He's got this sexy aura about him—longish dark hair swept to one side, a tight white T-shirt that tapers at his waist and ripped blue jeans. He'll definitely work— my mother would kill me if she saw me with him.

I stare at him.

He stares back at me, eyes roaming the length of my body.

I stand still, trying to work up the courage to approach him. Where's the liquid courage when I need it? Before I can talk my feet into moving forward, he pushes off the wall and starts in my direction. His eyes stay on me, dark and seducing. The whole thing plays like a movie in slow motion. My heart hammers—not like it does when I'm with Blake—but with heightening nerves.

Without a word, he grabs my hand and pulls me out in the middle of the packed dance floor. Calvin Harris pumps through the club as he wraps one arm around my waist. My body tenses just for a second, then the alcohol gets ahold of me. I'd be out the door if it weren't for the help of Jose Cuervo. Instead, I'm pressed against a complete stranger. Letting him touch me, feel every curve of my body. It doesn't feel right, but it doesn't feel wrong either. When I dare look back into his eyes, he's assessing me, silently begging me to relax against him.

I close my eyes, and I try.

He tightens his arm around my waist, bringing us even closer. This room is suddenly too warm. Too much Jose. Too much of the dark stranger. Too much of Blake. I'm not quite sure what to do with my hands so I wrap my fingers around his strong biceps. It's safe—not too inviting.

"Relax," he whispers against my ear.

I nod, drawing in all the oxygen my lungs will hold. He moves us together using his hold on me, and as the song switches, I find my groove. I slide up and down his body, enjoying how free I feel. I feel alcohol flowing in my veins.

The dark stranger glides his hands over the curve of my ass at the same time he leans in to whisper in my ear. "Is this what you had in mind when you looked at me like that from across the room? Because I had a little more than this in mind."

His lips skim my neck. My breath is stolen from me. The English language leaves me stranded. I wanted to play, to dance, to make Blake jealous, because maybe deep down inside, I want something more than he's given me.

"That's enough!" an angry, unforgiving voice yells from behind me.

Blake's eyes are something so fierce I can't hold them. It's too much but yet it's exactly what I wanted.

"She's with me." The helpless man is now just a pawn standing in front of an angry king.

Blake sidles up to him, holding on to the stranger's bicep so tightly his knuckles turn white. "Let. Go. Now. Asshole."

"And, what are you going to do if I don't?"

The grin on Blake's face is evil. "Trust me . . . you don't want to know."

"She isn't worth it anyway," the guy says as he lets go of me.

Something immediately washes over Blake's face, and he pulls his arm back and punches the guy. The whole scene flashes in front of me like lightning. My hand in Blake's. Him pulling me off the dance floor. My heels click as I try to keep up with him. My head spins from shock and alcohol.

He pulls me into a dark corner and presses me against the wall, his knee wedged between my legs. "Tease Blake time is over. Are you ready to get the fuck out of here?"

"Do you want me to look at your hand?" I watch him flex it over and over again between us.

"No." He shakes his head. "That dickhead was soft."

I pull my lower lip between my teeth. I'm a novice at seduction . . . it's the best I can do. "Dance with me." Twice in one night. *Good job, Lila.*

He kisses the corner of my lips, trailing down my neck. His mouth is the equivalent of silk against my skin . . . it's almost enough to convince me to skip all the nonsense and follow him wherever he leads.

"Blake," I say, pushing against his chest. "Dance."

He's stronger than me—a giant next to my small five foot three frame. He pins my arms above my head with one hand and trails the back of the other along my side. "We're going home. Now."

I'd argue if I could speak, but I can't. His thumb brushes the underside of my breast as his lips crash into mine. I never realize how much I like him, what he does to me, until we're like this. There's no denying *this.*

He grins. "What's it going to be, Lila?"

Holy hell. I can't say no to that gorgeous face. "Okay. Let me tell my friends."

He comes at me like he's going to kiss me again but stops just short. "Hurry."

As soon as he gives me enough space, I all but run away from him in search of Reece and Dana. I could just text them. They'd understand. Our booth is empty so I scan the dance floor looking for the two polar opposites. Nothing. Ready to give up, I head to the bar to settle my tab, spotting them taking shots at the end of the bar. *This isn't going to be good.*

"I'm leaving," I announce, sliding between them.

Reece stumbles into the guy next to her when she sees me. "Lila, we've been looking all over for you."

"Not really," Dana chimes in. "Blake wasn't going to take his eyes off you so we knew you were in good hands. He has good hands, doesn't he, Lila?"

Before I can reply, Blake comes to stand behind me, curving his hand around the back of my neck. "How are you guys getting home?"

Reece chuckles, leaning her weight against the bar. "The same way I got here. I think I took the train, or maybe a cab. Do you remember, Lila?"

I'm about to set her straight when Blake speaks up. "What's your address?"

"Umm. It's a tall building with bricks. By the way, you better not hurt my friend here, or I'm coming after you. She's amazing and beautiful and smart. You should be doing more than just fucking her brains out."

I wince, taken aback by my new friend's drunken threat. It's bold and full of truth I'm not brave enough to speak.

Blake curses under his breath. He looks down at me, half irritated, half troubled. "I'm going to run outside and get a cab. We need to make sure these two get home before we do."

I'm a little shocked by his gesture but can't place why. Blake was minutes away from hitting the homerun he came to score, but that's going to have to wait. Strange for a guy who's self-absorbed most of the time, but I like knowing there's a caring side to him. "Okay."

He squeezes my shoulder and walks away, his figure quickly being swallowed by the crowd. It takes a minute to soak in, to see him as more than the god of my desires.

"Where's he going? Do you think I made him mad?" Reece asks.

"He's getting us a cab. Let's pay up so we can get out of here."

I motion for the bartender, letting him know we're ready for the bill. While we wait, I practically pour a glass of water down Reece's throat in an attempt to dilute the alcohol. Not wanting to hang around, I settle the whole bill and pull my friends away from the bar.

Luckily, Dana can still walk a straight line. That much cannot be said about Reece who struggles to keep herself upright. She's so going to kill me when she sees me at work tomorrow . . . if she makes it.

Blake spots us coming out the door and comes over to help with Reece. He makes sure we're all safely tucked inside and slides into the passenger seat, giving the driver instructions on which address to go to first.

Reece's head falls against my shoulder as the car starts down the city streets. It's quiet except for the occasional voices coming over the cabbie's radio. Dana lives closest so we drop her off first, watching her disappear behind her door. Next is Reece.

"Wait here," Blake instructs our driver.

He points to the meter that steadily climbs with every minute we spend in here, but Blake doesn't respond. Something tells me this isn't a first for him. He's too good at it.

We help Reece out and hold onto her until we're standing in front of the door. "Can I have your key?" Blake asks, holding his hand out.

She unwraps her arm from Blake's, clumsily digging through her purse. It's painful to watch this bright, sweet girl struggle to do something so simple. I make a mental note not to do it to her again.

"Here," I say, reaching for her purse. "Let me help you." A few quick shuffles and I have her key chain between my fingers. I hand them over to Blake who makes quick work of the door.

"What apartment?" he asks.

I watch her struggle, going from a drunken awake state to half asleep. "Last door to the right," she mumbles. *Thank God it's the first floor.*

We get her inside and carefully tuck her into her bed before retreating back to the waiting cab. Blake hasn't said much, and my liquid courage is dissipating. He follows me into the backseat, giving the driver the address for his last stop.

Distance remains between us. His elbow rests against the door, his fingers running along his strong jaw as he stares out at the city lights. He doesn't talk. He doesn't look. That spark isn't burning as brightly, but that's what always happens when I think too much. What changed in the little bit since we left the bar?

He does this all the time, hot and cold, cold and hot. It makes it harder and harder to trust him, to know that he has the best of intentions with my heart. But then again, my heart was never supposed to get involved in this.

"You okay?" he finally asks when we pull up in front of our building.

"Why wouldn't I be?"

He shrugs. "Did you have a little too much to drink?"

"Maybe, but it's wearing off now." Everything is as clear as it should be. Besides, I don't think this much when I'm drunk.

Blake hands the driver enough cash for the whole ride plus tip and climbs out, holding the door open for me. He walks with me, but we don't touch. The chilly night suddenly feels a lot colder.

He follows me up the stairs and unlocks our door before I get a chance. He holds it open then makes sure it's locked again when we're both inside.

I want the other Blake back—the one who'd set me on the counter and fuck me until I can't walk tomorrow. The one who'd touch me in ways that would make me quit thinking again.

"You should probably go to bed," he says. He stares at the floor, combing his fingers through his hair.

"What if I'm not tired?"

He laughs—not from humor but from frustration—and looks up. "You have to work tomorrow, remember?"

I nod, disappointment stinging the back of my throat. I'm not ready to call it a night, but I can't stay here like this. This isn't how I wanted the night to end. I hurry to my bedroom, careful to close the door behind me. I turn on the shower and strip out of my clothes while I wait for it to heat up.

With a lot on my mind, I stay under the water a little longer than I should. The three corners of my world collided tonight, parts successfully, others not so much. If it weren't for a few drunken comments toward the end, things would have been perfect.

By the time I step out, my fingers are pruned. My skin bright red. Not wanting to dig around for pajamas, I pull on my robe and haphazardly run a comb through my hair. It's almost midnight, and I should be tired, but I can't shut off my brain. It drifts to Blake—why he is who he is, why he's not easier to read . . . why he doesn't want me. We all have a story. The more we let people know, the better they understand us.

Most of the things I know about Blake are drawn from what I know about Mallory. Their parents are professionals, still married and all in all good people. I know they pushed Mallory a little bit, but not in a sense that made her struggle under pressure. She drew from it. It helped her keep her focus. Maybe it was different for Blake, or there could be a whole other part of him that I don't know.

I want to know every part of him.

When I finally emerge from my room, Blake is standing in the kitchen with a beer bottle to his lips. His eyes land on me almost immediately, exploring every inch of my bare, exposed legs. If I'm going to get his whole story, I need to do it his way. I need to speak his language and pray that he eventually speaks mine. This isn't ideal—it's a flower that won't bloom, a tree without leaves. There could be so much more. It could be so much better. But if this is what I get, I'm going to keep it alive.

I walk toward him slowly, noticing the way his fingers tighten around the bottle . . . craving those hands on me. My robe slips off my shoulder, and I make no attempt to fix it. I take slow, calculated steps toward him. He strides around the counter toward me. A force stronger than either of us pulls our bodies together. Clasp. Glue. Desire.

My heart pumps faster when he's standing right in front of me. Neither of us has muttered a single word. We just stay . . . like this, eyes of lust speaking silently to one another.

The way his lips part, the way his eyes gloss over, is confirmation enough. He craves this just as much as I do. I run my fingers along my belt, slowly untying it as his hands clench at his sides. The cotton robe falls open just enough to give him a glimpse of what he's trying to deny himself.

I take another step, running my fingertips over my lower lip, pretending it's him. His tongue sweeps across his lips, and I swear if he doesn't touch me soon, I'll scream.

Seduction is new, but I'm finding it's like riding a bike—I just need to stop over-thinking it and move my legs. To him. To us.

One step closer, and our chests would be touching. I flush just thinking about his skin against mine. The robe slips further down my arm, and, this time, the pull is enough to take it to the ground. So I stand in front of him, naked and exposed, waiting for either the worst form of rejection or the elevator to sexual bliss.

A slow smile pulls at his lips as he cradles my face in his hands. His mouth crashes down on mine. It's not enough. I want him—no, I need him deeper. I need all that I know he can give me.

I run my fingers over his strained erection, wanting so badly to free him and push him into me. Sex has never been a necessity to me, but with him, I breathe it, dream it. I live for it.

"Not going to sleep?" he asks between kisses.

"I'm not tired." *Definitely not going to sleep after a taste of him.*

He pulls away, still holding my face. "I don't want you to think I'm just using you. What Reece said—"

"She was drunk."

He runs his thumbs over my cheekbones. "Do you remember what I said . . . about not getting your heart caught up in this? I meant it, but I don't know if you're that girl. I don't know if you can leave your heart at the door."

My finger covers his kissable pink lips. "Blake, you promised me counter sex. It's all I've thought about all damn day. Now, are you going to give it to me or not?"

"Promise me," he says, "Promise me that this is all there is. That you won't let yourself fall into something deeper, because Lila, I don't want to hurt you." His chest pulses. My heart clenches. "I can't hurt you."

If there's one thing I'm sure of, it's that Blake's loved before. To understand pain and hurt, you have to have loved first. Who hurt him so badly that he won't let himself go through it again?

"Touch me. Please." I inch my fingers up, brushing against his stomach, his sculpted chest. His body is a touchable masterpiece.

"Fuck," he mutters, claiming my lips with another kiss. My arms wrap tightly around his neck, pressing my body to his. It feels so right.

Standing on my tiptoes, I whisper against his ear. "I've been thinking about the feel of you inside of me all day."

His cock twitches against my stomach. "Is that what you want?"

I nod, too nervous to say any more. He's created a sinner. I'm addicted to the fire with which he burns my skin—a slow singe that spreads until my whole body is aflame.

The alcohol is starting to wear off. Just enough remains to give me the confidence for this—to initiate what Blake wouldn't when we walked through the door. He showed a little bit of nobility—a miniscule version of Prince Charming—with his concern for my heart. It just made me want him even more.

He lifts me off my feet and carries me to the kitchen, his mouth connected to mine. He holds me to him with one arm while using the other to clear a stack of newspapers from the counter. Before I even realize what's happening, I'm sitting on the edge with Blake between my legs. I'm done messing around . . . I need him inside of me.

Reaching between us, I work the button on his pants. There's not an ounce of patience left in me.

"Hey," he groans, gripping my wrist. "There's no rush, Lemon Drop."

I look up, using my free hand to run the back of my finger against his jaw. "Are you ever going to tell me why you call me that?"

He grins, pressing his index finger to my lips. "We're done talking." His hot lips replace his finger, but I pull back, earning myself a curious look. This back and forth thing . . . we do it a lot.

"Tell me, or maybe I'm not playing tonight." He better freaking tell me, because there's no way I'm going to be able to sleep with this hungry sensation between my legs.

He leans in, and I think he might kiss me. Try to silence me. But he doesn't. He pauses a few inches from my face. "I don't have to tell you a damn thing to get between those legs, and you know it."

"Not true," I mutter, shaking my head.

He grips my knees then skims his fingers along the inside of my thighs. I spread them wider, thinking it will interrupt his rhythm, but it works against me. His thumbs stroke the top my thighs and a thick groan escapes his lips. "I knew the second you walked out in that sexy little robe that I was going to fuck you."

When he slips one finger inside of me, I gasp. "You're so fucking wet and ready for me. I dare you to make me to stop. This pretty little pussy would hate you for it."

He pushes a second finger into me. Pressure builds quickly. He's winning, but when he's winning like this, I'm anything but losing.

He stills his fingers, using his free hand to lift my chin so my eyes align with his. The intensity within them burns into mine. "Want me to stop?"

I shake my head as much as I can against his touch. There's nothing but green lights when his hands are on me.

His fingers thrust into my body just once, causing me to shutter. "I didn't hear you."

I steady my breathing just enough, digging my fingers into his shoulders. It's not what I want, though. Not even close. "No, fuck me, Blake."

A smile spreads across his handsome face. "Good girl."

I sit completely naked in front of him, the light above the sink the only thing illuminating the dark space. The intensity in his eyes is worth drowning in.

"Lean back," he commands. I do as he asks, watching him strip out of his clothes. The moment I decided to step out of my room, there wasn't going to be any going back. Blake's an enigma. I want his body, but I don't need his heart, at least that's what I keep telling myself. It may be nothing but a sugar-coated lie, but as long as I still have him like this, none of that really matters.

He splays his hand between my bare breasts, slowly working it down against my flat stomach, circling my belly button. All I want is him inside of me, but he treats me like a wind-up toy—teasing and touching until I explode.

He uses his hands on my thighs to spread me, and then his hot mouth hits my core. His tongue laps my clit a few times followed by sucking. It's the most amazing feeling . . . the pressure he creates, his skill. I wrap my legs around his back and tug his hair between my fingers in appreciation. This man . . .

My walls clench, causing me to scream out of pleasure. "Blake. Fuck." I pull his hair harder, letting the silky strands fall from between my fingers.

"That was number one. Let's work on two and three." His words alone get the river of desire flowing again. Derek always made sure I had one. To him, that meant I got mine, but in actuality, it just made me want another.

Blake stands and kisses me, letting me taste myself on him. It's sexy as hell. With his lips still on mine, he pushes into me with one quick motion. I'm so wet and ready . . . for him. His mouth trails my neck as he rolls my nipples between his fingertips. The combination—having so many places touched by him—puts my body into overdrive. I dig my nails into his back as my second orgasm rips through me. It's better this time with his cock buried deep inside of me.

"Jesus," he groans, pumping into me harder. He reaches deeper than I ever thought possible. This is what it's like to be filled completely. "The guy at the club—he could never give you this. You were made for me. So fucking perfect."

I moan, letting myself fall back on the counter, on full display for him. My mind fixates on the emotional explosion our connected bodies create. I'm so lost in the feeling, my eyes close unintentionally, and then I miss him. I miss the intensity I see in his eyes.

I watch as he pulls open a drawer, still buried in me. I hear shuffling below but don't think much of it; the sensation of our joined bodies is enough to handle. He slams the drawer shut and puts his fingers to my lips. "Open."

I narrow my eyes at him in question, but he doesn't say anything more. He's going to win . . . he always wins. I part my lips and taste sweet candy on my tongue . . . a lemon drop. Sweet on the outside, tart inside, it's not my first choice but it has me thinking of him. He thrusts two more times then gently kisses my lips. "Pass me the candy."

Placing it on the edge of my tongue, I allow him to suck it between his lips. He rolls it in his mouth a few times before bringing his head down to my nipple, lapping it with the candy between my skin and his tongue. The texture does things to me that I never imagined, heightening the sense of arousal. He moves to my other breast, repeating the same.

"Blake," I cry.

The sticky candy falls from his tongue, slowly sliding down my stomach. He looks up at me, eyes hooded. "You want to know why I call you Lemon Drop?"

I nod, gripping his hair between my fingers. He moves his head back down, tracing circles around the candy with his tongue.

"Until I met you," he murmurs against my skin. The candy slips lower, and I imagine what it would feel like in his mouth while it's working my clit. "Life handed me nothing but lemons. Shit. Heartbreak. Bad Luck." It glides even further. So close. I don't even care why he calls me Lemon Drop anymore as long as he does what I want him to.

"And, since I met you, things aren't as black. I even catch myself smiling sometimes. Life's sweeter with you." He clenches the candy between his teeth. His cock slips out of me, and I want it back.

"Blake." His mouth covers my clit, licking and sucking. The lemon drop is cradled in his tongue, providing constant added pleasure. When he said three orgasms, he wasn't exaggerating.

When I'm mere seconds from falling back into bliss, he stops. I whimper. He's dangling something so freaking delicious in front of me, but I can't quite grasp it. He's a tease, but I keep coming back for more.

He works his way back up, licking a trail around my belly button and my breasts. He thrusts his cock back into me as his mouth trails up my throat. When our eyes are level, he brushes his lips against mine. "Take the lemon drop back, baby."

His endearment clenches my heart. It's nothing to him, but it's everything to me. No one has ever made me feel as wanted as Blake does, and he's not asking for all of me. With Blake, that will never come; he made that perfectly clear before we even started this.

He startles me from my thoughts when he sticks his tongue out, the lemon drop resting on the tip. I do as he did earlier, clamping it between my teeth. It's not as good as it was the first time. Most of the sweetness is gone and only the tartness remains.

"How does it taste?" he asks. The question is almost impossible to answer as he picks up his pace, pumping in and out of me. *So good.*

"Sour," I breathe, digging my nails into his back. I'm so close it almost hurts—the best type of pain. I've never wanted to take in my next breath as much as I do right now.

"That's how my life was before this . . . before you." A few more thrusts and my walls contract around him. He groans, burying his face in the crook of my neck. I clutch onto him like I might fall off the edge of a cliff if I don't.

He's going to let go . . . it's just a matter of time. We're just supposed to have sex—hot, intense, mind-blowing sex. Feelings and cuddles and long walks on the beach aren't part of the package, but the more we do this, the more I wish it were. I should have never started this, because once I did, there was no going back.

"Shit," he spits, quickly pulling out of me. "Shit."

I'm sitting naked on the edge of the counter, watching him pace across the kitchen in the same state. I don't understand how we go from one extreme to another so quickly. Somehow, I'm good enough to fuck, but not good enough to hold. I slip off the counter and start toward my room before he sees the unshed tears in my eyes.

"Lila." His voice is low, tortured. I want him to call me back to wrap me in his arms, but that's not going to happen. I turn around anyway.

Unable to speak without crumbling, I stare. He looks like the weight of the world has been dropped on his shoulders.

"I forgot to use a condom."

A million things flash through my mind but none of them are probably the same as what's going through his. If he got to know me a little better, he wouldn't be fretting over this. If I'm not worthy of a relationship with him, I'm definitely not in the running to carry little Blake babies.

"I'm on the pill. I never miss one."

He sighs, combing his fingers through his hair. "Oh, thank God."

"What about you?"

"Me?" he asks, eyebrows raised.

"I know you have more . . . experience than me. Are you clean?"

The curious expression switches to one of irritation. He assumed I was irresponsible; it's only fair for me to do the same. "I always use a condom. I'm not stupid."

I nod, feeling the reminder of our sex sliding down my inner thigh. This is crazy. Why do I keep doing this when it leaves me with so much regret?

Blake comes to stand in front of me in all his naked glory. His eyes search mine, and he sees it—the torment he's caused within me.

"Hey, I'm sorry. I didn't inherit the sensitivity gene."

"The pretend-to-care one would have been nice," I chide, folding my arms in front of my chest.

"Lila." He cradles my face in his hands. "I care, and I'm going to find a way to make this up to you. Do you want me to run you a bath?" He leans in to kiss my lips tenderly—a peck for each corner, then ending in the center.

As soon as he lets go of me, I start walking backward. "I think I'm just going to go to bed. Besides, it's going to be hard to top the lemon drop."

He laughs, real and throaty. "I already have that covered."

"We'll see."

He reaches out, running the back of his fingers along my jaw and down my neck. "I meant what I said earlier . . . why I call you Lemon Drop. This is all I can give you, and I hope it's enough for now because I don't want to lose this. I swear you're the only thing I look forward to these days."

I lean into his hand, buying myself time to form a response that won't give away what I'm really feeling. He's not equipped for that right now. "I don't want to lose this either."

"We need to be smart about this." I know he's talking about the condoms, and maybe even my falling heart, so I don't ask for any more explanation. I don't want to hear it.

I nod, and without another word, I turn to walk back to my room. The lemon drop was the most sensually sweet thing I've ever experienced, and he just ruined it. Realizing the tart remnants of the candy are still in my mouth, I roll it against my tongue. Still tart. When I stop and think about it, the tartness lasts longer than the sweet coating. Sex for us is the sweet coating, and everything else that comes with it, or doesn't come with it, is the unwanted tart center.

That doesn't mean I'm going to stop eating them.

"DO YOU HAVE PLANS FOR TONIGHT?" Reece asks, coming around the corner to my cubicle.

The sight of her makes me smile. She's dressed in a white camisole with little black eye glass graphics plastered all over it. It's a little cute and a lot quirky—reminds me of her whimsical personality.

I shake my head to wake myself up, remembering how much it aches from only sleeping three hours last night. My shift at Charlie's ran late, and then I had to come into the office. I'm dreading having to shift from here back to waitressing in just a few hours. At least it's Friday. "I have to work."

"That sucks. What about tomorrow night?"

She's pretty anxious for a girl who got shit-faced three nights ago. She was a zombie the next day—going through the motions and not noticing anything else that was going on around her. Yet, the way her eyes light when she asks makes me feel bad about having to turn her down. Her question also reminds me of my impending evening with Pierce Stanley. I still haven't said a word about it to Blake; things have been so . . . different between us.

Wednesday night he greeted me at the door after work and made me come hard against the wall. Then he fed me a pasta dish he'd made, and got me naked again in his bed. It ended like it always does. Every time, it hurts a little more, because every time, I fall further into him. Maybe, if I sink far enough, I'll be in his heart, and he'll feel the same.

He fulfills my physical needs and unravels my emotional ones. I have to be willing to let him go. If he can't give me what I ultimately want—what I've always wanted—then I need to cut the strings and move on. It's so much easier to sit here and think about how I'm going to do it than it is to actually do it.

He wasn't home last night, and that's the difference between us and a real couple. He didn't mention anything about being gone. I wonder if there's someone else . . . if that's why he's so secretive about everything. And that's one thing I don't think I can do—be one of his many.

Reece snaps her fingers in front of my eyes. "Earth to Lila."

"Sorry, I'm tired. I have an event tomorrow. I'm free Sunday through Wednesday night, though." Crossing my fingers beneath my desk, I hope she doesn't ask anything more about tomorrow. I'm not a good liar.

"What event are you attending tomorrow?"

Shit. "A benefit."

Her eyes narrow in on me. "For what?"

And secrets crumble. "I'm not sure exactly. It's for work . . . Stanley invited me."

"As in Pierce Stanley?"

"Yeah . . . that would be the one," I answer shyly.

Her mouth falls open. "Oh. My. God."

I place my finger over my lips, doing my best to quiet her. "It's not a big deal."

"Are you freaking kidding me?" she squeals. "It's Pierce Stanley. That's a huge deal. Why didn't you tell me?"

"This is why I didn't tell you," I reply, waving between us. "Besides, it's not a date or anything like that."

"Whatever." She rolls her eyes, crossing her arms over her chest.

"Drop it."

"Fine, but I'm calling you first thing Sunday morning, and I want details."

I raise an eyebrow, giving her a glassy stare. "There won't be much to tell. Now, when are we going to do girls' night?"

"What if we make a standing Tuesday night thing . . . you, me, and Dana?" she exclaims, clapping her hands together.

Smart girl. "I like that. I'll ask Dana about it tonight at work, but we might want to lay off the alcohol a little bit."

"Yay. Look, I've got to get back to work before Mr. Ryan starts looking for me. I think he's still reeling from the way I acted Wednesday. Text me later." As she walks away, I notice the red high heels she wears with her black and white ensemble. I have a whole new respect for that girl.

Before my thoughts drift back to Blake, I look back down at the color board I've been working on all day trying to decide what I'm missing. I never go for conventional because that's not what's going to set me apart. It's not what's going to help me achieve my ultimate goal—to become a top designer with a renowned national firm. I'm in the right place. I have award-winning people around me. The rest is up to me, and this is an opportunity I won't let pass me by.

The phone rings, startling me a few inches out of my chair. For unimportant people like me, the cubicle phone rarely makes a peep. I bring the phone to my ear, expecting it to be a misdial. "Hello."

"Ah, Ms. Fields, it's a pleasure to hear your voice." No introduction needed—Pierce's voice is as discernible as a church bell on Sunday.

"How was your trip, Mr. Stanley?" It's not like I'm going to tell him his voice or anything else about him is of any sort of pleasure to me.

"I believe I told you to call me Pierce."

"And I believe you just used a title before my name. Besides, don't you think that's a little inappropriate?"

"I didn't realize you had so much fire in you when I offered you the job." His voice tells of an obvious smile. Even though I'm not with him, I can practically see his dimples and the creases around his eyes when his lips curl.

"Hmm, was my hair color an oversight?"

He chuckles—deep and reverberating. It's enough to make me sit back in my chair and enjoy the banter-filled ride. "Nothing about you escaped me. Trust me."

"So, what can I do for you, Pierce?" I keep my voice low enough not to garner any stares or spark the office rumor mill. In five days, I've learned that it's not much different from high school as far as that goes.

"Come up to my office before you leave today. I have something for you."

My mind immediately wanders off to what it could be. Instructions for tomorrow? A new assignment? Then it dawns on me that I'm not rattled because of that little question; it's the thought of going up to his office. The way he looks at me. The tension hangs in the air like a thick fog. It's hard to concentrate, hard to form words or even think. Tomorrow night is going to be very interesting.

"Okay," I say nervously, "I'll be up in a little bit."

"I look forward to it." He's still got the smile . . . I hear it.

As I put the phone back on the receiver, the only smiling face I see is Blake's. Why should I feel guilty about this when he doesn't let me in? I know so little about him; he's too complicated to figure out.

Noticing that it's already half past three, I tuck my color board underneath my desk and head to see Pierce.

The elevator is empty, and the ride up to his floor lasts only seconds. I smooth my red pencil skirt and straighten the tuck on my black blouse before stepping out.

"Good afternoon, Lila. Go right back to Mr. Stanley's office. He's been waiting for you," Jane greets, smiling behind her well-appointed desk.

"Thank you." I smile back, and quickly make my way down the hall before I change my mind. My heels click against the marble, alluding to anyone around that I'm here. *Click. Click.* My heart pounds right along with it.

His door is open just enough that I hear his voice. Peeking inside, I see he's on the phone. I step back to give him privacy, but he waves me in.

I bite my lip in an attempt to extinguish my racing nerves. They speed even more so when he motions for me to close the door. When I turn back around, he's watching me with such interest—like a rare, classic car or an even rarer piece of art. I don't know what to make of it, but then, I don't know what to make of him.

I sink into one of the leather chairs in front of his desk and focus my attention out the window toward the cityscape. It's hard to see anything from where I am, but I pretend it's the most enthralling thing in the whole world. Anything to keep my eyes off him.

"Yes, we should have the deal done by next week," he says with such confident authority. Just because I'm not looking at him doesn't mean I'm not listening. His voice commands it.

"I'll be making a trip to New York next week to wrap it up," he adds, tapping his fingers on his mahogany desk. His eyes are still on me. I feel them.

"You too. We'll touch base next week." The phone clicks, my signal to look to him.

He leans back in his chair, loosening his tie just enough to undo the button on his collar. "You kept me waiting, Lila."

"I was working on something," I answer. His green eyes have a gray tint to them, accented by his suit.

"Maybe I have to rework the apprenticeship program to free up your time."

I cross and uncross my legs, not quite able to get comfortable under his stare. "I like being busy. It makes the day go faster."

"That it does," he quips. He pulls his desk drawer open and holds up a white envelope with my name scrolled at the top. "Since the benefit is a work function, I have a couple things for you."

He slides it across his desk, his eyes never leaving me. I hope he doesn't notice how my fingers tremble when I pick it up. The silence indicates that he expects me to open it right here in front of him. Maybe it's just a ticket or a copy of the invitation, I think as I slip my fingers inside. What I come out with leaves me gasping.

"It's a black tie affair," he says simply as I slide the black American Express between my fingertips.

"I can't—"

"You will. I invited you. I don't want to be presumptuous, but I'm assuming you weren't quite prepared for this kind of event." He raises an eyebrow as he surveys me.

"No," I whisper. I suddenly feel out of place and extremely uncomfortable. I hadn't thought that far into it—what I will wear, how I'm going to do my hair. I might have to call in Dana for this one.

"So we're set. I'll pick you up at seven." There's a twinkle in his eye.

"I'm not going to use this." I toss it on his desk, but he slides it back toward me.

"I insist."

"Pierce—"

"Lila." He grins, rising from his chair and coming around the front of his desk. The woodsy cologne he wears overtakes my senses, practically making me forget what I was fighting for.

"We're all set," he says again, crossing his arms over his muscular chest.

I nod, swallowing down the other questions that threaten to escape my lips. *Why are you taking me? Who's going to be there? Can you please not wear that cologne?*

"Good." He holds his hand out to me. I just stare at it for a few seconds, uncertain, and then place my hand in his. His skin is warm and soft against mine as he helps me from the chair and leads me to the door.

"I hate to cut this short, but I have a dinner I need to attend." He uses his free hand to open the door, and I don't miss how the thumb on his other hand brushes over my knuckles. It feels uncomfortably sensual, yet I can't pull away.

Before letting me go, he stands in front of me, brushing a strand of loose hair from my eyes. "Black looks nice on you, but I'd like to see you in green. See you tomorrow night, Lila."

My mouth hangs open as he releases me. He guides me out the door by placing his hand on my lower back. The whole walk back to the elevator is a blur. This whole city and the men in it are throwing me for a loop.

MY WHOLE LIFE IS A SERIES of complicated predicaments lately. I find myself questioning it more than I'm actually living it. Given the way things ended with Derek, I promised myself I wouldn't get in that position again. Not that I have that much control over it. Love is the greatest risk, but yet, it's the greatest euphoria one will ever feel. That's what makes it so hard to stay away from. I want to feel that way—like nothing else matters but that one person. Riches, beauty, prosperity . . . it all pales in comparison.

I'm not in love at the moment, but my choices are putting me at risk to fall back into it. Blake's not going to reciprocate, so why do I keep doing this to myself?

"Okay, what's going on in that pretty little head of yours?" Dana asks, standing next to me at the end of the bar. It's almost closing time and the crowd has thinned out.

"You'd think I was crazy if I told you."

"Are you kidding me? You're as normal and boring as they come. Spill."

I focus on the old bar top, tracing my fingers along the grain of the wood. It's mundane, but I need something not so exciting in my life. "You know how I asked for tomorrow night off?"

I glance over at her, waiting for her to nod. She does.

"I kind of have a date, or at least, that's what it feels like."
Her eyes narrow in on me. I see unasked questions there. I try
to silence her by guessing them. "He says it's not a date, but his
actions tell me something completely different. Anyway, I
don't know what I should tell Blake or if I need to tell him
anything at all."

She's quiet for a little bit, marinating on my words. Then
she says, "This is perfect."

"What?" I ask, surprised.

"He's going to be jealous. If he really wants you, you'll
know it after this." She waves for Charlie to come over, which
he does quickly since there's no one to serve. "Lila needs a
shot. Actually make that two."

"Wait," I say, putting my hand up. Charlie pauses, thinking
I'm talking to him, but I wave him off. "That's not why I'm
doing this. The guy's the CEO of the company, and he says it's
just a work thing, but the way he acts around me—"

"Stop! Will you quit thinking so much?" She shakes her
head, grabbing the shot glass Charlie sets on the bar.

The image of Pierce in a black tux flashes in my mind. My
breathing accelerates just imagining it.

Dana notices, passing me a shot. "Drink this, and I'll get
you another one. You're going to need it." I down it, realizing
just how much I do need it. I'll be lucky if I sleep at all tonight.

"What am I going to do?" I ask, putting back another shot
as soon as Charlie pours it.

"You are going to go out with your boss. It's not like Blake
gives a shit anyway, and if he does, this will wake him up. I
can't believe this," she says, practically dancing at the end of
the bar. One of the two guys still inside whistles, drawing a
sneer from her.

"I'm glad you find this amusing."

"Enjoy the ride, Lila. Most women would line up to be
where you are right now."

Maybe she's right. This should be fun, or at least that's what I'm going to tell myself to get through it. This is about fun and nothing more.

The whole ride home I ponder how I'm going to tell Blake. If he's home tomorrow night, I don't want it to be a surprise. I've witnessed his temper, and I don't need him swinging at my boss. Besides, I'd want to know—not get hit in the face with it.

When I walk into the apartment, I don't see Blake, but the light in his room is on. I set my purse on the kitchen counter and stare off at the wall, trying to decide what I should do next. I haven't seen him since Wednesday night, but I know if I go in there, I'm going to feel guiltier about accepting Pierce's invitation. Deep inside, I know it shouldn't be this way. What Blake and I have is an understanding, one that includes lots and lots of hot sex; it's getting weird, though, because I can't even think about him with anyone else, touching another woman the way he touches me.

Deciding I can just tell him tomorrow, I take a quick shower and slip into my flannel pajamas. My long red hair is a matted mess from being wrapped in the towel so I comb through it carefully, letting the damp strands fall onto my back.

"Hey," Blake says, surprising me by stepping in behind me. He wraps his arms around my waist, burying his face in the crook of my neck. It feels so intimate—so opposite of anything we've let our hearts be. It's impossible to stand here and not relax into it.

Looking up, I catch his reflection in the mirror. I can tell he's been painting. His hair is messed up, and his black T-shirt is covered in specks of red and blue.

"Hi." I smile, leaning even further into him.

His lips press to my sensitive, damp skin, moving from one shoulder blade to the other. "I didn't hear you come home."

"I didn't want to interrupt you." I cover his hands with mine, relishing in the feel of his lips.

"I've been waiting for you, actually. There's somewhere I want to take you if you're up for it."

"Tonight?" I have no idea what time it is, but it was after three when I came in.

"Or we can go tomorrow night," he says between kisses.

That brings what I have to tell him back to the forefront of my mind. I quickly push it away, wanting to stay like this a little longer. "Tonight works." *Not like I was going to sleep anytime soon anyway.*

He squeezes me, feathering my neck with more kisses before pulling away. "I'll give you a couple minutes to change. Wear something comfortable."

As he walks away, I can't help but think that this is the Blake I like. Sweet. Charming. The one who shows me that there's more to what we have than just meaningless sex.

There's no way I can tell this Blake about tomorrow night.

I quickly throw on a pair of faded blue jeans and a worn gray hoodie. Morning will be here before we know it, so I tie my unruly hair into a tight knot at the top of my head, anticipating the possibility of running into the early morning crowd. Before going to find Blake, I pull my jacket from the closet and slide my feet into my chucks.

I don't have to go far. He's leaning against the counter with his hands tucked into his jean pockets. "Ready?" he asks, smiling.

"Are you going to tell me where we're going?"

"Nope." He looks edible in an oversized gray sweater and charcoal beanie. Preppy was my type through most of high school and college. That's not the case anymore. My new type is sexy-just-kind-of-pulled-together bad boy.

When he wraps his fingers around mine, I hide my bulging eyes by looking down at my shoes. Something is different. This is a different version of us.

He leads us out of the building, not stopping until we're alongside an older, dark-colored car. "Lila, I'd like you to meet Frank."

I'm stupefied. It might be the vodka, or the fact that I've been up for almost twenty-four hours.

"The car, Lemon Drop. It's the only thing from high school that's still with me so I thought he deserved a name."

I slept with Blake before knowing what kind of car he drove, or that he even had a car. *Nice, Lila.*

"Are we taking him somewhere?" I ask, running my fingers over the smooth paint.

"Fuck yes." He places the key in the passenger side door, then opens it for me. "Get in."

After I'm safely inside, he runs along the front of the car and jumps in the driver's seat. The whole car vibrates when he turns the key.

"What kind of car is this?" I ask as he peels out into the street.

"1969 Pontiac Trans Am. I usually keep him in my parents' garage for the winter, but I missed him."

I laugh when it dawns on me that he's talking about the car the way I wish he'd talk about me. For the first time, I wish my name were Frank. "It's nice."

"Damn right it is."

The car purrs loudly as we make our way down deserted city streets. The farther we drive, the more curious I become about where he's taking me. I know he won't tell me, but I trust him.

A couple minutes later, the car comes to a stop in front of a row of old warehouse buildings. It's dark and quiet, a little scary actually. "Is this it?" I ask, running my palms over my blue jeans.

"Maybe," he replies before climbing out of the car. I watch him round the front then he's at my door. Without question, I stand up next to him, letting him pull me against his strong, warm body. "Ready?"

"As I'll ever be."

He guides us through the darkness, not once letting go of me. This isn't a neighborhood I'd go to alone, even during the day. There's one streetlight about a block away and not a house in sight. A creaking sound repeats in the distance, like an old wrought iron gate opening and closing. Definitely creepy.

Blake lets go of me just long enough to unlock an old metal door to one of the buildings. He looks back at me before opening it. "I've never brought anyone here before."

My mouth gapes. Under the faint streetlight, I see vulnerability. A man who always seems to know exactly what he wants doesn't look so sure.

"Why not?" I finally ask, not even sure where we are exactly.

He shrugs, tucking his hands deep in his pockets. "It's the diary of a mad man."

It's hard to know what to say to that so I say exactly what I think. "I can't wait to see it."

He reaches up, caressing my cheek with the back of his fingers. The night sounds are the only thing I hear. He the only thing I see. Then his fingers fall away . . . the spell between us broken as he pushes open the door.

I'm not sure what to expect as I step inside, but as soon as he flicks the lights on, the air leaves my body. There are paintings everywhere. Large. Small. Hanging. Resting against every corner and on easels. Some covered, some exposed. Every color imaginable is displayed within them.

"These are amazing." I'm awestruck as I circle the expansive room. I got a small peek at his work once, but nothing like this . . . this is the Museum of Blake in full display.

I pay more attention than I normally would, concentrating on every detail in hopes of drawing a piece of him from it. Abstract art is my favorite, but I don't like it on him.

I want to understand him.

To know *him*, not just every ridge of his body.

He's my personal Loch Ness. I know he's here. Sometimes I see him, and then I don't. When I do, only parts of him are exposed. He'll never let me see all of him at once.

Glancing over my shoulder, I notice him staring at me from just inside the doorway. If I didn't know better, I'd say the confident man I've come to appreciate is a nervous mess. His hand continuously combs through his hair—like what he looks like matters or something.

"How long have you been painting?"

He looks sheepish, as though what he creates here is nothing. "Since high school. My parents wanted me to take physics and calculus. I picked art instead."

"I'd say your rebellion worked to your advantage."

He grins. "I'm close to ending the argument. If Mallory would stop being so damn successful at everything she does, it would be a lot easier." Since I'm an only child, I can't even imagine.

I continue my walk around the gallery. Most of the pieces are colorful arrangements—swirls, lines, geometric shapes—painted to look like people, trees. He's brilliant; I'll give him that.

At the opposite end of the room from where we came in is a little nook. The one painting within it is different than the rest. It's as real as a portrait. A beautiful woman with dark, cascading hair, dark brown eyes with a speck of green, and porcelain skin. She's about my age, or she's painted to look that way. The way she's portrayed, like she's lying sideways in the bed with her arm twisted above her head, gives the impression that's she's staring at whoever is in the room. It's creative and terrifying at the same time.

Blake stands next to me, tugging my fingers between his to lead me in another direction. This time, I don't let him. "Did you do this?" I ask, still in awe.

He ignores me, changing his game plan so he's standing right in front of me, successfully blocking my view. He cups my face in his cold hands and presses his lips to mine. With that one move, he pulls me away from everything but him. He does that a lot—changes my frame of thinking.

"Come," he says, "There's a reason I brought you here."

"Can I ask about the painting?"

"No." He doesn't miss a beat as he pulls me along into another room. In the back of my mind, I know he painted that portrait. I also know that she must have meant something . . . something more.

"Close your eyes." The front of his body is pressed to my back as he walks us forward. He fits perfectly against me . . . every curve, every hollow. Just being like this is enough.

I hear a door creak and the flicker of a switch. On instinct, I open my eyes to get a look. This room is much smaller than the first. It shows like a blank canvas—bare white walls, a drop cloth of the same color covering the floor. It's a room without clear purpose. "What's this for?"

When silence is the only response, I look back over my shoulder. Blake stands like the statue of a god, brushing his thumb over his lower lip. He looks down, then up again, one side of his mouth pulling up along the way.

"What?" I smile back at him, tucking a piece of hair behind my ear. He stares at me like he's seeing me for the first time, or maybe I'm just looking at him differently. The guy who always has something to say has nothing.

He lifts a finger to my mouth, using it to draw my lower lip down. He doesn't stop there, trailing his knuckle down my throat, then between the swell of my breasts. My eyes hold his like my life depends on it. "Do you trust me?" he finally whispers.

I nod, because I do. He might be the last person in this city I should attach myself to, but it's too late. He has me even if I don't have him.

"Take off your clothes." His voice is low and breathes of bottled up sexual desire. There's absolutely nothing he couldn't convince me to do right now.

My sweatshirt goes first, leaving me standing in front of him in nothing but a black lace bra and blue jeans. He swallows visibly as I slowly reach behind my back to unfasten the clasp. This is fun—teasing and tormenting him, daring him not to touch.

He watches me as I slowly slide both straps off my shoulders. His fingers ache . . . I can tell because he keeps combing them through his hair, over and over until it has that sexy, mussed up appearance. Until it looks exactly like it does each time we're done having sex.

My bra falls to my feet, and then I slip my fingers into the band of my jeans, working the buttons.

"You're going to make me crazy." He groans, stepping into my personal space. He traces a circle around my breasts, using the side of his thumb. My breath hitches, my knees weaken. My panties were already damp simply from him watching me like he does.

He whispers above my ear. "I'm not going to fuck you tonight, but I will make you come." *Oh, shit. And the pool in my panties just got deeper.* "Work those pants off, Lemon Drop. I'll be right back."

As he steps around me, he trails his fingertips across my bare stomach. The screaming voice in my head begs me to grasp on to him and never let go. His promise resonates in my mind, and I wonder if it's one he'll be able to keep. I want to know if it's a form of magic he's capable of.

Without him watching me, my jeans come off quickly, leaving me in nothing but lacy black boy shorts. When he's with me, I can be like this and feel comfortable with who I am. His stare dresses me in confidence and sensuality. It gives me a courage I've never felt before.

The door opens and closes behind me, but I keep my eyes trained forward, to keep his surprise a secret a little while longer. Metal clinks. The plastic under our feet shuffles with him. My heart races. My fingers curl. I need him . . . I hate admitting it, but I do.

He presses his cold hand to the top of my spine, slowly trailing a finger down until he hits the edge of my panties. "Ready for your surprise?"

I nod.

"Turn," he commands, letting his hand fall away from me.

After taking one last deep, cleansing breath, I pivot to get a better look at the man who's putting my senses into overdrive. His shoes and socks are gone, as is his shirt. He's every sexual fantasy I've ever had wrapped in one.

"I don't do well with surprises," I announce quietly. His eyes burn, and words are the only way I can extinguish it.

He bends to pick up a paint palette from the floor, then closes all but a few inches of space between us. "Close your eyes."

I do, parting my lips to remind myself to breathe. When I was younger, I'd shut my eyes on the fair rides because I didn't want to see the world go by. I'd pretend it was just me on an epic adventure. It was my way of being anywhere besides where I actually was.

Tonight is different. I want to hear, see, and touch Blake. I want to press my nose to his skin and breathe him in. I need his lips on mine, to taste him.

When something cold makes contact with the skin between my breasts, I flinch. It shocks me . . . then it just feels right.

The contrast. The wetness. "Keep your eyes closed while I paint this gorgeous body of yours. Can you do that?"

I swallow hard, because that's all I can do. This is different—challenging me, exposing inhibitions I didn't realize I had.

"I want you to listen and feel. Nothing else."

Rolling my shoulders back, I try to relax, to sink into the moment as if it were a soft place to fall. His paint-covered fingers trace the underside of my breast. I know he's probably watching me, waiting for a reaction—a moan, a buckle, anything.

"I used to think these were the best part of a woman's body," he breathes, continuing to circle my breasts. "But they're not . . . not even close."

The pads of his fingers trace a line down my stomach, past my belly button, before gliding across the top of my panties. Warmth builds between my legs. I need him to touch me there, to feel the pressure of his fingers against me. To make me climb the stairway until I'm calling out his name and nothing else matters.

His feet shuffle against the plastic-covered floors. His fingers curve around my hip, traveling around to the small of my back. It's sensual—a mere caress—and if it weren't for the paint he trails with him, it would be difficult to make out.

The more he paints, the more desperate I become.

Desperate for him, and the way he makes me feel.

Desperate for us, and how everything else fades away when we're fitted together.

One stroke, and I'd be done. I'd be his.

The cold paint he leaves in his wake makes me shiver, the coolness contrasting with the warmth I feel inside.

"And I think . . . no, I know I could slide right into this sweet little body. I can practically smell how wet you are. Am I right?" He brushes across my other hip, completing the perfect circle.

I nod, biting down on my lower lip to hold back a moan. I'm dripping for him . . . in need of him.

When he's standing in front of me again, the heat of his body warms mine. His hand falls away long enough to be coated in more paint. I wonder what color it is. If it has anything to do with me, how he feels, or how he sees me.

When we reconnect, his whole hand is splayed across my stomach, covering almost the entire width of it. He keeps it there long enough to warm the liquid pigment between us. It's sticky, causing friction as he slides back up between my breasts.

"Is your heart beating for me?" His fingers curl around my wrist, bringing my hand to his bare chest. His heart pounds against my palm. "Feel that? Do you feel what happens to me when I'm touching you?"

I'm hanging onto every word, inhaling and letting every one hit me with more sexual potency than the last. He's wound me up so tight . . . he just needs to let me go. "Touch me, Blake." My voice is desperate. There's no hiding it.

"Where, baby? Show me where." His voice is strained, husky, making me want him even more.

I remove his palm from my chest, utilizing the wet paint to slide it down between my legs. "Here," I murmur.

He curls his fingers into me through the lacy material. It's exactly what I wanted . . . what I needed. Then he suddenly pulls away, and I can't help but open my eyes. Plastic crinkles under his feet as he picks up a white cloth to wipe his colorful fingers with. I fight the urge to scream out, to beg and plead for the feel of his skin on mine.

I hold back, rubbing my thighs together to sooth the ache.

As his eyes drink me in, the cloth falls from his hand. He steps closer, his shoulder brushing against me. My heart hammers, waiting. His soft lips tickle my ear, warm breath hitting me before words ever do. "Like this?" he asks, circling my swollen flesh with his fingertips. "Or did you want something more like this?" he adds, pushing my panties aside and inserting one of his long fingers inside of me.

The moans I've been holding in refuse to stay caged any longer. I close my eyes so all I can do is feel. He has me—inside and outside—I'm his. He adds another long finger, moving in and out of me while his thumb circles my clit. I just feel—the friction, the tension. Touch blacks out every other sense, and I come hard around his fingers.

ˑ He groans then kisses me hard, pulling me against him. His tongue presses between the seam of my lips, tangling with mine. It's different than the ones we've shared in the past—full of its usual passion but also wrapped in undeniable want. He punctuates it by lightly kissing each corner of my mouth, even the tip of my nose.

As he pulls away, I dare to open my eyes, wanting to see him and what he's created on my skin. He's only inches from me, watching me adjust to the light.

"And those are my new favorite part . . . your eyes. If you could see them right now . . . the sated, content look of them, you'd never doubt how sexy you are."

I stare, slowly believing every word because the same look he described is mirrored in his eyes. Somewhere along the way, I let him crawl into my heart. That was the easy part . . . letting him out, that's not going to be so easy.

MY ALARM SOUNDS TOO SOON. If I count the time I spent tossing and turning in my bed after Blake and I finally got home this morning, I maybe had five hours of sleep. Every lost minute was worth it when I replay the events of last night. What he made me feel. What he made me see without even looking. Being with Blake is like dreaming while awake. I want to stay locked in those moments—the ones where his touch makes me forget everything else—forever.

I want more than what he's given me. I want to know his history . . . all of it. I want so badly to know what goes through that head of his. I want everything . . . everything I know he's not ready to give. Or, maybe it's everything I'm too afraid to ask for.

After Blake took time to wipe the paint from my skin, he'd shown me a few of his favorite paintings. I saw them differently—more vibrant, full of color. Maybe it was because of the new way I viewed paint or the rasp in his voice while he spoke.

Behind the walls, he's thoughtful, intelligent and kind-hearted. I want to know what made him construct them in the first place. Why does he guard himself? Why does he push people away?

I thought about it a lot while he drove us home. The sun was rising on the horizon—a perfect cap to a perfect night. I pictured us, what we could be like if it was always like that. If he always made me feel that way. But like most good things, it couldn't last forever. We were both quiet when we entered the apartment, our eyes saying a silent good night. Maybe that's how it had to be. Things went too far. I'd felt too much.

Now, as I stretch my arms up, my thoughts flicker between that and what's in store for me tonight. If I'd met this Blake before Pierce asked me to accompany him to the benefit, I don't think I could have said yes. It feels wrong, even if there's nothing wrong about it.

My stomach growls as I roll off the mattress. It's been hours since I've eaten anything. If I'm going to spend hours getting myself beautified, I'm going to feed the monster in my stomach. I tiredly make my way to the bathroom and splash some cold water over my face, trying to salvage whatever I can of my youthful appearance. I smooth over my gray cami and pull my hair up in a tight knot. Hopefully Dana will be able to make something out of my zombie self when she gets here. I need her to bring a magic wand to banish my dark circles and ashen skin. Cucumbers, cold spoons . . . anything.

As soon as I open the door to my bedroom, I see Blake sitting at the kitchen table with a full bowl of cereal in front of him. From this angle, he looks reflective, focused on the little o-shaped grains. His hair is tousled. Muscled arms showcased by the way his elbows rest on the table. It brings back memories of last night.

"What? No eggs today?" I ask, sneaking up behind him.

He turns to face me, a cocky half-grin playing on his lips. "I thought I'd follow the rules."

"My birthday isn't until summer, so what's the occasion?" I tease, stepping closer.

He shrugs. "You followed my rules last night. It's only fair."

"That I did." I smile just thinking about his hands on my skin. I grab a bowl from the cabinet and sit next to him, helping myself to some of the cereal.

He watches me between bites, clinking his spoon against the bottom of his bowl. "Did I say you could have some of my Fruit Loops?"

"Umm—"

"Relax," he says, covering my lips with his fingertip.

I close my eyes and let my mouth curve into a smile again. "I knew you were teasing."

"No, you didn't."

There's something different about him this morning—more playful, light. He reaches out for my wrist, pulling me into his lap. He holds me close to his chest, arms wrapped tightly around my waist. It's something Derek used to do when things were good, before success and time got in our way. It gives me hope that there might me more to this than mind-numbing sex.

"Do you have plans this afternoon?" he asks, kissing the back of my neck. His question wakes me from the moment, reminding me that there's someone else who will be expecting me tonight.

"Blake, there's something I need to tell you," I confess, closing my eyes to brace myself for what may come. Maybe this will go over better than I think, but it could also go terribly wrong. I've put myself in his shoes, and I know that the female jealousy within me would be boiling over. The thought of anyone touching him, in any way, makes me bat shit crazy.

He pauses for a second then continues kissing me. "I'm listening."

How am I supposed to tell him that my hot, powerful, extremely successful boss is taking me out tonight with his mouth assaulting my skin like this? Things with Blake start to feel less and less like a benefits-only relationship and more and more like the semblance of a real relationship when he does this. It's in the way he kisses me. The way he looks at me—like he was last night when I finally opened my eyes. It's in the little ways he's changed over the last couple weeks.

If he asks me not to go, if he tells me this thing between us means something, I won't go. I wouldn't be able to enjoy my time with Pierce if I knew it bothered Blake. If I knew there was a chance for us.

"I was invited to attend a benefit tonight . . . for work." Watching him, I don't see any reaction, but that's not the part that's going to bother him.

"Not working at Charlie's?" he murmurs between showering my neck with kisses.

"No, I took the night off." I stop, tilting my head to give him better access. "Someone invited me to, umm, go." That stills him immediately.

His head comes up, his eyes cold—like they were when I first met him. He doesn't say anything. He just stares. If I could take those words back, put this whole scene on rewind, I would.

"When he asked, I said yes because there really wasn't any reason to say no."

He loosens his arms but doesn't completely pull them away from me. My whole world spins waiting for him to say something. This was a mistake; I feel it already.

"What do you mean when you say you're going *with* him?" he finally asks. He's got the same angry edge to his voice he had the night I left him in the bar. This time, there are more feelings to be destroyed.

I swallow the giant lump wedged in my throat. "I'm going to get dressed up, and he's going to pick me up. We're going to the event, and then he'll bring me back home."

"Are you going to fuck him?" The edge in his voice and harshness of his words propel me forward, wanting to be out of his arms.

"I'm not like that," I seethe, quickly standing from his lap.

"Really?" he shouts. "What are we doing then? We're fucking, and, from what I remember, it wasn't that hard to get you under me."

My blood boils. "Do you think I just fuck any guy who comes my way?" I pause, wrapping my hands into tight fists at my side to keep from hitting him. "That's the problem with this whole stupid arrangement. You don't know a damn thing about me."

He dares to come closer. "I've memorized every fucking inch of your body, and that's all I need to know for what we have."

My fingernails dig into my skin. I can't take it anymore. The way he looks at me like I'm nothing. With nothing else to add, I stalk back to my bedroom, throwing the door open with enough force to send it into the wall. I need to put space between us.

"Lila, I'm not done with you!" he yells.

"Oh, I'm sorry! I didn't realize we even started," I remark, not bothering to look back. Without warning, his body is flush against mine, pushing us both forward.

When we reach the wall on the opposite side of the room, he spins me around and pins my arms above my head. He's pissed, and I only have myself to thank for that. "Do you feel that?" he asks, grinding his hard cock against my stomach. "That's what you do to me."

Tears pool in my eyes. I gaze up at the ceiling, begging them not to fall. "I need more than that, Blake. I can't keep doing this."

"What do you want from me?"

"If you ask me to stay, I'll stay, but don't do it just because you want to fuck me. Or because you don't want anyone else to have me." Just voicing the last part makes me question how exactly I got here.

"I've given you everything I promised."

I wiggle against him, but it's no use. He's too strong, too determined. "What if I told you I'm falling?"

"You don't mean it."

My chest heaves against his. Hearts beat fast. "Yes, I do."

"Shit," he mumbles, letting go of me.

"I didn't mean for it to happen!"

"You didn't stop it either." He starts walking away, his hair gripped in his long fingers. A fool could see he's struggling against himself. I follow behind him, practically falling into his back when he halts suddenly. "Don't," he warns.

"I'm going. Unless you ask me to stay . . . unless you can promise me more, I'm going."

He smiles sadistically, lifting my chin to gain better access to my lips. He kisses me once, hungrily, darting his tongue between my lips just long enough to get a little taste. My mind races with the possibilities; they're all I have left. "Don't you dare forget that when you're out with your date tonight."

Without another word, he pulls away, heading straight out of the apartment, slamming the door behind him. If he's jealous, it doesn't have the effect that Dana said it would.

He didn't ask me to stay.

He didn't beg me not to go.

I thought what we have might mean something more to him, like it does for me.

I think every girl hopes she'll get her chance to tame a bad boy, to bring a soulless creature out of the darkness, but Blake isn't my salvation. There's not a part of him that's mine . . . there never was.

I sink back down into my chair and cross my arms on the table. I stare . . . forever, thinking about what I should do next, what this means.

 Butterflies multiply in my stomach as the hours tick by. Time brings me closer to Pierce and further from Blake.

He's been gone a couple hours . . . since we had our argument this morning. What if he disappears again? And when he comes back, will we go back to being enemies under the same roof?

I don't want that. I just want to be us. Kisses. Painting. Lemon drops.

I think about him constantly. The fact that this might all be over before it even really started is hard to swallow. I can't live with what could have been; I'd promised myself I would stop doing that the minute I stepped on the plane. He's just so hard to let go.

I'm lost in my wakeful nightmare when a knock sounds at my door.

When I'd told Dana about the invite, she'd offered to come over and help me with my hair and make-up. There was no way I was going to decline because getting all that done in Chicago would have cost a small fortune. And there was no way in hell I was going to use Pierce's credit card.

I fake a smile and open the door. "Hey." My eyes immediately focus on the small suitcase she lugs with her. "Did you bring the whole bathroom?"

"Almost," she replies, rolling it in front of her. "Take this. I'm going to grab the dress from my car."

I grab the handle from between her fingers and watch as she retreats down the narrow hallway. "Need any help?"

"Got it!" she yells back.

The suitcase must weigh at least twenty pounds, which scares the hell out of me. What could she possibly put on me that weighs this much? Twelve pairs of shoes? Eight curling irons? Four cases of make-up?

After rolling it to my room, I go back to the door to wait for her. She mentioned this dress she has for me—something she wore to an event a couple years back. This event is a big deal . . . for my career, for my future. And if Pierce Stanley is going, it's a big deal in general—a who's who of the Chicago scene. I'm trying to be excited. If for nothing else, what it could do for my career.

"No wonder you stay so skinny," Dana grumbles as she makes it up to the top of the stairs.

"I usually make it in one trip."

"Shut it. I brought my whole vanity because I didn't want to regret leaving anything behind. It's not often a girl gets her chance to be a stylist."

My eyes dart to the white garment bag she has wrapped over her forearm. She wouldn't give me much detail on the dress, and it's been killing me.

"Do I get to see it now?" I ask, clapping my hands together.

She stops just far enough away that I can't reach her, or the dress. "Hair and make-up first. Then the dress."

"Ugh, I'm sorry but I can't be your friend anymore."

"This isn't the third grade, Lila," she remarks as she walks past me into the apartment. It's impossible to even see the color of the dress through the bag.

"Oh, come on. It better not be pink, especially hot pink, because that looks hideous against my red hair." I close the door and follow behind her into my bedroom. I've already showered, shaved, and moisturized per my *stylist's* instructions, but all of this is making my stomach hurt. The closer we get to seven, the harder it is to keep my nerves in check. It all weighs too heavy—talking to people I don't know, being the girl next to Pierce, wondering where Blake is.

"If you sit still long enough for me to turn you into a glam queen, I promise to show you."

"Let's get this over with," I say, leading the way to the bathroom. It's not very big, but there is a vanity chair slid under the sink, giving her free reign on her blank canvas.

"This is going to be so fun!"

I can't match her enthusiasm. No matter what I'm saying or what I'm trying to concentrate on, Blake's there. Maybe it's just wishful thinking, but I've been waiting for him to come through the door and tell me not to go. That maybe time would put things into perspective for him.

With only a few hours until Pierce picks me up, it hasn't happened yet. I'm tired of fighting for something that doesn't want to be fought over.

Dana sprays sections of my hair, letting it all fall over my eyes. "I'm going to curl your hair first, then we'll do your make-up so it's fresh."

Closing my eyes, I attempt to fall back into better times. I try to imagine what the venue looks like. I've been to big weddings, but I have a feeling this will top all of them.

"Are you okay? You're kind of quiet." I didn't think it would take her long to notice. I'm not the definition of a social butterfly, but I usually have something to say when it's just the two of us.

"It's been a rough day," I reply simply. I want to keep what happened at the studio between Blake and me. I definitely can't explain what happened between us at breakfast without letting her in on my growing feelings for him.

"Where's Blake?" *She can't be that perceptive.*

"He left earlier."

"Oh," she says, "I take it the plan to make him jealous didn't really work?"

"I don't want to talk about it."

"Sorry." She picks up yet another section, wrapping it around the iron. "Maybe, you're just not meant to be."

Maybe we're not.

WHEN PREPARATIONS ARE DONE, I spin in front of the full-length mirror. The long, dark green dress Dana loaned me contrasts beautifully with my red locks. The form-fitting skirt and open back give it a sexy touch—not too much but just enough.

"Do you feel okay?" Dana asks, smoothing the edges of the sleeveless top.

"I'm just nervous. It feels like prom all over again, but even then, I was with someone I knew. What am I supposed to talk about all night?"

She pulls some of my curled locks over my shoulder. "He's successful in the design industry. Maybe you can talk about that. Have him give you some tips for your career."

"I'm sure he didn't invite me with him just to talk about work." I pause, deciding just how much I should tell her about Pierce Stanley. If I let her stay until he arrives, he won't need any explaining. "Most women find him charming. If I don't keep him occupied, someone else will."

"Does it matter?" she asks, taking one last look at me.

I shrug. "I honestly don't know what matters anymore."

"Are you going to tell me what happened with Blake?"

I shake my head. If I don't say it out loud, maybe it will just go away like it never even happened at all. I want to think he'll be here waiting when I get home tonight. He'll be leaning against the counter, just like always. He'll take me to his bed, making sure he's all I think about. He won't hold me afterward . . . he never does, but I'll leave knowing it will happen again.

I want the certainty that's missing right now.

"It's almost seven so I should probably get out of here before your date arrives." Through the mirror, I see her wince. "I mean, boss. Are you all set? Need more lipstick?"

"I think I'm good on the lipstick." I wasn't sure about the red at first; I thought I'd look like a glorified human Christmas tree with my green dress and red hair, but it pulls it all together.

She brings me in for a hug, careful not to flatten my curled hair. "If you need anything, just call. I have to work, but that doesn't mean I won't bail you out if you need it."

"I'll be okay. Thanks for pulling double duty tonight."

She steps back, surveying me one more time. "No big deal. Double tips for me." She winks, and then picks her stuff up from my bed. "Call me tomorrow. I want to hear all about it."

"I hope I want to talk about it."

"You'll be fine." As she walks toward the apartment door, I follow. I need all the practice I can get in these stupid heels. "Oh, that reminds me," she says as she turns the knob. "Did you run a background check on him?"

The door opens, and before I can respond, Pierce's grinning form is standing in front of me. He's a vision in a black tux, that's for sure.

"Google should cover the background check if you'd like me to wait out here." His dark eyes dance between Dana and me.

I sneak a quick look at Dana whose mouth hangs wide open, her eyes drinking in Pierce's perfect physique. I should snap her lips closed and push her out the door, but I don't blame her one bit.

His tux is complete with a black tie and crisp white shirt. His hair is styled, spiked up toward the front. Not only could he walk a red carpet, he'd own it. All sets of eyes, male or female, would be on him.

"Dana, this is Pierce. Pierce, this is Dana." I introduce them, hoping to break through the awkward silence we've all fallen into.

Pierce holds his hand out to her. "It's nice to meet you, Dana."

I wonder if she's screaming internally at the sound of her name coming from his lips. I know I did the first time.

She places her hand in his. He practically swallows her small hand up. "Nice to, umm, meet you, too." *I guess she stutters now.*

"You're early," I announce, pulling Pierce's attention back to me.

"Far better than late," he quips, tucking his hands into his pants pockets. I don't miss how they strain across his hips. He's pretty, there's no arguing that.

"I'm actually running late for work," Dana says, squeezing my arm before pushing through the doorway. "You guys have fun tonight."

"Thanks for everything, Dana!" I shout behind her. I watch her walk away until she disappears down the stairs. It gives me an excuse not to look at Pierce.

"I think she's gone now," he remarks, forcing my eyes back to him. He's obviously amused—head cocked, lower lip pulled between his teeth.

"Sorry," I say, tucking a loose strand of hair behind my ear. I quickly pull it back out, not wanting to ruin my beach-like waves.

He raises his eyebrows as he glances down the vacant hallway, then back to me. "Ready? My car's waiting downstairs."

"Yeah, let me grab my jacket. Do you want to come in?"

"I thought you'd never ask."

Pulling the door all the way open, I give him the space to step into my territory. The apartment isn't much. We have a futon as our only piece of living room furniture for God's sake. His master bedroom is probably bigger than this entire place.

"You can have a seat if you want. I'll only be a minute."

I turn to walk away but he grabs my elbow, stopping me in place. Fear courses through my veins, not of him, but of what he does to me when we're this close. He steps closer until I can feel the heat coming off his body. My eyes dart around the room. My mind wanders to all the possibilities of this.

"You look gorgeous," he says from behind me.

"You don't look so bad yourself."

He runs his hand down my forearm, slowly releasing me. "You like the tux?"

"No," I answer, spinning back around to face him. I tug on his tie. "I love the tux."

He grins . . . in a way that's bound to get me in a whole lot of trouble. The kind that reminds me why this might not be a good idea.

"I'll be right back." I disappear behind my bedroom door, inhaling the air needed to fill my lungs, then repeating until I feel like I have enough control to be in his presence again. He unnerves me in ways I can't describe, and he's too perceptive for me to let him see me this way.

After grabbing my long black coat from the closet, I swallow the last of my anxieties and walk out to the living room where he stands peering out the lone window. He defines power—perfect posture, broad shoulders and taut muscles. The man has everything going for him from what I can see. He's just not Blake.

"Ready?" I ask, careful not to scare him.

He looks back, eyes surveying me. "Just waiting on my beautiful date."

I open my mouth to argue, but pull myself back. He probably didn't mean it in the way it sounded. "Let's get out of here then. I didn't get all dressed up for nothing."

He laughs, deep and throaty. "That makes two of us."

I pick up my clutch from the table and head toward the door, opening it for him. He comes to stand next to me but doesn't exit. "This is the only door I'm going to let you open tonight."

I glance down, running the toe of my heels against the hardwood floors. This guy is a complete gentleman. I should be swooning, picturing myself as his better half. Dreaming of it at night and falling at his feet during the day to make it happen.

It may be the biggest mistake of my life—clinging to a guy who'll never truly let me in when the epitome of male perfection is standing right in front of me.

When I come back to, he's standing out in the hallway looking down at me with his eyebrows drawn in. "You all right?"

"Yes, sorry," I reply, shaking my head. "I probably should have slept more last night."

He holds out his hand to me, and I take it, pulling the door shut behind me. His fingers are warm, entwining with mine. It's intimate but doesn't push me too far from my comfort zone. As we walk down the long, narrow hall, I keep my head down, afraid that my heels will catch and I'll go tumbling across the old, worn carpet.

If I let it, tonight could be fun. If only it were that easy.

Pierce stops suddenly, yanking me back with him. I look up at him, confused, and notice his fiery eyes staring forward. Curious, I follow them, and in that one moment, my whole world spins.

"What are you doing here?" Pierce asks, gripping my hand a little tighter.

"I fucking live here," Blake answers. His words are meant for Pierce, but he's staring straight at me. The pain and confusion that emit from his eyes don't go unnoticed.

"Do you know each other?" My voice is so timid, I'm not sure if my words even registered with them.

"You could say that," Pierce says. He lets go of my hand, moving it to the small of my back. "How do you know him?"

I swallow, attempting to bury the weariness in my voice. "He's my roommate."

Blake laughs maniacally, rubbing the back of his neck. "Roommates? That's fucking great."

Now I'm mad. Pissed. Frustrated. Resentful. I'm a big fucking ball of destruction that wants to roll toward Blake and make him feel every ounce of what I'm feeling. "We talked about this earlier. Remember?"

I sense Pierce's eyes on me, but I don't dare look. I could have gone a hundred life times without this moment.

Pierce's hand squeezes mine again, lightly tugging me forward. "Let's get out of here. I think we both know this asshole isn't worth our time."

"Take your hands off her!" Blake yells. I don't get this. He knew I had plans tonight. I was upfront with everything, but obviously there's something between these two that I'm completely oblivious to. A game changer.

"Pierce," I say quietly, placing my hand on his forearm. "Can you wait outside? I'll take care of this."

"I'm not leaving you."

"Yes, you are, or you can go ahead and leave without me."

Pierce obviously isn't used to being ordered around. He releases my hand and comes to stand in front of me. The carefree, sexy smile he wore earlier is long gone. "Lila, what is this?" he whispers so only I can hear.

"Please, wait outside. I'll explain later."

He nods, brushing my hair off my forehead. "If you're not out in five minutes, I'm going to come looking for you. I don't trust this asshole."

"I'm a big girl."

He shakes his head at me before walking away. I don't miss how he bumps his shoulder against Blake's as he walks by. Or the way Blake looks at him with venom in his eyes. It's as if I'm witnessing the final seconds before a MMA fight.

Just when I'm about to step between them, Pierce breaks away and continues down the hall. I inhale a deep breath, relieved that whatever that was is over . . . at least for now.

Blake stands with his hands on his hips, staring up at the stained, white ceilings. He seems unapproachable—anger rolling off him in epic proportions.

"How do you know Pierce?" I ask, not waiting for him to look back down.

"I just do," he replies, eyes roaming the walls. He's trying hard to see anything but me. I don't like it.

"Will you at least tell me what that was all about?"

He shakes his head. There's not a sound. Not a whisper or an audible breath. Nothing.

There's nothing else I can do here . . . nothing else to say. I swallow my foolish dreams and start past him . . . to find Pierce before this day lets me down any more than it already has.

I've tried hard not to be a naïve woman—not to put myself in situations where my heart will be broken—but that's all I seem to accomplish. Just when I feel like my life's going somewhere, I'm pushed back on my ass.

"Don't go," he says quietly as I walk past.

I stop, glancing toward him. His eyes finally meet mine, glossed over from too much alcohol or not enough sleep. Or both. "Then tell me to stay. Tell me you're ready to give me more."

When he breaks eye contact again, I know the answer. He doesn't want to see my heart shatter and fall to little pieces on the old, worn carpet. "You already know what I can give you."

I nod once, glancing at his broken profile one last time. When I walk out the door, that's going to be it. He's going to know I made my choice just as he did a few seconds ago.

With every step I take, I wait for my name. I wait for him. And as I make my way to the top of the steps, I realize I waited for something that will never be.

AS SOON AS I OPEN THE front door, I see Pierce perched against the side of a sleek black Escalade. The chrome rims sparkle under the moonlight. It screams for attention in the same way the guy standing next to it does. He could step right into an Armani ad, and no one would blink an eye.

"Are you okay?" he asks, slowly moving toward me.

I cross my arms over my chest to chase away the unbearable cold. "I'm ready to get out of here." Explaining the rejection I just went through wouldn't be right. He's my boss, and this isn't the place or the time. Tonight was supposed to be fun, different, a way to advance my career, but instead, it feels like something I have to do in order to save face. And I'm losing everything in the process.

He places his hand on my back to guide me to the car. Not to my surprise, an older gentleman in a nice black suit comes around the back to open the door.

"Good evening, ma'am." He nods his head, and I smile in appreciation before climbing into the back seat. Pierce follows, leaving just a few inches of space between us. His proximity, the herb, wood, and fruit scent that emanates off his body reminds me just how intimate this is. I turn my attention out my window, wanting to avoid him and his assessment of me.

The door clicks shut, and I wait for him to ask me questions, for the inner confidence to ask him questions about how he knows Blake. What are the chances that these two corners of my life would intersect? Chicago was supposed to be different than my hometown.

"How do you know Blake?" he asks, saving me. His name comes off Pierce's lips like a language he'd rather not speak.

I look him in the eyes, knowing it's what he expects. "He's my best friend's brother. I thought I was moving into an empty apartment because she's in Europe. Surprise was on me."

He assesses me. Reads me. Calculates my pluses and minuses. He's not dumb—he can do a simple math problem. "Is that all it is?"

I chew on my lower lip, buying myself time to decide what to say. How much of my world I want to open to him, keeping in mind he's not the average man who I can feed full of falsities.

"It is now." It's telling without saying much. He can read between the lines.

"Are you sure?"

"Never been more sure about anything." I don't need to look away because it's true. Blake's dangerous, and little by little, I caught myself falling. Luckily, I was able to pull myself back up before I hit the ground. Just like I've done over and over the last few months, I'll bury away the negative and focus on whatever I have left.

"How do you know Blake?" I ask, realizing I have just as many questions as he does.

He studies me, eyes narrowing in. "I've worked with him in the past."

I ponder my next question carefully. What went on back there was about more than work. It was personal. It was hate.

He interrupts my thoughts before I get a chance to interrogate him further. "You look stunning, in case I didn't make that clear earlier." My cheeks heat from his praise, from the sexy tone of his voice. *Thank God for darkness.*

I smile genuinely, not so used to being complimented. Maybe my questions about Blake can wait until later . . . he's not who tonight is about. "You clean up pretty well yourself."

"Oh, this," he says, pulling at his lapels. "I drag it out every once in a while for a special occasion . . . when I want to look good for someone special."

"Like once or twice a week?"

"Not nearly as often as you think," he replies.

I know so little about Pierce Stanley. His professional success is clear, but everything else is a mystery.

"How old are you?" I ask. I kind of regret it as soon as it leaves my lips. Too personal maybe?

"Guess."

Shit. If I guess too high, he's going to be offended. If I guess too low, well, I don't know. "Thirty-two?"

He chuckles, leaning in closer. He smells so good, I just want to bury my nose in the crook of his neck and breathe him in until I fall asleep with nothing but that memory. Only problem: I still want it to be Blake's arms wrapped around me when I wake up. "I'm thirty-six."

I recover quickly from my dreams. "You look younger."

"You're not saying that just to get a raise are you?"

"Nah, I like the challenge of surviving on peanuts. It gives me something to think about when I have nothing else going on in my life," I say, smoothing my hands over my dress.

"Smartass."

"Oh, how nice, I already have a nickname. Maybe by the end of the night, I'll have one for you." This banter is just what I need to take my mind off Blake.

"I'm totally fine with Handsome, Master, Oh Great One . . . unless you can come up with something better."

I laugh . . . for the first time in a long time. "I think I have one already. How about Mr. Full of Himself."

"You have me pegged already."

I'm about to reply when the SUV pulls up in front of a brightly lit building. There's a group of reporters outside snapping pictures of well-dressed people who walk in front of an Urban Arts banner. Watching it all makes me extremely nervous. Limelight, cameras flashing . . . it's not my thing.

"You ready?" Pierce asks, squeezing my knee. It distracts me at first, but I'm quickly drawn back to the chaos outside.

"Do we have to stop for pictures?" My fingers shake against my clutch. Gripping it is the only way to keep them away from my hair, from ruining Dana's hard work.

"We'll take a couple then move on. Just smile and let me do all the talking. It will go quick, I promise," he says soothingly.

I nod. He signals to the driver who swiftly opens the door, exposing us to the crowd. As Pierce steps out, I inhale the fresh winter air until my lungs can hold no more. He is by no means a celebrity, but he's one of the 'it' men on the Chicago art scene. Being with him comes with limelight and elevated social status because of his money and success.

When he holds his hand out to me, I hesitate for just a second, doubts flooding my conscience. It all goes away when he bends down so I can see his smiling face. "Coming?"

"You got me this far, I can't back down now." I slip my coat off and then place my hand in his, letting him hold on to me as I slide across the seat. I make sure both of my feet are firmly planted on the ground before revealing myself to the waiting crowd. It's overwhelming—the flashes and screams. One of Chicago's most eligible bachelors is in their midst.

"Pierce! Pierce! Mr. Stanley!" It's all I hear as he grips my elbow to guide me up the curb. As soon as we're on level ground, he wraps his arm around my back, resting his hand firmly against my hip.

"Who's your date?" one screams, loud enough I hear it over the rest of the crowd.

"Her name's Lila!" he answers between pictures. My smile falters, but I quickly recover.

"What's her last name?" the same one yells.

To my relief, Pierce is quiet, guiding us down the carpet toward the glass doors. The doorman opens it just in time for us to step inside without breaking stride. There are a few people gathered in the entry, but nothing like outside.

"You okay?" he asks. He stands in front of me, hands lightly caressing my forearms.

I nod. "Yeah, I just wasn't expecting it to be quite like that."

He smiles, squeezing my arms once. "I promise we can sneak out the back when it's time to leave."

"You should have that same arrangement for your arrival."

"That's why expectations are rarely desires." His words don't make sense at first, but then they do. As soon as something hits a list of things to do, it loses its luster. Another responsibility added to our hectic, busy lives.

"You know what I desire?" I ask

His lips part, eyes holding mine firmly. "What's that?"

I lick my lower lip, drawing his eyes down momentarily. "Wine, red preferably."

The corners of his eyes crinkle. "Pinot noir? Merlot?"

Isn't red wine just red wine? The only option I've ever been given before was between red and white.

"Merlot for now," I answer, not recognizing the other one. I have no idea what I'm getting myself into, but it's a sipping drink . . . it can't be that bad.

"Let me show you where the ballroom is. Then I'll grab us something from the bar."

Showtime version 2.0, I think to myself as Pierce rests his hand on my lower back to once again guide me forward. Hopefully the cameras aren't allowed inside, and all I'll have to deal with are the other artsy folks who were invited tonight.

"You're going to do great," he whispers in my ear. "Stay by me. I'll introduce you to some people, we'll eat dinner. The night will go by quickly . . . they always do."

We cross the threshold into a room full of well-dressed people—men all in black suits, women in dresses that probably cost more than I make in two months. It's overwhelming, especially when heads turn in our direction. We keep moving, but the rest of the room seems paralyzed.

My nerves are raw. My ears pound to the point that I swear all talking has ceased. Being the center of anything, especially attention, is absolutely terrifying to me. It's worse here . . . where I feel so little and unimportant.

I'm torn from my thoughts by the stunning blonde in a gold satin dress standing in front of us. She's probably old enough to be my mom but could easily pass for thirty. "Pierce, I'm so glad you made it."

"Diane." He reaches his free hand out, gripping her shoulder while quickly pecking her cheek. "Everything looks fabulous as usual."

"I can't take all the credit. The whole committee pitched in for this one." She looks over his shoulder to me. "Are you going to introduce me to your friend?"

Friend. Nice. I hope Pierce isn't the type who usually brings pretty, low IQ women to these things. I don't want to be categorized with them.

"This is Lila Fields. She's an up and coming designer who just relocated to the city."

I hold my hand out, letting her swallow it up in her well-manicured one. "It's nice to meet you. I'm Diane Rector. I oversee the board that put this together."

"From what I can see so far, you did a fabulous job." Years of working in customer service gave me the gift of being able to make small talk with just about anyone.

"Wait until you sink your teeth into the dessert." She winks, letting go of my hand. "I'll catch up with you two later. I need to check how everything is coming along."

"It was nice meeting you."

"You too," she says as she starts to walk away.

"That wasn't so bad," I mumble under my breath as she sashays to the next set of guests.

"You're a natural," Pierce says next to me. I hadn't meant for him to hear my inner jargon. Tonight is just as much about making a good impression on him as it is connecting myself with my peers. I don't want him to see me as an immature woman or think I can't handle all of this because I know I can. The skill is there; it just seems to be buried under a layer of shattered confidence.

He steers us toward the bar, probably well aware that I'm not ready to be left alone in the sea of perceived sharks. I'm careful not to make eye contact along the way, needing at least one glass of that liquid courage before we get too far into this.

It's not a surprise that the bar is packed with people. Pierce picks a spot toward the end where the bartender can easily see him waiting.

After the bartender takes our order, Pierce turns to the guy next to him. "Long time, no see."

"Stanley, I was starting to think you'd moved out of town. What have you been up to?" Pierce has at least six inches on the older, balding gentleman standing next to him.

"Been out of town, working on a couple large hotel projects," Pierce replies.

He turns his attention to me. "And who's this lovely lady?"

"This is one of my apprentices, Lila Fields. Lila, this is Wade Adams."

"Interesting," he says. "If she has even half your eye for design, she'll do just fine." He winks, sipping a glass of wine. *Where's mine?*

"She has a great start." I don't think Pierce has seen any of my work; at least, I haven't shown him anything.

"Look, I was actually hoping I'd catch you here. I'm remodeling the 5th Avenue location in New York, and I'd like you to head the project."

I glance up at Pierce who looks taken back by the statement. He quickly recovers, pulling his business card from the pocket of his tux. Watching him work makes me respect him even more; he's hard to shake and blends in easily with the variety of personalities. "I'd be honored. I'm sure you have my contact information, but take my card just in case."

Wade nods, taking the card from between Pierce's fingers. "I need to get back to my date before she calls a search party, but I'll call you sometime this week."

"I'll be in town all week. It would be a pleasure to work with you."

"Likewise." Wade gestures to me before slowly disappearing into the thickening crowd. I guess this is just as much about making deals as it is about charity and goodwill.

"You seemed surprised that he wanted to work with you," I say.

Pierce's eyes narrow in on me. "We have a bit of a history. Not necessarily a good one."

"Ah, maybe he's going to lure you into an empty building and have his way with you."

He laughs. "Doubt it. He hates to get his hands dirty."

I'm curious, but I don't push for more. I'm not going to share my deepest and darkest secrets so I can't expect him to.

Before anyone else can introduce themselves, a glass stem is placed between my fingers.

"Let's toast," Pierce suggests, holding up a glass of whiskey.

"To?"

"To new friendships."

"To new friendships," I repeat, clinking my glass against his. I swish the red liquid once, then lift it to my nose, inhaling. When I finally bring the glass to my lips, I tip it back just enough to get a tiny sip. It tastes of vibrant black cherries and plums, sliding easily down my throat.

I take a second sip, then a third. Pierce just watches as I finish off the last of it and signal for a second.

"Slow down, at least until we've eaten," he breathes against my ear, making the hair on the back of my neck stand up. It's the wine. It's the warmth. It's the smell of a man wrapped in an expensive black tux.

"We're going to have to do something to keep me busy then." I lick my lower lip, bringing the full glass to my mouth. This stuff is dangerous—it's what one-night stands and surprise babies are made of.

"Dance with me," he says, squeezing my hip.

"Where?"

He nods toward the side of the ballroom opposite of where we came in. A band with classic instruments in hand plays the soft music I hear overhead.

I drain the rest of my wine and set the glass on the bar. If I think too much, I'll never get the courage to forge ahead with this. Pierce understands my wordless answer, wrapping his fingers around mine to lead me out to the wooden floor. This time, if people are staring, I don't notice. That's the difference between being sober and slightly buzzed.

He faces me, wrapping one arm around my lower back and keeping his other hand entwined with mine at our side. Our bodies melt together until we're chest to cheek. So close . . . so intimate.

"I'm so glad you came tonight," he says, his lips brushing my hair.

"Me too." I mean it. This pushed things with Blake to a boiling point, but it was going to go there at some point anyway. Maybe it's better to have gotten it over with than attach myself to him even more—before I fell in love.

Besides, I'm enjoying my time with Pierce. Tonight hasn't exactly been perfect, but he has been.

"After dinner, I'll introduce you to some more people."

I don't reply. I don't think he needs one. We sway back and forth, turning ever so slightly along the way. He leads us with expert rhythm.

"What's your favorite type of music?" he asks out of the blue.

"Angsty rock. I reflect on life when I get lost in the music."

He leans back, looking down into my eyes. "Good or bad?"

"What?" I ask.

"Your reflections."

I shrug, thinking back to how normal and great everything was until a few months ago. "I think about the painful ones the most. They're the ones I still need to let go of."

He smiles sympathetically. "I think we all have a few of those we're carrying around."

"How do you know it's okay?"

"When you can still live with it on your back." He's right, because if we can handle it, it's not too much. The space between us closes again as we continue to move to the music. "What's your favorite band?" he asks.

"That's easy. Coldplay. Yours?"

"Chopin and Horowitz are more my speed."

The song switches as I press my cheek to his chest. The wine and my lack of sleep have brought me to this state where all I want to do is pull on a pair of comfy sweats and crawl into my nice, warm bed. Being with Pierce, like this, is just as good.

"Do you know what my favorite part of tonight is going to be when it's all over?" he asks.

"Hmm?"

He hesitates for just a second. "Being here . . . like this with you."

"Why do you say that?"

He slides his hand up my back, then down again. "There's just something about you. Something I've been thinking about since I sat next to you on the plane."

"I need to ask you something, and I need you to answer honestly," I say, feeling the familiar nerves creep back up.

"It's the only way I know how to be."

"Did you offer me this job because I had the skills or because you wanted to be like this?" I close my eyes . . . waiting. I've been second-guessing myself since I started at Stanley Development, and I hate it.

His grip on my hand tightens. "A little of both. It takes ambition to risk a move to the big city, and I'd be lying if I said I didn't have my own selfish reasons. I kind of like you, Lila."

My eyes widen as my heart bottoms out. I shouldn't be here. As soon as he says those words, I think about paint, tequila, and kitchen counters. I think about my blond artist— the man I've never had, but yet lost tonight.

That's what I'll always think back on.

THE MUSIC STOPS AT JUST the right moment, when this doesn't feel right anymore.

"Please take your seats. The first course will be served shortly," a female voice sounds over the loud speaker. Inner panic momentarily paralyzes me.

Pierce loosens his grip enough for me to step away. When he looks at me, I think he knows my mood has shifted. The wine and the dance—they aren't enough to banish the heartbreak from earlier. I'm not ready for this.

"Are you okay?" he asks, grabbing hold of my elbow.

I shake my head, searching for the right words. A reason to escape from here. "Can you take me home? I'm not feeling well."

His brow wrinkles. "Is it something I said?"

"No," I answer quietly, wishing I could simply fold myself back in his arms . . . and everything would be okay.

"What's going on?"

"I have a headache." My voice is meek, lacking assurance.

Pierce is at a loss for words, looking down then away. This room is filled with hundreds of people, but it feels like it's just us. Two people at a crossroads. He's not convinced, but I'm not either. Trying to crawl back into Blake's bed will more than likely end with me suffering from more than a bended heart. And Pierce continually crosses the professional line. What he's trying to accomplish, what he sees in me . . . I have no idea.

I can't stay.

Yet, I feel like I shouldn't go.

Life is one big tangled mess after another.

"Let's get you home then," he finally concedes. He steers us away from the dance floor, through a side door, and out into a quiet hallway. He pulls out his cell phone and makes a quick call to have the car come pick us up.

After it's tucked back into his pocket, he envelops my hand in his and leads us through a pair of swinging doors. A huge kitchen full of staff in black chefs' coats appears, and without seeking permission, Pierce ushers me through it. The staff barely blink an eye, like this happens all the time.

"Where are we going?" I ask, walking faster to keep up. That's not an easy feat in heels.

"Back door."

There's a metal door that leads to a dark alleyway. The black Escalade pulls up just in time to rescue us from the cold. Pierce pulls the door open, letting me climb in first. He follows.

"Can I at least take you for a quick bite? I'm not one to send a girl home hungry."

"No, I just want to get home."

Silence ensues. I count the minutes, trying to remember how long it took us to get here . . . how long it will take to get back home.

"How much do you know about him?" Pierces asks. *Him* doesn't require any clarification. His sense of perception is really starting to get under my skin.

"Enough."

"What if I told you to stay away from him?"

"I'd ask you to give me a good reason."

More silence. That seems to be the theme for tonight—a teeter-totter between conversation and nothing at all.

I watch out the window as we speed down city streets. Downtown slowly turns into the more residential area where I live. Seeing familiar houses and street signs calms me . . . just a couple more minutes until I can put this all behind me.

When we finally pull onto my street, I sit up straight, ready to make my escape. "I'm really sorry about tonight, Pierce."

"I'll let you make it up to me sometime. I think you owe me dinner."

To that, I can only smile. Maybe I do owe him something, but some debts are never paid.

The car comes to a stop in front of my building. I contemplate opening my door and hurrying out to avoid any more conversation, but Pierce opens his first. "At least let me walk you to your door."

I nod, sliding across the seat. The driver's waiting for me, coat in hand. "Here you are, Ms. Fields."

"Thank you," I reply, slipping my arms into it.

As soon as it's on, he disappears inside the car, leaving Pierce and I alone. The only thing that separates me from home is about ten feet of sidewalk; it seems much longer now than it ever did before. Pierce's hand splays against my lower back like it has several other times tonight, startling me. "If it's any consolation, I had a good time with you tonight."

"So did I."

"Hmm, I hate to see your version of a bad date."

I laugh. "Guy takes you to an expensive restaurant, leaves you paying for dinner. Or better yet, he talks about his ex the entire time, audibly comparing you to her."

"Damn. You must have dated some winners."

He's doing that thing he does again—making me forget. It's just a little too late because we're standing in front of my door—the only thing that separates me from the guy who holds a piece of my heart in his hands.

Pierce surprises me, cradling my cool cheeks in his warm hands. "For the record, I'd never leave you with the bill, and there's no comparison to make between you and my past."

"That's good to know," I reply, chewing on my lower lip. The way he stares down at me makes me uncomfortable. It reminds me of a defining moment in the movies . . . before a kiss. "I should get inside."

"Remember what I told you about staying away from him," he says quietly, rubbing his thumb along my cheek. He reads the undying question in my eyes. "And if that's not enough for you, ask him about Alyssa." There's undeniable pain in his voice when he says the name.

"Who?"

He kisses my cheek. "I'm going to leave it up to him to tell you."

I nod, feeling a sting in my chest. What if there's someone else? What if that's where he disappears to? It's been a doubt that's lingered for far too long already, and Pierce just planted a seed to make it grow.

"Good night," he says as he lets go of me.

"Good night and thank you." I wave as I slip inside. For the second time tonight, I wonder if I'm making a mistake by leaving a man. They're so different; Pierce probably the safer choice. I just can't give him a second thought when every part of me is hooked on Blake.

Sometimes, it takes a moment of intolerance to realize where your soft place is. Everything Pierce did tonight was perfect yet I couldn't be with him because deep down, I was with Blake . . . I never actually left him.

My feet ache from a few hours spent in heels as I make my way up the last flight of stairs. I script exactly what I want to say to Blake—how I want to package my bid to get him back.

Anger makes people say things they wouldn't otherwise. Nothing happened between Pierce and I to change the way I feel about Blake. Nothing happened to make me feel guilty about tonight except for going in the first place.

The apartment is dark when I push the door open. He's either away or asleep; I'm hoping for the latter. I need him, and I'm not going to let myself fall asleep until I have him in my sight again. I peel my heels off and flick on the kitchen light.

My stomach turns.

My legs buckle.

Life isn't fair.

It certainly hasn't been kind.

They say the awful things that happen to us in our lifetime only make us stronger. I think they just harden us until we can't feel anymore.

Clothes are scattered in a clear path from the door to Blake's bedroom—not his clothes. My eyes stick to them. Maybe if I stare long enough, they'll just disappear. Turn into nothing but a wicked game my mind played.

I step over the tiny black skirt first, then the thin red sweater. I reach toward his doorknob as if it might burn me. I don't want to know, but I have to. Was moving on this easy?

Before the door even opens, I hear the sounds—the grunts and moans. I see two dark silhouettes, and I know. I know I ruined everything we had, or maybe we never had anything at all.

It only took four hours for him to replace me with someone else—for him to replace me in his bed.

I should close them out of my view, but I can't. My body is paralyzed, but my heart bleeds as the show of emotions slide down my cheeks. This I can't erase. I want to take this pain and inflict it on someone else—on him.

It only took him weeks to fix me, and now, I'm broken again. I want him to hurt as much as he's hurt me.

I step back, slamming the door shut. The moans stop, replaced by hushed whispers.

I wait, needing to see what makes her better than me. Who was worth throwing everything away for? I swipe my fingertip under my eyes. Even if I'm weak, he's not going to get the satisfaction of seeing it.

While I wait, I pour myself a glass of wine to try and numb the pain. Minutes tick by, and just when I'm thinking they may have picked right back up where they left off, the door inches open.

A thin brunette with long, mussed up hair steps out first in nothing but a black thong and matching bra. Our eyes connect, but she quickly looks away, picking her trail of clothes up off the floor. Blake follows in nothing but his gray boxer briefs. His cock is still swollen—probably a symptom of unfinished sex. Years from now I'll still think about it. How it felt inside me . . . how it felt to come hard around him. I hate myself for even thinking about it.

"Sorry," the girl mutters as she reaches around my legs to grab her skirt. I watch her shimmy into it, her cheeks blushing more with each passing second.

"Do you want me to help you find your shoes?" I ask.

Out of the corner of my eye, I catch of glimpse of Blake staring at me curiously.

She looks up through her lashes, her doe eyes studying me.

"They're at the foot of my bed," Blake answers for her. His voice hints of annoyance but not an ounce guilt. "Why don't you go get them for her, Lila?"

I hate him. I hate that he called me Lila instead of Lemon Drop. Because I don't want him to know what I'm thinking or feeling, I walk past them to his room. He won't expect this. It'll throw him off . . . make him wonder. I flip the light on, instantly spotting the black stilettos. I grab them up quickly, wanting to escape the lingering smell of sex.

The walk out to the living room is just long enough to take a breath, to clear up my emotions again. "Here," I say, holding them out to her.

"Thanks," she says quietly, slipping them off my fingers.

"Not a problem. I'm used to it."

Her eyes double in size, but she quickly recovers, slipping the shoes onto her feet. I muster everything I have in me to keep myself together. I promised myself I wasn't going to let anyone take the best of me again. I'm definitely not going to let this woman I don't know, who probably just met Blake a couple hours ago, take it. I'm not going to let him get away with it either.

When she's done, she turns to Blake as if I'm not in the room. "Do you want my number?"

Even I know the answer to that.

He shakes his head, walking to the door and opening it for her. "I told you this would be nothing more than this."

She sidles up to him, tracing a small circle onto his chest. "But can't we do *this* again?"

He shakes his head again, more definitive this time.

Her finger quickly falls away. "Okay," she says, sounding on the verge of tears. "I guess I'll just catch a cab then."

To my utter disgust, he reaches his hand out, a rolled up twenty between his fingers. "For the cab," he remarks.

"Fuck off!" she seethes, pushing past him. "You're an asshole."

With no reaction from him, she walks away. I wonder if this is how his hook-ups usually end. If there's a long path of pissed off women in his wake.

He closes the door, staring at it for longer than necessary. I want to run away, but there's nowhere for me to go. Besides, I ran here and look where it got me. "What the hell was that?" he finally asks.

"I have no idea what you're talking about. I just got home from my date." I put extra emphasis the last word. "I heard noises, and I went in to make sure you were okay."

He tugs at his hair, lifting his eyes to the barren ceiling. "Don't fucking toy with me, Lila. What the fuck was that?"

He needs to feel the sharp edge of the blade. He needs to know what he's done to me. Reaching my hands back, I work my zipper down, feeling the tight bodice loosen around my stomach. I slip one sleeve off my shoulder, then the other. My breasts exposed. My lacy, green panties the only thing that covers me.

His eyes find me, full of want . . . finally hinting at guilt. Or maybe that's just what I think I see. He saunters to me, I take a couple steps toward him. I rest my hand flat on his bare chest; his heart beats viciously against it.

I imprison my heart to try to keep it from feeling as my fingers slide down his taut stomach. My eyes cloud over anyway.

He grips my hips. I stare up at him, remembering how good it can feel to be with him like this.

"What are we doing?" he asks in a low voice.

I slip my hand lower, wrapping my fingers around his swollen cock. His breath hitches, his fingers digging deeper into my skin.

Standing on my tiptoes, I bring my lips to his ear. "This is me saying goodbye, Blake. I'd say fuck you, but she already did."

My hands fall away from him as I step out of his grasp. I never had the strength to do this with Derek—put a painful, sharp period at the end of our relationship. I gather the silky dress from the floor and stalk off to my bedroom without another word.

I don't look back. I can't let him see me fall apart.

He doesn't come after me or call my name. All I have left to do is lie in the bed I made for myself . . . the one he tore the covers off for me.

3

"LILA!" REECE PRACTICALLY SQUEALS, coming around the corner of my cubicle. "Why didn't you answer when I called you yesterday? I've been dying to hear about the benefit."

I bury my face in my hands, trying to hide the disappointment I know shows as clear as day. Friday night with Blake was possibly one of the best nights of my life—most memorable anyway. Saturday night—the part after the benefit—was a perfect view straight into hell. It's a bad memory, permanently burned in full color into my mind.

"I'm sorry. I spent the day in bed," I answer, finding the courage to uncover my eyes, exposing my dark circles from lack of sleep. I spent the morning telling people that I wasn't feeling well. If I keep at it, it'll probably become true. Karma is a spiteful little bitch.

"With Pierce?" She sounds so enthusiastic about it, I almost want to lie, go with her fairy tale. Tell her he carried me up the stairs to sooth my aching feet, then slowly undressed me and made sweet love to me until the sun came up.

Shaking myself from my thoughts, I say, "No, Pierce drove me home Saturday night. The closest we were was a dance . . . I promise."

"You're kidding me. He didn't invite you to his place? I bet he has a huge penthouse, with an amazing view and a king size bed."

"I didn't exactly give him a chance."

Her brows wrinkle as she takes me in. I'm a mess; I don't need a mirror, or her, to tell me that. "Have you had lunch yet?"

Looking down at the clock on my computer screen, I notice it's almost one. "If you're inviting me, I guess I can peel myself away from this desk for a few minutes."

"You can, and you will. You're losing weight, I swear."

I roll my eyes. Life has been so busy since I've moved here that it's become normal to skip meals, especially on days like today when I don't feel much like eating. "I'll choke down a banana."

"You'll do more than that. A sandwich and a banana. Let's up that and make it a fried chicken sandwich."

I log off my computer and grab my purse from under my desk. This is going to suck. It's why depressed people close themselves off; they'd rather not talk about any of it. She's going to push—ask me what I wore, what he wore. She's going to want to know what it was like when he dropped me off . . . did he try to kiss me. And if she even thinks about asking about Blake, I'm a goner.

We make our way to the cafeteria, discussing our current work projects instead of men. Our passion for doing our best no matter what is the one thing we have in common.

We keep conversation to a minimum while we pick up our lunch, but all bets are off when we're seated at our usual table in the corner.

"So, you haven't mentioned Blake. How is he?"

Shit. Shit. Shit.

"He's Blake."

She sighs. "Start talking."

Quadruple shit. "He's a jerk."

"You're going to have to give me more than that," she says, slipping a grape between her lips.

I inhale a deep breath, looking around to make sure no one is listening. "Okay, so I thought I could do this whole . . . I don't know what you call it . . . no-strings-attached relationship. I forgot that I'm a woman, and we can't control our feelings."

She nibbles on the edge of her sandwich, watching me intently.

"And he does things . . . says things. I just can't keep sleeping with him without getting more out of it. I mean, I spent Friday with him, and it was amazing. Like beyond anything I've ever imagined, but when I told him about Pierce and the benefit, he couldn't commit. So here I am." I throw my hands up in defeat. That's what I am I've decided—hopelessly unlovable. Derek didn't even want to marry me after spending seven years together.

Her eyes look like the grapefruits I passed in the lunch line. "He didn't care that you were going with Pierce?"

I think back to the other night . . . the look in his eyes, his words. "I wouldn't say that. But I did find out they know each other."

"Seriously?"

"Yep, and they hate each other." The scene in the hall replays in my mind. Definitely no love lost between them.

"Well, that is interesting. Do you know why?"

"Not really. Except they worked together once."

My mind wanders to that and the parts of this weekend I left out—the parts that make me not want to care about Blake or how Pierce knows him. Men keep fucking up my life little by little.

"Lila." I lift my gaze to Pierce who stands next to our table with his hands stuffed in his slate blue suit pockets.

"Hi," I answer, feeling every bit a high school girl when a hot guy sidles up during lunch. I even tuck a lock of hair behind my ear. *Nice, Lila.*

"I hate to interrupt, but when you're done with your lunch, can you join me in my office for a few minutes?"

Reece's legs bounce against mine under the table. If I say no, she'll haul me out to the parking lot and beat me until all my sense returns. "I'll be up in a few. We were just finishing up here."

He smiles, one side of his mouth lifting higher than the other. "I'll be waiting. Enjoy your lunch, ladies."

We both watch him walk away. In fact, the whole cafeteria watches him in hushed silence. Pierce Stanley doesn't hang out in the cafeteria. Ever.

"You're one lucky bitch," Reece finally says when he disappears through the door.

"He just wants to talk."

"Call it what you want. I'd do anything to get that man alone in his office."

"Reece?"

"Yeah?"

"You need your pipes snaked."

She scrunches her nose. "What?"

"Sex. You need sex."

She blushes. "Some of us don't have men falling at our feet like you."

I laugh. "They don't fall at my feet. They sit next to me on airplanes and invade my apartment."

"Whatever."

We spend the next ten minutes talking about Tuesday girls' night. It sounds like I'm doomed for a sad love story on the big screen. It's probably a good thing after what happened last week at the bar. I need controlled, safe, and drama free.

When we're done, we climb in the elevator together. I can tell by the way Reece fiddles with her purse strap that she's dying to ask me more. It's probably better if she doesn't; it wouldn't be appropriate with the other occupants.

They're still on when it comes to a stop on her floor. "I'll call you this afternoon," I say, reassuring her that she won't be left in the dark. My life's become just another romance novel to her.

"I'll be waiting," she replies, waving as she exits. I wait until she's out of the elevator then rest my head back against the wall. I need to catch a break—from men . . . from life in general.

Before my mind carries me too far, the elevators dings at the twelfth floor—Pierce's floor. I straighten up, smoothing out my skirt as I step off. The receptionist sees me right away, nodding down the hall toward Pierce's office. I guess he really is expecting me.

I concentrate on the click of my heels on the marble floors. From the front desk to his office is exactly forty-three steps. Enough time to let all the possibilities of what he could want run at feverish speed through my mind. I felt comfortable around him the other night, but we're back in the office. Expectations are different. Personalities shift. I'm not sure who I'll get when I open the door.

I knock twice.

His mellifluous voice rings through the thick wooden door. "Come in."

My trembling fingers grip the knob tightly, but I wait a couple seconds to turn it. Getting in is easy. Dealing with what awaits me inside isn't so much.

He isn't sitting behind his desk like he usually is. He's every bit a masculine statue standing in front of the floor-to-ceiling window, his back to me. "How was lunch?" he asks.

"Good," I answer, not quite sure where to go since he's not even looking at me.

"How was the rest of your weekend?"

"Uneventful," I lie, weaving my fingers together, slowly bending my hands back and forth.

When he finally looks at me, the expression on his face hints of disappointment. The kind that makes me wish I hadn't come up here at all. "You're a woman of many words."

"Sorry. I'm a little out of it today."

In three strides he's behind his desk, wrapping his long fingers around a tumbler half full of amber-colored liquor. He lifts one finger, signaling for me to take a seat. I do as he asks, watching him drain the last of his glass.

This Pierce is different than the relaxed one I enjoyed the company of the other night. This one intimidates me.

He sits back in his oversized leather chair, staring at me intently. "You don't look so good, no offense."

"Rough weekend."

"I take it things didn't go well after I dropped you off?"

"You could say that." He's crossing the line of professionalism again. The one I wish we'd never stepped over in the first place.

"Did you ask about her?" I wonder why he can't just say her name, but I'm not as free with my line of questioning as he is.

"Not that it's really any of your business, but we got in a fight before I had the chance."

He sizes me, running his forefinger along the top of his empty glass. "That doesn't surprise me. He tends to fuck things up."

"Why don't you just tell me?"

His skin pales. Pierce Stanley likely has very few sore spots, but I've hit one. "It would be better coming from him."

Still, I push. "Will you at least tell me why you hate him so much?"

"Let's just say we had a similar interest at one point," he replies, narrowing his eyes.

I dig deeper. "Work related?"

He shakes his head. I'm young and naïve, but I'm not stupid. This all has to do with a woman . . . one likely named Alyssa. Whatever it is, I don't want to get caught in the middle of it.

"That's not why I called you up here anyway," he says, changing the subject.

"Is there another benefit you'd like me to accompany you to on short notice?" I tease.

He smiles. "No, but I'll make sure you get the invite first next time. By the way, I have some good news. Do you remember Wade who I introduced you to the other night?"

I nod, listening more intently.

"He wants me to bid a project in New York, and he requested a fresh eye—your eye, to be exact."

I stare at him, dazed. There's no way he asked for me. I'm as green as they come. "I don't understand."

Pierce leans forward, forearms resting on his desk. "He wants us to fly to New York on Wednesday. We'd arrive early, see the site and then fly home Thursday."

"Do you really think I'm ready for this? I—"

"You're ready, Ms. Fields," he interrupts. "Your mentor showed me some of the stuff you've been working on. I like what I see."

Successful businessmen. New York. First big project. It all spins like a wheel in my head. This is what I've always wanted—what I went to school for—but having it within my grasp scares the shit out of me. Failure is a feeling we get from not accomplishing something, but when it's our dreams that go unrealized, it's something far worse that burns us inside.

"It's settled then. I'll pick you up at seven Wednesday morning."

He's so sure of himself, leaving no room for argument. "Okay," I say quietly.

"Good." He relaxes back in his chair. "I want you to put together a mood board for a new boutique hotel. He likes modern and planet-friendly. Remember that."

What the hell have I gotten myself into?

I ALWAYS MAKE THE WORST decisions when I feel as if my life is unraveling. When I feel as if I have no control, I grasp for any thread of power I can get my fingers on. Most of the time, I end up regretting rash decisions. It's impossible to anticipate the consequences when my mind is surrounded by dense fog.

What I'm about to do might end up being one of those decisions I'll regret when I wake up in the morning.

I open the door to Charlie's, hurriedly stepping inside to escape the cold December weather.

The bar isn't anything like it is on the weekend—maybe it's because it's Monday or maybe it's the snow. Charlie stops what he's doing as soon as he notices me. I never come here when I'm not working; I don't even want to be here when I'm getting paid.

"Did you get fired from your boring day job? Coming to beg me to give you more hours?" he teases. I had to tell him about my job at Stanley to get the night of the benefit off. He's been waiting for me to quit ever since.

"What are you talking about, Charlie? They'd never get rid of me." I slide onto one of the empty barstools away from the other patrons.

"Bad day at work?"

"More like bad week in life."

He leans on the bar in front of me, watching me curiously. Charlie's not a bad guy . . . just a little rough around the edges. "Can I get you something to drink? Alcohol solves all problems."

I should say no, tell him what I came here to say, and leave, but alcohol sounds pretty damn good right now. "Vodka water with lime, please."

"You got it."

He leaves me alone to make my drink, giving me more time to process everything that's happened recently. It's probably not a good idea—giving me time to reflect. It leaves me feeling rejection, confusion, and sadness. Why do I keep doing this to myself? I shouldn't let myself get hung up on men who are complicated, who I know are just going to leave me in worse condition than when they found me.

I need safe, reliable, and romantic, which just sounds boring as hell.

"Here you go," Charlie says, placing my drink on a napkin.

"Thanks."

"You look like you might need a couple."

"That's actually what I need to talk to you about. Do you have a few minutes?" I ask, feeling a little nervous. I'm not a quitter so this has been wearing on me.

He glances around the bar and smiles. "It's pretty busy, but I can make time for you."

His good mood leaves me feeling even guiltier. Charlie the asshole would have been so much easier to quit on. "My boss informed me that I need to go to New York later this week, which means I'm not going to be able to work on Thursday."

He nods, but I think he senses there's more because he doesn't say anything.

"It's becoming obvious that I'm not going to be able to keep two jobs . . . not with the demands of my new job."

He nods again.

"I appreciate everything you've done for me . . . giving me this job when I first got to town. I can work the next two weekends on Friday and Saturday to give you time to find a replacement." I keep rambling. It's safe to say I suck at this.

"Are you done?" he asks.

"I think so."

"Look, Lila, I knew when I gave you this job that you wouldn't stick around forever. You're a bright woman who has dreams and all that other shit you all move here for. I get it," he says, staring at me with softness in his eyes that I've never experienced from him.

I release the air I'd been holding in my lungs. "Whew. I thought you were going to yell at me."

He laughs, tossing a bar towel over his shoulder. "Nah, I learned to control myself when I was locked up."

My eyes widen unintentionally.

"Relax. It was almost fifteen years ago. I'm a changed man." He winks, and then continues, "If you can work this Friday and Saturday, I can cover the rest. There was a young lady who stopped by earlier to fill out an application . . . another dream catcher. And I always have Dana."

I thought about Dana a lot this afternoon when I was tossing this idea around in my head. It's as if I'm abandoning her, but I know if I asked her, she'd tell me this is the right thing to do.

"Thanks, Charlie."

"No problem. Just don't forget me when you're rich and famous."

I roll my eyes. "That's probably not going to happen, but I promise not to forget you anyway."

He starts walking to the other end of the bar where a customer is waving his empty glass in the air. "See you Friday."

I polish off the rest of my drink and head out before I can talk myself into having another.

After pulling my jacket tightly around me, I start the short trek toward home. It's just before seven, but darkness has fallen, the sky only painted by the light dusting of snow falling in front of the streetlights.

This is usually my favorite time of year—all the Christmas decorations—especially the bright lights. Dad went outside the day after Thanksgiving—a few days before I left for Chicago—to put lights around the house. I kind of miss staring at them while driving up to the house at night . . . I miss home.

The only thing holding me back from my peaceful place is the uncertainty with Blake. Will he be home when I get there? If so, what kind of mood will he be in? We just left things—me pissed off, him with his head spinning.

On my way up to the apartment, I make a list of all the things I need to pack for New York to take my mind off what might await me. It's useless because after each skirt, shoe, etc., Blake peeks through. That's how it's been all day.

When I reach the door to the apartment, light filters underneath, preparing me for what I might find on the other side. I brace myself against the wall, letting my mind get used to the idea. It doesn't take long to realize that thinking about it is just making matters worse.

I take a deep breath and turn the knob, relieved to see that Blake's not here . . . not where I can see him anyway. After stepping out of my boots and throwing my coat over a dining chair, I disappear into my bedroom to put on some comfy clothes. Nights like this call for sweats and thick wool socks.

When I emerge to find something to eat, I'm in my comfort zone. It doesn't take long to get knocked right back out of that by Blake who stands with his back to me, looking into the open fridge.

Hoping he didn't hear me, I slowly walk backward through the doorway to my bedroom. It's too late, though. The memories have surfaced. The thoughts I've tried so hard to bury come up for another breath. And then he glances over his shoulder, looking straight into my eyes.

"I know you're there," he says, catching me off guard. I kind of expected him to ignore me even if he did hear me. It would be easier on both of us.

"And . . ."

He shuts the fridge, rubbing the back of his neck. "The fridge is empty."

I've only been to the store once since I moved here, and I feel kind of guilty. Then I remember everything that's transpired between us over the last few days, and I'm not sorry. "Go out and get something to eat then. Don't hurry back."

I start to walk away, but his voice stops me. "Is that how it's going to be now?"

Now I'm pissed—white walls turned red. "You did this, Blake! If you don't like it, that's too damn bad!"

He looks down at the floor then back at me. "You're the one who left with him."

Blake, who comes off as the most confident person I've ever met, looks lost. Torn. Mentally obliterated. I can't deny that I still feel things for him. After everything we've done, it would be hard not to.

I walk to where he stands. He needs to hear me. He needs to feel every ounce of pain he's caused me. He stands in front of me, the vision of every man I should run from. "I came back for you. I was with Pierce, comparing everything he did to everything you did to me. I picked you."

His expression crumbles, but it's not enough. "If your goal was to hurt me . . . if you wanted to see how easy it was to break me, mission accomplished, Blake. You can move on to your next plaything now."

I wonder if my words are cutting deep enough. In a way, I want to hurt him more than I wanted to hurt Derek. At least he was honest. "I'm sorry," he mumbles. He brushes past me without another word, without waiting to hear my reaction. My eyes stay on him as he grabs his jacket from the chair and walks out of the apartment, slamming the door behind him.

I almost wish I'd just left it alone, because in the end I think I hurt myself more than I did him. I watched him fall apart, but I'm the one who shattered.

Needing some added comfort, I order a veggie pizza from the place near Charlie's, and pour myself a big glass of wine. I try to chase Blake out of my mind, and when nothing else seems to work, I pick up a book. I can't concentrate on the pages. It's just a bunch of words I'm not really taking in. I keep drifting for there really is no distraction that can peel me away from him.

Nights like this should be relaxing. I should use the time to find myself, to figure out what I really want. But there's no guarantee I'd get it, so what's the point.

A light knock sounds at the door. Pizza—that will make everything better.

I open it and immediately regret not using the peephole.

Pierce smiles at me, and for once, I can't match it. Smiles have been as rare as warm days in winter since the night of the benefit.

"What are you doing here?" I ask, straightening my messy bun. Not a conventional hello, but not much about my life is conventional anymore.

"I still owe you dinner, and I was in the neighborhood." This is the first time I've seen Pierce in jeans. He wears them just as well as a suit. His thick gray sweater highlights his eyes.

"You should've called first."

He shrugs, hands buried in his jean pockets. "You would have said no. This was a better bet."

I chew my lower lip. He's right. He's always right, and I hate it. "I ordered a pizza a little while ago." I pause, weighing my options. "You're welcome to stay. It's not like I can eat the whole thing myself."

He peers over my shoulder into the vacant apartment. I know what he's thinking. The same thought flashed through my mind when I saw him standing on the other side of the door.

The thought of Blake coming home and seeing us petrifies me, but I don't think he will. He hasn't been gone long enough yet; it wouldn't fit his pattern.

"He's not here."

"I guess you twisted my arm, not that you had to try too hard," he says. I step back, allowing him to enter. He's wearing his usual cologne. It's seduction in a bottle.

"Would you like a glass of wine?" I ask, pulling a glass from the cupboard.

"Red if you have it."

He watches me from the other end of the counter. I feel self-conscious—completely underdressed. At least I'm still wearing make-up.

I hand him his glass. "What are you really doing here, Pierce?"

"I wanted to see you."

"Pierce, I don't—"

"No," he says, coming around the counter. "Don't. I like spending time with you. I'm not asking for anything else."

I close my eyes tightly and bring my wine glass to my lips. Maybe this is what I need . . . someone to take my mind off everything. "Well, I hope you like veggie pizza."

His smile is back. "It's not so much about what you eat . . . it's the company you keep while doing it."

Before I can reply, there's another knock at the door. *This better be the pizza this time,* I think to myself. When I open the door to a deliveryman holding a brown box, I feel just a slight sense of relief. I hand the guy some cash, and bring it to the kitchen, quickly making us each a plate.

"Can you tell me a little bit more about the New York project?" I ask when we're seated at the table.

"I didn't come to talk about work."

"Humor me for a few minutes, and then we can talk about whatever you want," I say, popping a portabella mushroom into my mouth. They're the reason I love this pizza.

"Wade wants something unique, something that will draw in the young and rich." He sips his wine, never taking his eyes off me. "I can't stand the guy, but I can't walk away from this project either."

"I don't know if I'm ready to be on a stage that size yet," I say, honestly. It's been eating me up; I hate failure or even the threat of it.

He leans in, gently brushing his thumb across my cheek. His touch is soft—comforting. I can't turn away. "The only thing that's going to hold you back is self-doubt. Don't let it."

"It sounds so easy when you say it."

"That's because it is." He drops his hand, and I have to admit I want it back.

We talk a little bit more about the project while we finish our pizza and the whole bottle of wine. Any reservations I had when I first opened the door are gone. This is natural, easy.

"Were you planning on sitting here alone all night?" he asks when the plates have been cleared.

"It's what I do: eat, drink, and read."

"You deserve more," he says, softly.

"It's not that easy."

"What's the real reason you moved to Chicago?" he asks. I could speak lies and half-truths, but he'll see right through them.

I hesitate, nervously folding the corners of my napkin. "To run away from the past."

"What was his name?"

"Why are you so perceptive?" I inquire.

"This isn't about me."

This is forbidden territory. A tall wall I'd never dare climb. But wine makes me more apt to accept a dare. "His name is Derek. We dated for seven years, were engaged for one. One day he decided he could live without me."

Pierce studies my features, taking in every word. "He's going to regret it. Maybe not now but someday."

I nod. Months ago, I wished he'd come crawling back to me with a heartfelt apology, but I don't even care anymore. I've moved on . . . I just don't know if it's a better place yet.

"How do you feel about him now?" Pierce asks, resting his elbows on the table.

"I'm over it. I think it started to unravel long before he ended it anyway."

He shows his two sexy dimples. They've probably gotten him out of a lot of trouble over the years. I could see them getting a girl like me into trouble. "At least I stand a chance."

"Pierce?"

"Yeah."

"Sometimes I wish you would've called me sooner, or that I had called you right away."

"Why's that?" he asks.

"Because I would've fallen for you first."

He shuts his eyes, but they quickly find me again. Brow furrowed. Jaw set. "That doesn't mean anything."

There's nothing to say to that. Pierce should be my choice whether he touched me first or not. He's gorgeous and smart. He could make me happy if I let him, but he's the right guy at the wrong time.

Maybe it's not too late.

"It's getting late," I say, standing to clear the dishes from the table.

He follows, grabbing the empty glasses and bottle. "Let me help you with these, and then I'll get out of your way. You filled your dinner obligation, so you're off the hook for now."

I look back over my shoulder.

He winks.

Being with him like this would be so easy.

After everything is put away, I walk him to the door. Honestly, I don't really want him to go.

"I'm looking forward to New York," he admits.

"Me too."

He surprises me, gripping my chin between his fingers. I stare up into his eyes, watching them come closer until his warm lips brush my cheek. I close my eyes, relishing in his sweetness until he lets go. "Goodnight, Lila."

"Goodnight, Pierce."

And as I watch him walk down the hallway, I wonder what could be . . . if maybe my heart has been wrapped around the wrong man.

No one ever said love was easy. If it were, it wouldn't be worth it.

"HOW DID YOU GET SO LUCKY?" Reece asks as she polishes off the last of her second Cosmo. We decided to grab an early dinner and drinks before the movie, and the one and only topic of conversation has been my upcoming trip with Pierce. I miss being the one with the boring life.

"I wouldn't call it luck. I'm scared out of my freaking mind. This isn't a small project . . . I haven't even had a small project yet. On top of that, I have to spend two days alone with Pierce."

Reece rolls her eyes. "Have to? Really, Lila? The man is a god."

"He's just intense. And after what happened last night—"

"Wait," Reece says, holding her hand up. "What happened last night?"

Shit. I didn't necessarily want to bring this up. "He came by the apartment, and we had dinner."

"No way!" Reece exclaims, eyes widening.

"He confuses me . . . I mean, the way he makes me feel confuses me," I admit.

I think back to the night of the benefit, and the time I've spent with him in the office. He's not a bad guy. In fact, if I let myself, I could fall for him.

"What are you going to do in New York?" Dana asks, interrupting Reece's interrogation.

I shrug, not quite sure myself. "We're meeting with a potential client. A hotel project I think."

Dana lifts a brow. "And the meeting is going to take two days?"

"Okay, Reece One and Reece Two. I'm going to New York for two days with Pierce Stanley for business. There's nothing romantic about it."

"New York is romantic," Reece says dreamily. "Have you ever been?"

I shake my head. "No, but even if it were Paris, nothing would happen." If I don't watch it, I'm going to be the only one who needs convincing.

"You're a tough cookie," Reece says, shaking her head. "No wonder you have man problems."

"You seem to enjoy my man problems," I chide. She opens her mouth, but when I narrow my eyes on her, she closes it.

"She doesn't need Pierce anyway. She has Blake," Dana pipes in.

I groan, burying my face in my hands. My life is such a crazy ride; I can't keep up with it, let alone keep my friends up to date. "That's over."

Dana looks at me with question in her eyes. "What? How can it be over? I thought you guys were just fucking." Leave it to her to magnify the crudeness.

"It wasn't working out. Besides, the second he got angry with me he took it as a hall pass to go screw someone else he met in a bar. I'm not going to play those games with a guy who refuses to commit. There are other guys I can get benefits from without the drama."

"Oh my," Dana says, shaking her head.

"What?"

"I warned you, and you did it anyway . . . you fell for him."

I open my mouth to correct her, but I can't. She's right . . . the only reason Blake being with another woman bothers me is because in my mind, he's mine. Or he *was* mine.

"Can someone explain to me what Blake has that Pierce doesn't?" Reece asks. "I don't see it."

That one I have to think about. Blake has this whole other side that surfaces every now and then—one I can't seem to let go of. He's the definition of a damaged man, and I think a part of me wanted to fix him . . . to find the man he is underneath.

"Pierce is successful, and when we're together, I know exactly what I'm getting. I guess I liked the mystery with Blake. Every time we were together was different. New. Exciting. It just didn't end the way I envisioned it."

Reece sits with her head resting in her hand, staring at me dreamily. "You make fucking sound so romantic."

Dana looks at her like she's someone she doesn't even know. "You just said fucking. We just might turn you into a bad girl yet. And you," she says, turning her attention back to me, "the reason your benefits-only relationship didn't work was because you wanted more than benefits."

I roll my eyes, but deep down inside, I know she's right. I wasn't made for that type of arrangement and failed miserably. "Is it time to go to the movie yet?"

"Who needs a movie when we have you?" Reece asks.

"I do. You two can't talk there."

With only ten minutes before Pierce arrives, I push down on the lid of my small suitcase in order to zip it shut. It's one night, but without knowing everything he has planned, I over-packed a bit—three pairs of shoes, two changes of business attire, and a dress just in case we have dinner somewhere nice.

I roll it to the door and put on my shoes and coat. I opted for a sleek black pantsuit with a low-cut white blouse underneath. Not too sexy, but risqué enough to show I have some edge and taste. I pair it with a low black strappy heel, hoping my feet won't fall off by the end of the day.

In the rush of everything, I almost don't hear my phone ringing from inside my purse.

"Hello," I answer without checking to see who it is first.

"It's so good to hear your voice." Mom. I smile to myself, imaging her sitting at the table on the other end, sipping from her large black coffee mug.

"Sorry I haven't called in a few days. Things got a little hectic at my new job." I don't add anything about my personal life because that's the last thing I want her to know about. She'd probably try to convince me to come home to a 'nice country boy' as she calls them. I tried her idea of nice, and it didn't work out so well for me.

"Is everything all right?"

"Yeah, I'm actually leaving any minute to go to New York for a few meetings with the CEO." Saying it out loud gives me heart palpitations. This trip isn't just another meeting . . . it's a potential multi-million dollar business deal.

She laughs. "You don't sound all that excited. Haven't you always wanted to go to New York City?"

"Yes, but on vacation. Not my first ever business meeting."

"You'll do fine. Besides, they wouldn't have invited you if they didn't think you could do it."

"How are things back home?" I desperately need to think about something besides two days in New York with Pierce.

"Just trying to get ready for Christmas. Have you decided if you're coming home yet?" Worry drips from her voice.

"I'm not sure. It depends on work and stuff, but I should know by the end of the week."

"Well, I hope you do, but I'll understand if you can't."

"I'm really going to try." I glance up at the clock, feeling the nervousness that faded while talking to Mom creep back up. "I need to get going. My ride will be here any minute, but I promise to give you a call sometime this weekend."

"Remember to have fun, and Lila, I know you can do this. You're a smart girl, and you deserve everything that comes your way."

"Love you."

"I love you, too."

By the time I throw my phone back in my bag, the weight on my shoulders isn't quite as heavy. In a way, Mom is right . . . if Pierce didn't think I could handle this, why would he risk losing such a big business deal. I honestly don't think he'd put everything he's worked hard for in jeopardy.

The doorbell rings, and my heart rate picks up again. Using the glass in the microwave, I straighten my hair then head to the door, opening it to Pierce, who stands suited in his signature gray. No matter how many times I see him like this, I stare longer than I should.

"Ready?" he asks, breaking my visual spell.

"I think so."

"Here," he says, stepping around me. "Let me take your bags."

"You don't have to do that, but thank you."

He appears to be in a hurry, which is understandable since we have to make it through Chicago rush hour traffic in order to get to the airport. He strides a few feet in front of me, trailing my suitcase behind him.

"I need to lock the door," I announce, pulling the key from my purse. Blake hasn't been home since he left Monday night. My guess is he holes himself away in his studio, painting until he has no choice but to crash. Even after everything that's happened between us, I still worry about him no matter how much I try to convince myself I shouldn't.

When I finally turn back around, Pierce is waiting for me, eyeing me cautiously. "Are you okay?"

I wonder if my expression changes when Blake runs through my mind. "Yeah, it's just early."

"If you hurry, we have time to grab coffee."

"Ah, how did you know I was an addict?"

He tilts his head, grinning. "I saw the k-cup collection in your apartment the other night. I assumed you were the addicted party."

"Let's get out of here then. You'd hate to see me if that addiction doesn't get fed."

"Good idea," he says, starting down the hall again. As we make our way down the stairs, I wish for the hundredth time this building had an elevator. He's carrying the suitcase, but I have the stupid heels.

The same black Escalade from the other night waits out front. The driver greets me. "Good morning, Ms. Fields."

I smile in response. "Good morning."

"I'll take that from you." He points to my briefcase. I hand it to him, grateful to have my shoulder back.

I step into the SUV, relishing in the warmth it offers. Pierce follows, taking the seat next to me. As the car starts down my street, he holds a venti Starbucks cup out to me. "Here."

"I thought—"

He interrupts, "You shouldn't underestimate me."

"Do I need to tell you that I'm not very talkative until I've finished my coffee, or do you know that too?" I ask, feeling bold.

One side of his mouth turns up. "I would have figured it out in a minute or two, but thanks for the warning."

"No problem."

For the rest of the ride to the airport, I sip on my soy latte. How he knew how I liked my coffee is a mystery to me, but I'm not going to question it. It's relaxing not to have to take the train, being crowded in with a bunch of people I don't know. However, that same uncomfortable feeling will creep right back up when the wheels touch down in New York. People I don't know. Meetings I'll squirm through because I have no idea what's going on.

We pull up in front of a building I don't recognize. There's only a few people standing on the sidewalk, and O'Hare is usually bustling with people.

"Where are we?"

"We're taking the company jet."

Confusion only leads to questions. "If you have a jet, why were you riding coach from Omaha to Chicago?"

He smiles. "My plane was being serviced. Besides, it all worked out, didn't it?"

I brush his comment aside, feeling a lump form in my throat as I remember the hundreds of stories I've read over the years about small plane crashes. "Are those jets safe?"

"I've had this plane for six years, and between me and the rest of the Stanley execs, it flies two to three times a week. Never had a problem."

I nod, but that doesn't mean I'm okay with it. I'm not. If I'd known, I would have taken an anxiety pill or two before leaving the house this morning. Now, I'm screwed.

"We're clear for take-off in about twenty minutes. They'll just need to see your ID."

My head spins so fast that the next few minutes are a total blur. I hand the lady inside my driver's license and use the restroom . . . twice. I don't really recall getting on the plane or buckling my seatbelt.

"Do you need anything before we take off?" the female flight attendant asks.

When I don't answer, Pierce does it for me. "Bring her a water. I'll take a coffee, black."

She smiles warmly. "My pleasure."

I can't tell you what happened the rest of the flight . . . it's all a blur.

My legs shake as I take the final step off the plane. Never in my life have I been this happy to walk on solid ground. I've taken it for granted.

"That wasn't so bad, was it?" Pierce asks, coming up behind me.

"We survived."

"That we did, and, lucky for you, we get to take a car to our first appointment." He surprises me, placing his hand on the small of my back to guide me to a waiting car. I should be used to it by now, but it still sends a little tingle down my spine. Even more so after dinner the other night.

"What's on the agenda?" I ask as soon as we're inside the waiting town car.

He displays a wide grin. "Not a fan of surprises?"

"Not usually."

He runs his finger across his chin. "We're going straight from here to meet with Wade. More than likely, we'll grab lunch with him and tour the site. If we make it through all of that, I have a dinner reservation at New York's most exclusive steakhouse. Thought if we were in the city, we might as well experience it." He rattles it off without blinking an eye. Just listening to it makes me want to fall back onto my pillow.

"Does this schedule ever wear you out?"

He stretches his legs out, his tall frame taking up half the backseat. Everything about him commands my attention. His suit. The strong jaw framing his handsome face. "I don't have anything else to do with my time, although I'm hoping that changes soon."

The way he's looking at me—eyes glossed over, touching his lower lip—defines the meaning of his words. It makes the hair on the back of my neck stand up. His words from the other night ring through my head. It's one of those moments where I'm not sure what to say, so instead, I stare out my window. The movement probably says more than I ever could. After all, the possibilities play in my head too. I just won't admit it.

I relax back into the seat watching New York City fly by my window. I've always wanted to come here, but I envisioned seeing the Statue of Liberty and walking through museum after museum until I couldn't stand to be on my feet any longer. I'd also get one of those frozen hot chocolates from *Serendipity*; I've always wondered if they are as good as they look.

"What's going through that head of yours?" Pierce asks, breaking through my big city dreams.

"Frozen hot chocolate," I answer.

He doesn't say anything until I glance over at him. "Have you ever had one?"

I shake my head. "No."

"We might have to change that."

We spend the next several hours in meetings, going over budgets and design concepts with Wade Adams. After ten minutes, I knew I wasn't going to be a fan of his. He's on some sort of power trip over Pierce, displaying a constant stream of arrogance and defiance. There's obvious history between them, and I'm starting to wonder why we're even here.

"If I have to spend ten more minutes with that asshole, I'm going to punch him," Pierce remarks as we climb into the waiting car. We just finished our tour of the site, but made plans with Wade to meet one more time before we leave tomorrow. It's safe to say neither of us is looking forward to it.

"Do you need me to hold you back?"

He laughs, eyes wandering my small frame. "Good luck with that."

"There are ways to distract you." The glimmer in his eyes tells me that it wasn't the best choice of words. "What's the plan now?" I ask, hoping to lead his mind on a detour.

"We have a couple hours before our dinner reservation. I thought we'd check into the hotel, and then you can take a nap or attempt to make yourself even more beautiful than you already are. It's up to you."

He's smooth . . . really smooth.

He's sexy and intense, yet harmless. He hints, but he doesn't push. He's not the type to take what I haven't offered.

"Where are we staying?" I ask.

"Four Seasons."

He doesn't spare an expense. I've only ever heard about it but never stayed anywhere like it. Not even close.

The car pulls in front of the sleek and elegant high-rise hotel. "This is amazing," I say, all but pressing my forehead to the window.

Pierce slides across the seat until his body touches mine. I glance over, noticing him look out the window right along with me. "Wait until you see the inside." He whispers the words so close to my ear, I feel his warm breath against my skin.

"What are we waiting for then?"

The driver shifts the car into park and comes around to open my door. "Go on inside, miss, and I'll send your luggage in with the bellman," he says as I step up onto the curb.

"Thank you." I smile at him, watching Pierce slip money into his hand.

The revolving door opens to something just as magnificent—a multi-story entry, columns, and patterned limestone floors. Even if I'd had twenty years of design training at the best schools, I couldn't have come up with this.

"What do you think?" Pierce asks.

"I don't think I ever want to go back to Chicago." It's the truth.

"We could arrange that too."

I tug my lower lip between my teeth. "Let's revisit that at the end of the night."

I'm joking, but I'm not. Chicago is nice, but New York City is magical. The culture. Everything.

While Pierce checks us in, I stay back, looking at more of the décor and people. New York is so diverse. In this lobby alone, I hear several languages, see different types of people. I could spend hours, listening and observing.

"Ready?" I jump, holding my chest as I glance over my shoulder at Pierce.

"You scared me."

"I'm sorry." He smiles, swiping his thumb across my cheek. "We're on the thirty-fourth floor."

A million thoughts flash through my mind. He wouldn't have booked us for the same room, would he? My gut reaction is to offer to get my own, but there's no way in hell I can afford this place.

"Do you need help up with your bags, sir?" a bellman asks.

Pierce glances at the two small suitcases being swallowed by the oversized cart. "I think I can handle it, but thank you." He hands the guy some cash and picks up our bags like they weigh nothing. "After you," he says, nodding toward the elevator.

I walk on shaky knees, my mind still taken with possibilities and how I'm going to react to each one. When the door opens, I step inside, with Pierce following me close behind. To my dismay, the elevator closes with only the two of us within its four walls.

"Did someone steal your voice?" he asks.

"Are we both on the thirty-fourth floor?" I blurt, looking up just long enough to see his bewildered expression. *I'll stick to memorizing every inch of the limestone floors.*

"Of course" he answers, matter of fact.

Shit. For the rest of the ride up, I fidget with the strap on my purse. I hate being pushed into uncomfortable situations.

I concentrate on the climbing floor number lit above the door. The elevator moves faster than normal—too fast—then it jerks, coming to a stop with a bright thirty-four blinking up high.

"Are you going to get out?" I'm standing like a roadblock in the center of the elevator, caging Pierce and our bags in the corner.

One foot in front of the other, Lila.

"It's room 3410," he announces from behind me.

I look up to make sure I'm going in the right direction then get lost in my own inner madness again. It's a crazy place where I seem to spend a lot of my time lately.

3406

Shit.

3408

Double shit.

"Here we are," he says. I stand like a woman of stone as he sets the luggage down and grabs a key card from his pocket. The door opens to a light, airy room, accented by oversized windows and beige and white fabrics. It has a spacious living area on one side and a king bed on the other. My panic hits a high . . . *there's only one bed.*

"Will this room do?" Pierce asks, opening the curtain a little wider.

I swallow. I'm not good at this—the games and the lies. Crossing my arms over my chest, I carry my heavy feet to stand in front of the window that looks over the hustle and bustle of the city. "No," I finally answer, my voice just above a whisper.

I sense his presence behind me. His warmth. His strong masculine scent. And when I'm about to turn and face him, his fingers curve around my upper arms then slowly slide down. "Are you cold?"

I shake my head, but his hands stay on me, continuing to cover the chill that doesn't exist.

"Are you hungry?"

"No."

"Do you want me to order you a bottle of red wine?"

Tempting, but I shake my head again. Being alone with a guy like Pierce with alcohol flowing through my veins would have consequences—especially with one bed. "I think I'm just tired."

He squeezes my arms one last time then releases me. "I'll leave you alone to get some rest. Meet me at the hotel steakhouse at eight. Reservation is under my name."

I spin around, confused. "Umm . . . where are you going?"

He looks at me with narrowed eyes. "To my room."

"To your room?"

"Yes, to my room. I'm in 3411."

"So you're not sleeping here?"

He grins wide, showing his perfect white teeth. "Not unless you want me to."

"I think I'll be okay."

He shrugs.

My eyes fixate on him as he makes his way across the room, picking up his suitcase along the way. "Oh, before I forget, do you have something to wear tonight? It's black tie."

"I got it covered."

Before exiting the room, he winks. "I'm sure you do."

As soon as the door clicks, I fall back onto the pillowtop bed, every muscle in my body relaxing.

PACKING THE COCKTAIL DRESS was a good call, I think to myself as I slowly walk into the eloquent dining room. It's the type of place where even the wait staff looks ready to attend a fancy event, dressed in black linen.

"Are you waiting for someone?" a man with a slight British accent asks. I'm guessing he works here by the way he's dressed.

"I'm dining with Pierce Stanley. I'll wait here for him if that's okay."

He smiles warmly. "Actually, he's waiting for you. Follow me."

My eyes wander the room looking for Pierce as I follow behind the host. I don't see him. When we reach the far corner, the reason is obvious—he's tucked away in a small booth surrounded by three half walls. He picks up his glass of whiskey from the table, but the second he lays eyes on me he sets it back down. The power of his stare forces me to shift in my heels. Sometimes, he's too much.

His lips part as he stands to greet me. "You're stunning," he says, lifting my arms to get a better look. I blush, looking down at my dress. It's black, form fitting, and hemmed right above my knees with long sleeves and a deep V-neck. I'd bought it to wear to the rehearsal dinner Derek and I never had.

"Thank you," I reply quietly. He doesn't look bad himself, dressed in a tux similar to what he wore to the benefit. I'd bet he wears a tux more in one week than most men do in their lifetime.

He pulls a chair out for me. "I hope you're hungry. I went ahead and ordered a couple appetizers."

"I'm starving." I sit in the chair he offered, unfolding my white napkin onto my lap. His fingers trail along my neck on his way back to his seat, giving me goose bumps.

"Can I offer you some wine?" Looking up, I see the host is still standing there watching our exchange.

I blush, tucking a strand of hair behind my ear. "Yes, red please."

"I'd like the lady to try a glass of your best," Pierce instructs.

The host nods, disappearing around the corner, leaving Pierce nowhere to look but me. I pick up the small water glass, sipping it only to avoid conversation. It won't last forever. All the flirtatious words, all the little touches throughout the day lead to this.

"Your water glass is empty."

I choke on the little bit I still hold in my mouth, my eyes watering.

"Do you like filet?" he asks out of the blue.

"What's that?"

The corners of his mouth turn up. "Filet mignon, or in English, a tender, lean steak."

"Oh yeah, sorry. I guess I'm a little out of it tonight."

The waiter comes to fill my wine glass, and Pierce places our order, kindly asking the waiter to leave us until our dinner is done unless a wine glass needs to be filled.

"I'm introducing a rule for the night," Pierce announces as soon as the waiter is out of earshot.

"What's that?"

"We're not to talk about work."

"Okay, what do you want to talk about? We covered quite a bit the other night," I answer, bringing my wine glass to my lips. It's rich and delicious, one taste leading to another.

"Tell me about where you grew up."

Just thinking about it makes me happy. I grew up with something as close to a sitcom family as you can get. "My dad farmed, and my mom worked part-time as a receptionist in the doctor's office. After they had me, they found out they couldn't have any more children, so I was it, but it all worked out. I ended up a spoiled child."

"You don't seem spoiled at all."

I shrug, taking yet another sip of wine. "Emotionally spoiled, I guess. We didn't have a lot, but I felt like I had everything."

He stares at me, lips parting slightly. "That's one thing money can't buy."

"What's that?"

"Love," he says simply.

That's one thing I've never thought much about. We assume that money equals happiness and that it allows a person to have everything they want, but it means nothing in the grand scheme of things.

I wet my lips, picking my next words carefully. "What about you? How was your childhood?"

He sits back in his chair, eyeing me warily. "Lonely."

"Were you an only child?"

"I have one sister. My parents decided they needed to fail more than one child."

My mind wanders in so many different directions. Was he abused? Did they abandon him? All of it makes my heart ache.

"My dad was a successful district attorney who eventually got a seat on the judge's bench. I'm sure he was a nice guy at some point, helping so many people, but he was always too busy to spend time with us. I remember the things he bought, but nothing more." His voice shows a vulnerability I'm not used to.

"And your mom?"

He sighs, running his hands over his face. "She didn't work, but being the wife of a successful lawyer meant keeping up appearances. She was more concerned about how we looked and what activities we participated in than anything else. But don't feel totally sorry for me, I had a very nice nanny."

"I'm sorry."

"For what? You didn't raise me."

I hesitantly reach my hand across the table, covering his. His eyes go to where our bodies are connected then back to mine. "That doesn't mean I'm not sorry."

The waiter chooses that moment to reappear, setting our sizzling steaks in front of us as well as a dish of grilled asparagus and roasted baby potatoes. "Anything else I can get you?"

I look to Pierce to answer, but he's staring at me the same way he was a few seconds ago. "More wine, please," I answer for him.

Our conversation turns to our high school and college days while we devour our dinner. I even let him in on more details of my life with Derek, how hard I fell, and how it all fell apart. Pierce alludes to a couple serious relationships, but nothing that went too far.

I've had him on this pedestal because of everything he's accomplished at a relatively young age. Since the other night, I've seen a new side to him—one that makes being around him easier. He has way more than I do, but inside, where it counts, he's just another guy. A nice, sophisticated guy who happens to be really easy to talk to.

"Wine?" Pierce asks, pointing to my empty glass. My thoughts and opinions are already swimming in a sea of alcohol. It's too good. "Come on," he urges, "I bought a whole bottle, and there's just a little left."

"You don't have to ask me twice." Every glass has been going down easier than the last.

The waiter clears everything from the table. "Can I interest you in some dessert?"

I'm about to say yes, but Pierce interrupts. "No, thank you."

I want to argue, but the look on Pierce's face warns me not to. I wait until the waiter walks away with Pierce's credit card to bring it up. "I really wanted chocolate." I sound like a typical woman, but I don't care. Plus, I've had wine, and nothing goes better with wine than chocolate.

"You'll get your chocolate."

When we walk out of the restaurant his hand takes its usual position on my back. "There's somewhere I want to take you. Do you want to grab your coat?"

"Are we walking?" If we are, I'm in trouble. The alcohol makes it almost impossible to feel my legs. I could have gone without the fourth glass.

"The car is out front."

Thoughtful.

Smart.

Charming.

He helps me safely into the car and climbs in the other side. I shiver against the cool leather seats, missing the warmth of the restaurant and red wine.

"Come here," he instructs, holding out his arm.

Without hesitation, I scoot over to him, letting his arm fall over my shoulders. He tucks me against his body. Blame it on the alcohol or whatever, but it feels nice. "I'd offer you my jacket, but I like this better."

"Me too."

It's completely dark outside, but the Christmas and city lights give it a layer of romance. I hate myself for even thinking this way, but this is one of the most perfect moments I've ever experienced. The company. The setting. The peacefulness.

"We're here." Pierce nudges me. If I thought tonight couldn't get any better, it just did. "You said you wanted chocolate."

We're parked right outside of Serendipity. Thoughtful, definitely thoughtful. "I can't believe you did this."

He shrugs like it's nothing, but it means everything to me. Our eyes lock under the faint streetlight. I can't remember the last time anyone did this for me—taking a simple comment and using it to surprise me. He's unlike anyone I've ever met, in the best possible way.

An invisible string pulls me to him until my lips brush against his. Light as a feather. Tender. I pull back, but he grips my chin between his fingers, holding me close to him. He covers my mouth with his, working his fingers back into my hair. My body has the warmth it didn't have a few minutes ago, but it isn't the fireworks I felt with Blake. It's a slow simmer . . . it's just different.

He puts a period at the end of the kiss by pressing his lips to mine three times over. As he pulls back, he smiles, running his thumb over my swollen lower lip. "Ready for some frozen hot chocolate?"

"Yes," I answer. That little voice that keeps whispering doubts in my ear is back, but I quiet it. I'm living every woman's dream in New York City; there's nothing to be confused about.

I MOAN FOR THE HUNDREDTH TIME, scooping every last bit from the bottom of my crystal dish. The hot chocolate is as delectable as I thought it would be.

"I don't think I've ever heard a woman moan quite like that, and certainly not over chocolate," Pierce teases, swiping his thumb along the corner of my mouth. "You had some whipped cream there."

"You should try some. It's by far the most delicious thing I've ever put in my mouth."

A wicked grin spreads across his face. "That's unfortunate."

We've been playing the flirtation game since we sat down. I bait. He catches. I really took off when I found out he doesn't like chocolate. Who doesn't like chocolate?

Licking the whipped cream from my upper lip, I find his attention on my mouth. The movement wasn't intentional, but the look in his eyes tells me he believes it was. "Do we need to stop somewhere to get you dessert?" I ask.

He leans in closer. "I had my dessert . . . in the car."

My cheeks heat, probably turning as red as the maraschino cherry on my frozen hot chocolate. "It's a good thing you're such a cheap date," I shoot back.

"The best things in life don't cost a thing."

There's been a weird buzz between us since the kiss in the car. I'm waiting for him to bring it up, but the only reminder I get is in his eyes—the constant glimmer. There's a new look of adoration within them, more intimate.

And while the frozen treat gives me a reprieve from conversing, I let my crazy mind roam free again. Since I moved to Chicago, actually since things ended with Derek, I don't have a clear picture of who I am anymore. Maybe I really did leave the old me behind and come into a new life completely. I had only given away a few kisses before meeting the guy I spent the last seven years with. The guy I gave my heart, soul, and remaining firsts to. Now, I feel like I'm just handing my affections away, or maybe I'm just tasting a little bit of everything while I decide what it is I really want.

The waitress sets the check on the table, shaking me from my thoughts. I reach for it, but Pierce grabs it before I get a chance, his warm fingers brushing mine. "My treat."

"You didn't even eat."

He winks. "But I did."

He pays, and we make our way to the door. This time, as we exit the building, he wraps his jacket around my shoulders, running his hands over the wool sleeves. "You have goose bumps."

"December isn't the best month to be indulging in frozen hot chocolate."

"You have a point there."

Our car pulls up to the curb, and Pierce quickly opens the door for me to climb in. He follows close behind, forcing me to scoot to the other side. "Four Seasons," he instructs the driver.

The second the car starts down the road, I know this trip will be different than the others. No endless daydreaming. No peaceful quietness. Pierce's hand comes up, gently caressing my cheeks, eyes searing into mine under the streetlights that flood through the window.

"It's been a long time since I felt this comfortable around a woman," he remarks, tucking a strand of hair behind my ear.

"I have a hard time believing that. You make being with you so easy." It's true. Since the initial butterflies wore off tonight, I've had a good time. He takes my mind off things it shouldn't be dwelling on.

He closes the remaining space between us. "Can I kiss you again?"

If he'd asked me the first time, I would've had to think about it more. Now, the pendulum swings but only for a second. The line has been crossed—any anti-fraternization policy that Stanley Development defied.

"You don't have to ask," I answer, staring at his lips. He kisses me—one long, lingering kiss that would make the most ordinary of places feel romantic. His lips are warm against mine. The more he takes, the more I want to give . . . the more I want to want him.

As he pulls away, he looks down at me with hooded eyes. I crave more . . . so much more. I want to take what he offers, forget about all of my other missteps. Nuzzling the crook of his neck, I inhale the sexy scent that's tormented me all night. I could get lost in it, sleeping for hours just like this.

He wraps one arm around my shoulders, pulling me tightly against his body. His other hand grips my knee, and ever so subtly slips between my thighs. My muscles go rigid at first, but then I relax into him.

His hand slides higher, and on instinct, I look into the rearview mirror. The driver is only feet away. He probably sees everything. Hears every sound we make.

"He can't see this," Pierce whispers above my ear.

I tense, trying to find it within myself to let him in, to let adrenaline control me for once. His long fingers curl between my thighs, keeping them from traveling any higher. "Do you want me to stop?"

Every decision has a consequence, big or small. Kissing him earlier was one thing, but this is different.

The answer becomes clear when I look up, catching the lust in his eyes. Desire must be contagious because I hunger for him, for his lips, his hands.

"Don't stop," I answer. I close my eyes as his hand slips up higher, his fingers a light brush against my skin.

And as he kisses me, he works his way up to the edge of my panties. His lips are more urgent, pressing harder, almost punishing. "Do you know how long I've wanted to do this?"

I moan into his mouth, tugging his hair between my fingers.

He runs his fingers against the tingling spot between my legs. I gasp, ready for whatever he wants to give. "You're going to undo me if you keep making sounds like that."

I part my lips to apologize, but he uses the opportunity to press his tongue into my mouth. His chest touches mine, caging me against the seat. I'm completely under his spell, captivated by every stroke of my skin. He lowers my defenses. And, he makes me forget . . . that's the best part. When I'm with him, I'm just . . . with him.

Our tongues caress.

Our bodies collide.

The spark is there, igniting my hands on him, his on me.

The car comes to a stop. Pierce groans, reluctantly breaking away. I miss his warmth. "We're here," the driver announces.

I rub my fingertip around my mouth, checking my lipstick. Pierce helps the cause, smoothing down my skirt and tucking a strand of hair behind my ear.

"Where's the traffic when you need it?" he grumbles under his breath.

The driver startles us by opening the door. Pierce begrudgingly he climbs out, holding his hand out to me. The cool air feels good against my flushed skin as I step onto the sidewalk, but the warm tingle between my legs doesn't go unnoticed. The thought of asking to take a few more laps around the block crosses my mind. That thought rings louder when I notice the impressive bulge that tugs at his zipper. I imagine what he'd be like in bed—a true gentleman with immeasurable confidence. I imagine his lips on every inch of my body . . . the pleasure he'd give me.

Those thoughts melt away as he tucks me under his arm, quickly ushering us through the lobby to the elevators. We wait quietly for the doors to open, his arm never leaving me.

When it finally dings, we step inside, alone again. His lips descend on mine—hungry, wanting. My back is pushed against the wall, his hips grinding against mine. I wish this were the movies . . . that the elevator would suddenly stop so we could finish what we started.

We reach our floor far too soon. Our hands stop their exploration when the door opens, but our bodies remain glued together, neither of us wanting to make the first move out of the elevator.

"Come to my room," he pants, eyes reading mine.

I hesitate, my chest heaving against his. He leans in, kissing me again. It's a plea—one I'm having a hard time denying with his warm body against mine. Blake's needing eyes flash through my mind like a burst of lightning, but I let the vision fade. Pierce is here, not pushing me away. No games. He even cared enough to take me out, which is something Blake never did.

I wrap my arms around his neck, washing away any doubts. He practically carries me to his door, only letting go to take out his key card.

He sets me down, carefully slipping the jacket from my shoulders. The slow caress of his fingers against my skin makes the simple move seductive. I'm ready to feel his hands on me . . . everywhere.

He leaves me standing alone while he loosens his tie from around his neck and tosses it on the dresser. His eyes roam over my body as he kicks off his shoes. His stare holds me, and even though I'm fully clothed, I feel naked. To escape it, I build a wall, crossing my arms over my chest.

"Arms down," he commands.

I shift on my feet, searching for the confidence I'm not sure I've ever had. Especially with his dark, piercing eyes on me.

He strides toward me. I take it as a warning, letting my arms fall to my side.

Maybe I'm here for all the wrong reasons—too much wine, a heightened need to feel wanted. I couldn't have picked a better man to rebound with. Not that I can really call it that; I'm rebounding from my rebound. I don't know a whole lot about Pierce, but I trust him not to hurt me, not to use me for his own selfish needs and discard me like I'm nothing. I don't want to feel that way again.

I want what every woman wants . . . to feel wanted.

Pierce slides his fingers along my collarbone then between my covered breasts. He moves slowly, calculating my reaction to every touch. He's an expert at everything he does.

"Are you sure? Because if you're not, I need to know now," he whispers against my ear. I had a lot to drink, but I'm present in the moment. I want him, to know what he can do to me.

I answer without words, running my hand along his hard length. He groans, sliding his hands around my back to work my zipper down. The dress slips with his fingers, leaving me standing in nothing but green satin bra and panties.

He steps back to get a better look. "You're stunning. Absolutely stunning."

I watch him under the moonlight that illuminates the room. It's sexually exhilarating—the way his eyes stay on mine. The way they communicate his desire and desperation.

"Turn around," he instructs as he unfastens the buttons on his dress shirt.

I want to question him, but I know better. Instead, I turn so my back is to him, oblivious to what's going on behind me.

"Jesus," he growls. I hear shuffling behind me but don't chance a look. The anticipation leaves me wet. Maybe this is part of his game—to cause an ache so intense I want to beg for him.

I hear his footsteps on the marble floors. I inhale a sharp breath when his hands cover my hips, sliding under the curve of my ass. On instinct, my head falls back against his shoulder, allowing me to sink into him. To give him the control I know he craves.

He kisses the side of my neck while his hands splay against my stomach. "Lila," he murmurs against my skin. "Do you know all the things I want to do to you?"

His fingers slip into the front of my panties. I moan, rocking my head back. His actual touch is so much better than the anticipation.

"Tell me what you want. Tell me where you need me," he demands, teasing me by sliding his fingers a little lower.

"Touch me," I beg, wiggling against his palm.

"I think I'm already doing that. You're going to have to be a little more specific."

He's so in control, and I'm so out of it. I grip his wrist, placing his hand lower, exactly where I need it. He takes the hint, curling his finger into me. "Feel what I do to you."

I whimper, wanting more. Fast, slow . . . I don't care. He uses his body pressed against mine to move us forward to his bed. It's the first time I panic, or maybe the wine is starting to wear off. When my knees touch the bed, the thoughts of the two other men I've been with flood my mind. It shouldn't be this hard, but I just got over one, and then Blake . . . I still think about him all the time.

Closing my eyes, I push all those thoughts away, bringing myself back to the moment. Pierce isn't Derek, and he's definitely not Blake. I press my lips together to keep myself from stopping him.

He craves me.

If I let him have what he wants, maybe he'll make me crave him too.

Before I get a chance to crawl on top of the bed, he unclasps my bra, letting it fall to the floor. His hands come around, rolling my nipples between his fingertips. I'm wound tightly, the pressure between my legs increasing.

"I have rules," he says, still teasing my sensitive skin. "I don't come until you come. Your eyes stay on me while I fuck you. And . . . you sleep naked in my bed when we're done. That is, if we ever finish."

I swallow, gripping the high thread count sheets between my fingers. "I only have one rule."

His fingers still. "What's that?"

"Don't hurt me," I whisper.

His hands slide down the curve of my back then curl around my hips. "I couldn't," he answers, pressing his lips to the center of my spine. His voice is smooth and comforting. I wish I could wrap my arms around it and hold it tight.

Without warning, he flips me on my back. He slowly stands back up, holding me to him with his eyes. I watch as his shirt falls to the floor first followed by his suit pants. My gaze falls to his muscular chest before going further to his defined, narrow abs.

"Are you staring?"

"Maybe," I answer, squirming under the weight of his eyes.

He ups his game, slipping his thumbs into the waistband of his boxer briefs and slowly inching them down his thighs. He's magnificent . . . there's no other way to put it. Watching him is making my stomach twist into knots. I wonder how many women he's had before me, and how I even compare.

"I see you thinking. Stop thinking." He kneels in front of me, hooking his fingers in the side of my panties to slide them off.

This is it.

This is that make-me or break-me moment.

He comes back up the length of my body, peppering my stomach and breasts with soft kisses. "Just feel," he says against my lips before moving back down. He laps at my breasts then sucks my nipples. I curve into him, threading his hair between my fingers. The light stubble that covers his jaw line feels amazing against my skin.

He moves down, brushing his lips over my stomach. I know where he's going, and I want it . . . I want him. He slips down out of my reach, kissing between my thighs. I whimper, buckling under him. I literally ache for more.

His mouth works me perfectly, sucking, teasing with his tongue. The build-up from everything else he's done only allows me seconds before the familiar tingle has me breathing faster, gripping the sheets tightly. Lapping. Sucking. He's pushing me up Mt. Everest. I wrap my legs around him, throwing my head back as the orgasm rips through my body.

"Oh God!" I scream as the last current flows through me.

My body is pliant. He traces his tongue up my stomach between my breasts, and when he kisses me, I remember why.

"I love hearing you scream." He nibbles on my neck, brushing his palms over my nipples.

He sits up, staring down at me. "Eyes on me." I watch as he picks up a condom from the side of the bed, carefully rolling it on his hard length.

Something inside me shifts. I realize that for the last few minutes, it wasn't Pierce between my legs. It wasn't Pierce who'd carved his way into my subconscious. Old wounds haven't healed enough to allow new ones.

Tears fill my eyes. What have I done? What am I doing? This girl is lost somewhere in a dark, unforgiving hole . . . and she just wants out.

I feel him at my entrance, and I panic, bracing my hands against his chest. "Stop! Please, stop!" I yell.

He's paralyzed, looking down at me with concerned eyes. "Am I hurting you?" he asks, his voice trailing off.

"Yes," I say honestly.

He flinches.

"It's not what you think." I pause, squeezing my eyes shut to hide from the disappointment in his eyes. "I'm not ready. I thought I was, but I can't. I just can't."

He lifts off my body, withdrawing from me. The tears spill over. God, I hate this . . . all of it. Why couldn't I have fallen for Pierce first? What if he would have asked to see me again when we got off the plane? What if I would have called him sooner? Life is a bunch of stupid what ifs.

"Does this have to do with him?" Pierce asks, standing with his back to me.

I could lie. Tell a figment of the truth, but I'm already lying naked in his bed. There's no point in hiding.

"Yes."

THIS HAS TO BE THE WORST silence I've ever experienced. Like a coward, I don't want to wait to see his reaction. I carefully scoot to the edge of the bed until my feet hit the cold, hard floor. The room is dark, and my clothes are scattered everywhere. I pick up my bra and panties near the foot of the bed and put them on as fast as I can with trembling fingers.

My dress is in a heap on the floor where Pierce slid it off me. It was so hard to squeeze into in the first place; there won't be anything quick about putting it back on.

"Here," Pierce says, tossing me his dress shirt. I eye it curiously, not sure what he expects. "You're just across the hall. I'm sure you can make it without anyone seeing you."

I roll the soft cotton between my fingers, hating him for being so casual and mature about this.

I quietly watch him pull his pants back on, not bothering with his belt. I want him to yell, tell me I'm ridiculous for letting myself fall for Blake. He's thinking it. He has to be thinking it.

Nervously, I slip my arms in and then fumble with the buttons. The first tear escapes, rolling down my cheek. I don't want to be this woman I've become, and I can't rely on a man to find me.

"Will you let me help you?" I hadn't even noticed Pierce standing in front of me. I let my hands fall away from the buttons. *God, why won't he just yell at me and get it over with.* I need it to erase some of my guilt.

He takes my non-answer as acceptance, buttoning the shirt to cover my exposed body. His fingers brush my skin a couple times, a painful reminder of everything that just happened. I should want a man like Pierce Stanley, and I'm angry with myself because I don't. Not in the way he wants me.

When the shirt is perfectly in place, he cups my face in his hands, forcing my eyes to his. "I need you to know that you're making a mistake. When you finally come to realize that, I hope it's not too late."

I shut my eyes tightly. It's my only escape. "Some choices we don't get to make."

"Then how am I supposed to win?" he asks, his warm breath hitting my cheek.

Warm tears fall down each cheek. "I don't know if you can."

I open my eyes to find him looking down at me. In another time, Pierce could have made me happy. There's no doubting that.

He rubs his thumb across my lower lip. My chest tightens. I hate what I'm doing to him . . . I hate feeling like I lead him on. "Promise me something, Lila."

"Anything."

"Don't become someone you aren't just to be with him."

I nod against his touch, but I know it's too late. Blake's already turned me into someone I don't like. Pierce deserves better than that. "Goodnight, Pierce."

"Goodnight." He kisses my forehead before letting me go.

I head straight for the door, picking up my purse along the way. I don't want to look back, but I do anyway. He hasn't moved from where I left him, standing with his hands tucked in his pockets. "Thank you for tonight." I attempt to smile, but I'm sure I look ridiculous with tears falling at the same time.

Without another word, I open the door, and make my way across the hall. When I'm finally shut inside my room, I crumble to the floor. For what could have been minutes, or maybe hours, I fall back to the heartbroken woman I was months ago. This time, I have no one to blame but myself.

Blake warned me. I didn't listen.

Pierce offered to catch me, but I'd already fallen.

The worst thing to wake up with is guilt. My swollen, tired eyes remind me of everything that happened last night. Dinner. The kiss. Dessert. Everything after. It all plays over and over again until I don't even recognize myself.

Rolling to look at my clock, I realize I only have forty-five minutes until Pierce and I have to meet with Wade.

I tie my hair up and turn on the shower as hot as I'm able to handle, letting the steam fill the room as I unbutton Pierce's shirt. I didn't have the strength to take it off last night after my meltdown. Besides, it still carries that scent that always seems to comfort me, which only compounds my guilt. In a way, I used him. I took from him when I had nothing to offer in return.

Closing my eyes, I let the stream of water beat down on my face. I remember the expression on Pierce's face when I told him to stop. If I let myself, I can still feel his skin on mine, and it disgusts me, because when he was with me, I was with Blake.

Not able to take anymore, I quickly dress, not too concerned about how I look. When you feel like a rainstorm just pounded your heart, it's hard to look like anything less than that happened on the outside.

I untie my hair, pinning it into a more professional bun and do my best to cover the circles under my eyes.

I grab my luggage and coat, ready to make the journey to the lobby. When I pull the door open, Pierce is standing against the wall. My heart skips a beat or two. He's well dressed, as always, in a gray suit with a lavender button-up underneath. I shouldn't stare, but I can't look away. If we could go back a month—before Blake—Pierce would be a force I couldn't resist. I loathe myself for having to distance myself from him because I'm glued to the one person I should have stayed far away from.

"Do you need help with your things?" he asks, pushing off the wall toward me.

"I'm okay, but thank you."

He rubs the back of his neck, avoiding my stare. "How did you sleep?"

"Okay." I tuck a strand of invisible hair behind my ear, needing the distraction.

He nods toward the elevator. "We should get going. The quicker we get there, the quicker we can leave."

He starts walking. I follow.

He takes one corner of the elevator. I take the other.

And when I climb in the car, I stick as close to my door as I can, knowing the ride won't be anything like last night.

The silence is lonely, but loneliness is welcome.

I've never thought there could be a positive side effect of amnesia, but this one time, I wish I could choose it. There are so many things I'd just rather forget.

I wish Pierce and I could both forget, to go back to what we were before.

I dared to cross that line. Now, there's no way to get back over.

Pierce finally breaks the silence as the car parks in front of Wade's office building. "The jet is ready to leave as soon as we're done here."

I nod, wondering if he had something else planned originally . . . before the mess I made last night.

He holds the door open for me, but he doesn't place his hand on my back like usual. Anger may not be Pierce's thing, but the temperature between us is cold. He walks next to me without a word. It's almost worse this way, wondering what he's feeling instead of having him say it.

"Pierce Stanley for Wade Adams," he announces to the receptionist before it even dawns on me that we stopped in front of her desk.

"You can go on up to the twenty-fourth floor. His assistant will show you to the conference room."

My phone vibrates as the elevator closes, but I don't move to retrieve it from my purse. It vibrates again a few seconds later.

"You going to check that?" Pierce asks, staring up at the elevator ceiling.

I pull it out, sliding my thumb over the screen. I have a slew of missed texts, but the one that catches my eye first is from Blake.

Blake: I might not be here when you get back. Going out of town for a few days.

I think about ignoring him but reconsider.

Lila: When will you be back?

When there's not an instant reply, I start typing another message. It shouldn't matter to me. We're unfixable. Too much has been done and said that can't be forgotten.

The elevator dings, interrupting my thoughts.

"Ready?" Pierce asks, narrowing his eyes on my phone.

I shove it back in my purse. "Sorry."

This will be the second time in two days I've been in this suite, and it holds bad memories of the testosterone battle I witnessed yesterday between Pierce and Wade. I'm not expecting fair play today either.

Wade's Barbie-like assistant appears to greet us. "Mr. Stanley. Ms. Fields, please follow me this way."

We end up in the same conference room as yesterday, the one with the line of windows overlooking Times Square. Instead of taking a seat at the expansive marble table, I walk toward the picturesque view, placing a finger on the cool glass. I need a break from Pierce, from seeing him and hearing the smooth sound of his voice. Even more than that, I need a reprieve from myself, because, at the end of the day, it's not Blake or Pierce who got me here . . . it's me.

Professionals flood the sidewalks below. Posters and billboards line the street. It gives me something to focus on, a place for my thoughts to wander. It works until I see a man—who has the same hair color as Blake—walking. He creeps into my thoughts so easily. A part of me wishes he only existed there . . . that I could mold him into what I need him to be.

I'd keep his edge. The sides of him that people warned me about are the ones that make me feel the most alive. All I'm asking is for him to let me in, to give me a chance to see if everything I feel inside is valid, or if it's a fucked up mirage I've caught myself in.

"Good morning." I startle, glancing over my shoulder to see Wade entering the room. I already want to slap the smug look off his face.

"Sorry. Just admiring the city," I say. Out of the corner of my eye, I catch him watching me as I walk to my seat. The guy gives me the creeps, but I put up with him for Pierce. That's what I get paid to do after all.

Pierce hasn't said a word since we walked in here. He sits at the end of the table like a king witnessing our exchange. He's probably waiting for Wade to eat me up and spit me out after what I did to him. "Did you make a decision?" Pierce asks.

Wade clears his throat, leaning back in his leather chair. "I did."

"And?"

"The project is yours with forty percent ownership under two conditions."

Pierce lifts a brow but says nothing. I feel like a spectator at a powerful ping pong match.

Wade continues, "She stays on the project." He points his pen in my direction. "This hotel is going to be the future of New York City hotels, and it needs her fresh eye."

Both sets of eyes are on me, but it's not my decision to make. Pierce pays me, and I don't think I'm his favorite person at the moment. Then there's the whole apprenticeship—nothing more permanent has been promised.

After a long pause, Pierce finally says, "She's on the project. What else?"

Wade smiles. It has an evil undertone. "I want Blake Stone to work on all of the murals and art pieces. His style will blend in perfectly with what Lila presented yesterday."

My breath catches, and my gaze whips to Pierce. The muscles in his jaw pulse, his teeth bared. "No fucking deal," he barks across the table.

"Are you sure about that?" Wade asks, smugness washing over his face again, "There's a lot of money in it for you."

"I don't need your fucking money! We're done here." Pierce stands from the table, motioning me to join him. I comply, too afraid of his current emotional state not to; I've never seen him like this.

"Hey, Lila!" Wade shouts behind us. On instinct, I glance back over my shoulder. "If you're fucking him, be careful. He has a penchant for using things once and then letting them go, especially things that aren't his to begin with."

Pierce releases me, striding across the room to where Wade sits, relaxed in his leather chair. A gap between two speeding trains is closing before my eyes, but I can't look away. Pierce grips Wade's shirt, pulling him up a couple inches. "Who the hell do you think you are?"

"You know exactly who I am, Stanley. You took something from me, and I don't think you've paid me back yet. Now, I'm just going to take it."

Pierce swings his arm back but hesitates. "You're not worth it." Just as quickly as he went to Wade, he walks away. "Let's go," he says as he passes me.

He moves quickly toward the elevator as I struggle to keep up in my heels. We step inside, him on one side, me on the other. Anger radiates off every tense inch of his body.

"What was that all about?" I ask, my voice low.

"This isn't the time, Lila."

I open my mouth but quickly shut it again. He's right.

When the elevator reaches the first floor, Pierce surprises me, grabbing my hand in his. Behind almost sleeping with Pierce and frozen hot chocolate, elevator rides are going to be the most memorable part of New York City. It's where everything starts, or ends, or where my thoughts get me all worked up.

Before I know it, we're in the car, all the space in the world between us. It's strange going from lovers one night to distant acquaintances the next.

"So, you want to know what that was all about?" he asks, rubbing his hand along his jaw.

I nod. Obviously I do. Who wouldn't? "If you want to talk about it," I answer.

He laughs sadistically. "I feel like I owe you some explanation, so here it is . . . a couple years ago, I slept with his girlfriend once after a night of having too much to drink." He continues, "I didn't know who she was at the time and had no intention of ever seeing her again. He can't seem to let it go."

"Were you friends before?"

255

He shakes his head. "No, business partners in some aspects."

"Maybe you shouldn't work with him anymore."

"I wouldn't, but he's a smart asshole. We can either work together or be enemies. I guess the latter is where we're heading."

I fidget with the buttons on my jacket, not sure what to say. I pull my phone out and check for messages. There's one from Blake.

Blake: I don't know.

"Who's that?"

I tear my eyes from the screen, looking into Pierce's. "No one."

"I hate being lied to, Lila."

"I hate when people keep things from me," I bite back. Frustration boils to the surface. There can't be two sets of rules between us.

"And what exactly am I keeping from you?"

"Tell me what happened between you and Blake. Why do you hate each other so much?"

He stares at me long and hard, reading me as if I have some complex definition. "Have you asked him about Alyssa?"

Shaking my head, I glance out the window and watch New York City go by. I haven't asked him because I'm scared. If it weren't a big deal, Pierce would just tell me.

"Ask him. Tell me what he says, and I'll fill in the blanks."

"I don't get why you can't just tell me," I respond. If we weren't stuck in this car right now, I'd probably scream.

He shrugs. "There's no way I can explain it and come out sounding like a nice guy, but if you want a glimpse into the past, let's just say, when two men love a woman and both lose her, it turns into one fucked up mess."

I contemplate his words—roll them around. In the end, I'm just left wondering if I should just walk away from both men. If the baggage they carry is more than I can take on my back. And even more than that, I wonder if I can ever compete with Alyssa . . . whoever she is.

BY THE TIME THE CAR PULLS up in front of my apartment building, the sky is completely black. I'm happy to be home—ready to climb into my warm bed and sleep the night away, but there's still a Pierce hurdle I have to jump: goodbyes.

"Let me walk you to your door," he says.

I don't argue. I don't have the energy. Instead, I stand quietly on the sidewalk and watch as Pierce takes my bag from the driver. The air is frigid, so much so it seeps through my jacket, peppering my skin with goose bumps.

"What did you think of New York?" Pierce asks as we make our way up the sidewalk.

"The hot chocolate was good."

He opens the door, allowing me to step inside first. "Hmm, just the hot chocolate? You're low maintenance, Ms. Fields."

We make our way up the flights of stairs, and all I can think about is how I'm going to handle things when we get to my door. I need to smooth things over with Pierce. I've enjoyed the little bit of time I've spent at Stanley Development, and I want to be able to go into work without this giant cloud hanging over my head. Even if I know it won't dissipate completely.

Then there's Blake. I don't know if he's still going to be here when I open the door. Part of me hopes yes, the other no. It makes me nervous as hell. To top it off, I need to keep the two of them apart. When they're together, it's like watching a lit match hit gasoline, and I'm the one who seems to get burned.

"Pierce."

"Yeah?"

"I know we've already talked about this, but I want to make sure that what happened last night isn't going to affect our work relationship." I stop walking, closing my eyes to clear my head. "I don't want it to ruin what could be a really great friendship between us."

I don't want to look up, but I don't have a choice when he uses his finger under my chin to lift my eyes to his. "Nothing has changed for you at Stanley."

I nod, breathing out.

He continues, "And as far as friendship goes . . . if that's what you want, that's what I'll give you, but I'll always want more."

"I can't give you that. Not now," I say, shaking my head.

His thumb brushes my lips. "I know, but I'm not going to be able to watch you with him either. You deserve better."

"And so do you," I whisper. Pierce has so much to offer. If he found the right woman, he could show her the world and give it to her too.

He kisses me gently on the forehead before letting me go. "Love isn't defined by what you deserve. It's about finding that one person you know you can't live without and never letting them go."

He's right, in a way. I've known lots of great guys who I classified as a woman's dream—successful, kind, good-looking—but it didn't equate to me falling at their feet.

"Get some sleep, Pierce," I say, picking up my suitcase. "I'll see you in the morning."

"Take tomorrow off. You deserve it." He winks, but the playfulness doesn't show in his eyes. He looks tired and mentally worn. Not the powerful man I'm used to.

"You don't have to do that. Besides, I don't do well when I have too much time on my hands."

"It's up to you, but the offer stands." He runs his long fingers through his hair. "I'm going to wait right here until you're inside. Have a nice night, Lila."

I step back, waving one last time before sticking my key in the lock. I feel him watching me but don't look back. My heart aches enough from staring into his forlorn eyes just seconds ago. He tempted me last night, and I led him on—made him believe there was a chance at something that just can't be. Not now.

After closing the door behind me, I notice the apartment is dark. Disappointed, I carry my luggage into my bedroom and rummage through my drawers for something more comfortable to wear. It's going to be another night where I sit alone and wonder what I actually escaped by moving to Chicago. Two cities. The same problems.

I curl up in the center of my bed, wrapping the thick comforter around me. Blake's absence shouldn't bother me, but it does. I need closure. I need to know if I ever meant anything to him, or if he was just a waste of a broken heart.

I grab my cell phone from the nightstand and dial Mallory's number, tapping my finger on my knee as I wait for her to answer. She's my voice of reason—the sanity to my insanity. And maybe, she'll have some answers.

"Hello," she answers, sounding a little out of breath. I wonder what the weather is like there, if she's out for a run.

"Hey, we haven't talked in a while so I thought I'd give you a call to see how things are going."

"That's funny because I was thinking about calling you after the gym. It's been crazy busy. I swear the tests here are ten times harder than they were at UCLA. I'm either in class or studying. How are you?"

"Not too bad. I quit Charlie's the other day. Doing that and working at Stanley was getting to be a little too much. I actually just got back from New York an hour ago."

There's nothing but silence on the other end . . . rare Mallory silence.

"Are you there?" I ask after seconds have passed.

"Sorry, did you say you're working at Stanley? As in Stanley Development?" She sounds a little panicked. I start to panic.

"Yes, they hired me for an apprenticeship."

Another long pause. "You're working with Pierce Stanley?"

"He hired me," I say simply.

"Shit."

Mallory never swears. Ever. "What?"

"Does Blake know?"

"Yes. What's the matter, Mallory?" There's so much I want to know about Pierce and Blake. Most importantly, why they hate each other so much.

"There's a history between them."

"I've already gathered that much, but why?"

She sighs. "There was so much heartbreak when it all happened . . . so much. You need to leave it alone."

Begging.

Pleading.

I have no idea what to do next.

Then I remember what Pierce said. "Does it have something to do with Alyssa?"

"Who told you?" she asks, practically choking on her words.

"Pierce."

She whimpers. "Oh God. Have you mentioned her to Blake? What did he say?"

The way she reacts makes me want to know even more. It's worse than waiting to see what's wrapped for me under the Christmas tree. "I haven't mentioned it to him. Should I?"

"No!" she yells. "You know how much you hate it when I bring up Derek? How much you hated when people asked you about him after you broke up? This is the same type of situation. Sometimes the past just needs to be left alone."

I close my eyes, allowing her reaction to soak in. Whatever happened was big. Big enough to leave deep, emotional wounds and cause an even deeper hatred between two men who I've become caught between. "I'm sorry. I didn't mean to upset you," I finally say.

"It's not your fault," she concedes, letting out a heavy breath. "I just wasn't expecting this. What are the chances you move to Chicago and run into the president of Blake's hate club within a few weeks."

"It's just the kind of luck I have lately."

"Can you do me a favor?" she asks.

"Anything."

"Keep them away from each other, and whatever you do, do not mention Alyssa . . . not to Blake," she pleads. Curiosity killed the cat. It's going to kill Lila Fields too.

"I'll do the best I can. I've learned that men aren't as controllable as we'd like them to be."

That brings a short laugh from her. "Truer words have never been spoken. What are you doing for Christmas?"

"I haven't decided yet. I want to go home, but I don't have the money to buy a plane ticket."

"I guess we're in the same boat. Worst-case scenario, we can have a Skype date."

"Sounds like a plan, and there's always *A Christmas Story*," I say.

That brings back memories of our first year at UCLA. We thought a California Christmas would beat out the snow and cold, but when the holiday finally rolled around, we were both depressed and homesick. We stayed in our pajamas and cozied on the couch, watching *A Christmas Story* over and over again. It was the best and worst Christmas I've ever had.

"It's a date."

"Hey, Mallory, can I ask you one more thing?"

"Shoot."

"Where does Blake go when he disappears? What does he do?"

"He paints. It's his therapy. Is he gone now?" she asks.

"Yeah. He said he was leaving for a few days." I run my fingers across the soft cotton comforter, remembering the time I spent in the studio.

"He'll be back. Look, I should get going. I'm covered in a layer of sweat."

I laugh. "You work out while I lay in bed and read a book. Some things never change. I'll talk to you later."

"Take care."

Dread. It's the only word that comes to mind as I walk into Stanley Development. It kept me up last night, rehearsing what I would say if Pierce wandered by my desk or called me to his office.

I'm not an actress, and this isn't the school play.

I hide away in my little cubicle, doing my best to keep my mind occupied. He said nothing had changed for me at Stanley, but I've changed. How I feel about him . . . how I think whenever he's around.

"Hey," Reece says, coming around the corner. "Are you going to lunch?"

I finish shading the edge of my mood board and look up. "I'm not hungry."

"You're not getting by with that excuse today. Come on." She picks up my purse and holds it out for me.

"Can we go to the little café down the street? I need some fresh air."

"Are you going to fill me in on New York?" she asks.

I cringe; I should've guessed this was coming. "As much as we can cover in one hour."

"Now I'm excited," she says, watching me pull on my coat. I lift my purse from her fingers and follow her to the elevator. As we step on, I glance around for Pierce. He's not there. And again, when we walk through the lobby, I search for him. I don't know what I'd say if he walked up. And within seconds, Reece would know something is up. She's too perceptive.

The café is small and dimly lit. It's one of the few places around here that isn't often used for business lunches between important executives.

We each order soup and find a table in the back, away from the busy counter. "You're quiet," Reece says, staring me down from across the table.

"I'm tired. Two days of traveling and meetings wore me out more than I thought it would."

"So, what was it like?" Not knowing is killing her. I'm surprised she didn't convince me to join her for coffee this morning.

"What part?" I ask, delaying the inevitable.

"Let's start with New York."

` A smile actually plays on my lips for the first time today. "If you haven't tried it, you need to make time for the frozen hot chocolate. Hands down, one of the best things I've ever put in my mouth."

"And the meetings?"

I sit back, trying to get comfortable in the wooden chair. "Interesting. The guy we met with is a complete asshole. It ended up being a pissing match between him and Pierce."

"Did he end up picking Stanley for the project?"

I think back to how the meeting ended yesterday. "Umm . . . probably not."

"That sucks. It would've been a nice excuse for all of us to visit New York." She takes a bite of her soup, then continues, "And Pierce?"

"What about him?" I ask.

"What was it like being alone with him for two days?"

It depends on which part, I think to myself. "He's charming and sweet . . . easy to talk to."

She sets her spoon down, studying me. "And?"

"Can we talk about something else?"

"Nope," she says, shaking her head for extra emphasis.

Pierce and I crossed over so many boundaries, but I'm not going to admit to all of them. But I need to talk to someone. "He kissed me."

"Shut up!"

After looking to make sure no one is listening, I turn back to her. "I can't do it, Reece. I can't be with him like that, and I hate myself for it."

"Do you know how crazy you sound right now? What do you mean?"

Good question. "I moved here to get over a broken heart, and when I started messing around with Blake, I thought I could do it. I thought someone else still owned my heart . . . that it wasn't mine to steal. I was wrong; I had it, and Blake took it right out of my hands. I know he's not the right guy, but I'm having a hard time letting him go."

"And Pierce?" she asks quietly, hanging on my every word.

"I wish things were different. I wish I'd fallen for him, but it's hard to fall when I'm already down."

"Is it impossible?"

"What?"

"To fall for Pierce?"

I close my eyes, thinking about what it would be like to be the woman on Pierce's arm. To have him worship me . . . to take care of me. How safe it would feel. It's what I imagined last night, lying in my quiet, dark apartment. *It should've been him.*

"No," I say honestly. "I just can't have a future with someone when I haven't closed the book on my past."

"Have you talked to Blake, to try to work this all out?"

I stare down at my full soup bowl, stirring my spoon along its edges. "No. He's out of town for a few days."

"Lila, you know you can trust me, don't you?"

I nod.

"When he gets back, you need to talk to him . . . you need to let him go."

I nod again. It's all I can do. She's not telling me anything I don't already know. It's just not that easy.

We head back to the office, and I get lost in a sea of fabric samples for the rest of the afternoon. The day speeds by, giving way to a much-needed weekend. I'm actually looking forward to Charlie's, to the distraction it provides.

As I step outside, I wrap my arms tightly around my stomach. It's dark, and light snow flurries blow across my face.

I'm about to round the corner to the train stop when I come face to face with the man I've been trying to avoid all day long.

I've never been very good at hide-and-seek.

"Hey," he says quietly, tucking his hands in his pockets.

"Hi."

"I haven't seen you all day. Have you been avoiding me?"

He's standing so close the light breeze carries his scent toward me. The lies that want to slip from my lips fade from memory.

"Maybe," I answer quietly, brushing my hair from my face.

He reaches up, hesitantly, helping with a strand I missed. "I don't want it to be this way."

"I'm good at running."

"Don't run from me."

"You don't know me, Pierce."

"I want to," he replies quickly, brushing his thumb across my cool cheek. "Friends, Lila. That's all I'm asking for."

I nod against his palm. It feels too good to pull away.

"I was just about to grab some coffee around the corner. Do you want to join me?" he asks.

"I have plans."

His hand falls away. "Have you talked to him?"

He doesn't need to clarify. My whole world revolves around *him* right now. It also doesn't get past me that he assumed my plans were with Blake. I guess I can't blame him. "No, he's out of town for a while, I guess."

His expression softens. "Can I at least give you a ride somewhere?"

I think about it for a few seconds, hearing the train leaving in the distance. It will be at least fifteen minutes before the next one. "Yeah, if it's not too far out of your way, that would be great. Thank you."

He makes a quick call and two minutes later his black Escalade pulls up. We both jump in, leaving downtown Chicago as a backdrop.

"Are you going home for Christmas?" he asks, breaking through the silence. I feel him staring at me but fixate my eyes on the passing buildings.

"No, not this year." I've been so consumed by everything that's going on in my life, I almost forgot it's only days away. It's too late to make plans now, even if I could afford it.

"You better not be spending it alone in that tiny apartment of yours, Ms. Fields." I kind of like when he calls me that. It brings me back to when we first met . . . when things were normal.

"Don't worry about me. There's Skype."

"Seriously?"

I laugh, thinking about *A Christmas Story* and horrible take out. "You should try it."

The rest of the ride is quiet, and when we pull up in front of my building, he climbs out before I get a chance. He keeps his hands to himself as he walks me to the door.

"Have a nice weekend, and Merry Christmas, Lila."

"You too," I answer back, walking through the open door.

Before it closes all the way, he pushes his way in. I walk back to give him space, my heart thudding against my ribcage. He comes close, and when I think he might kiss me, he stops, his warm breath hitting my lips. "I have one more thing I need to say."

I swallow, looking up into his warm green eyes.

"When you're lying in bed tonight—thinking—remember that I'm here and he's not."

Before I can respond, he's gone.

WHEN I WALK INTO MY APARTMENT, my thoughts are so wrapped around Pierce's words that I almost miss Blake leaning against the counter. He's the opposite of the man who dropped me off just minutes ago—fitted long-sleeve white T-shirt, faded jeans that mold to his body in all the right places, his blond hair curling under his gray beanie. Times like this, I get why I fell for him so hard. I wish he'd stop reminding me.

He speaks first. "Hey."

"Hi."

"How was New York?"

I shrug. That's a loaded question. "It was a quick trip. I didn't fall in love. I didn't fall in hate."

"How's Pierce?"

He doesn't really want to know this, does he? I contemplate, watching him.

He pushes off the counter, taking slow steps toward me. "I hated that you were alone with him."

This should be the time that I tell him nothing happened. I should be able to say that, but I can't. If I let myself, I could easily fall for Pierce.

And the guilt . . . I don't deserve it. Blake is the whole reason I can't fall for Pierce. He fucked me. His touch reached deeper than my skin to my heart, but he couldn't fill the need he created. He couldn't commit, and now I'm the one who finds it impossible to give myself to anyone else. That brings the bitterness back.

"You let me go, remember?"

He winces but doesn't break his slow stride. I step back to get more space between us, but just like so many other times with him, I find my back against the wall. He reaches me, caging me in with his hands against the wall on either side of my head. "Do you trust me?"

"No."

"I need you to. Even when I hurt you . . . when you hate me, I need you to know I'm only doing what's right for you."

I swallow, trying to keep my eyes on his, but they always seem to find their way down to his lips. I hate how my body reacts to him. "You confuse the hell out of me, Blake."

"There's somewhere I need to go tonight, and I want you to come with me."

"I can't keep doing this. Nothing has changed between us."

He comes even closer yet, his lips inches from mine. If he tried to kiss me, I don't think I'd be able to stop him. My brain may scream at me to run away, but my heart wants me to stay. Even when just hours ago, I'd convinced myself it was time to break away.

"Come with me," he begs.

I open my mouth to argue, but his finger covers my lips. "Come with me."

"I have to work."

He shakes his head, running his fingertip along my lower lip. "I already talked to Dana. I got you covered."

Everything goes black. *You shouldn't do this. He's just going to leave you flying high again without a safe place to fall.* Then, as things come into focus, and all I see is him—the

Lisa DeJong

one guy I shouldn't want but can't seem to forget. He's managed to ruin me in just a few short weeks.

His eyes soften as he removes his hands from the wall. He won this battle, and he knows it. "Grab your coat."

I struggle to find the right words. My throat is dry. My head aches. It's as if I'm stuck on one side of a fence with no way to get over and no time to strategize. I just want to disappear into my bedroom and bury myself under the thick covers, but I can't. Not when he's looking at me like this. "Give me one good reason why I should."

"Because if you don't, you'll always wonder what could have been." He motions between us. "You feel this connection, but just like me, you're not quite sure what to do with it. This gives us a chance to figure it out together."

He makes it hard to argue when he says the most perfect words. He's right, but he's not. Just days ago, I knew what I wanted from Blake, but he was on a completely different page. For all I know, he still is.

"I'm not going to let you hurt me," I finally whisper.

"I don't intend to."

"I need more than that, Blake. I don't care about your intentions."

He cups my face in his hands, leveling our eyes. "I'm not very good at this stuff, Lila, so listen to me carefully. For two years, I've been trying to get a contract to restore historic murals in Paris, and I finally did a few days ago." He pauses, brushing the pads of his thumbs across my cheeks. "I turned it down because I couldn't leave you . . . I couldn't let you go."

His admission melts me. Maybe I do mean something to him. "What does that mean . . . for us?" I ask, holding back tears.

"I don't know, but I want you to figure it out with me. Please . . . just come with me tonight."

A long pause. A potentially life-changing decision. "Do I need to change?"

He looks down, surveying my dress and heels. "You might want to throw on some jeans and grab a warmer jacket."

As I move around the apartment, changing and gathering my things, I'm in a fog. Thoughts come then quickly fade away only to be replaced by others. Reece's advice repeats in my head. Pierce's words play over and over. Yet, before long, I'm standing at the door next to Blake.

He smirks. "Are you going to put on your shoes?"

"Shit," I mutter under my breath.

I run into my bedroom and tug on my black wool boots. When I come back out, he's leaning against the wall, arms folded over his chest. "Much better," he remarks, lacing his fingers with mine. He never lets go, pulling me along as we quickly move out of the building.

This is all so crazy—with Pierce one minute then Blake the next. I don't even recognize myself anymore, but I push it all away to stay in the moment.

A cab waits out front. Blake opens the door, allowing me to climb in first. "Are you going to tell me where we're going?" I ask when the door shuts.

"No."

"I haven't eaten yet," I announce. Even with my heightened nerves, my stomach grumbles. I should've eaten more of my soup at lunch.

"We'll take care of that."

I nestle against the seat, watching the Christmas lights through my window.

"Can I ask you something?" Blake says out of the blue.

"Only if I get one, too."

He actually has to think about it, eyes exploring my features along the way. He's scared of something, but I don't know what. "There are stipulations."

"Like?"

He rubs his chin. "I ask now, and you get yours at the end of the night."

"What's the point in that?"

"Maybe yours will be answered along the way."

I nod, but I'm not exactly sure what I'm agreeing to. I have no idea what we're doing, or how anything is ever going to get answered.

He continues, "Has Pierce mentioned me?"

By the way he rubs his hands together, I can tell he's nervous. I am, too. "Just that I should stay away from you."

"That's fair enough."

I don't mention Alyssa . . . that's something for later.

Before long, we're pulling up next to Navy Pier. I'd read about it when I'd decided to move here but was waiting for warmer months to visit. Blake passes the cab driver a couple folded bills then climbs from the car, holding the door open for me.

"This isn't quite what I expected," I say without thinking.

He wraps his hand around mine, pulling me forward with him. "What were you expecting?"

I shrug. "A gallery or something."

He laughs—something I rarely hear from him. "I paint because I'm good at it, and it helps me work through my shit. It doesn't mean it's the only thing I know."

"Isn't Lake Michigan frozen this time of year?"

"Lemon Drop?"

I grimace at the sound of my nickname rolling off his lips. He hasn't said it since, well, since everything. "Yeah?"

"You'll get your question at the end of the night. Now, please, just enjoy this."

I smile to myself, remembering how I came to love this side of Blake.

He points out little attractions here and there as we walk hand in hand. I get lost in his love for Chicago, for the pier in general.

"Still hungry?" he asks.

"You have no idea," I answer. There's not much I wouldn't put in my stomach right now.

"Have you tried a Chicago-style dog yet?"

"No."

"That's about to change."

I despise hot dogs, but I'm so hungry I don't care. I watch as he walks up to a stand and orders two dogs and two Cokes. Even I have to admit the aroma in the air smells amazing.

"Here you go," he says, handing one off to me. I hesitate before sinking my teeth into it. It's better than anything I've had in a while, better than the filet I had a couple nights ago. The taste of onions, relish, and tomatoes hits my tongue, playing together beautifully in my mouth.

"That good?" he asks, swiping his thumb across the corner of my mouth.

"What?"

"You're moaning like you do when I'm buried inside of you."

I attempt not to choke on the bite I just took. "We don't have to worry about that ever again, do we?"

"We'll see."

The cold breeze batters my cheeks, but it doesn't faze me with the hot food to keep me warm. We finish and head toward the amusement park. It's dark and deserted—almost a little spooky, like a scene from a horror film.

"We're not going in there, are we?" I ask.

"That's another question. We talked about this."

I grip his hand tighter as we walk toward the ferris wheel. I'm sure when this place is open at night in the summer, the lights are a beautiful addition to the glistening lake water.

A man stands next to the gate with two paper cups in his hands. "Mr. Stone."

Blake nods.

"The bottom bench is ready for you."

"Thank you."

To my surprise, he leads us to the loading pad of the wheel and motions for me to get on. I hesitate for just a second before complying. I've never been on one like this before—at night when the park isn't open.

"Take this," he says, tossing me a thick fleece blanket. I wrap it around me, trying to keep my hands underneath. "Here," he adds, handing me his gloves. He climbs in next to me, taking his side of the blanket.

The man who greeted us hands us each a cup and pulls the bar down over our lap. "Ready?" he asks.

"Let her roll," Blake replies.

The wheel jerks once, then we start our ascent. When we reach the top, I notice we can see most of the city from here. "This is amazing."

"I was hoping you'd like it."

"How could I not?"

We go round a few more times. I almost forget about the paper cup wrapped in my hands. "What's this?"

He smiles shyly. "Hot chocolate."

I put it to my lips, letting the velvety hot liquid coat my tongue. It's perfect—just the right amount of sweet. "Thank you for this."

Before he can reply, the wheel suddenly comes to a stop with us seated way up top. It scares me, making my heart race considering the fact that we could be stuck up here.

"Relax," Blake says, "this is part of the plan."

I sit back against the seat, trying my best not to look down. Heights have never been my thing, but the view just might make it all worth it.

"What are we doing?" My voice is a little shaky.

He shrugs. "Maybe I just wanted you all to myself."

I glare at him.

"I'm kidding. There's so much to see up here and nothing to block the view."

"Have you been up here before?" I ask between several deep breaths to calm myself.

"Not like this," he says quietly.

"How did you get them to open it?" I remember how dark and empty everything had been when we entered.

"A few dollars will get you just about anything."

Looking around, I notice I'm swimming in a sea of stars and lights. Something far more breathtaking than the sunset, and from here, it's as if we're the only ones who can see it.

"What do you think?"

"It's nice . . . really nice." Honestly, the thought behind this has me close to tears.

"I missed you, Lila . . . talking to you."

"I missed you, too." I stop short of telling him I threw away a chance with someone else because my heart was still stuck on him.

"I fuck up a lot, but I'm going to try not to do that with you anymore."

My heart leaps. Nothing seems to work out the way I want, but maybe, just maybe, this is different. "What are you saying?" I hold my breath, waiting for his answer.

"I can't lose you, but I'm not the man you need either. Not the one who deserves you, but I want to try." He pauses, looking up to the sky . . . thoughtful. "I've said more to you in the last few weeks than I have to anyone else the last couple years. There's got to be a reason for that. We just need to tread slowly."

His words pang my heart. Whatever it is he's carrying around with him left deep scars, easily detected by anyone who spends more than a few minutes with him. "Blake."

"Don't," he says, tucking away a piece of hair that had blown across my face. "I don't need anyone feeling sorry for me."

"I don't," I lie. In the beginning, when I hadn't met this side of him, I didn't feel sorry for him. I think I hated him. "I need you to promise me you won't cross that line—the one between where we are now and where we've been the last few days. I can't do that again."

"I can't promise anything except that I'll try." His fingertip brushes my cold cheek.

The situation between us isn't perfect, but it's as perfect as we're going to get. And I'm not ready to let him go.

"Is it my turn to ask a question yet?"

He smiles, but I know it might not be there long. "Go for it."

"Who's Alyssa?"

As soon as the words leave my mouth, I regret them. Not just because I'm afraid of the answer, but his reaction too. Under the lights of the ferris wheel, his skin pales. His eyes flick from the sky back to his hands, and when I think I might be shunned from the truth again, two shaky words leave his lips. "My wife."

"WHAT DO YOU MEAN *WIFE*?" My voice vibrates with anger and confusion.

"Lila—"

"No. No. No. Don't you dare step around this one. How the hell can you sit up here with me, telling me all these lies, when you're married? Tell me how the fuck that works, Blake."

He's quiet longer than is tolerable. If we weren't up here, he'd be running away just like he always does. It's probably killing him that he can't.

"Blake."

He slams his hand down on the metal bar meant to keep us safe. "Why do you always have to push, huh? Does constantly digging into my failures make you happy? What the fuck do you want from me?"

I flinch, scooting to the edge of the seat. "I didn't think asking the guy who kind of admitted he had feelings for me earlier about his *wife* was an issue. If it is, I want off. Now!"

"Lower us!" Blake yells over the side.

My stomach drops. My heart aches. Every thread of hope is lost. If I'm smart, I won't grab at it the next time it's dangled in front of me.

Our cab rocks at the bottom, and as soon as the metal bar is loose, I stumble out. I don't stop there, walking as fast as my shaky legs will carry me. Blake made his choice . . . his last choice.

"Lila!"

I speed up, eyes locked on a taxi parked along the street.

"I met her my first year of college."

His words stop me. The taxi speeds away.

"She was majoring in literature, me in art. We were so young, maybe too young, but we made it through four years. When I asked her to marry me, I did it because I couldn't imagine what a day would be like without her."

When he's quiet for a few seconds, I turn around, wondering if he's still there. He is, and he looks so freaking wounded that I feel like the villain. "So what happened?" I ask, feeling there's got to be more to the story.

"I failed."

"At what?"

He shrugs. "Everything."

My heart's not just sinking . . . it's lying at my feet. There's not much I can say to that. "Is that why you don't do relationships?"

"It's why I don't do a lot of things."

A cool breeze blows between us. Nighttime out here is as quiet as it is dark. It's been a long day—for both of us—and though there's so much more I want to know, I've had enough. Emotionally spent doesn't even begin to describe it.

"I think we should go," I finally say, pulling my jacket tighter around my body.

He walks to me slowly like he's not quite sure what to expect. His eyes glisten under the moonlight. "Let's find a cab."

Without a single word, I walk by his side. We exist, but not together, and all I want to do is make us better.

On a late, cold Chicago night, there's not much competition at the pier. He hails the first cab that roars down the street, holding the door for me to slide in first. I focus my attention out the window, at the streetlights. I wonder what she's like—does he compare me to her? Does he ever think about her when he's buried inside of me? And how is Pierce connected to all this? Was he with her too?

"I'm sorry," he murmurs. "Tonight wasn't supposed to end this way."

"I'm sorry, too."

It's my last night at Charlie's. I thought I'd struggle to get there, to finish out my last night, but I'm feeling a bit nostalgic. Charlie's welcomed me to Chicago even if it wasn't always in the best way. It's where I met Dana, who has quickly become one of my best friends.

It's also the last time I'll make this walk between my apartment and the small line of shops I've come to love. I know I'll still make it up here from time to time, but it won't be like this.

Pulling my coat tighter around my body, I speed up my pace, eager to escape the cold. My thoughts shift back to last night. It was late when we got back from the pier, and after the ups and downs—the apologies and revelations—I was exhausted. I still don't know everything, but what he told me was enough to scare me into thinking I may not want to know more. And beyond that, I'm pissed that he kept this from me for so long. He owed me the truth. Especially one that big.

Blake wasn't home when I woke up this morning. I'd assumed he was at the studio, or doing whatever he does when he disappears. And after what he confessed, I wish I could do the same. Disappear and forget. I wish I could unhear everything he told me, but I need to face the facts.

Blake has a wife he's made no mention of. He's taken me, and other women, to his bed without blinking. I pushed him for more information on the way home, but he stopped me. Said we would talk about it later.

Now, here I am—wondering.

Opening the door to Charlie's, I notice the crowded bar and rowdy college students packed around tables. The college jerks are the one thing I definitely won't miss.

"Lila!" Dana practically runs up to me, wrapping her arms tightly around my neck.

"Hey." I hug her back. "Ready to rock this place for my last night?"

She pulls back, holding my forearms. "Are you sure you don't want to stay? It won't be the same." She sticks out her lower lip like a child.

"If Pierce fires me, I might not have a choice." I'm still worried about how things might change. How will everything that happened in New York affect what I worked so hard for? He's a man of integrity, but he's already broken a few rules when it comes to me. What will he think of me if I end up with Blake?

"I'm catching the hint of a juicy story. Go clock in, and we'll talk about it between tables."

"I'm going to miss this," I admit as I walk to the back to hang my coat and punch the clock. I jump right into the swing of things—grabbing drinks for a couple groups that walked in.

When Dana and I finally have a couple minutes of downtime, she begins her usual line of questioning. "Now, why would Pierce even think about firing you?"

"New York was . . . interesting."

She raises her brow. "Keep going."

"He kissed me."

Her brows shoot even higher. "And, what? You're a horrible kisser? I'm still not following."

"We ended up in his room, and naked in his bed," I answer, tracing the rounded wood grain on the bar top—anything to avoid seeing her reaction.

"Holy shit! You fucked your boss? I didn't know you had it in you . . . no pun intended."

"I didn't sleep with him!" I try to keep my voice down, but it's hard when I'm wound up.

When I glance back over at her, she's smiling. "Say you didn't fuck him."

I roll my eyes, sick of being talked to like this. "I didn't fuck him."

"How far did it go then?" I narrow my eyes at her. She continues, "If I'm going to help you out, I have to know."

I move closer to whisper in her ear. "His head was between my legs."

"Oh God, so what happened?"

After looking around to make sure no one's listening, I tell her the rest—about how I'd imagined Blake, about the awkwardness that followed, and our dealings with Wade.

When I'd first met Dana, I never imagined my life would be of any entertainment to her. It's amazing how fast things change.

"He won't fire you," she decides after processing it all.

"You don't know him."

"From everything you've told me, Lila, he likes you. He's not going to jeopardize that as long as he thinks he has a chance. Besides, he can't fire you; it's sexual harassment."

She's right . . . about everything. I hate and love her for it.

I'm about to ask her for some Blake advice when Charlie slaps his palm against the bar. "Are you ladies ready to work now? Just because it's Lila's last night doesn't mean you can fuck around."

"Sorry, Charlie. We're just catching up," I reply.

"Finish later. Two tables walked in while you hens were clucking."

Turning around, I immediately spot the new table of thirty-somethings looking our way, but the other is harder to find.

"Did you know he was coming?" Dana asks, bumping her shoulder against mine.

"Who?" Still scanning, I see nothing.

She points to the far corner, the one partially hidden by the entryway. "There."

He looks lost, staring blankly out the window. I wonder what he's thinking about—if it's her or me or no one at all.

"Do you want me to grab him?" Dana asks, cutting through my thoughts.

"I'll take it," I say, pushing away from the bar without another word.

My ears ring as I slowly weave my way through the tables. I have so many questions.

"Hi," I say quietly, taking a seat across from him.

Blake's eyes briefly lock with mine then out the window again. "Do you need a ride home tonight?"

I shake my head then realize he probably can't see me. "No. It's my last night so Dana wants to sit around and have a drink or two."

His mood hasn't changed much since we got home last night.

"Can I get you something to drink?" I ask, needing to carve into the silence.

He studies me like we've never met before. "Ask me," he finally says.

I hate seeing him like this—a mess of emotions I can't place.

"About last night . . . I can tell you're dying to know more, so ask me," he continues.

Shaking my head, I say, "Not here, Blake. Not right now."

He pounds his fist against the table. "Now!"

I hesitate, because deep inside I know he won't handle this well. One question, and I'll be done . . . he'll be done with me. "Where is she?"

"She's gone. She left me," he says, eyes never leaving mine.

That makes sense, I guess. Why mention her if she's no longer in the picture? "Are you still in love with her?" I ask, knowing I'm pushing my luck.

"I love her, but I'm not in love with her. There's a difference."

Truer words have never been spoken; I know that from experience. Love comes in many forms, and once you feel it for someone, I don't think it's possible to ever completely let it go. It lingers in its most simple state, taking a permanent place in your heart.

"I'm sorry," I reply when nothing else comes to mind.

He pulls his hair between his fingers. "Don't be. Just bring me a bottle of Absolut."

"A bottle?"

"Yes," he answers on edge. He dismisses me by staring out the window again. Maybe I should be angry about him coming here, but I can't be. Not when he's finally turning the pages of his story, answering some of my questions about why he is the way he is. Besides, friends stick by each other's sides, even when things aren't picture perfect.

I leave him alone, walking back to the bar to read Charlie Blake's order for self-medication. "Did you tell him how much it's going to cost?" he asks, standing on his toes to grab a bottle from the top shelf.

"I don't think he cares. Besides, this one's on me."

"Well, in that case, I suggest you get your ass out to your tables a little more often to earn your tips." Charlie's not joking either.

"Thanks for the advice. Can I get a shot glass too?" I ask, tightly gripping the neck of the bottle in my hand. Someone's bound to bump into me, and I can't exactly afford another. Charlie slams a glass on the counter; I grab that too.

My palms sweat against the glass as I make my way back over to Blake. His eyes follow me like a stalker in the night, yet I want his attention. I want to know he's thinking about me.

"Here," I announce, setting the bottle in front of Blake. I don't even recognize him tonight. I've caught glimpses of the charming one and more than my fair share of the asshole I'd met first, but this distant, sad version is new to me.

He wastes no time twisting the lid off the vodka bottle and filling his glass. He throws it back, and tops it off again. "Have you ever been in love?" he asks.

"Once," I answer, taking the seat next to him so I can keep an eye on things at the bar.

He grips my chair, pulling it closer until our knees touch. Then he takes his second shot. The alcohol doesn't seem to faze him. "What happened?"

"He decided he didn't want to be with me anymore."

He nods, pouring more of the clear liquid in his glass. "Well, he's an idiot."

When he goes to lift the glass to his lips again, I grab hold of his wrist. I'm not willing to watch him self-destruct. He's just going to wake up tomorrow in this same messed up state; the alcohol only temporarily drowns the memories. "Take it easy."

"You don't get it, do you?"

"Don't get what?" I ask.

He frees his hand from my grip, knocking back another shot.

"You're the type of woman that men don't know they want until they've already fallen. You're there, and then you're just . . . everywhere."

I swallow, fumbling for words. I heard what he said, but processing it is a bit harder. I ask the first thing that comes to mind. "And is that the type of woman Alyssa is?"

His mouth falls open, but he quickly recovers. "No, that was a conscious fall."

I nod, debating which could possibly be better. I start to ask another question, but Charlie shouts my name from behind the bar. After waving him off, I turn back to Blake. "I need to get back to work."

He swirls his shot glass around, eyeing it like it's the most interesting thing in the world. "I'll wait."

Because I know there's nothing I can do to free the glass from his hand, I walk away without trying. Tomorrow morning, or even trying to get him home tonight, is going to be a challenge.

I busy myself with drink orders and bussing tables. As the night wears on, my pockets fill with cash, and the room slowly begins to empty.

"I barely got to talk to you tonight," Dana remarks as she helps me clear my last table.

"My last night would be the busiest. At least Charlie hasn't had time to convince me to stay, because with all the cash in my pocket, he'd have a good chance."

She laughs. "Maybe I should go tell him because I'm a selfish bitch, and I want you to stay."

Narrowing my eyes at her, I say, "You wouldn't."

"Don't test me."

"Closing time, ladies! Let's get this place cleaned up so I can get to bed!" Charlie yells across the room.

As I turn with a full tray in my hand, I notice Blake's still sitting in the back corner. He looks like shit—slouched shoulders, head buried in his hands.

"You still up for a couple drinks?" Dana asks, coming up behind me.

I look back at Blake, slumped over, and my conscience pulls at me. "I need to get him home. Can I get a rain check?"

She sighs. "Need me to give you a ride?"

"If you don't mind. I don't think he's up for the walk."

"Get him moving. I'm going to grab our coats and clock us out," she says, taking the full tray from my hands.

I walk to him slowly, like I might wake an angry un-caged lion if I make a sound. His head comes up, but then slumps forward again.

Upon closer inspection, I note the liquor bottle is empty. I'll be lucky if he can even walk his ass out of here. "Blake," I say softly.

He lifts his eyes but nothing more.

"Let's get you home." I cradle his elbow in my hands, but he's almost twice my size. Unless I suddenly get Superman's powers, this isn't going to work.

"Shit," I mutter under my breath.

"Here," Dana says, bumping her shoulder against mine.

I pull my coat from her arm and quickly throw it on. "I'm going to need some help with him," I admit.

"You take one arm, I'll grab the other. My car is right out back."

"Don't need help," Blake mutters, rubbing his fingers along his forehead.

I sigh, anticipating what's ahead as Dana and I each grab hold of one of his arms. "Let's get you home and into bed."

"Only if you're coming to bed with me, Lemon Drop," he stutters, trying to hold himself up. I ignore him; he won't remember any of this a few minutes anyway.

We sneak out back without more than a simple goodbye to Charlie.

Blake shifts between carrying some of his weight and being completely dead weight. Almost too much for two girls coming off a long shift.

"She's not coming," Blake remarks when he catches his first glimpse of Dana.

"She's driving."

He grumbles. I swear to God if he gets sick, I'm going to kill him. "I mean . . . she's not sleeping with me. It's just you and me now, baby."

I don't reply because there's no reason to. I manage to keep him on his feet while Dana opens the back door. My intention was to lay him down inside, but he won't let go.

"Blake."

His cold fingers tighten around mine. I give up, climbing in behind him. His head rests on my lap. On instinct, my fingers tangle in his hair. When you care about someone, even if it's the crazy way I feel for Blake, you want to take care of them when they're hurting.

In the short ride to our apartment, he drifts off. It gives me a chance to reflect on the last twenty-four hours. On exposed secrets. Truths still unspoken. The heartbreak it caused. When it's all said and done, it's going to be the things I still don't know that determine the outcome of this. Of us.

Dana pulls in front of our building, shifting the car into park. "Umm, has an elevator been installed since the last time I was here?"

I groan, not having thought about how I'm going to get him up the stairs until now. "Unfortunately, no."

She crawls out, coming to open my door. "You know this is going to suck, don't you?"

"Yep," I answer, carefully lifting his head from my lap.

I start to climb out but not before Blake grabs hold of my wrist. "Wait for me. I got this."

With doubt, I step out onto the curb and wait. He'll probably fall flat on his face the second his foot hits the ground, but it's not like I'm going to be able to pull him from the car when he's like this.

To my surprise, he makes it out, standing on his own two feet. For security, I wrap his arm around my shoulders in order to balance his weight against me.

"I'll walk behind you in case he starts to fall backward," Dana says as she locks up the car.

"You realize you're not going to be able to catch him, don't you?"

"It gives me purpose."

I laugh at her ridiculousness but keep moving up the first flight of stairs. It's not so bad—his legs almost keep up with mine.

"Let me know if you want to trade," Dana chimes from behind us.

Blake beats me to answering her. "Not a chance."

When we finally reach the door, he leans against the wall while I dig out my key. He looks as if he's falling asleep—eyes shut, shoulders falling forward. I motion for Dana to hold the door so I can get him inside.

"Do you want me to stay?" she asks.

"No, I got it. I'll give you a call tomorrow. Thank you for everything."

She hugs me. "I'd tell you to have a good night, but that would be stupid."

I want to laugh and cry at the same time. Instead, I push all the feelings away and watch her walk out the door. It's only then that I feel completely, utterly lost. No idea what I'm doing or where to go from here. This guy who I think I love is half passed out beside me. Alcohol chased his worries away, but there's no way to escape mine.

I usher him to his room, letting him fall onto his unmade bed with his feet hanging over the edge. I carefully pull off his shoes and slide the comforter up over his shoulders. Watching him lying there motionless makes my heart twist in ways it shouldn't. I can't stand it. Slowly I back away, flicking off the light before going to close the door.

"Don't go," he whispers, rolling to his side.

"You need to sleep."

"Sleep with me."

Just like so many other times since I've met him, I open my mouth to argue but can't find the words. Instead, I slip off my shoes and climb in next to him . . . where I've wanted to be.

WHEN I WAKE, IT TAKES ME a few seconds to adjust to my surroundings. I'm in my apartment but not my bed. My warm down comforter has been replaced with a heavy, muscled arm. The smell of fabric softener is masked with stale alcohol.

Looking back, I see Blake fast asleep. He looks so peaceful and innocent. His long lashes make me want to kiss him, especially the lids of his eyes.

I shift underneath him, attempting to roll onto my stomach to get a better look. It backfires—he startles, lifting his arm from my waist. For a moment, I lie quietly, selfishly hoping he'll wrap his strong arm back around me. Instead, the bed shifts, and I hear his feet padding across the wood floor. The bathroom door opens.

I debate whether I should lay here and see if he comes back to me, or if I should cut my losses and disappear into my room. Then I remember my promise to myself to not let this happen again.

Blake steps out of the bathroom then starts opening and closing dresser drawers. All I can do is sit up and watch.

The muscles in his back tense as if he can feel my eyes on him. I want to go to him and wrap my arms tightly around him. If he'd let me, I'd never let him go.

After coming out of the last drawer empty handed, he stands stiffly with his hands on his hips. "Lila." His tone is sharp, and instantly, I know I'm just another regret. A seed of misery plants itself in my stomach. "I need you to go."

I wrap my arms around my folded knees, otherwise unmoving. "Can we talk first?"

I hear him breathing. His jaw ticks. "Did you hear a single word I said last night?"

"That's why I want to talk," I admit, hugging myself tighter.

He forces a laugh, poking his tongue into his cheek. "I'm leaving for a few days. I don't know exactly when I'll be back."

I jump off his bed, anger boiling over. "That's it? I told you if you did this again . . . if you leave when things get tough, this is over." I try to keep my distance, but my increasing frustration won't allow it. He needs to see me . . . see what he does to me with his hot and cold routine.

"I was drunk," he seethes, gritting his teeth.

I groan out of frustration. "Not at Navy Pier. Not when you spilled a bunch of crap about falling for me. Not when you told me you were married. Can we talk about that for a second? I need a little consolation that I'm not your side piece being kept at your fuck pad."

He pushes past me, grabbing a duffel bag from the floor. He walks around me like I'm not even here, throwing two drawers of clothes into it.

"Blake, please don't go." A tear slides down my cheek as I stand in the middle of his room. I'm tired of the back and forth. I'm tired of him running when he starts to feel too much. He doesn't realize he's making me feel worse along the way.

He zips the bag, throwing it over his shoulder. He starts walking out the door, but then changes his mind, coming back to me. "I meant what I said about trying to figure out what this thing is between us."

He starts to walk away again. "How is that ever going to happen if you leave whenever things don't go your way?"

My words stop him. "Nothing has gone my way in almost three years. Whether I'm here or not, that's not going to change until I get my shit straightened out."

He's going to leave.

And, I'm going to have to let him go—forever.

He's almost out the door.

And, I'm out of my mind.

"Blake!"

He breaks stride but then keeps going. *Try harder, Lila . . . if you really want this.* "Blake! I can't keep doing this. If you walk out that door, I'm leaving, and I'm not coming back."

That gets his attention. He turns back around.

I stand silently, reading the pain in his tired eyes. It's hard to stay mad at someone with that much visible ache.

He walks toward me. "I've spent weeks trying to convince myself I don't want you. When I leave . . . when I paint . . . you're all I think about." He comes closer, skimming his thumbs over my cheeks. My eyes close in an attempt to hold in tears. "I can't give you everything you want . . . not yet . . . but I need you here with me."

"Why? Why do you need me, Blake? Tell me," I cry.

"Because, without you, it hurts to feel. All the bad memories—the nightmares—they're suffocating me. You steal them away, Lila. Don't you understand? You give me good memories to cover the bad ones." He wipes my tears away while staring down into my eyes.

If it were that simple—if I didn't have my own bad memories—I'd be putty in his hands. "Then stay. Let me help you."

"I don't know, Lila. I just don't know."

I throw my hands up in frustration. "What do you want from me?"

"To be your friend, for now."

"And if that's not enough?"

He moves his face closer to mine. "Then I guess I'll need to work through my shit a little sooner."

I want to believe in him . . . in every word he says. "Can I ask a question?"

"I'll answer anything if it'll make you stay."

"How does Pierce know Alyssa?" I ask, knowing I'm the one with the upper hand.

His hands fall from my face. I think he might just walk away, but he doesn't. He shakes his head, staring down at his feet. "I can't do this now. I—"

I shake my head. "No. You can't keep doing this to me. Either you tell me now, or I'm leaving. "

He glances back up at me, eyes glossed over. "Alyssa's maiden name was Stanley. She's Pierce's sister."

Shock rips through me. Knowing Blake and Pierce, I'd imagined some complex love triangle—one guy taking the other guy's girl—but not this. Why was this a secret? "And why does he hate you so much?"

He winces, combing his fingers through his hair. "He doesn't think I did right by her."

"Is he right?"

"If I were in his shoes, I'd probably agree."

My selfish need screams for me to push him further, but common sense pulls me back. If the past is a predictor of the future, he'll run, and I might not see him again. "If you leave again, I'm done."

"I don't want to leave you."

"Then don't," I answer, the tears starting to dry up. "Does this mean you're staying? Besides, Christmas is in two days, and I wasn't looking forward to spending it alone."

He wraps his arms tightly around me. "I'm not going anywhere."

MONDAY MORNING COMES TOO SOON, but it's okay when I realize I'm wrapped in two strong arms in a nice, warm bed. Even better, it's Christmas Eve, which means I have the next two days off.

Blake feels me shift and pulls me further into him. We talked most of the day yesterday, cleared most of the skeletons from the closet. We can only go forward from here. I let him know what I need, and he promised to stay. It can only get better from here.

His lips press to my neck, sending a tingle down my spine. "Good morning."

"Morning."

His hand slips under my T-shirt, tracing small circles around my belly button. "I like waking up with you in my arms."

"I like waking up in your arms," I admit. It's the best sleep I've had in a long time.

"I forgot to ask you yesterday . . . what are we doing tomorrow, for Christmas?"

"Mallory and I were going to Skype and watch *A Christmas Story*."

"Are you fucking kidding me?"

"That would be a stupid thing to lie about."

"Look," he says, brushing his thumb along my hip. "Pencil me in. We'll order a pizza and watch a real Christmas movie."

I smile. "There is no other Christmas movie."

"We'll see about that," he says, kissing the back of my neck again.

After a few moments, he starts to drift back to sleep as I cozy into him. Falling asleep in his arms last night was nice. No sex. No arguments or hurt feelings. It was just us being us for the first time.

When I'm convinced I won't fall back asleep, I slide out of his arms. I make myself some coffee and curl up on the end of the couch, enjoying a rare peaceful morning. The holidays are a time to look back, and this year has certainly given me plenty to think about. I have so much to be thankful for.

"Hey," Blake mumbles, stepping out of the bedroom. "My bed is cold without you."

"Sorry. You're welcome to join me," I say, patting the spot next to me.

"Breakfast . . . I can't live without my breakfast."

"I guess you're allowed since I'm awake," I tease, watching him rummage through the refrigerator. He fries eggs while I watch the snow fall outside. If this is domestication, sign me up.

"I kind of wish I'd gone home for Christmas," I say when he finally joins me on the couch after breakfast. He brings a full box of chocolate-covered cherries with him. I'm happy being here with him, but it's not the same.

"What would you be doing now, if you were home?"

I smile, thinking about sitting at the table, watching Mom prepare dinner while she hums her favorite holiday music. "I'd probably be helping Mom in the kitchen and then talk Dad's ear off while he attempts to watch football."

He raises an eyebrow. "And you miss that?"

"Yeah, I do." It's not like Nebraska is a rare diamond that can't be found anywhere else. It's just where my heart is. "Why didn't you go home?" I ask, curious.

He shrugs. "Since Mallory wasn't coming home, my parents decided to go to Hawaii. I really can't do Christmas in a Speedo. Besides, the holidays aren't the same without snow."

"I'm the same way. I think one of the things I miss most is our house—the way it looks when it's covered in snow. It's beautiful this time of year." I stand, setting my coffee on the table. "Let me grab a picture so you can see what I'm talking about."

I pull the scrapbook from my nightstand and hand it to Blake. Pages don't have to be turned because it's front and center on the cover. "It sort of reminds me of the mountain cabin my parents used to take us to in Colorado," he remarks, running his finger along the photo's edges.

"I thought I was a city girl at heart, but the longer I'm away, the more I wonder if there's any truth to that."

He studies the photo for a second longer then looks up at me through his thick lashes. "It's not the place you miss; it's the people. When it comes down to it, they're all that matters."

"When did you start writing for Hallmark?"

He grins, sliding my scrapbook off his lap. "You think my thoughts are worth a greeting card?"

"They're worth something."

His eyes search mine, the way he looks at me pulling at my heart like a magnet. I want so badly to kiss him, to let his lips erase all the bad and remind me of when things were good. It's one thing we haven't done yet. This whole taking it slow thing sucks.

We watch a couple movies, laughing a lot along the way.

"Are you getting hungry?" he asks, breaking the spell.

"Eating something besides chocolate would be good."

"I'm going to jump in the shower quick. Why don't you order Chinese?" he suggests.

"Anything in particular?"

He laughs. "I'll let you have your way since it's Christmas Eve."

"How kind of you," I say as I watch him walk away.

"Don't say I didn't give you anything!" he yells as he disappears into his bedroom.

I order the Chinese and settle back into my spot on the couch. As I look toward the window, I'm surprised to see the snow falling harder. Oversized flakes stick to the glass. It's the kind of quiet view that let's you pretend you're anywhere. Not that there's anywhere else I'd rather be right now.

Laying my head against the back of the couch, I listen to the shower run in the distance. I wonder if Blake thinks of me while the warm water washes over his body like I'm always thinking of him.

Home Alone plays on mute. Frank Sinatra croons softly through my iPod, drowning out the sound of the shower whenever Frank hits a high note.

I relax.

My mind drifts.

And just as I'm about to fall to sleep, the doorbell rings, causing me to jump. The food is here, and Blake's not even out of the shower.

"Coming!" I yell, making my way to the door.

When I finally open it, the shock of my life waits on the other side. Pierce is standing there, holding a gift bag in his hand.

"Lila." His eyes roam the length of my body before coming back up.

"I wasn't expecting you."

He grins wide. Sexy. Charming. *Pierce.* "I didn't like the thought of you spending the holiday alone."

I'm not, I think to myself. *Shit.*

"I brought you something," he adds, handing me the red and silver bag.

"You didn't have to—"

"I wanted to. Open it."

I fiddle with the silver ribbon, pulling it loose. Inside is a thermos with *NYC* scrolled across the center.

He laughs nervously, combing his fingers through his hair. "There's more. Twist the lid."

My fingers tremble as I do. The sweet smell hits me as I stare down at whipped cream with a maraschino cherry on top. "Frozen hot chocolate." He's so thoughtful I almost want to cry.

"I ordered a whole canister online." He holds out another bag. "This should get you by until you make it back to New York."

I set everything down on the counter near the door and throw my arms around his neck. "Thank you."

He returns the hug, pressing his nose into my hair. "You're welcome. Hey, I was thinking about going ice-skating in the park. Do you want to join me?"

"What the hell is he doing here?"

I jump at the sound of Blake's voice. From the look in Pierce's wide eyes, he's just as shocked to see Blake as Blake is to see him.

"I stopped by to give her a Christmas present," Pierce answers for me.

"Fuck off, Stanley. You've caused enough trouble as it is." Blake's chest rubs against my shoulder, but I don't dare look back.

"Me?" Pierce shouts, stepping closer so I'm wedged between them. "Look at yourself, Stone. You wouldn't know the truth if it hit you in the ass." He looks back down at me. "Did you ask him about her yet?"

I nod, throwing my hands up in the air. "Will you guys please stop? This is ridiculous, and yes, Pierce, he told me about your sister."

He looks like I slapped him. That wasn't my intention. I look over my shoulder at Blake, recognizing the familiar fire in his eyes. "Give me two seconds."

He doesn't budge. "I'm not going anywhere," I mouth, hoping only he can hear me.

Blake steps back. "I'm only going to warn you once. Stay away from her."

I watch Blake disappear into the apartment before turning my attention back to Pierce. The boyish grin he wore a few minutes ago is gone. He's pissed or confused—maybe both.

"I'm sorry." It's all I can say.

"When did he come back?"

"He was here Friday when I got home."

He flinches. It was the same night he dropped me off. If things were different, if Blake hadn't come home when he did and opened up, this could all be different. I know it . . . he knows it.

"And now everything's all better again?"

Tears well in my eyes. "Love allows us to forgive a lot of things."

He spins around, hands on his hips. He stares at the wall for several quiet seconds, then turns back to me. "Merry Christmas, Lila. I hope you get everything you wished for."

He walks down the hall, disappearing down the stairs. My heart aches for him, but I have to let him go. I haven't played fair.

After I have time to catch my breath, I step back into the apartment.

Before I can react, Blake has my back pressed against the wall like he did the first time his lips touched mine. He cups my face in his hands and crashes down on me in the best way. His mouth is hot on mine, melting away the lingering hurt and pain from the last few weeks. It's possessive, reminding me who I belong to.

He's a wizard, a god—everything imaginary coming to life.

Shutting my eyes, I soak up every bit of what I've missed. They say you don't know how much you miss something until it's gone, but it should be you don't know how much you miss something until it's gone and then you have it again.

The tip of his tongue presses the seam of my lips, licking and teasing while warm drops of water from his soaked hair hit my skin. It's the kiss to end all desire for kisses from another.

He sucks my lower lip between his before pulling away. A line is drawn between our eyes. I see *I'm sorry.* I see promises of never leaving me again. I see everything I've been waiting for, but that he couldn't give me . . . until now.

He clings to me, and my thoughts of Pierce slowly start to disappear. I shouldn't feel so guilty. I've been honest with him every step of the way. I can't help what my heart wants.

"I don't want you near him," he says softly.

"I didn't know he was coming. I'm sorry."

Someone clears his throat next to us. "I need to make deliveries to this building more often." Through all the chaos, we hadn't noticed the delivery guy standing out in the hall staring at us through the open door.

"I'll take that," Blake says, handing him some folded bills. He takes the bag, closing the door before the guy has time to comment any further.

I watch Blake set the bag on the counter. Then he walks past me, locking the deadbolt. When he turns back to me, I can't help but wonder if he knows how sexy he is—taut muscles, glistening chest.

"I've been wanting to do that since last night," he says.

"What?"

He takes small steps toward me. "Kiss those perfect lips."

The way he looks at me makes my heart race at a record pace.

His bare feet pad across the floor until the tips of his toes touch mine.

His hands cup my face, staring down at me with those blue eyes. Two fucked up people trying to decide if our hearts could ever beat to the same rhythm. "You're mine, Lemon Drop."

I can barely breathe. "I think you already know that."

He grinds his hips against mine. I whimper. "I want to hear you say it."

"I'm yours."

"Again," he whispers, his lips brushing against my ear. "Make me believe it."

"I'm yours, Blake. All yours." The words come out as a plea—one begging him to stop talking and touch me.

He lifts me up. My legs have nowhere to go but around him. His lips trail my neck as he walks us to his bedroom. It feels like forever since we've been like this. I think about what's happened since—where he's been, where I've been.

For the second time tonight, my back is pressed against the wall. His body holds me in place while he pulls my arms from his neck, pinning them above my head. Not having control, not being able to touch him . . . it just turns me on even more. Blake's never disappointed me when it comes to taking care of my body—he owns it.

He nips at my collarbone then soothes the bite by tracing it with his tongue. "I missed how you taste."

He trails kisses up my throat to my lips. "And these," he whispers, kissing me softly, "I've missed them too."

He stares into my eyes, the back of his finger brushing my cheek. "And your skin . . . I love the soft feel of your skin."

I tighten my legs around him; it's the only way to express the crazy emotions he's freed inside me. He reacts, pressing his lips to mine again.

As he kisses me, I rock my hips, creating friction between our bodies. He groans, which just fuels me. "Lila," he mutters against my lips. "Stop, or we aren't getting any further than this tonight."

"Blake," I pant, needing him . . . wanting him. Tilting my hips toward him again, I elicit another throaty groan.

"That's it," he says, wrapping his arms around my waist. He throws me down on the bed, watching me with raw hunger in his eyes while he undoes the button on his jeans. I squirm against his soft cotton comforter, admiring the way the streetlights cast a glow on his well-sculpted body. He's easy to get lost in, and once I do, I never want to be found. Not by Pierce . . . not by anyone.

When his knee hits the end of the bed, my eyes make their way up, locking with his. Intensity burns like a wildfire between us. I grip the comforter tightly, anticipating his hands on me—the brush of his cool fingertips against my skin.

"Blake."

He presses two fingers to my lips. "No more talking."

I wither beneath him, waiting for that moment when I feel the weight of his body on mine. The moment I feel him pressing into me, filling me. It's the only time when all the other bullshit between us seems to melt away.

He pulls off my leggings in one swift move, leaving me bare, then pulls on my arms to lift me up. Within seconds, we're facing each other, completely naked. Weeks of memories—some good, some I wish I could erase—flicker in my mind, but I push them all away. The world stops spinning. It's just me and Blake in this moment.

I want to stay here.

Live here.

To always breathe the air here.

His palm presses to the center of my chest. I feel my heart beating hard against it. And more than that, I feel warmth building within me—inside the cage. Love isn't easy—no one ever said it would be—but maybe if it withstands this torrential rain, it's worth fighting for. Not just once. Not until I'm badly bruised, but until my last breath.

Blake is worth it.

He lowers me to the bed slowly with the soft press of his hand. He kisses me, leaving nothing behind. His tongue traces the seam of my lips—exploring and tasting—before dancing its way to mine.

I lift my hips, craving all of him, but he ignores it, kissing his way down my throat. My hands slide up and down his spine, smoothing over his rigid muscles. When his mouth covers my breast, I whimper. The pressure between my legs is undeniable.

"Please," I whisper. His fingers curl around my head, massaging my scalp. Maybe it was meant to pacify me, but every nerve in my body is lit.

His lips travel lower, trailing toward my stomach, while his hands slip from my hair. His hot mouth covers the pulsing spot between my legs, and his fingertips trace my nipples. It's sensational overload. It wasn't enough, and now it's too much. He alternates between sucking and flicking his tongue against my center.

"Blake," I moan, reaching for his hair. I hold it between my fingers, pulling it as I lift closer to heaven. And then he pinches my nipples, and I fall apart. He holds me down, his fingers burning into my hips as I scream out his name. The entire way through, he stays with me until all that remains is the rapid drum of my heart.

"That will never get old," he murmurs as he kisses his way back up my body.

I dig my fingernails into his shoulders. "What?"

"Hearing you scream my name."

He softly kisses my lips, and without warning, he thrusts into me, filling me in one quick motion. "Tell me he's never been in you like this."

I look up into his eyes. He stills above me. "Only you, Blake. Since the day I met you, only you."

He pushes back in—all the way in. I feel the burn in my chest . . . I love him. On our good days and bad days, I love him.

And this time, it's different than the others. It's raw. It's sensual. It's two souls searching at the same time, slowly finding their place in this world.

My legs wrap around his waist.

His lips cover every inch of my neck.

I fall apart first, my body squeezing his. He's only moments behind, filling me. Our bodies tremble as we hold onto each other tightly. Right away, I want to do it all over again.

"I'm sorry," he whispers.

I cradle his face in my hands. "For what?"

"For letting you go. For leaving you. The moment I walked out that door tonight and saw you with him, I saw my life without you. I hated every second of it."

I shut my eyes then open them, staring him straight in the eye. "I won't leave you unless you leave me first."

He pulls out of me, rolling to my side and wrapping his arms around me. "I'm not going anywhere."

A smile curls onto my lips as I rest my arms on his. We lie together, drawing off each other's warmth, and drift to sleep.

ONE AMAZING NIGHT WITH an amazingly unconventional guy has me waking up with a huge smile plastered on my face. The first thing I realize is his body isn't pressed to mine like it had been yesterday when I woke up. I miss it—crave it like an addict. Rolling over, all I see is an unmade bed.

My heart shrinks until it's invisible. My stomach clenches in the worst possible way. I listen for a sound—anything—but there's only silence.

He's left so many times. It's the first place my mind wanders off to . . . the worst-case scenario. He made a promise, but I learned way back when I was still with Derek that those mean nothing.

I crawl off his bed, tiptoeing naked toward the kitchen. The hope of finding him seated at the table eating breakfast dissipates, and then I start to think that maybe he left me to get coffee up the street. There's no note, but I still hold on to hope—barely.

Deciding I need something to keep my mind occupied, I step into the shower, letting the hot water wash over my skin. I let memories of last night consume me. The way he made me feel so much by barely touching me at all, the pads of his fingers brushing against my skin. It was lustful worship, a feeling of complete appreciation. He filled my heart without using any words at all.

As I turn off the shower and step out onto the soft cotton mat, I pretend Blake is out there waiting for me because in my mind, he is. He has to be. I take time drying myself off and throw on my clothes. While I work on my hair, I think about all the things I'd want to do with Blake today when he gets back—it's Christmas after all.

With hesitancy, I walk back out into the living room. It's just as I left it before. Maybe I'm overreacting. Maybe he'll walk through that door at any moment with a ridiculously sexy grin on his face, but I can't escape that feeling that something is wrong. I can't help but wonder if it had to do with last night. Was it too much, too soon? Did we cross a line he wasn't ready to cross?

I can't sit around all day wondering. I need answers. Walking back to his bedroom, I look for anything that might tell me where I can find his studio. Mallory won't tell me so this might be my only hope. Searching the top of his dresser first, I find nothing but loose change, receipts and an old White Sox baseball cap. I open drawers next. The top one holds nothing but an old, tattered picture. It's a woman about my age. She's sitting in tall grass in a white sundress, her arms hugging her knees. Her long, dark hair blows past her shoulders from a light breeze. She looks content—contemplative. As I trace the edge of the picture with my fingertip, I realize I've seen her before. She's the woman in the painting that hangs in the corner of Blake's studio. There are things I know now that I didn't know then. Things that give new meaning to the painting. She has to be Blake's Alyssa, and to hold on to something like this, to still have the painting . . . she still means a lot to him. She's more than just a faded piece of his past.

I lay it back in the drawer where I found it and search the apartment for my phone. He can't just leave like this . . . he'd tell me. As soon as I spot it on the counter, I hit the button to light up the screen. Nothing. No texts. No voicemails.

I have to know . . . I have to try.

Lila: I'm worried about you. Where are you?

Staring at the bright blue digital clock on the microwave, I wait five minutes. Nothing comes. Desperate, I dial the one person who might be able to help me.

"Merry Christmas," she answers, sounding extra chipper.

"Mallory, I need your help."

"What happened?" she asks, picking up on the tone of my voice. "Oh my God. I almost forgot about today. It's Blake, isn't it?"

My heart beats rapidly. I hate the tone in her voice. "What do you mean? What's today?"

She whimpers. "I can't believe I forgot. Have you seen him yet?"

"No," I answer, losing some of my patience. "That's why I'm calling you."

She's silent for several long seconds. When she finally speaks, her voice is low. "You need to find him."

"Where's his studio?"

I find a piece of paper and write down exactly what she says. I hope he's there. If he's not, I don't know what I'll do.

"When are you going?" she asks.

"I'm going to call a cab as soon as I get off the phone with you. Mallory," I say, making sure I have her full attention, "can you please tell me what all this is about?"

"He lost someone who was very special to him three years ago today. He's probably thinking about her . . . searching for something that reminds him of her. Honestly, Lila, you're the first person he's let in since her, and there's got to be a reason for that. You need to find him."

"How do you know he's let me in?"

"Because you care. If you only saw the side of him he lets everyone else see, you wouldn't."

I pause, thinking back to how Blake was when I first met him, and how he's changed. "I'll call you when I find him. I didn't mean to scare you, but he usually says something before disappearing. This time, there was nothing." Tears well in my eyes when I think about the promise he made me last night. Didn't take him long to break it. "Is he going to be all right?"

She breathes out heavily into the phone. "I hope so."

Before hanging up the phone, she makes me promise at least three times that I won't forget to call her.

While putting a call out to the cab company, I quickly grab my coat and purse. I don't recall taking the stairs or walking out the building. My eyes are trained on the street waiting for yellow. A few minutes feel like hours. I climb inside, wasting no time reading the address Mallory gave me.

I slouch down in the seat, playing every scenario over and over in my head. Every part of me wants to be pissed off at him, but Mallory's words and sorrow reside in the forefront of my mind.

There are pieces of Blake I still don't have, that is obvious, but I can't shake this feeling. The way he kissed me. The way his hands traveled every inch of my skin . . . I thought it meant something, but it turns out, it was all lies unspoken.

He made a promise to me, and he already broke it.

Tears fall from my cheeks as we finally pull into an industrial park—not an area I'd run off to if I had a choice. "Can you wait here?" I ask, noticing there aren't any people around.

He points to the meter. I nod; I've lived here long enough to know that he's going to charge me for every minute I spend inside the tall brick building.

My heart races as I climb out of the car and up the metal stairs. He's either here, or he's not. I haven't decided what I'm going to say if he is. My mind is a complicated jigsaw puzzle, unable to fit a piece in until I can see the edges.

I turn the cold metal knob, holding my breath. Surprisingly, it's unlocked . . . he has to be here. I slowly step inside, like there are shards of glass I'm trying to walk over. It's dark and quiet . . . neither a good sign.

I flip on the light, and a pit instantly forms in my stomach. There's not a single breath of life. Nothing. I go farther, opening the door to the small studio we'd spent so much time in when I was last here. The happy memory now burns—everything hurts without him here.

Unable to think about it anymore, I close the door. I'm about to walk back outside when I remember the painting—the one that mirrors the picture in Blake's room. I know the pain behind his eyes has to do with her.

When its edges come into view, I'm paralyzed. It's not her at all . . . it's me. Looking into the mirror, I'm lying in a sea of blankets, one pulled just above my breasts. My red hair fans out, framing my face. My expression is sleepy, yet content, my eyes staring into whoever looks at the painting. It's beautiful; it's the first time I've ever seen myself as more than ordinary.

"Blake!" I cry out, covering my mouth in an attempt to regain control. It's no use. I stare at it for what feels like forever, memorizing every last detail. It leaves me feeling more confused than I was just minutes ago.

He wants me, then he doesn't.

He makes me believe that he's everything, then he's nothing at all.

He tells me all the things I want to hear, then takes it all back.

I gave my heart to the wrong guy, or at least that's what I thought until I saw this. It means something—a sliver of hope.

My mind races as I run back out to the waiting cab. Where would he go? Looking at my phone, I still have no new messages or texts. My knees shake as I glare out the window at the passing buildings. I play the events of the last few weeks in my head. Chicago. Blake. It's been such a winding road, and there's no fucking way I'm going to let it end here.

The journey takes me to Pierce, and it hits me. I quickly find his name in my phone and hold my breath waiting for him to answer.

One ring, then two . . ."Hello." His voice is hesitant.

"I need your help."

"What is it? Where are you?"

"You said you would tell me," I answer, trying to swallow back my emotions.

"Tell you what? What's going on?" His voice is panicked.

"About Alyssa. You said if I asked him, you would tell me the rest."

He's quiet for a few seconds. "Where are you?"

"In a cab."

Another pause. "Have the driver take you to Saint Mary's. I'll be waiting."

"The church?" I ask.

"Yes."

"Okay." I hang up without another word. Time moves slowly before we pull in front of the massive church.

I throw money at the driver and step on the sidewalk, taking a deep, cleansing breath before walking up the cement stairs. There's a part of me that wants to know the truth and another that doesn't. Once it's heard, I know it won't easily be forgotten.

I walk down the aisle of the dimly lit chapel, scanning the pews for Pierce. There are several people sitting quietly toward the front, head bowed in silent prayer. Pierce is hard to spot at first—dressed in a thick black sweater instead of his usual suit. He sits by himself on the left side of the expansive room. He looks up as I get closer, his eyes sad and swollen. My heart swells, bracing itself against the protection of its cage.

"Is this how you always spend Christmas?" I ask as I approach him.

"It's how I've spent the last three."

"You don't look good," I say honestly, taking a seat next to him. I hope it doesn't have to do with me, and everything that happened last night. My heart can't take it.

He shrugs. "I wasn't planning on company."

"I'm sorry about last night."

"None of that matters right now. I have other things on my mind."

I nod. "Do you want to talk about it?"

"I take it Blake didn't tell you everything he should have."

My heart pounds, begging for escape. "Where is she?"

He lowers his head, running his fingers through his dark hair. My anxiety multiplies with each passing second. Every possible answer flashes in front of me, but none of them make sense.

"She's dead," he mumbles, sounding like he might be sick.

"What? When?" Maybe I didn't hear him right.

He looks at me, eyes glossed over. "She died three years ago today."

His heartache radiates through my own chest. Pierce is so strong—in control. I never imagined him like this. "I'm sorry. I'm so sorry, Pierce. What happened?" I ask, a tear slipping down my cheek.

Pierce uses the pad of his thumb to wipe it away, unknowingly freeing more raw emotion I'd tried to keep locked inside. "I thought it would get easier as time passed, but it hasn't. I was supposed to protect her."

I cover his hand with mine. "It couldn't have been your fault," I cry.

"It wasn't," he says, weaving his fingers with mine. "He killed her, Lila."

"No." I can't think. I can't hear. I can't see. My words are temporarily lost, but then I find just one.

"He did. Blake killed her, and nothing has ever been the same."

And I don't think it ever will.

MY EYES ARE SWOLLEN, and my head is reeling when Pierce drops me off at my apartment. There were so many questions I wanted answered, but I couldn't take any more of his truths. Besides, he's dealing with the anniversary of his sister's death, and the last thing he needs is my peppering him with questions when the wounds are already torn open.

After he'd told me about Alyssa, we'd sat quietly for a while, listening to "Silent Night" play quietly in the background. Then he told me stories about their childhood. I listened, while in between, I wondered why no one said anything to me about this until now. Why didn't Mallory tell me what her brother had done? Why would she set me up to be alone with him . . . to fall for him? I feel so stupid. If I'd known all this before, I would have never let Blake get close. I would've never set myself up to be hurt like this.

Tomorrow, I'm going to get as far away from any memories of him as I possibly can. It's something I should have done a while ago. It would have saved me from *this*.

As I cross the room, I skim my fingers along the wall. The empty apartment is like the bottom of a deep, dark hole. Blinds drawn. The only sound, besides the heavy pounding in my head, is the quiet hum of the refrigerator. It's eerie—the worst kind of lonely.

"Where've you been?"

My whole body stills. My heart is paralyzed. *He can't be here. I can't face him and pretend.* Fear entraps me, making it impossible to escape.

A dark shadow crosses the room, not stopping until I'm caged between it and the wall. His familiar scent envelops me, and stark reality hits me, lending me back my voice. "You need to go," I whisper, bracing myself against the wall, anything to put distance between us.

His fingers playfully pull at the ends of my hair. He's been drinking . . . I can smell that too. "I've been trying to call you. Been waiting around here for hours, worried about you."

"Please go," I beg. My voice catches. Tears would fall so easily if I let them.

He leans in, his forehead pressed to mine. So many times I wished we could be like this—him wanting me. A real relationship . . . not this pile of lies. "Are you mad at me?" He nuzzles the cool tip of his nose against mine. "Don't be angry with me, Lemon Drop. I left for a few hours to work on your Christmas present. I've been trying to call you for the last two hours, but it went to voicemail every time."

I swallow the giant lump that's lodged itself in my throat, carefully choosing my next move. This isn't a chess match . . . it's my life. "I know. I know everything."

"Know what, baby?" His lips journey along my jawline then down my neck. My body shakes from nerves, but I'm too afraid to stop him.

"About Alyssa." I choke on the words, wondering how he did it. Wondering if I'm making the biggest mistake of my life confronting him like this. I know too much, but yet I know nothing.

His body freezes against mine, rendered powerless by two words.

Time passes.

The world tilts too far.

It's just him and me and everything in our little world is wrong.

He backs away, tugging his hair between his fingers. "Who?" he seethes, pacing the floor.

I cower, the weight of situation hitting me like an avalanche. I should never have come back. I should never have come here in the first place.

"Who fucking told you?" he yells louder this time.

"Pierce. I tried calling, even went to your studio. When I couldn't find you, I met him at the church," I admit, slowly inching my way toward the door. So many times in my life, I've thought this might be it. This might be the moment I close my eyes never to open them again. Pierce warned me, and I walked right into the mouth of the raging tiger anyway.

He grabs the lamp, hurling it at the wall opposite me. I flinch. By now, I've adjusted to the darkness, able to see the angry glow in his eyes. They lock us in a silent game of truth or dare—me begging for the truth, while he dares me to leave. I dare myself to leave.

"Why would you go to him? Why?"

"I thought you'd left."

He paces again, more frantic this time. "Shit. Lila, I was at that studio all fucking morning. I only left for maybe thirty minutes to get more paint."

"Why did you do it?" I ask. I keep inching, ready to run at any moment.

He stills, and I think he might swing at me, but he doesn't. "Do what?"

The logical voice in my head screams for me to leave, to cut my losses before I have nothing left to lose. "Why did you kill her?" My voice trembles.

He stalks toward me, my heart pounding against my rib cage. All I've ever wanted is to feel true love, and this is all it's gotten me—heartbreak. His warm, calloused hands cup my face, holding me still. "I. Didn't. Kill. Her."

The anger that pours off him is immeasurable. And the denial . . . I didn't expect anything less. "Then where is she, Blake? Why would he say something like that if it weren't true?"

"You should've answered your phone," he whispers. I open my mouth to speak, but he beats me to it. "You should've heard it from me."

"You wouldn't tell me! No one would fucking tell me anything!"

He lets me go, turning his back to me. Silence cuts through panic, lending space to curiosity. "I didn't kill her . . . I could never hurt her. But it's my fault she's not here."

Shock steals my voice, but I quickly recover. "What do you mean?"

"She was sick."

"Sick?"

He spins back around, keeping the space between us this time. With the faint light of the moon, I see a tear running down his cheek. "Depressed."

Confused and mentally drained, I let myself sink down against the wall. Tonight—this whole day actually—isn't going as I'd planned.

Blake follows my lead, sliding down next to me. "When I first met Aly, everything was great. She saw the positive in everything, and that was what I'd admired most about her. She was everything I'm not." He shakes his head. "Christ, I even wondered what the hell she was doing with an ass like me."

It's as if my whole future hangs in the balance. As if his words are the tight rope for which I'm walking. All I can do is hold my breath and wait.

"She had one of those laughs you recognize in a crowded room, and as college came to an end, I heard it less and less. Then, after we got married, I barely heard it at all."

"Do you know why?" I ask hesitantly.

"She hadn't been okay in a long time. She'd been on medication when I first met her, but went off not long after we met."

"What happened?"

"I don't talk about this, Lila. Ever."

I nod in defeat—this ship has sailed far enough away that I can't see it. Even if it came back for me, I don't know if I'd get on. Standing, I walk off to my bedroom without another word. I throw my suitcase on the bed, piling it full of random things from my closet. I'm so lost in the fog of thought, I don't hear Blake coming up behind me. I don't know until he's sitting in front of me on the edge of the bed, staring at me with pained eyes.

"I left her," he says quietly.

"You left her?"

He glances down at my haphazard suitcase then back to me. "She tried to take her life one day when I was at work. I came home and found her laying in the bathtub with an empty pill bottle in her hand." His voice breaks as he stares up at the ceiling. "I got there just in time. I'd never been so scared in my life."

He takes a deep breath. I've never seen him more vulnerable. It reminds me that there's a beautiful soul inside him . . . one I fell for. "She was in the hospital for a few weeks while they worked on her meds, trying to make everything right. When I took her home, things were better, but I wouldn't leave her side. She was my responsibility, you know? I'd made a promise to always keep her safe when we said our vows."

My hands ache to touch him—to comfort him—but the crazy cocktail of emotions I've felt today holds me back. I'm to the point where I've felt so much that I feel nothing at all. "So you saved her?"

He stands, pacing once again. "That time I did. I spent every second with her. For a few weeks, it felt like when we first met. That's when I painted that picture of her . . . the one you saw in the studio. She was the Aly I fell in love with, and I wanted to capture it just in case . . . fuck. It was two days before it happened."

"What happened?" I ask. My fingers run along the edge of the suitcase to keep from reaching out to him.

"There was this concert I'd been talking about for months. I wasn't going to leave her, but she wouldn't let it go. She told me she was going to crawl into bed with a book. She said I deserved a break. Fuck, I had no reason to doubt her. She was my Aly."

So captured by his words, it doesn't dawn on me that he's crying. He's hunched over, tracing circles on the hardwood with his foot. "I came home that night. God . . . I remember it. Every fucking detail of it. "Blood Bank" by Bon Iver was playing loudly. Until that night, it was my favorite song. The one I could listen to over and over."

"I love that song," I reply. It now plays in my head, a backdrop to the story he tells. The one that I know locked the demon inside him.

"I hate it."

Silence falls over us again. The shell he's enclosed himself in cracked . . . I cracked him. Only I can put him together. Slow steady steps. Left foot then right. I hesitantly place my hand over his heart, feeling the heavy weight of his past in my palm. "What ruined the song?" I know the answer, but I need to hear it, and I think he needs to hear himself say it.

"It was the one that played when I found her lying dead on our bedroom floor. The one that played when I realized the best thing that ever happened to me wasn't mine anymore."

His tears mix with mine, a manmade lake forming at our feet. You think you know a person, but then you really don't. Turns out, they're a better person than you ever could be.

"Sorry doesn't sound like enough," I whisper. "Not when it can't change anything."

His arms pull me in, holding on for dear life. I want to be wrapped in him, to know he's still here . . . that maybe everything will be okay.

"They all blame me . . . I should have been there."

I bury my face in his chest; I swear I hear his heart breaking. "Sometimes love just isn't enough."

For seconds, minutes, hours, we stay like that, holding onto each other. His tears soak my T-shirt. Mine soak his. I never knew the version of Blake that lived before all this, but it defines this version so clearly. He's guarded because it's who he needs to be to protect himself. He's a jerk to keep girls like me away; the clingy type who fall too easily. He's not an asshole by nature, but by nurture. Life and its shitty circumstance made him this way, but I fell for him anyway.

And now, I'm embedded to him. I never want to let this beautifully broken man go.

Without warning, he loosens his grip on me. "That's true, isn't it, Lila? Love isn't always enough."

"It can't be," I admit, remembering every bad relationship I've ever had. Every one that led me here.

"Kiss me."

I stare, not sure how we got back here.

"Kiss me," he says again.

Without another thought, I stand on my tiptoes and press my lips to his salty, tear-stained mouth. What's meant to be a taste turns into so much more. Our bodies pressed together, singing a soulful duet while our tongues dance. He's my air, my water . . . everything I need is right here.

He pulls away slowly, tugging my lower lip between his teeth. When he done, he stares at me like I'm the window to something he's been waiting his whole life to see. "You were right. Love isn't enough. It wasn't enough to make you believe the best in me."

"Blake—"

Holding his hand up to stop me, he says, "No. I love you, Lila, and sometimes when I look at you, I think you feel the same. It just wasn't enough." Anger replaces sadness in his voice.

I swallow hard. "What are you saying?"

"I'm saying you deserve better than me. You deserve someone you can believe in."

"I don't want anyone but you," I cry, doing my best to hold on.

He steps back, leaving me cold. "I'm going to accept the contract in Europe."

"No." Panic. Fear. Sadness. I feel it all.

The back of his finger brushes my wet cheek. Small, sweet caresses. "Someday, you'll look back at this and thank me, or maybe you'll just realize that we fucked up the best thing that's ever happened to us."

"Stop!"

"No, don't you get it? Love isn't always enough, but trust is, and it's gone now. I left for a few hours, and you ran straight to him. You made your choice, and this is mine." His finger drops as he slowly backs away. We all have that one moment in our lives we wish we could take back, and this is mine. This will always be mine.

"Stay," I beg, following him to his bedroom.

He ignores my pleas, picking up a duffel bag from the floor and throwing clothes inside. He walks to the door, wrapping his hand around the door handle that's going to take him right out of my life. I can't let him . . .

"Blake . . . please. If you'd just told me—even just a little bit of it—I wouldn't have had to search for the truth. This can't be the end."

He turns back around one more time. I'll never forget the look in his eyes. "It can be, because it is. Have a nice life, Lila."

And just like that, he's gone. I don't run after him because deep in my heart, I know he won't stay. If I've learned anything at all about Blake, it's that I can't win around him, and this is my worst loss.

For the second time tonight, the dam breaks and tears fall. For the second time, I fall to the floor because my legs can no longer hold me. Self-induced misery is suffering in its worst form. If I could go back to when I woke up this morning, I would wait for him. I would have enough faith to know he'd come back. Now I'm left with nothing, unless you count a shredded heart.

Wiping my cheeks, something across the room catches my eye. From the outline, it appears to be a canvas . . . one that wasn't here just hours ago. I stand back up, flipping the light switch by the kitchen table. My breath catches. It's my home—the one I grew up in—covered in a sheet of snow. Golden light shines through the front picture window, the one I used to stare out as a kid, watching snowflakes fall for hours, and just inside is the colorful Christmas tree my family put up every year. It's the same one I told Blake about last night . . . the one I missed.

And it hits me, while I was out thinking the worst—thinking he'd left me again—he was doing this. It makes everything inside me twist a little more, and then I notice an envelope at the bottom of the easel with my name scribbled on it. I hold my breath and rip it open without giving much thought to what's inside.

To my Lemon Drop,

Since you couldn't go home, I brought it to you. Some day, you just might find that there's more than one place to call home. Merry Christmas!

Love Always,
Blake

That's when I completely lost it . . . lost him.

The END

Lila's story continues in
Love Unspoken
out March 1, 2015.

ACKNOWLEDGEMENTS

FIRST, I HAVE TO THANK THE ONE person who made this—and ever other book I've written—possible: my husband, Michael. If it weren't for you, I wouldn't have the courage to keep at this, or the time. Thank you for everything you do to keep the household going while I'm "working".

To my kids, I love you more than words can ever express. Thank you for understanding when Mommy has to work instead of play. It just makes every moment I get to spend with you that much better.

To my assistant, Melissa, thank you for putting up with me on a daily basis. I appreciate everything you do to give me more writing time. Hopefully, I'm not the worst boss you've ever had . . . hopefully!

I have to thank my bestie Jessica C. for helping me make this story what it is. Without her, you would've had a little less Pierce. Besides that, she has the biggest heart and is always there when I need her.

To my Jennifer, Taryn, Elizabeth, Jessica, Bridget, Lisa, Allison, Kara and Michelle, thank you for helping me shape this book into what it is. Teams are a little divided at the moment, but I promise you'll all be happy in the end.

I also have to thank my editor, Madison, for keeping me away from clichés. My formatter, Kassi, for always making the pages pretty. Regina for giving me a cover that I love. And my agent, Jill Marsal, for supporting me along the way.

And last but not least, the bloggers and readers who have been with me over the last couple years . . . you helped make my dreams come true. THANK YOU!

22480600R00192